CAUGHT BETWEEN TWO STORMS

Federal Deputy Sullivan Hart stood with his back against a tall jut of rock and levered a round into his rifle chamber. Water ran freely from the brim of his battered Stetson. Across the trail from him, his partner, Twojack Roth, ventured a look up along the trail, then ducked back behind the thick trunk of a cedar tree. Sullivan Hart watched the big Cherokee tracker adjust his sopping hat and let out a restless breath.

"I'm ready when you are."

Hart slid down the tall rock and leaned back against it for a second, tipping his hat brim up and feeling water steam down the back of his rain slicker. He cradled his rifle across his lap, took his wet bandanna from around his neck, and wiped streaks of splattered mud from his face. "Listen up, boys," he called out above the rain. "You know how this works. Throw out your guns and walk down here with your hands raised. The sooner we get this done, the sooner we'll get out of this storm and dry off."

The deputies waited a moment for a reply. When none came, Hart looked over at Twojack Roth, then called out again, "Joe? Lloyd? Hand? We're not going to sit here all day. Throw out your guns, and show yourselves. Let's go home."

Lightning forked down, followed by a deafening burst of thunder. Once the pealing thunder subsided, Joe Marr shouted, "We're not going back, Hart. You want us? Come and get us. You won't take us alive. . . ."

DEVIL'S DUE

Ralph Cotton

A SIGNET BOOK

SIGNET
Published by New American Library, a division of
Penguin Putnam Inc., 375 Hudson Street,
New York, New York 10014, U.S.A.
Penguin Books Ltd, 27 Wrights Lane,
London W8 5TZ, England
Penguin Books Australia Ltd, Ringwood,
Victoria, Australia
Penguin Books Canada Ltd, 10 Alcorn Avenue,
Toronto, Ontario, Canada M4V 3B2
Penguin Books (N.Z.) Ltd, 182–190 Wairau Road,
Auckland 10, New Zealand

Penguin Books Ltd, Registered Offices:
Harmondsworth, Middlesex, England

First published by Signet, an imprint of New American Library,
a division of Penguin Putnam Inc.

First Printing, August 2001
10 9 8 7 6 5 4 3 2 1

 REGISTERED TRADEMARK—MARCA REGISTRADA

Printed in the United States of America

PUBLISHER'S NOTE
This is a work of fiction. Names, characters, places, and incidents either
are the product of the author's imagination or are used fictitiously,
and any resemblance to actual persons, living or dead, events, or locales
is entirely coincidental.

For Mary Lynn . . . of course

Chapter 1

Lightning licked down from the low boiling sky and flickered on the mud-slick trail. Joe Marr flung himself from his wet saddle and slapped the spent horse on its rump, sending it upward among brush, rock, and braided streams of water running the color of iron rust.

"Damn Sullivan Hart!" Marr stood for a second in the blowing rain, his bare feet slipping in the mud, his breath pounding hard in his chest.

Lloyd and Hand Crenshaw slid their stolen Appaloosa to a halt midtrail and watched Marr's horse gallop away in a spray of mud and disappear out of sight. They looked at one another, stunned, then down at Joe Marr. "I mean it, boys!" Marr shouted, water running down his bare forehead. "They ain't takin' me alive! Not this time!" Marr's grimy prison clothes clung to him, wet and heavy. Above the hills, thunder exploded, jarring the earth. "I'll die first!" Marr ran from the trail into the cover of rock, a stolen sawed-off shotgun in his hand.

"He'd die first?" Hand Crenshaw turned in his wet saddle, staring into his brother's eyes. "He's lost his mind! We've got to make a run for it."

But Lloyd Crenshaw shook his head and jumped down from the Appaloosa. "No. We sided with him.

When you side with a man, you don't run out on him. Come on!"

"But, Lloyd, this horse has got plenty of run left in him," Hand said, holding the Appaloosa in place. "We can make it out of here."

"There comes a time you've got to make a stand, Hand." Lloyd Crenshaw stepped back, jerking the big rusty English pistol from his waistband. "If Marr's willing to die like a man, so are we."

So are we? Jesus! "Wait, Lloyd!" Hand called out to him, but Lloyd had already disappeared into the cover of rock. Another clap of thunder split the sky. "Damn it!" Hand Crenshaw looked back and forth, bewildered. Then he jumped down from the mud-streaked Appaloosa and jerked it along behind him. He had to talk some sense into his brother and Joe Marr. This was neither the time nor the place to butt heads with the two deputies who'd been dogging them for the past three days. Their only weapons were Marr's stolen shotgun and the rusty pistol they'd found in the Appaloosa's saddlebags. The pistol only had three rounds left. Marr had only one shot in the shotgun, and that would be the end of the fight.

"You both better think about this," Hand shouted above the storm, joining them behind a stand of rock. He reached out to tie the Appaloosa's reins to a scrub juniper.

"There's nothing more to think about!" Joe Marr snatched Hand's Appaloosa's reins, flung them away, smacked the horse's rump with a loud yell and sent it pounding away up the mud-slicked trail.

Rain whipped in sideways at Hand Crenshaw's face as he watched their last means of escape gallop away. "God-almighty. Joe! What did you do that for?" If he had a gun he would have shot Marr dead.

Defenseless, he just stood staring, shaking his wet head back and forth. "Now we've got no choice but to give up."

"Like hell we will." Joe Marr glared at him. "There comes a time, you have to decide whether you'll crawl like a coward or die like a hero." He looked back and forth between Hand and Lloyd Crenshaw. "I ain't spending one more lousy day in a stinking jail cell. What about you?"

Lloyd Crenshaw nodded in firm agreement. The two of them turned their gaze to Hand. He slumped and let his arms fall to his sides in submission. "Hell, I reckon."

"Good then." Joe Marr peeked over their rock cover, down along the trail behind them. "Now let's have no more talk about giving up."

Thirty yards down the trail, Federal Deputy Sullivan Hart stood with his back against a tall jut of rock and levered a round into his rifle chamber. Water ran freely from the brim of his battered Stetson. Across the trail from him, his partner, Twojack Roth, ventured a look up along the trail, then ducked back behind the thick trunk of a cedar tree. Sullivan Hart watched the big Cherokee tracker adjust his wet hat and let out a restless breath.

"Stay put, Twojack," Hart whispered from fifteen feet away, "they've about spent themselves. They're not going anywhere."

"I know," Roth replied softly, his gloved thumb across the hammer of his Winchester rifle. "I just wanted to look things over."

"What did you see?" asked Hart.

"They've let the horses go. I expect they'll be turning themselves in any time now."

Sullivan Hart nodded. "Yeah. Joe Marr is no fighter. Neither are the Crenshaws. That was stupid, letting the horses go. Now they'll have to walk back to Fort Smith."

"It was their decision. They'll just have to live with it." Twojack Roth shrugged, crouching down behind the big cedar as he spoke. "I'm ready when you are."

Hart slid down the tall rock and leaned back against it for a second, tipping his hat brim up and feeling water stream down the back of his rain slicker. He cradled his rifle across his lap, took his wet bandanna from around his neck and wiped streaks of splattered mud from his face. "Listen up, boys," he called out above the rain, "you know how this works! Throw out your guns and walk down here with your hands raised. The sooner we get this done, the sooner we'll get out of this storm and dry off."

The deputies waited a moment for a reply. When none came, Hart looked over at Twojack Roth, then called out again, "Joe? Lloyd? Hand? We're not going to sit here all day. Throw out your guns, and show yourselves. Let's go home."

Lightning forked down, followed by a deafening burst of thunder. Once the pealing thunder subsided, Joe Marr shouted, "We're not going back, Hart! You want us? Come and get us. You won't take us alive!"

Sullivan Hart looked over at Roth, this time with a puzzled expression on his face. "They can't be drunk, can they?"

"Not unless they found some liquor in their saddlebags." Roth jacked a round into his rifle chamber, looking up at the low turbulent sky, then at the trunk of the big cedar tree. "We're going to have to do something though. I'm not going to lay here and get fried by lightning."

Sullivan Hart called out, "Joe! Quit acting a fool. Even with this jailbreak, you'll be out in three, four years at the most. Don't make us kill you. I need you as a witness."

"Nothing doing, Hart." Joe Marr's voice faded in a gusting sheet of sidelong rain. "We've made our stand. Come and get us!"

Beside Joe Marr, Hand and Lloyd Crenshaw looked at one another, water running down their faces. "A witness? What's he talking about, Joe?" Lloyd Crenshaw asked. "A witness to what?"

"It's nothing," Joe Marr said over his shoulder, squinting out through the howling deluge. "I can identify the man who killed his pa a while back. Without my testimony, Hart's got no solid proof against him."

"Lord have mercy," Lloyd whispered, his jaw going slack as he and Hand stared at one another. Both of their faces took on sickly expressions. Lloyd's eyes cut to the slick trail where nothing remained of their horses but washed-out hoofprints in the rust-colored mud. "You never told us nothing about it. You said you were in for cattle rustling!"

"It's not important," Joe Marr snapped, running his palm along the glistening blue of his shotgun barrel. "I told you, I ain't going back."

Lloyd flashed his brother an even more dour expression. "But still, Joe, damn it to hell! You might have mentioned it before getting rid of our horse! Hart ain't about to kill you! But look at me and Hand here! We're dead sure as hell!"

"It slipped my mind, all right?" Joe Marr spoke without facing them.

"Slipped your *mind*?" Hand Crenshaw shrieked, lunging at him, his wet hands clawing at Marr's throat like talons. "Why you dirty son of a—!" But Lloyd caught his brother midair, holding him back as Joe Marr swung the shotgun around and leveled it at them. Lloyd Crenshaw pushed his brother back, the big rusty pistol in his other hand cocked and pointed at Joe Marr, three feet away.

"Hand is right, Joe! Damn you to hell! This whole jailbreak was your idea! We both would have been out in another three months! What in the *blue living hell* did you mean, getting us into this?"

From their cover of tree and rock, Sullivan Hart and Twojack Roth both flinched and hunkered down as the sound of pistol fire and the blast of the shotgun split through the storm. The firing came on suddenly in rapid succession. Yet, at the end of it, when the deputies had heard no bullets hit close to them, Hart looked over at Roth. "What was *that* all about?"

"Beats me." Twojack Roth rose slowly, his rifle ready in his hands, peering around the trunk of the cedar as lightning twisted and curled. "Boys, we're coming in! Either drop the guns or get to using them."

Joe Marr lay sprawled in the mud behind the cover of rock. His hands clasped the two bullet wounds in his chest, dark blood turning pink as the rain thinned it out down his side. Six feet away, the bodies of the Crenshaw brothers lay broken and bleeding, smoke still rising from Lloyd's chest. Hand lay face down, the rain beating his bloody back. Sullivan Hart stepped in from one side of the rock, Twojack Roth from the other. They looked around with their rifles cocked and ready. Then Hart let out a breath, stepped over to Joe Marr and stooped down beside him. "What happened here, Joe?"

"We had . . . a disagreement. They just . . . went nuts on me, Sully," Marr said in a weak voice. "I kept wanting us to give up. But they wouldn't hear of it. Lloyd run our horses off . . . acted like they wanted to shoot it out with yas." His eyes cut from Hart's face to Roth's, then back. "I told them no . . . but you know how they—"

"You're lying, Marr," Twojack Roth said, cutting him off. "These boys would have been home in time for Christmas. Why would they want to do something this stupid?"

Joe Marr shrugged. "Restless, I reckon." He winced as Sullivan Hart pressed his wet bandanna to the man's gaping wounds. "Sully, I'm sorry I got myself killed, before testifying for you."

"Take it easy, Joe. You'll make it. We'll get the bleeding to stop, then get you back to Fort Smith. You're right about one thing, though—I've got to have you identify J. T. Priest. You might be my only hope." He laid Marr's hands in place on his chest atop the bandanna. Then he looked closer at Marr's face. "Why did you do this, Joe? I told you I'd speak on your behalf. You would have gotten off with a year or less."

"Hell, if I knew why I done things, I'd never been an outlaw in the first place."

"That's no answer, Joe." Hart stood up in the pouring rain, the wind finally slackening up now, the storm pulling slowly away. "Come on," he said to Roth, "let's get him out of this downpour and see what we can do for him."

Their boots slipping in the mud, they carried the wounded outlaw between them, back down the trail to where they'd tied their horses beneath a deep cliff overhang. Twojack Roth shoved the horses to one side, clearing a place for Joe Marr on the ground. By evening the storm had blown itself out, and Joe Marr lay asleep with a wet saddle for a pillow and his chest wrapped in strips of cloth Hart had torn from an old shirt he found in his saddlebags.

*   *   *

"He looks bad," Roth said, nodding toward Joe Marr. "It'll be a miracle if he makes it back to Fort Smith." Beneath the overhang, they'd scraped together enough dry pine needles, twigs, and wood kindling to build a small fire and boil some coffee.

"He's got to make it," Hart said with determination, holding both hands around his tin coffee cup. "Without his testimony, Judge Parker said there's a good chance J. T. Priest will go free."

"The Hanging Judge is not about to let Priest off the hook." Roth sipped his coffee, considering it.

"But it goes farther than Judge Parker," Hart said. "Parker has had a lot of his decisions reversed on appeal. Things aren't like they used to be. You can't just hang a murderer and be done with it anymore." Hart shook his head and gazed into the low lapping flames. "We've spent most of the summer tracking down the *Los Pistoleros* gang—still haven't caught all of them. If we lose J. T. Priest in court, we'll be starting all over again."

"At least we've got them on the run now," Roth offered, sipping his coffee. "We haven't heard a thing out of Cleveland Phelps since we shot it out with him and his boys at the Old English Spread. Maddog William Mabrey has dropped out of sight. If we have to start all over again, we'll do it." He shrugged. "This time, we'll know more about what we're dealing with."

"Yeah . . ." Hart let his words trail down for a second. Then, gazing into the flames, he said, "Parker says *Los Pistoleros* is an example of how crime is going to be in the future. Says by the turn of the century, there'll be more banks robbed by businessmen with pencils than there will be by outlaws carrying guns. Says if you expect to bring a killer to justice, you best shoot him down yourself, or else his lawyer will be keeping him alive after you're dead of old age."

Twojack Roth spread a thin smile. "Parker's got some strange ideas about the future. Let's hope he's wrong. The day we start shooting men down without a trial is the day we might as well take off the badge and become gunmen ourselves—it pays better."

"Law is a real tricky thing," Sullivan Hart said in contemplation. "Parker says it's all based on public opinion. When he came out here, this territory was so wild, all the public wanted to hear was how many men he had sent to the gallows. Now that it's settled down some, all they talk about is how ruthless his methods are." Hart shook his head and sipped his coffee in silence.

Finally Roth broke the silence, saying, "Speaking of tricky things, shouldn't we be seeing Quick Charlie Sims roll into Fort Smith any day now?"

"Yep. Parker said Sims headed here from Chicago over a week ago."

Roth nodded. "He probably got his foot caught in a poker game in St. Louis and couldn't shake it loose. Now that his bank robbery charge is dropped, there's no telling when we'll see Quick Charlie again."

"I figure he'll show up sooner or later," Hart said. "He seemed real anxious to get to Fort Smith the last time we talked to him. He was convinced J. T. Priest would try to bust out of jail."

"Well," Roth said, sitting his empty cup down and lying back on his blanket near the low flames, "Sims was also convinced that Mad-dog Mabrey would come gunning for him in Chicago." He lowered his damp hat brim over his forehead. "So that's two things Sims was wrong about. As far as I'm concerned, I'd just as soon work with the devil as work with Sims again."

Hart smiled, finishing his coffee. "Be careful what you ask for. Sims could probably arrange it."

Roth chuckled. "Yeah, I don't trust him, but I've got to give him his due. Sims manages to stay a few steps ahead of every game. Wherever he's at right now, he's not sleeping on a blanket."

"That's a sure bet." Hart slung the coffeegrounds from his cup, set it beside the fire and leaned back on his damp saddle. He flipped half of his blanket across himself and settled his hat over his eyes. "Wherever he's at, I'm sure he's not in any strain."

Chapter 2

Quick Charlie Sims looked across the table at the barrel of a cocked derringer pistol in the tight fist of Dirk LeMaster. There had been some serious cheating going on in this game. LeMaster had been dealing crooked all night, ever since the train pulled out of the St. Louis rail station. Quick Charlie Sims had only started cheating an hour or so ago, once he saw that LeMaster wasn't going to let up until he'd broken everybody in the game. "You heard me, Simpson," LeMaster growled. "I'm calling you a lousy card cheat!"

"And right you are, LeMaster." Sims smiled, lifting his gaze from the cocked pistol and looking deep into Dirk LeMaster's eyes. "I was wondering just how clumsy I'd have to get before a fool like you would notice it."

LeMaster was taken aback by Sims's words, as were the other four faces around the table, except for C. B. Harrington. "You're right about him cheating, LeMaster," Harrington said, taking the thick cigar from between his lips and blowing out a long gray stream of smoke. "But he's cheating because I paid him to." A short gasp rose from the other seated players. "Easy, gentlemen," Harrington said to them. Then he spoke to LeMaster again. "His name is not

Simpson—it's Charlie Sims. Perhaps you've heard of him?"

"Charlie Sims? You mean, *Quick* Charlie Sims?" Dirk LeMaster swallowed hard, the derringer still cocked and pointed less than two feet from Sims's face. It took him a second to recover, but once he did, he drew in a deep breath and said, "Well, it makes no difference who he is. He's been cheating. I've got every right to kill him."

"I couldn't agree more, LeMaster," Quick Charlie Sims said, still wearing the calm confident smile. "When a man cheats at cards, he deserves to be shot. Wouldn't you agree, Louisville Ike Woodsen?" As Sims spoke, his left hand suddenly came up beside the man sitting beside him. Now another derringer was in the game, this one in Sims's hand, cocked and pointing into Woodsen's ear.

The man beside him froze, his half-lens spectacles lying low across the bridge of his long nose. "I—I don't know what you're talking about, sir! I'm not Louisville Ike. My name is Morris . . . Jack Morris. I'm from Nashville, Tennessee!" The players around the table sat tensed, their mouths agape.

Sims kept the pistol in the man's ear beside him as he spoke to LeMaster, saying, "You and I have a couple of things in common, LeMaster. We've both been cheating in this game, and we're both ready to kill a card cheat. You're ready to kill me . . . I'm ready to kill your partner."

"Partner! Sir, I swear to you, I'm Jack Morris!" The man beside him had started to sweat. "I've never seen Mr. LeMaster before in my—"

"Shut up, Louisville Ike." Sims poked the small pistol deeper against the trembling man's head without taking his eyes off of Dirk LeMaster. "The difference between us, LeMaster, is that my derringer has two shots in it. Yours isn't loaded."

LeMaster blinked, almost taking his eyes off of Sims for a second to check the pistol in his hand. But then he caught himself, tightened his grip, and said with a sneer, "You're out of your mind, Sims."

"Oh?" Sims lifted a brow. "Then pull the trigger— of course when that hammer drops on an empty chamber, I'll put one bullet through Louisville Ike, then the next one through you."

LeMaster's expression wavered with the slightest trace of uncertainty. Sims saw it and went on. "Yep, I unloaded it for you a while ago. Remember when the train swayed? I fell against you on my way out back to relieve myself? Then I fell against you again on my way back?"

LeMaster recalled the incident and swallowed down another hard knot in his throat. "You didn't do that, Sims. Nobody is that slick. You're bluffing!"

Sims shrugged one shoulder. "Suit yourself then. Pull the trigger, and let's see who wins this hand."

"Jesus, Dirk!" Louisville Ike pleaded, breaking down, a sliver of a nervous tear leaking down his long nose, beads of cold sweat shining on his forehead. "Don't let him kill me here—"

"Shut, up, Ike!" LeMaster snapped, his eyes still boring into Sims's, not reading a thing there but cold dark resolve. "All right you smooth son of a bitch . . . I'm calling your bluff. Any last words?" He stiffened his arm out toward Sims, watching him for any sign of fear or doubt. But Quick Charlie Sims only sat there staring, calm, cool and silent. This was the last play in the game—the next man to speak would be the loser. Sims wasn't about to say another word.

"I mean it, Sims! Here it goes!" LeMaster's face swelled red, his hand tight around the derringer.

"For God sakes, Dirk!" Louisville Ike whimpered. Sims sat smiling, nothing changing in his demeanor. He knew the outcome now. All he had to do was wait. The other players sat braced, their breath collectively held.

Dirk LeMaster clenched his teeth, his gunhand so tense it had started to tremble. Sims watched the man's final surge of rage and determination sweep across his face. LeMaster's knuckle had turned white on his trigger finger. He gave a low, gut-wrenching growl. "Damn you, Sims . . . !" Then his pistol hand slumped to the table and he let the cocked derringer spill from it as if it weighed a ton.

With his own derringer still pressed into Louisville Ike's ear, Sims reached his free hand out and picked up LeMaster's pistol. He looked at it, smiling, then raised it and fired two shots into the ceiling of the Pullman car. Then he lowered the pistol and slid it across the table to LeMaster. Bits of splintered wood showered down from the ceiling. Sims brushed them from his shoulder as the players sat slack-jawed. "Bad call, LeMaster. No wonder you have to cheat at this game."

"You dirty son of a—!" Dirk LeMaster leapt to the coatrack on the wall where his .45 caliber Colt stood in its holster, hanging from a peg. The players—except for Sims and C. B. Harrington—scattered from the table, their abandoned chairs tumbling over onto their sides.

"Look out!" one of the players cried out as LeMaster spun with the big Colt, cocking it and pulling the trigger. When the hammer fell on an empty chamber, LeMaster clicked it again, then again. Then he slumped with the empty gun hanging loose in his hand, seeing Sims turn his cocked derringer toward him.

"I forgot to mention," Sims grinned, "I really did unload your Colt." As he stared at Dirk LeMaster, the smile on Sims's face vanished. "Start running, LeMaster. You too, Louisville Ike. But leave those half-lens spectacles behind. I'll call them a keepsake."

After LeMaster and Louisville Ike had scurried out the door, Sims uncocked his derringer, tossed it over to C. B. Harrington, and stood up, straightening his vest. "Now then, gentlemen," he said, smiling at the other players, "Mr. Harrington has been keeping count on the losses." He nodded at the pile of bills and gold coins on the table in front of LeMaster's empty chair. "What say we take back our shares and get down to some *real* poker playing?"

C. B. Harrington had broken Sims's derringer open in his hand. He gasped, then held it up for the others to see. "My goodness, Sims! This thing isn't loaded either!"

"Oh that . . ." Sims spread his hands. "What can I say? I always seem to work better under pressure." He smiled. "Besides, those little pistols are dangerous—imagine if one happened to go off in your trouser pocket. Ouch!" His smile widened.

C. B. Harrington stared, aghast, a thick finger pointing back and forth from LeMaster's empty chair, to the door, then back at Sims. "But . . . I mean, that is . . . you just—" Harrington swayed a bit, then righted himself as the train went into a wide curve.

"There was never any danger," Sims said with a wave of his hand. "Let's face it, gentlemen. If they understood the finer aspects of playing the game, they wouldn't have been cheating in the first place."

Near daylight, after the game had broken up, Quick Charlie Sims and C. B. Harrington stood on the rear deck of the private Pullman car. They smoked cigars and watched the first streak of morning light seep over the far edge of the earth. The train clacked along at a comfortable twenty-five miles an hour, its wake of air causing Sims's string tie to flutter sideways.

"I have to say, Mr. Sims," Harrington beamed in satisfaction, "I can't recall a more stirring game. You certainly brought something to the table. I've been bursting to ask you how they were cheating, and why you chose such a dramatic way to expose them."

"The main thing I wanted was for them to admit they were partners, because that's something hard to prove. While they never admitted it, it became obvious at the end." Sims drew on the cigar, taking his time, watching the smoke stream away. "Now the word will go out—they won't find themselves welcome in any game of this quality."

"But how were they doing it?" Harrington asked.

"Louisville Ike's half-lens spectacles," Sims said, taking them from his inside lapel pocket. He handed them to C. B. Harrington. "I noticed after every new deal he would push these up on his nose and cock his head both left and right, studying his hand. Then he'd lower them and go on with the game."

"And?" Harrington looked bewildered. "He was somehow signaling LeMaster?"

"No, Ike was showing LeMaster what the players on either side of him had—me on his right, the elderly Caldwell gentleman on his left." Sims nodded at the half-lens spectacles in Harrington's hand, then paused for a second as if to see if Harrington could figure it out on his own. When Harrington didn't seem to get it, Sims went on. "When Ike raised his nose and cocked his head just so, the overhead lamp caught the reflections of the cards from his spectacles like a mirror."

"My goodness! I would never have guessed it!" C. B. Harrington stiffened at the revelation.

"Because you were busy watching your game," Sims said. "I was paid to watch theirs."

"Good show, sir!" Harrington chuckled, shaking his head. "But that must've been awfully difficult for LeMaster, only seeing those tiny reflections, and for only a moment at that."

"Very difficult." Sims grinned. "They were so busy cheating, all I had to do was palm a few discards, build a low hand for them to see, then play my better cards after they thought they knew what I had. It started driving them crazy after a while, but what could they say? Finally I started palming cards so slow, LeMaster figured he could expose me on it, get me thrown out of the game and go back to business as usual." Sims drew on his cigar.

"I have to admit, I feel a bit foolish being taken so easily." C. B. Harrington lowered his eyes.

"You shouldn't, sir." Quick Charlie Sims exhaled a long stream of smoke. "You're used to playing a gentleman's game in honest surroundings. These two were just a couple of sharks who slipped into your pond. It can happen to anyone."

"Kind of you to say so." Harrington let out a tired sigh. A silence passed between them before Harrington said, "Speaking of one's game and one knowing how to play it, I have something to tell you that I think you'll find very interesting." He glanced back and forth as if to ensure their privacy. "I heard through the grapevine that you were involved in that nasty shooting incident in Chicago a few weeks back. The one between those two federal deputies and some hired gunmen working for J. T. Priest and Wil-

liam Mabrey?" He cocked a brow at Sims, hoping
for some acknowledgment. But Sims offered no
change in his expression, giving C. B. Harrington his
flat, gambler's stare.

"Come now, Mr. Sims," Harrington said, wagging
his thick hand, the glowing ash on his cigar dancing
like a firefly in the gray darkness. "Don't make this
a one-sided conversation. I assure you this is in the
utmost confidence. There are things I need to tell you
about a particular gang called *Los Pistoleros*. But I can
only do so in an air of openness and trust."

Sims considered it, then said, "All right, but first
tell me what you know about the shoot-out in
Chicago."

C. B. Harrington spread a patient smile. "My, but
you are the cautious one."

"I'm listening," Sims said, interested in how Harrington was going to play this.

"In a nutshell," Harrington shrugged, "you escaped from Deputy Sullivan Hart and took up with
J. T. Priest. Hart was on Priest's trail because Priest
killed his father. Deputy Hart caught up with you
and Priest in the Chicago railyard. Somehow you
changed sides, took up with Hart and his partner,
and the three of you shot it out with a bunch of
Priest's gunman. Am I right so far?"

Sims only nodded and said, "Go on."

Harrington shrugged and drew on his cigar. "You
took a bullet in the back and Priest ended up in
Judge Parker's jail." He raised a thick finger for emphasis. "But word has it that before the shooting
started, you managed to trick Priest into signing his
shares of Midwest Investment over to you. So now
you're a major shareholder of a powerful corporation, one that happens to have strong ties to *Los Pistoleros*, the biggest secret society of killers and

criminals in the country." He stopped and studied Sims's face in the grainy light. "J. T. Priest and William Mabrey ran the gang. Now Priest is in jail, and nobody seems to know where Mabrey is. I've even heard rumors you might have killed him."

"Not bad," Sims said. He wasn't about to admit that he'd killed William Mabrey. "You've kept your ear to the ground. So assuming any of this is true, what's your interest in it?"

"Purely financial," Harrington said. "I want to buy that stock from you. It's no secret Judge Parker's deputies are out to put an end to *Los Pistoleros*. Once they're out of the picture, I want control of Midwest Investment. With my business expertise I can do something with it . . . something you could never do. The best thing you can do is sell it to me, make yourself a sizeable amount of money, and forget about it."

"So you're making a legal offer?" Sims cocked his head slightly, watching Harrington's eyes.

"Yes. That's what I *prefer* doing." Harrington's firm tone of voice offered a hint of force behind it. "But knowing the way you took possession of the stock in the first place, I'm determined to get it by whatever means necessary. Name your price, Sims— money is not an object. Let's be gentlemen about this."

"Sorry. It's not for sale." Sims puffed on his cigar. Harrington took a surprised step back. "I've always wondered how it would feel to own part of a big business. I think I'll hold on to the stock—see what it goes up to over a few years' time."

"I was afraid you'd say something like that." As Harrington spoke, he stepped to one side, raised a hand, and snapped his fingers toward the door as if summoning a table waiter. The door flew open and

Sims saw a large silhouette standing in the darkened doorway, a pistol raised and pointed at him from six feet away. "Meet my newest employee, Arch Radner," Harrington said. "Folks call him Steelhead—you don't even want to hear why. Steelhead has a way of making people listen to reason. Believe me, it's best you give me a price, and see if we can't reach an agreement. This is the part of doing business you don't have a knack for."

Sims smiled, not seeming too worried. "Maybe not, but I learn something more about business everyday. No wonder you have a reputation for always getting your way. What happens now if I turn you down? Steelhead here kills me? That won't get you anything."

"Kill you?" Harrington tossed the suggestion aside. "Of course not. One reason I've hired Steelhead is that he's assured me he can inflict an awful amount of pain without actually killing someone." He looked Steelhead up and down with admiration. "I'm sure most people would come to their senses before things get that far. Steelhead enjoys his work and goes about it in an extraordinary way. He likes to start at a person's little finger with a pair of wire cutters and work his way over to their thumb. Care to see him at work?"

The tall, broad figure stepped out of the doorway, keeping the door open with the side of his foot. Sims looked up at him, but didn't back an inch. "So the whole thing about the card cheats was just your way of getting me out here alone . . . no witnesses?"

Harrington offered a flat grim smile. "Don't feel foolish, Sims. Even the best of us can be tricked. To use your own words, 'You were so busy watching your own game . . . you never saw this coming.'"

Sims shook his head. "I have to admit, you're

good, Harrington. I fell for it, hook, line and sinker. Looks like you win." He puffed the cigar, still not seeming too concerned. "But tell me this—just how big is Midwest Investment that you'd go this far to own it?"

"Come now, Sims, you'll only hate yourself if I tell you." Harrington and Radner shared a secretive smile. Then Harrington added to Sims, "Let's march back inside. I have some ownership papers already drawn up. All I need is your signature—while you've still got all your fingers to sign it." He reached out with an arm and gestured Sims toward the open door. But Sims took a firm stance.

"Uh-uh, Harrington. You got me, you win. But I've got to know what it is I'm losing. Either tell me, and we finish this thing on a peaceable note, or I'll go down kicking and screaming right here. I've got a right to know, don't you think?"

"Let me have him, boss," said Steelhead Radner, inching forward, his voice sounding like low thunder coming from deep within a cave. He stared down at Sims. "I was watching everything in there. I hate a slick turd like you." He took a step toward Sims.

"Wait, Arch." Harrington stopped him, then looked at Sims. "All right, since you've given in so easily. It's going to break your heart, but I'll tell you just how big Midwest Investment is." He took out a folded leaf of paper from inside his coat pocket. Although it was too dark to read it, he held it up and referred to it as he spoke. "In the Northwest, they own Breakfield Mining and Logging. In Texas and California they own Danford and Moore International Shipping. In South Africa they own three diamond mines." He stopped and chuckled at the sunken expression on Sims's face. "See? I told you it would only break your heart. Now, come on, Sims, let's go."

But Sims hesitated. "All that, and Priest and Mabrey were still running *Los Pistoleros*? Still out robbing banks, running guns to the Mexican *Federales*, shooting and killing people? Why?"

"I'll tell you why." Harrington raised two thick fingers, his cigar glowing between them. "Because they were always outlaws at heart. Because no matter how much money Priest and Mabrey had, they could never get enough. Because they needed large amounts of unaccounted cash to buy politicians in Washington. It shouldn't surprise you, Sims, that most great fortunes have a certain element of corruption to them. It's the American way."

"And now you'll be doing the same thing, I suppose?" Sims asked, then drew on his cigar.

"No, Sims. Like I told you. I'll run the business end, forget the outlawry. That day is dead and gone. Instead of robbing one bank with a gun and getting away on horseback, I prefer robbing a lot of banks all at once legally, with accountants and attorneys, from a thousand miles away." He chuckled once more, casting a sidelong glance at Steelhead Radner. "That *too*, is the American way . . . only more sophisticated, and hopefully, less bloody."

"I'm glad we agree on the less bloody part," Sims said, finishing his cigar and tossing it out into the rushing wind. "But how do you know I won't come back at you later?" He looked back and forth between Harrington and Radner.

"I'll just have to take my chances, won't I?" Harrington said, stepping to the side. He gestured again toward the open doorway behind Steelhead Radner. His voice turned sarcastic. "Now I suggest we go get settled up with one another . . . unless of course, you have any more questions for me?"

"No, that's about all I wanted to know. You've been a big help, Harrington." Sims still didn't move toward the door. Instead, he turned to Steelhead Radner. "Don't get alarmed, Mr. Steelhead, but that cold metal you're about to feel on the back of your neck is my partner holding a cocked pistol on you. Since we're all being gentlemen here, I'm going to ask you just once, to lower your gun."

Harrington laughed under his breath. "Nice try, Sims. I have to admit, you are a remarkable gamesman. You never give up. Only this time I'm afraid you've met your match—"

"Uh, Mr. Harrington," Steelhead whispered, cutting him off with a nervous tone, "there really is something cold against the back of my neck."

"You'd better believe there is," a woman's voice hissed behind him in the darkened doorway, "but it won't be cold for long if you don't lower that pistol, you son of a bitch!"

"Oops," Quick Charlie Sims said to C. B. Harrington in mock surprise. He stepped forward, snatched the pistol from Steelhead's lowered hand, then stepped back and leveled it on C. B. Harrington. "I'm sure you remember my friend, Kate McCorkle? You met her earlier this evening. I can't stress strongly enough what a volatile temper she has, especially toward someone who meant to kill me."

"Jesus, Sims, wait a minute," C. B. Harrington said, his voice turning shaky all of a sudden. "We weren't going to kill you! You have my word as a gentleman! This was only business. I only meant to persuade you!" As Harrington spoke, Sims stepped in and took the folded leaf of paper from his coat pocket.

"So this has all the locations of Midwest Invest-ment Company's holdings?" Sims stepped back with the paper in his hand, running his eyes over the names.

"Yes, most of them . . . Don't kill me, Sims! Take the list, keep it. But don't kill me. I was only trying to—"

"Shut up, Harrington," Kate McCorkle called out from the darkness behind Steelhead Radner. She shoved Radner forward with her pistol barrel. He staggered with the sway of the train. "Put a bullet in him, Charlie," she added. "He brought it all on himself."

"Easy, Kate," Sims said. He grinned at Harrington, easing back another step as Kate shoved Steelhead Radner over beside his boss. "She does have a point, you know. But I have to admit, Harrington, if it hadn't been for this list it could have taken me months just to find out what I own. Since you know so much about *Los Pistoleros*, where would a person manage to find most of the gang together in one spot?"

Harrington swallowed a nervous lump in his throat. "If we tell you . . . you promise not to shoot us?"

"You have my word," Sims said.

Harrington slid a glance to Steelhead Radner, then back to Sims and Kate McCorkle. "Arch here used to ride with them. He said most of them are up north somewhere, right, Arch?"

Radner hesitated. "For God sakes, Steelhead!" Harrington rasped. "Tell him! I'll pay you extra for it!"

Radner raised a brow, seemed to think it over, then said, "All right, it's true. Cleveland Phelps is in charge. He's put the word out everywhere. Anybody who's a part of *Los Pistoleros* is meeting up north in the territory."

"Where in the territory?" Sims asked.

Radner gave Harrington a glance for reassurance. Harrington nodded his head vigorously. "Go on, tell him!"

"At Cold Ridge . . . a mining town up along the Columbia, near the border," Radner replied. "*Los Pistoleros* owns the whole town, mines and all. They've even got their own sheriff running things for them. He's an ex-stock detective named Harris Sweet."

"I've heard of Sweet," Quick Charlie Sims said. "He did his share of killing in Kansas, years back."

"That's the one," said Radner.

"Tell me about him," Sims said.

"What can I tell you about him?" Radner darted a bewildered glance back and forth.

"Think of something," Sims insisted in a clipped tone.

"Well . . . Sweet's an old, mean, crazy son of a bitch. He don't get along with nobody, except for a big one-eyed cat he calls Scratch."

"Oh? A cat?" Sims took keen interest.

"Don't ask me why," Radner shrugged his broad shoulders. "Sweet used to feed him whole chickens at a time. He'll sic that damn hellion on a feller, too! I've seen him do it. But you've got other problems besides Sweet. Cleveland Phelps is offering a five hundred dollar reward for anybody who kills you or those two deputies of Judge Parker's. If the three of yas are smart, you'll clear out of this country and change your names." Radner offered a flat crooked smile that was more like a sneer.

"What about you, Mr. Steelhead?" Sims asked. "Were you going to claim a reward after killing me?"

"No. I work strictly for Mr. Harrington. I was going to kill you, but it wasn't for no reward—"

"Shut up, Arch," Harrington snapped at him. Then

he turned to Sims. "That's all we can tell you. Now let us go. We'll forget this whole ugly incident ever happened."

Beneath them the train swayed into a curve, lowering its speed. Sims shook his head. "Sorry, Harrington, it's not that easy."

"But you gave your word, Sims!" Harrington pleaded.

"I said I wouldn't shoot you." Sims's smile disappeared, his expression turning deadly serious.

"Then what are you going to do?" Harrington began to tremble, already getting an idea what Sims had in mind.

Sims gestured the pistol barrel toward the grainy darkness of the passing land. "Get off the train."

Harrington and Radner looked at one another. "Jump? From a moving train?"

"LeMaster and Louisville Ike did. I'll count to three," Sims said. "One . . ."

Harrington's voice quivered. "You can't be serious! In the dark? We don't know what's out there! We could be passing over water! Over a canyon, for God sakes!"

"Life's just one big gamble, Harrington," Sims said. "Two . . ." He raised the pistol and took a close aim on Harrington's forehead. Beside him, Kate McCorkle did the same with Steelhead Radner.

"Okay, Sims, we're going." Harrington and Radner turned, facing the rush of wind, trying to steady themselves on wobbly legs. Harrington clamped a hand down on his hat and said without looking back at Sims, "You better hope you never see me again. I'm not the kind of man you can treat this way—"

"Three!" Sims fired the pistol straight up in the air.

Two long screams faded back along the side of the moving train. For a moment Sims and Kate McCorkle stood in silence. Then Kate lowered her pistol and said, "Think they rolled away okay?"

"Sure. I waited until the train slowed down." Sims uncocked the pistol in his hand, unloaded it, and threw it out into the wind. "Kate," he said as if in after thought, "you worry me sometimes. You were about to shoot those two, weren't you?"

"Oh, most definitely," she replied.

"See? Even though I told you earlier not to do it unless I gave you a signal? That throws my timing off, Kate. I'm wondering whether or not you're going to play the game the way I set it up."

"But it all worked out," Kate shrugged. "Anyway, we were right about this card game being a setup," Kate said. She pushed a dark strand of hair back from her face. "You took a big chance going along with it."

"Not as much as you think," said Sims.

"What is that suppose to mean?"

Sims seemed to consider something for a second. Then he dismissed it. "Nothing, Kate. I needed to hear what he knew about *Los Pistoleros* and Midwest Investments, that's all." He patted the pocket of his jacket where he'd put the folded paper he'd taken from C. B. Harrington. "How else could I have found out?"

Kate McCorkle only stared at him, a concerned look mantling her brow. "Charlie? Why don't we clear out? Forget about Fort Smith, Sullivan Hart, Twojack Roth, and Judge Parker. Let them handle this their way. You don't owe them anything. We can go wherever we want to."

"Now, Kate." Sims stepped over, pulling her close to him. "You know I can't leave until my business with J. T. Priest is settled once and for all. Besides,

what would Hart and Roth do without us there,
cheering them on?"

"Don't make jokes, Charlie. I'm afraid of *Los Pistoleros*. I know what they can do. They're dangerous
killers, Charlie. There's too many of them. Look at
that big monster Steelhead Radner, and all the things
Harrington said he would do."

"Radner was no problem. I can handle them,
Kate," he whispered near her ear.

"Handle them? How? You don't even like carrying
a gun."

"But I will carry one, if it'll make you feel better,
Kate. I'll carry a big Colt on my hip . . . and another
one up under my arm. I'll carry a sawed-off shotgun,
a bowie knife, a pair of brass knuckles, and a club.
There, will that do it?"

"Stop it, Charlie. I'm serious. This is a large and
dangerous gang."

"Okay, I'll bring in a gang of my own."

"Don't make jokes about this." Kate drew him
closer to her and held him, feeling his face against
hers. "We're together now. I want us to stay this
way."

"We will, Kate, you'll see. I'm getting all my chickens in a row. When everything's right, I'll start plucking them." He moved back, cupped her cheek and
looked into her eyes. "Now quit worrying and let's
go inside. We have C. B. Harrington's private Pullman car to ourselves now, all the way to Fort Smith
in the morning. It would be a shame to let all of this
go to waste."

Chapter 3

J. T. Priest stood at the bars of his cell and listened to the sound of heavy footsteps draw closer down the narrow corridor. The dimmed glow of a single lantern came to a halt outside his cell, and Priest squinted for a second, then looked into the guard's eyes. In a lowered voice, the guard said, "Two hours, Priest. Be ready."

"Two hours?" Priest spoke in a whisper. The guard had already started to turn and leave, but he stopped as J. T. Priest reached through the bars and clasped his arm. "Wait, Tooney. Are you sure about this?" The guard's rough, pockmarked face looked down at J. T. Priest's hand on his forearm until Priest turned it loose. Then Priest added, "I mean, this is cutting it awfully close, after those three escaping the other night."

"This is the perfect time, while the deputies are out chasing Joe Marr and the Crenshaw brothers," the guard hissed. "We go in two hours, Priest, unless you'd rather call off the whole deal."

"No, Tooney! Forget I mentioned it," Priest responded in a harsh whisper. "I'll be ready. Just make sure everything's all set. I don't want any slip-ups."

Sergeant of the Guards Martin Tooney looked J. T. Priest up and down. "There won't be any slip-ups, unless you make them. Don't forget, I'm going with you. Part of the deal is you getting me into *Los Pistoleros*. Think I'm going to let something like this go wrong?"

J. T. Priest eased a bit. "Don't worry, Tooney. You get me out of here, you *are* a member of *Los Pistoleros*."

Tooney nodded. "Then relax and let me handle this. Just be ready in two hours when I come back for you."

"Don't worry, I'll be ready." Priest stood in his darkened cell and watched the lantern fade back to the iron door at the end of the stone corridor. When the iron door opened and closed, Priest let out a breath. You better believe he'd be ready. He'd been ready ever since he'd arrived. As far as bringing this jail guard into *Los Pistoleros*? He'd have to wait and see. The truth was, J. T. Priest wasn't even sure where he himself stood with the gang. He hadn't heard a word from his partner, William Mabrey, since he'd been here—wasn't sure if Mad-dog Mabrey was dead or alive.

One thing was for certain: Priest was still the leader of the gang, and as soon as he busted out of this joint, he'd pull *Los Pistoleros* back together. Priest had made a couple of wrong moves, but nothing that couldn't be corrected once he was on the outside. His first mistake had been killing Federal Deputy Coleman Hart and slicing off his ears, not realizing that Coleman's son, Sullivan Hart, was also a federal deputy and that Sullivan and his partner, the big Cherokee Twojack Roth, would track him down. Well, that problem would be solved. He'd have them both killed.

Priest's biggest problem was that he'd allowed himself to be taken in by Quick Charlie Sims. Sims had forced him to sign over his interest in Midwest

Investment, the corporation that was the backbone of the whole *Los Pistoleros* criminal empire. Without his shares in Midwest Investment, J. T. Priest was no better than any other outlaw with a gun and a fast horse. He'd worked too hard for too long to go back to the life of a common thief. There was a bloody reckoning coming between him and Quick Charlie Sims, and this time J. T. Priest would take back what was his.

When two hours had passed, Priest eagerly stood at the bars of his cell and listened for the sound of Tooney opening the iron door. When it came, Priest felt his pulse quicken. He watched the glow of the lantern sway back and forth with Tooney's footsteps until the big guard stood at his cell door with a blue guard's uniform under one arm. When Tooney reached out with the cell key, unlocked the door and swung it open, he pitched the uniform against Priest's chest. "Hurry up, put this on," Tooney whispered.

Priest didn't question him. He stepped into the trousers without bothering to first remove his grimy striped prison trousers. Tooney looked him up and down and handed him a crumpled blue guard's cap. As Priest shook out the cap and put it on, Tooney said, still whispering, "Stay behind me when we get to the main door. I'll do the talking. Keep your face down. Nothing happens unless we get through the main doors. Do you understand?"

"I understand," Priest said in a hushed, somber voice.

Tooney dimmed the lantern and walked out of the cell and along the stone corridor, J. T. Priest staying close behind him. At the end of the corridor, they passed through the first iron door and walked slowly and calmly toward the main iron doors. At the main doors, Tooney reached out and banged his fist on the iron plating covering a six-inch peephole. "Guards coming out," he said as the plate slid to one side and a pair of eyes looked out through the opening.

"Sergeant Tooney?" a voice asked.

"Yes, Vertrees. Who the hell else would it be?" Tooney responded in a gruff tone. "Open up. We haven't got all night."

Priest stood behind Tooney with his face lowered, holding his breath until he heard the sound of a metal bar slide across the other side of the door, then the door creak open. "Sorry, Sergeant," said the guard. "I always ask, just in case. After that break the other night, you can't be too careful."

"Of course," Tooney said, stepping past and slightly behind him, seeing the guard's eyes go to Priest and look him up and down. Priest kept his face turned away from the guard, but Tooney knew it would only be a second before Vertrees saw something was wrong. He let Vertrees take a step closer, his expression already changing, catching a glimpse of the ragged striped trouser legs sagging beneath Priest's blue uniform.

"Hey! What the—" Vertrees's voice abruptly stopped as Tooney swung a powerful arm around his throat from behind, then lifted him up on the hilt of the dagger, its long blade sliding in between his ribs and finding his heart. Tooney held him up on his tiptoes, the guard's feet struggling for a second, then going slack.

"There now, you little peckerwood," Tooney chuckled under his breath. "I always told you this was a dangerous job." He backed up a step and let Vertrees's limp body collapse into a wooden chair beside the door. J. T. Priest watched, grinning to himself, liking the feel of getting back into the action. Maybe there was room in *Los Pistoleros* for Tooney after all. "Let's go, Priest," Tooney hissed, seeing Priest stare transfixed.

"Oh yes," Priest said, turning and following the big man to the wooden door at the rear of the building. "We're going to get along just fine, you and me." Beyond the last door lay the backyard of the courthouse, cloaked in darkness.

Without looking back, Tooney said, "That's real comforting to know, J. T."

Priest thought he caught a trace of sarcasm in Tooney's voice, but he was too busy scanning the grounds to let it bother him right now. He moved along quickly behind Tooney in a crouch, both of them looking back and forth in the darkness. At the rear of the yard they moved into the darker shadow of the small livery barn and stood with their backs pressed against the wall. Priest whispered, "Keep watch, I'll get some horses." He started to turn toward the door of the barn, but Tooney grabbed his sleeve.

"It's already taken care of." Tooney pulled him forward, then coaxed him farther into the darkness toward an alley at the rear of the yard. "Hurry up."

Priest glanced back as he moved along. "What about more guards?"

Tooney grinned. "There's only one more—he's taken care of too."

A few feet farther along, Priest saw the body of a guard lying face down at the base of a tall maple tree. He started to step over and reach for the pistol in the dead guard's holster, but once again Tooney stopped him and pushed him forward. "You don't need it," he whispered, hurrying him along.

Inside the mouth of the dark alley, they stopped

and pressed their backs to the rough boards of a rickety shed. "What gives, Tooney? Where's our way out of here?"

"Right there," Tooney said, gesturing at the four riders who stepped their horses forward from around the corner of another shed and moved silently toward them. The front rider led two horses by their reins. Priest squinted and tried to make out the faces in the darkness. Tooney stepped forward, took the two sets of reins and pitched one set to Priest. "Say hello to some friends of yours, J. T."

"Stanton? Is that you?" Priest stood still with the reins in his hand, his eyes moving across the faces. He wasn't sure if he liked this or not.

"Yep, it's me," said the gruff voice beneath the lowered hat brim. "Cleveland Phelps sent for me and the boys. Told us to do whatever it takes to get you out of jail." A silence passed, then the voice of Denver Stanton added, "Well? You coming, J. T.?"

"You're damn right I'm coming." Priest snapped out of it, swung himself atop the horse and reined it back and forth in place, the horse already wanting to run. "Who else is here? Bobby Crady? Is that you?"

"It's me," said the dark figure. "Me, Earl and Carl White. Now are we going or what?" Crady's hand came out with a length of riding quirt and slapped Priest's horse on the rump. Priest righted himself in the saddle, managing to hang on as the horse shot forward. All right, Priest thought, he was out now. That was the main thing. Now he had to get a feel for how he stood with the others.

The trouble with a big gang like *Los Pistoleros* was that everybody was always jockeying for position. If Cleveland Phelps wanted him out of jail, it wasn't because of loyalty. Phelps had something in mind for him. It was up to Priest to reestablish himself as a leader—something he would have to do as quickly as possible.

They pressed the horses hard for a full hour, non-stop, until finally Stanton brought the group to a halt atop a hillside and stepped down from his saddle. "Rest your horses, boys," Stanton said, looking back along the dark trail behind them. The men stepped down and stretched. They drank from their canteens, then poured water into their cupped hands for their horses.

"We've got nothing to worry about until the changing of the guards," Tooney said to Stanton. "It'll be another hour before anybody knows we're missing."

"You do good work, Tooney," Stanton said. He took a mouthful of water from a canteen one of the men handed him, swished it around in his mouth and spat it out.

"Yeah, he does," Priest cut in, making sure he wasn't excluded from anything. "I told him I'd put him in *Los Pistoleros* for doing this."

"That's funny. I told him the same thing," Stanton chuckled.

Priest looked back and forth between the two of them. "Let's get something straight, Stanton. Cleveland Phelps might have hired you to get me out of jail. But now that I'm out, I'm still the top dog in this bunch. Don't anybody here forget that." He looked from one face to the other in the pale moonlight.

"Ease up, J. T.," Stanton said. "Cleveland Phelps asked us to get you out, so we did. Whatever problems you and Phelps have is none of our business. All I know is, somebody better get to running things before *Los Pistoleros* goes out of business."

Priest nodded, reaching out for the canteen in Stan-

ton's hand. When Stanton gave it to him, Priest took
a drink then ran a hand over his mouth and said,
"Make no mistake about it, boys. I'm back, and
you're going to see some changes. Nobody's heard a
word from William Mabrey since he went to Chicago. I figure he's either dead or he's run out on us.
Either way, I'm drawing my best men close around
me. That means you boys, if you all want a piece of
the action."

"Now you're talking, J. T.," Stanton grinned. "Me
and the boys have been working for *Los Pistoleros* off
and on for the past three years. It's about time somebody took notice of us. Phelps only hired us to get
you out of jail. But if you're saying you need us to
back your play full time, you've got yourself some
gunmen." Stanton looked around at the others for
support. They nodded in agreement.

"That's exactly what I'm saying." Priest stepped
closer to Stanton, reached out and lifted one of Stanton's pistols from its holster and shoved it down into
his own waist band. "As soon as we get up into
the high country, I'm doubling whatever Cleveland
Phelps agreed to pay you for getting me out. If
Phelps has any problem with it, he'll have to take it
up with me. Any questions?"

"No," Stanton said, speaking for the others.
"You're the boss, J. T. If you're going to run this
gang the way it should be run, you can count on us."

Priest turned to Tooney. "What about you,
Tooney? Are you going to have any problems working for me? If you are, we'll pay you off and you
can leave right now."

As Priest spoke, his hand went to the pistol at his
waist and rested there. Tooney took note of it, seeing
how things worked with these men. Priest hadn't
been out of jail over an hour, and already he was

back to being top dog. Tooney liked that. He spread a flat smile. "I work for whoever is bold enough to take what he wants without asking anybody a damn thing. Looks like that's you, J. T. So count me in."

Priest chuckled, looking back at Stanton and the others. "Then what the hell are we waiting for? Let's ride!"

Chapter 4

The next morning Judge Parker was in his chamber, at his desk, and on his second pot of strong coffee when Deputy Dan'l Slater brought Quick Charlie Sims to see him. Parker looked up at Sims with red-rimmed eyes, not bothering to stand up as Sims took off his bowler hat, walked over and stood looking down at him. "I suppose Deputy Slater told you what happened?" the judge said.

"Yes, he told me." Sims gestured toward a clean coffee mug sitting bottom up beside the pot on the serving tray. "May I?"

"Help yourself." Parker spoke with a sound of defeat in his voice. "I suppose Slater also told you that Deputies Hart and Roth are still out hunting for Joe Marr and the Crenshaw brothers? That means I don't have any experienced deputies to put on Priest's trail . . . for the time being anyway."

Sims poured himself a cup of coffee, stepped back, and sat down in a wingback chair. "Slater filled me in on everything. He said a guard named Tooney helped Priest escape."

Parker winced. "Tooney got his job through a political connection—some congressman from Maryland. That's the third time I've gotten stung hiring someone as a political favor. But enough of that . . ." He sipped his coffee. "I want to thank you for help-

ing capture Priest in Chicago. You took a bullet in
the back trying to help my deputies. That was highly
commendable."

"You're welcome." Sims shrugged. "Although it
all seems a little immaterial now. How long before
Hart and Roth will be on Priest's trail?"

"Soon, I hope. They've been gone over a week.
The moment they arrive I'll send them out. I've sent
telegrams out in all directions, advising local authorities to keep a lookout for Priest and Tooney, but I
doubt if they'll be showing themselves."

"No idea which way they're headed?" Sims sipped
his coffee.

"No. You can't pick up tracks in a town this busy.
Once Roth gets out on the open range, maybe he'll
get a lead on them."

"I have an idea where Priest is headed," Sims said,
almost cutting the judge off.

"Oh?" Parker stared at him. "Hart told me you
had a feeling Priest would try to escape. But what
makes you think you know where he's headed?"

"Something I heard on the train coming here,"
Sims replied. "I met a gentleman named C. B. Har-
rington. He and his hired hand, an ape named
Steelhead Radner, seemed real familiar with Midwest
Investment and *Los Pistoleros*. Radner told me about
a place up in the Northwest—a mining town called
Cold Ridge. They said *Los Pistoleros* always head up
there when things get a little too hot for them."

"I've heard of C. B. Harrington—a big business
lord from New York. Where is he and this Steelhead
Radner? I'd like to speak to them at once." Parker
rose slightly from his chair.

"Sorry, Your Honor." Sims offered a slight smile.
"They both got off the train unexpectedly. If they
make it here, I imagine you'll be hearing from them

soon enough—some crazy accusation about me stealing his Pullman car." Sims shrugged it off. "But I think what they told me was true."

"You stole his Pullman car?" Parker asked, stunned.

"Well, he'll say I did. But it's nothing, Judge. He's just one more sore loser, trying to stay in the game. This Steelhead Radner said he'd ridden with some of the gang in the past."

"Should I arrest Harrington and his ape? Hold them here for safe keeping?"

"No," Sims said, "they're no problem. Harrington's just bargain hunting. You can't blame a man for that. As far as Radner, he's just one of many thugs. I've got a feeling Harrington only has him along because Radner can introduce him to the others without Harrington getting his head shot off."

Parker rubbed his forehead. "See? That's the trouble with this gang. Every hardcase in the country rides with them at some time or other. They're more like a secret society than a bunch of outlaws."

"They're hard to catch," agreed Sims, "I'll give them that. But if it will help you any, Your Honor, I'd be glad to head Northwest. I already have my game into play. It might save your deputies some time and trouble."

Parker cocked his head to the side. "And if Priest is there? What will you do? I'm told you don't even carry a gun."

"Well, that's not quite so, Your Honor. I don't like carrying a gun. But if need be, I will. The main thing is, if Priest is in Cold Ridge, maybe I can hold things down until Hart and Roth get there. If things go the way I plan, I'll take J. T. Priest into custody and bring him back. You'll need Hart and Roth to take down the rest of the gang."

"Oh? You'll take Priest into custody? Just like that?" Judge Parker snapped his fingers.

"Well, not *just like that*," Sims said. "Priest and I have some unfinished business—then I'll deliver him to you, personally." Sims grinned.

"I think you've lost your mind. But why are you offering, Sims?" Parker asked. "What's your angle in all this?"

"Angle?" Sims's smile widened a bit. "What about just civic duty, Your Honor?"

Parker shook his head. "Uh-uh. I don't buy it, Sims. I know you went after Priest the last time because he framed you for the bank robbery up in Creed. But that charge against you is dropped now. Why are you still so interested in Priest and *Los Pistoleros*?"

Sims considered it for a second. "All right, Judge, I'll be honest with you." He took a deep breath. "When I was a small child, my folks were killed crossing the desert to California. A band of traveling Roma found me, took me in, and raised me as if I were their own."

"Gypsies?" Judge Parker asked, interrupting him. "You were raised by gypsies?"

"Yes, Your Honor." Sims continued. "Years later, while I was seeking my fortune at the gaming tables in New Orleans, that band of Roma made the mistake of stopping for a few days on land owned by William Mad-dog Mabrey." Sims's expression turned grim. "Mabrey and some of his gunmen killed them all—men, women, children alike. He killed them and left their bodies and wagons to rot out in the badlands." Sims paused for a second. "The next day, he must've got worried. So he sent his top gunman, Tuck Javin, to clean things up for him."

"I remember that name," said Parker, thinking

about it. "Javin was a killer. But I heard he'd died years ago."

"Not so, Your Honor." Sims leveled his gaze on Parker. "Tuck Javin, you see, is J. T. Priest. Once he and Mabrey started *Los Pistoleros*, and channeled their robbery money into starting Midwest Investment Corporation, they both wanted to look respectable. Mabrey is still trying to drop the nickname Mad-dog, and Tuck Javin changed his name all together."

Judge Parker shook his head slowly. "That's quite a story, Sims. If it's true."

"It's true. Mabrey sent Priest out to clean up and bury the bodies and get rid of the wagons. But instead, Priest piled the bodies into their wagons and drove all four wagons into a large cave. The wagons and bodies have been there ever since. William Mabrey told me all of this in Chicago—told me he had it done, but he had no idea where that cave is. Only Priest knows that. And it's something I need to find out."

"But why?" Parker asked. "If they've been dead this many years, why not let them rest in peace?"

"It's a Roma custom, Your Honor. When a Roma dies, all the possessions, wagon and all, are burnt. It's up to me to set this thing right."

"Then why didn't you just ask Priest while you had him captured in Chicago? What did he have to lose by telling you?"·

"If you understood the Roma, Your Honor, you'd know why I can't ask him. To be honest, I knew Priest would escape your jail. I had hoped to be here when he did. My plan was to make him take me to that cave, so I could finish what I have to do."

Parker's face took on a wily expression. "You mean to take him there and kill him, don't you?"

Sims didn't answer for a moment, as if working that part out in his mind. Finally he said, "No . . . I won't kill him if I can keep from it. Mabrey was the one who killed my people. Priest only did the cleanup work."

"And William Mabrey? That's why no one has heard from him. He didn't just disappear to avoid prosecution—you killed him, didn't you? An eye for an eye, as it were?"

Sims studied the judge's stern face for a second. "Let's put it this way, Judge Parker. I'd be *very* surprised if you ever see William Mad-dog Mabrey again. Other than that, I won't comment."

"So, your interest in all this is strictly personal?" Parker studied Sims's eyes, but could read nothing from his practiced gambler's stare.

"Yes . . . strictly personal," Sims said, deciding not to let the judge know that he now owned J. T. Priest's interest in Midwest Investment, and that J. T. Priest would do anything to get it back.

"I see . . ." Judge Parker fell silent, contemplating all of this in his mind. Sims sipped his coffee and waited.

Finally, the judge nodded. "Okay, Sims. Suppose I send you up to Cold Ridge ahead of Hart and Roth? Can you control your revenge and keep them there until my deputies arrive?"

"Your Honor, I don't even call it revenge. It's just something I have to do." He finished his coffee and set the empty mug down on the serving tray at the edge of Parker's desk. "Let me remind you, Your Honor, I don't have to ask anybody's permission to go to Cold Ridge. I'm only asking you out of respect, sir. I prefer going there with your blessing, just to keep Hart and Roth from showing up there wondering whose side I'm on."

"Good thinking, Sims," Parker smiled, "especially since Sullivan Hart seems convinced that you're in cahoots with the devil himself."

Sims chuckled under his breath. "Sullivan Hart and Twojack Roth are fine lawmen. We just got off on the wrong foot—what with me stealing Hart's horse. But believe me, I wouldn't attempt this without them on my side."

"They might be upset if you really do succeed in capturing J. T. Priest before they do."

"They can have the rest of the gang all to themselves, Your Honor. That's a promise."

Judge Parker thought about it again, then concluded, "You'll be working for me without *Los Pistoleros* knowing it. Consider yourself deputized, Sims," Parker threw in with a toss of his hand, as if in afterthought, "All they will know is that there is bad blood between you and J. T. Priest. I see unlimited possibilities to what a man like you could do in this situation."

Quick Charlie Sims let Judge Parker play out the scenes in his mind for a moment. Then Sims said in a quiet tone, "My thoughts exactly, Your Honor."

Moments later on his way back to the hotel, Quick Charlie Sims stopped in an apothecary shop, and as he browsed a short aisle of herbs in glass jars, he tried to think of the best way to tell Kate McCorkle that she wouldn't be making the trip up to Cold Ridge with him. *For one thing there are bears and cougars in the Northwest, Kate,* he thought, rehearsing it out. He smiled to himself, lifting a lid from a jar and reaching down into it with a small metal scoop. *For another thing, at this time of year, you never know when a blizzard is going to sweep down out of the Canadian Rockies and—*

No, Sims thought, stepping to the counter, laying

a small brown paper bag down for the clerk and taking a dollar from his pocket to pay for it. Neither of those things would do. Kate McCorkle had no fear of such things as blizzards or wild animals. He would just have to tell her bluntly, flat out, that she wasn't going, and that was all there was to it. Yet, when he arrived at their hotel room and told her, Kate's eyes flashed as wild as that cougar he'd imagined, and her voice turned as icy as any blizzard.

"I didn't come this far to be left in Fort Smith like excess baggage," she said. "If I'm not going, neither are you." She swung the big Colt up from the nightstand beside the bed, taking both hands to hold it steady.

Sims only shook his head. "What are you saying? You'll kill me just to keep me from going?" He smiled. "Don't be ridiculous. You, of all people, should know I'm hard to bluff."

"No, I won't kill you," she said in a firm voice, "but I'll put a bullet through your foot. That should keep you here for the next week or so. Meanwhile I'll go to Cold Ridge and take on J. T. Priest and *Los Pistoleros* on my own." When she saw how lightly Sims was taking her, she added, cocking the hammer for emphasis, "I mean it, Charlie. Don't try me."

"Kate, dear Kate," Sims said, taking a step toward her, his arms spreading out affectionately, "we both know this is something best done by—*Whoa!*" He stopped short as the pistol bucked in her hand and the explosion rattled the panes in the window. In a gathering cloud of smoke, Sims looked down at his feet just to make certain. An inch from his right boot, ragged splinters stood up from the bullet hole in the pine floor. He looked back up at Kate in time to see her cock the big Colt .45 again.

"I'll do better this time," Kate said, taking aim

down the long pistol barrel. She squinted one eye shut, a lock of dark hair coiling loosely down her left cheek.

"Jesus, Kate." Sims stared at her, stunned. "See, this is the very reason I want you to stay here. You've got a terrible temper. I know you don't realize it, but it's true. There's no telling when you're apt to fly off the—"

"Don't tell me about my temper. I don't want to hear it!" she raged, cutting him off, the pistol still leveled down toward his foot. "All I want to hear from you is, 'Kate, be sure and pack something warm, it gets cold where we're going!'"

Sims studied her eyes, his hands spread in a cautious show of peace. Then he swallowed down the dry knot in his throat and said in a calm clear voice, "Kate, be sure and pack something warm. It gets cold where we're going . . ."

J. T. Priest sat atop his horse, looking down on the wagon-rutted main dirt street of Summit in the early morning light. He had taken the lead and beside him on his right sat Denver Stanton; on his left, Martin Tooney. Behind the three of them, Bobby Crady, Earl Mellon and Carl White reined their horses to a halt. "Listen up, gentlemen," Priest said. "It's been a long time since I've sacked a town." He looked around at the others, grinning. "But you can bet your shirt I haven't forgotten how."

J. T. Priest knew he needed to make some bold moves, let these men see that he was the man in charge. He needed to put some money in their pockets, give them the taste of blood, show them how ruthless he could be. Over the past few years he'd grown a little soft, traveling in his private Pullman car, living the high life. Now he was back on the run, living in the saddle like in the old days. He had to prove himself.

"We're not only going to rob the bank," Priest said, "we're going to seize the entire town." Lifting the big pistol from his waist, he gestured toward the row of telegraph poles running up alongside the trail. "Earl, you and Carl get up there and cut those wires."

When the two men stalled for a second and looked at Stanton, Priest asked them from behind a frosty stare, "Is that going to be a problem, boys?"

"He's in charge. You heard him," said Stanton. He looked away, offering no further guidance on the matter.

"No, sir, J. T., no problem at all," said Carl White. He kicked his horse forward. Earl Mellon fell in behind him.

Priest looked at Stanton, then at Tooney. "As soon as we rob this bunch of hayseeds, I'm heading to the mercantile, getting myself some decent clothes and boots. Then I'm getting a nice hot bath while the rest of you get acquainted with the womenfolk. Whatever Cleveland Phelps has going on up north will just have to wait a few days." He nudged his horse forward, down toward the trail into town. "We might as well kick up our heels a little on the way."

On the way down the dusty trail, Earl Mellon and Carl White trotted their horses back in and joined them. "It's done," said Carl, drawing a rifle from his saddle boot and laying it across his lap. At the beginning of the dirt street, they stopped six abreast. At the edge of town, Priest nodded toward a sign that read: TOWN ORDINANCE # 110 PROHIBITS THE CARRYING OF FIREARMS WITHIN TOWN LIMITS.

"I love it," Priest chuckled. "I believe every town should have such an ordinance." He batted his heels to the horse's sides, letting out a yell. Raising his pistol, he leveled it on the first person he saw stepping off of the boardwalk and shot him dead in the street. For a lingering second the town seemed to freeze in place at the sound of gunfire and the sight of the man falling dead beneath a spray of blood. Then a woman's scream rose amid the roar of pistol and rifle fire. The sound of her shrill voice became the warning signal that caused the townsfolk to leap for cover as the six riders bore down on them in a rise of dust.

Out front of the blacksmith's barn, a man stepped forward wearing a badge on his vest. But no sooner had his hand clamped around the pistol at his hip than a rifle shot from Carl White's Winchester sent him flying backward, crashing through a rail fence. Horses bolted from the corral, filling the street. Priest laughed and yelled and gunned an elderly woman down as she tried to hurry around the corner of an alley. "There's the bank, boys!" he shouted, pointing his pistol toward the only brick building on the dirt street. "Skin her down!"

Bobby Crady and Carl White jumped off their horses, up onto the boardwalk and through the open doors of the bank. Shots resounded from inside. A teller staggered out through the doors and fell facedown on the boardwalk. Earl Mellon cursed, kicked the teller's body out of his way, and hurried into the bank on foot, his horse left to wander the street amid the murderous melee. "You and Tooney keep everybody pinned down out here," Priest yelled at Stanton. "I better make sure there's enough money to go around." He laughed and gigged his horse forward onto the boardwalk and through the doors.

Inside the bank, Priest straightened up in his saddle as soon as he cleared the door frame. He saw another body, this one draped across a mahogany desk that sat off to itself behind a polished handrail. "How's it going, Bobby?" he called out, guiding his horse around the corner of the counter and back to where Bobby Crady and the other two stood inside an open vault, stuffing money into their saddlebags. Their horses milled back and forth among spilled files and overturned furniture.

"Lord have mercy, J. T.!" Bobby Crady held up two fists full of dollar bills. "There's too much money here! We can't get it all."

"We've got all day if need be," Priest grinned. "One of you go get some burlap bags from the mercantile. We're not leaving a red cent behind."

"What the hell is a two-bit town like Summit doing with this kind of money on hand?" Carl White asked. He pitched a handful of bills in the air and watched them flutter down around them.

"Why don't you just show up here next council meeting and ask them, Carl?" Bobby Crady shrieked and laughed. He hurled a banded stack of dollar bills at White, the paper band busting as it hit his chest and spilled open. Money showered down around them.

"See, boys," Priest said, swinging down from his horse, kicking dollar bills across the floor. "There's some people who promise big money. But I don't just promise—I *deliver*!" He raised his pistol and fired it into the ceiling.

Outside, three townsmen had armed themselves with shotguns and came running down the middle of the street. "Damned fools," Stanton growled. He and Tooney fired as one. One townsman fell limp in the street, another spun to the ground with a bullet through his shoulder. The third emptied both barrels, hitting nothing, then simply dropped his shotgun and ran away.

"I think I'm going to like this kind of work," Tooney said, smoke curling from the barrel of his pistol.

"It's all what you get used to, I reckon," Stanton said in a serious tone, his eyes scanning the empty street. "You people listen up!" he called out. "We're going to spend a little time here getting to know you. If there's any whores in town, they better get on out here and make themselves known. If not, we'll go door to door and pick who we want. It makes us no difference."

At the sight of Carl White running from the bank with his pistol in his hand, Stanton called out to him, "Where you going, Carl?"

"J. T. said to get some bags!" Carl White yelled over his shoulder without stopping. "You ain't seen so much money in your whole life!"

"Is that a fact?" Stanton said, almost to himself. He chewed on a wad of tobacco, spit a stream, and ran a gloved hand across his mouth. "Well, I'll be damned . . . maybe ole J. T.'s the man to pay attention to after all."

Martin Tooney eased his horse over closer to Stanton. "Does this mean Cleveland Phelps ain't going to be running things after all?"

"Hell, who knows? Who cares?" Stanton turned a flat expression toward him. "I say we let Phelps and J. T. work that out between themselves. Main thing is, we did our part. We're full-time *Los Pistoleros* now. That's a good thing to be no matter how you slice it." He spat once again into the dust.

Chapter 5

By evening a fire raged in the middle of the dirt street where broken furniture from the bank had been dragged out, piled high, then lit with a dose of kerosene. The striped barber pole had been ripped from its place on the boardwalk and now lay flaming beneath the remnants of a blackened rack of calf ribs on a spit. Bones and gristle lay strewn around the fire. A few feet away lay the body of a spotted hound with a bullet hole in its head where Carl White had shot it over an hour ago, after the pesky dog ventured in for scraps of meat.

At the alley where J. T. Priest had shot the elderly woman, two other dogs growled and snapped at one another above the hind leg and ragged hide of the slaughtered calf.

J. T. Priest stood at the fire in his new suit and knee-high riding boots, a crisp white straw skimmer hat cocked at a jaunty angle on his forehead. "I think we've about worn out our welcome here, gentlemen." His lapel pocket bulged with cigars. He ran a hand along his freshly shaved jawline and looked around the littered street at broken whiskey bottles and spent brass cartridge shells. His right hand rested on the butt of a big new Colt .45 in a hand-tooled Mexican loop holster on his hip. "By now, somebody is wondering why there's no telegrams getting through to here."

"Yep, you're right." Stanton stood up from a rocking chair and pushed a cork into a half-full bottle of rye. "All right, you heard the boss," he said, reaching out with his boot and nudging Carl White, who lay sprawled on a feather mattress in the dirt. A naked woman lay passed out beside him, flat on her back, her flaming red hair slung sideways across her face. "Get up, Carl, before you wind up married. Come on, boys, let's go!" Stanton raised his voice and clapped his hands together. "We didn't come here to settle down and raise families. Move it!"

Farther back from the fire, Earl Mellon stood up from a blanket and moaned, rubbing his head with both hands. A dark-haired woman with a rose tattooed on her right breast stood up, staggered in place, then swept the blanket up from the dirt, covered herself with it and trotted away. "Jesus," Earl rasped, "somebody *please* get her name." When the woman reached a doorway on the boardwalk, two women stepped out, took her in their arms and hurried her inside. The door slammed shut with a rattle of broken glass.

Priest looked around at the gunmen gathering like lost souls from some distant netherworld. "Anybody who doesn't want to live like this all the time best clear out now and not ride with me." He laughed. "Who else has ever treated yas this good, huh?"

"You've got my vote if you ever run for office, J. T.," Tooney said, staggering in, his new shirt front stretched wide with his share of the bank money stuffed inside it. The other men uttered their approval and staggered toward their horses at a hitch rail out front of the sheriff's office; the sheriff lay dead in the empty livery corral.

"I'm glad you all feel that way," Priest said, standing as if posing for a picture while Denver Stanton led his horse in the street to him, "because there's another jerkwater town just like this eighty miles up the trail. We'll do the same thing all the way up north." He took his reins from Stanton and swung up into his saddle, beaming at the men. "That is, if you don't mind upsetting Cleveland Phelps with us being a little late."

"To hell with Phelps," one of the men said.

"That's what I thought." Priest turned his horse in the dirt street and led the men forward like a Prussian general at the head of his troops. They rode out of Summit slowly, looking around as if in pride at the destruction they left behind them. Outside the town, Stanton sidled his horse up closer to J. T. Priest. Priest stared straight ahead with a black cigar between his teeth.

"I know a couple of ole boys living over on the flats not far from here—Luther Ison and his son, Bert. What do you think?"

"About what?" Priest asked without looking at him.

"About them joining us," Stanton replied. "Bert's what you might call a little touched in the head. But his daddy, Luther, is meaner than a snake. He's rode off and on with the James-Youngers ever since the war. I know he'd fit right in with *Los Pistoleros*, especially if this is the way things are going to be going. Luther likes it wild and wooly."

"How far?" Priest asked.

"Thirty, forty miles maybe."

"Think he's got anybody besides his idiot son with him?"

"You never know, he might have. Luther's always got three or four gunmen hanging around."

"Point the way then," Priest said. "We're always looking for a few good men."

Quick Charlie Sims and Kate McCorkle were three days out of Fort Smith by the time Sullivan Hart and Twojack arrived with Joe Marr, lying low in his saddle. They'd stopped at a missionary doctor's clinic in the Indian Nation and spent a full day there getting Marr's wound attended. Marr looked bad, his chest the color of fruit gone to spoil. As soon as they turned Marr over to the young doctor at the jail hospital ward, they went straight to Judge Parker's chamber in the courthouse upstairs.

Deputy Dan'l Slater met them at the door to the judge's chambers, a shotgun cradled in his arm. He spoke in a hushed tone, leading them a few feet away from the door, "Fellows, walk a little wide of the jailbreak matter. Parker's fit to be tied over it."

"I don't blame him," said Sullivan Hart. "So are we. This place is getting worse every day. One of the orderlies said a guard was responsible for Priest getting away?"

"Not just a guard," said Slater. "This was Tooney, sergeant of the night watch. Parker's ready to strangle him with his bare hands, if he's ever caught."

Twojack Roth shook his head in disgust. "There's no point in us rounding them in, if all they have to do is walk away."

Slater looked at him with a knowing expression. "Parker's not talking like he wants Tooney rounded in, if you know what I mean."

"We know what you mean," Hart said. "Take us in to see the judge, Dan'l. I imagine he'll want us on Priest's trail right away."

"Yep. But let me warn you before you go in there—Parker sent Quick Charlie Sims out looking for Priest. Him and his woman left here three days ago by rail, heading northwest."

"Sims?" Twojack Roth looked at Slater in disbelief. "Sims is no lawman!"

"Don't blame me, boys. I'm just telling you what I know." Slater backed up a step from the irate deputies. "Sims told the judge he knew where Priest was headed. Parker sent him on."

As Slater spoke, Sullivan Hart loudly rapped his knuckles on Judge Parker's door. Deputy Slater stepped in front of him. "Calm down, Sully. This ain't no time to go in there with your bark on."

Hart settled down, looked around at Roth, then nodded. "You're right, Dan'l. Take us in. We'll be all right."

Inside the judge's chambers, Hart walked to Parker's desk with his battered Stetson hanging from his hand. Roth followed a step behind him. "I can see by the look on your faces that you've heard what's gone on here," Parker said, rising slightly. He gestured them toward two wingback chairs, then settled back into his seat. "Before you say something you'll regret, sit down and take a breather."

"We're fine," Hart said in a firm tone, not moving from the edge of the desk.

Parker's expression hardened. "I said sit down." He stared at Hart with his eyes ablaze. "I've got enough on my mind. Don't come in here with a bad attitude."

Hart relented, letting out a breath. He and Roth stepped back and sat on the edge of the chairs. "First things first," Parker said. "Did you bring in the prisoners?"

"Only Joe Marr, Your Honor," Sullivan Hart replied. "Things got out of hand. Him and the Crenshaws shot it out with one another. Marr's down in the infirmary. He's touch and go with a chest wound. The doctor gives him a fifty-fifty chance."

Parker shook his head. "The Crenshaws would have been out of here in no time—the fools. Too bad about Marr. He's not a bad sort. He just can't keep his hands off other men's cattle."

"So much for Joe Marr. What about Quick Charlie Sims and his woman, Your Honor?" Twojack Roth asked, going straight to the subject. "Where do those two swindlers play into this?"

Parker raised a pacifying hand toward him. "Apparently Sims met a man on the train who says he knows *Los Pistoleros* is gathering up in the northwest, near the border—"

"Met on the train, Your Honor?" Hart cut him off, an astonished look on his face. "Sims had to have made that up, sir. How are we supposed to work with him and that woman? They're both slippery as eels in a bucket."

"Let me finish, Deputy," Parker said. "At the time I had no deputies to send out. Maybe Sims's information is good, maybe it isn't. But it costs us nothing to find out. He let me know I had no hold on him if he wanted go. But I deputized him. At least this way, maybe we'll have some idea what he's up to. If Cleveland Phelps or any *Los Pistoleros* are up there, we'll know where to look for Priest. You two will be on the trail anyway. If it leads northwest, so be it. If not, Sims will let us know. It can save you some time, either way."

Hart and Roth considered it. "Besides," Parker continued, "Sims holds you both in high regard. I think he wants to cooperate with us." Parker just stared at the two deputies for a moment, wondering whether or not to tell them about Sims's personal reason for wanting J. T. Priest. He decided not to mention it, not now anyway.

After a second of silence, Parker went on. "I know this sounds crazy, but Sims thinks he can arrest J. T. Priest and bring him back to jail. Says he needs you two to bust up the rest of *Los Pistoleros*." Judge Parker stifled a dark laugh. "You have to give Sims credit . . . he's not afraid to play his hand."

"They'll kill him," Roth said under his breath.

"Sims doesn't stand a chance, Your Honor," Hart threw in. "He's no lawman . . . he's just gotten too full of himself."

Parker shrugged. "Give him a chance. I have no idea what you should expect to be waiting for you up there. I'm certain to catch fire and brimstone from Washington for even sending you." His gaze tightened on Sullivan Hart. "The only reason I'm doing this is out of respect for your father. If you rather I turn this matter over to another district, just say so." Parker paused again, knowing better.

"No, Your Honor, we'll handle it," Sullivan Hart said, a trace of submission in his voice. "Who was this man Sims supposedly met, if you don't mind me asking."

"It was two men actually," Parker said. "One was a businessman by the name of Harrington, the other was his hired hand, a big fellow by the name of Arch Radner. Sims said Radner used to ride with some of *Los Pistoleros*. Said Radner often goes by the name Steelhead—I dare not wonder why."

"Steelhead Radner. That name sounds familiar . . ." Sullivan Hart ran the name through his mind, looking at Roth for help.

Roth worked on it for a second. "I once heard of a seaman called Radner who could break boards with his forehead. He learned it in Shanghai from some oriental wrestlers. They say he could kill a man just by butting heads with him."

A silence passed, then Judge Parker cleared his throat. "Well, at any rate, that's all I can tell you. I doubt very much if you'll run into those two. It sounded as if Sims might have thrown them off of a moving train."

"Why?" Hart asked, a bemused looked on his face.

"To keep Kate McCorkle from shooting them would be my guess, based on Sims's sketchy details," Parker shrugged. "Charlie Sims has a way of never giving you the complete picture. I get the impression he does so in case he may need to alter his story at some future time."

"And this is who we're supposed to work with?" Hart shook his head. "I hope we can round in Priest and his bunch without Sims's help. I'd like to keep him, his woman, this Harrington and his Steelhead friend out of it. Things just seem to happen anytime Sims is involved. I want to keep this whole thing simple, if that's at all possible."

Along the railroad tracks leading into Fort Smith, C. B. Harrington and Arch Radner rode the aged Indian ponies at a slow walk. Harrington had long given up on trying to make any time on the rundown animals. The spotted ponies flopped along, seeming to have trouble lifting one tired hoof behind the other.

When Harrington and Radner had found the party of Cherokee camped beside a stream the morning after Sims forced them from the train, luckily he had six hundred dollars in his pocket—the exact price the old chief had asked for the animals. Neither Harrington nor Radner had noticed that the two old ponies were being kept in a meat pen along with a couple of goats and a worn-out sow.

At the rail station in Fort Smith, Harrington tucked in the rip on the shoulder of his ragged suit coat and stood at the ticket window until the young man in the green visor cap stepped forward. "May I help you, sir?"

"Yes, I'm looking for a private Pullman car with the letters CBH Enterprises on the side of it in bold English Gothic? It was on the train from St. Louis, and should have arrived here on the eighteenth."

"The eighteenth . . ." The clerk consulted a clipboard full of paperwork, then turned back to the window. "Yes, sir, it came in on the eighteenth, was cleaned, safety checked, and resupplied with bourbon and food staples as per forwarded instructions."

"Good then," Harrington sighed. "Where is it?"

"Where—? Oh, yes." The clerk licked his thumb and shuffled through the paperwork again. "Mr. Harrington and his lady companion left here three days ago, headed north."

"Damn it to hell, no!" Harrington slammed a thick fist down on the narrow counter.

The clerk looked startled, then quickly turned the clipboard around for Harrington to see. "Oh yes, see?" He pointed a thin, trembling finger down on the paper. In a burst of rage Harrington swept the clipboard aside. Paperwork fluttered. "I mean, *I'm* Mr. Harrington, you imbecile!"

"Oh . . ." The clerk looked frightened and confused, touching his shaking fingertips to his lower lip. "Your brother then, perhaps?"

Arch Radner caught Harrington's arm in time to keep Harrington from clutching at the clerk's throat. The clerk jumped back with a short rasp.

"Easy, boss!" Arch Radner pulled Harrington

away from the counter and out of view of the curious gaze of travelers along the boardwalk. "You can't start letting Quick Charlie Sims get to you this way. You said yourself he has a way of getting under everybody's skin, making them slip up, doing exactly what he wants them to do."

Harrington settled down a bit, ran a hand across his dirty face, across scratches and bruises he'd taken from his leap off the speeding train. "You're right, Steelhead. Thanks. I'm okay now. Just give me a moment." He raised a quaking hand and took a deep breath.

"Serves you right, you fine-haired sonsabitch," said a voice behind them. Harrington and Radner turned to face Dirk LeMaster and Louisville Ike. "Where's our damned money?"

C. B. Harrington stared at them, wide-eyed. Arch Radner stepped in between the two men and his boss, and shoved LeMaster back. "Keep your distance or I'll keep it for you." Radner's broad shoulders seemed to bristle like a fighting dog's hackles.

"Wait, gentlemen!" Harrington said. "Hold everything." He stepped from behind Radner, facing LeMaster. "Do you realize what happened out there?"

"No, and we don't care," said Louisville Ike Woodsen. "You was supposed to have somebody pay us as soon as we left the game. We damned near got ourselves shot by that gypsy swindler, Sims. Now pay up! We don't care how many apes you have swinging in your tree." He cut a harsh glance up at Steelhead Radner. Radner seethed but held himself in check.

"All right, everybody, stay calm," said Harrington. "I apologize for you not getting paid right away. I'll go to the telegraph office, wire my bank in New York and have money sent—"

"We're going with you," LeMaster cut in. "Just to make sure you don't get sidetracked again."

"That won't be necessary, I assure you." Harrington lifted his chin and tugged at his ragged suit coat. "You may wait here with Mr. Radner until I return. It could take a day or so before the transaction can be completed."

"Yeah? Well meantime, we're sticking close to you like grass in a pig's droppings, Harrington," Louisville Ike said, "so don't get any ideas."

Harrington stood silent, staring at them. Then he said, "It might interest you to know about the pistol Sims held on you. You remember—the one that almost caused you to soil yourselves? It wasn't even loaded!"

Louisville Ike and Dirk LeMaster looked at one another blank-faced. "Yes, it's true," Harrington continued. "It turns out Sims doesn't like carrying a loaded weapon. He made blithering fools of both of you with an empty gun. So chew on *that* while I go have some money wired to me."

"So? We had no way of knowing the gun wasn't loaded," Louisville Ike shrugged.

"Of course not," Harrington said, "all of which tells the world he is by far better at poker than either of you."

"Makes no difference. The game was a setup anyway," LeMaster said, jutting his chin. "As far as Sims goes, we'll get our hands on him someday."

"*Someday* seems a bit vague, don't you think?" Harrington looked from one to the other, thinking something over. "However, if you'd like to get more specific, Mr. Radner and I are heading north to go after Sims immediately. If you'd *truly* like to get a hold of Quick Charlie and break his knees for him, you'll never get a better opportunity."

"You're offering us work?" LeMaster gave him a skeptical look.

"That's right, if you're both able to handle it. Mr. Radner and I are going after Sims for another reason. He and his woman threw us off the train. I can promise you when we find him, we're going to set things right." Harrington paused, then leveled his gaze on them and added, "There's five hundred dollars in it for you."

"Five hundred a piece, or for both of us?" Louisville Ike cut in.

Harrington tossed Radner a shrewd glance, Radner catching it and spreading a thin smile at how fast Louisville Ike had jumped for the figure. "That's for the both of you, naturally," Harrington said. "But that's two hundred and fifty dollars each, plus the money you have coming for the card game." He raised a finger. "Think about it. All you'll probably be doing is watching my back, helping Radner keep a few people busy while I conduct my business with Sims. Afterward, Sims is all yours."

"The same business you were supposed to conduct with him on the train?" LeMaster still looked skeptical.

"Yes . . . only this time it's going to turn out different. I'll get what I want or I'll have Sims's head on a stick. Are you two coming or not?"

"It sounds easy enough." Louisville Ike turned to LeMaster for his take on the matter. "What do you say, Dirk?"

LeMaster considered it. "Where is this place up north?"

Harrington hooked his thumbs into the pockets of his dusty suit vest. "Actually it's northwest, up along the border. A pleasant little mining town called Cold Ridge." He cut another shrewd glance to Steelhead

Radner, who grinned, liking the way C. B. Harrington was letting him in on everything, and keeping these two fools in the dark. He knew C. B. Harrington wasn't about to mention *Los Pistoleros*—not yet anyway. Not until they got there.

Chapter 6

Sheriff Harris Sweet stood at his office window and watched Cleveland Phelps and his six gunmen swagger across the rope footbridge. The bridge separated the small town of Cold Ridge from the scattered miner shacks standing on stilts against the steep hillside. Many of the shacks would be empty now, if it weren't for Phelps and his gunmen taking them over for the coming winter. Ordinarily, Sweet liked it here in winter, not having to put up with the miners or the occasional drifter—and not having to crack a drunken head now and then. Winter here was his vacation time in a sense.

But not this winter. This winter he would be putting up with Phelps and his bunch, something Sweet didn't like doing even in the summer when folks were more spread out. The biting cold pressed people closer together, made them huddle in a circle of woodstove heat and fireplaces. Sweet could smell them just thinking about it, the odor of dried and crusted body sweat, greasy hair and fermenting wool socks. He winced at the thought.

The company mine fell to a skeleton staff during the long winters. Most of the miners trekked down the mountainside by mule or on foot and spent weeks at a time in the whorehouses and whiskey swills down at Longbaugh or Brody. That was the natural order of things here. But now Cleveland Phelps and his men were upsetting that order.

"Look at you sons of bitches," Sweet whispered to himself, watching Phelps and his men coming closer. He raised the Colt Peacemaker from his holster and tapped the tip of the barrel gently against the pane of window glass. "Pow, pow, pow," he whispered, picturing Phelps and the next two men behind him falling to the ground, their hands clasped to their bleeding stomachs. "Gut-shot." A thin smile formed on Sweet's lips beneath the scant mantle of a wispy gray mustache. Then he lowered the pistol back into his holster and gently patted the butt.

In a moment, when he heard the sound of their boots step up and rumble low along the boardwalk, Sweet walked over, sat down behind his battered desk, and managed to busy himself with a stack of wanted posters as Phelps swung the door open. Sweet raised his eyes to Cleveland Phelps, an ink pen poised in his hand as if in the middle of writing something important, pertaining to keeping the peace in an empty mining town. "Have you ever heard of knocking, Phelps?" Sweet gestured a sharp nod at the stack of wanted posters. "I'm kinda busy here."

Cleveland Phelps knew better. "I bet," he said, stepping forward and cocking his head slightly to look down at the wanted posters, his long silver hair swaying out from his shoulder. He smiled through his salt-and-pepper beard. "What are you expecting, the James Gang? Jesse and Frank going to ride in here, pull your bridge down?" Phelps shot a glance at the men gathering around him at the edge of the desk, the lot of them chuckling at his remark. Phelps didn't like Sweet and he gave little attempt at hiding it. Harris Sweet didn't fit the image Phelps had of a rough, hard-boned old lawman. In spite of Sweet's reputation, he almost had the look of a dandy—clean cheeks, narrow eyes, thin shoulders, a fine nose that didn't look to have ever been broken. His voice wasn't even deep or gravelly enough to suit Cleveland Phelps.

Harris Sweet looked up at them somberly, each in turn—*pow, pow, pow*—then back at Cleveland Phelps. "What can I do for you, Phelps? Keep it short."

Cleveland Phelps's smile left his rough face. "Now that's more like it, *Sheriff*," he said with more than a touch of sarcasm. Phelps's fingertips rested down on the desk, tapping lightly, a big diamond ring shining, looking out of place on a weathered hand at the end of a rawhide coat sleeve. "Me and the boys are going to be gone a few days. We're riding up to the mine, looking things over." Phelps's right hand rested on the bone-handled Colt .45 lying against his stomach in a plain slim jim holster. "If J. T. Priest arrives whilst we're gone, tell him to sit tight here. I'm also expecting my kid brother, Darby, and a man named Chester Meins. If they show up, make them at home for me."

"Will that be all?" There was a tightness in Harris Sweet's voice.

"Hmmm . . . now that you mention it." Phelps's smile returned. He liked knowing that he got under Sweet's skin, an old killer like this, forced to sit guard on a cold lonesome mountainside. He liked the idea of a man like Sweet having to take orders from a bunch of outlaws. "If that steam engine gets here today, tell them to bring up some more beefsteaks and rye whiskey. I'm not going to spend the winter living on elk and blacktail. Gets to where somebody passes gas you're afraid to strike a match around them."

The men chuckled at Phelps's little joke, but Harris

Sweet bypassed it. "We'll be lucky if the engine makes another trip after today. The weather's moving down to us. You want beef all winter, you might think about heading south." Sweet returned Phelps's stare.

Phelps nodded, getting it. "We like it right here, *Sheriff*. We just want good provisions."

Sure, Sweet was paid by Midwest Investment, but he knew *Los Pistoleros* was part of the deal. Phelps liked rubbing Sweet's face in it—a little at a time, not too much at once. Harris Sweet might be getting old, but he still packed a lot of reputation.

"I'll tell them, Phelps. Now, if you don't mind . . . ?" Sweet cut a glance at the stack of wanted posters, then leveled his gaze back at Phelps.

"Well, no, sir *Sher-iff*," Phelps said, his sarcasm even more pronounced. "We don't want to get in the way of you upholding the law." Phelps stepped back from the desk, his right fingers tapping on his pistol butt as if he were sizing Sweet up. "Any *known* felons show up, you just holler real loud. We'll come running."

"I'll do that." Harris Sweet rose slightly, his stare boring right back at Cleveland Phelps, his eyes telling Phelps to go ahead and do it instead of just thinking about it. "You leaving now or what?"

Sweet's cold blue eyes focused on a spot just about center of Phelps's forehead. He'd been here too many times before to let some finger-tapping punk worry him.

"Yeah, we're leaving." Phelps's stare lingered, before he finally stepped back. "Come on, boys." They moved toward the door and left.

Pow, Pow, splat! bang! Pow! Sweet smiled thin and flat, getting a glimpse in his mind's eye of the other five down on the floor—Phelps the only one left standing, his eyes wide with fear, his gun only half out of his holster, Sweet's smoking pistol cocking for the sixth time. He rose the rest of the way from his desk, walked over to the window and stood watching until they filed across the swinging footbridge and headed to their horses. *So long, Cleveland Phelps . . . Kapow!* Sweet turned to face the empty office, eyeing the one open cell and the thin layer of rust that had formed across the lock plate. Suddenly he snatched his pistol from his holster, aimed it cocked at the cell door; then uncocked it, reholstered it and snatched it out again. Not bad. A little slow perhaps. But then he'd always been more deadly than fast.

He turned the pistol in his hand, examining its smooth sheen. Fast or slow, he'd love to kill Cleveland Phelps. Just thinking about it brought a rise in his chest. It would be just like in the old days. He could see the bullet hole in the center of Phelps's forehead as he went down like a sinking ship, his eyes already vacant and flat, deader than lumps of coal. *God, that felt good*, he smiled to himself, holstering the pistol.

When he turned back to his desk, he heard a rustling sound beneath it. Instinctively, he reached for his pistol again, the thought of killing still fresh in his mind. But then he let out a breath as the big furry black tomcat came rubbing around the desk leg and looked up at him with its one good eye. "Scratch, you sneaky old bastard," Sweet said with affection. "Get up here." He stepped forward and bent to pick up the big tomcat and tried cradling it on his forearm. The cat hissed and barred its long teeth at him, its one eye sharp, deep and yellow, the color of polished gold. The other eye was cloudy, white and dead, a jagged scar running through it like a river on a map. "Hush now, you don't mean a word of it."

Sweet struggled with the resisting cat, pressing it down on his forearm, the cat sinking its foreclaws through the sleeve of his shirt, letting him feel its protest. "Settle down now." Sweet ignored the claws until the tomcat eased them back into its paws. The big cat gave in and relaxed, slinking against the palm of Sweet's hand as it stroked its furry back. Eventually it began a low rattling purr.

"There, you see? You're just mean and restless. That's all you are." He ruffled the cat's head. "I hate a damn cat worse than anything—" He lowered his face and burrowed it into the thick fur. "—*Yeees* I do, you *knoooow* I do." The cat rattled and hummed and nestled against Harris Sweet's chest as he paced the small office, cradling the tomcat like a baby in his arms.

In the next town over from the one they'd just hit, J. T. Priest stood in the open doorway and adjusted the dead mayor's heavy wool coat on himself, brushing lint from the sleeve. "I swear it gets colder every mile farther north this time of year." He gazed out and up into the gray sky. "Don't get me wrong, what I was saying about Cleveland Phelps." He half turned to Denver Stanton, who stood one step behind him in the gutted lobby of the bank. "I've always said Cleveland Phelps is a good enough gunman. But . . ." Priest stopped, reached down and pulled the long wool muffler from the dead man's neck, shook it out then draped it around his shoulders. "There, that'll do," he murmured to himself.

Then he turned the conversation back to Stanton. "When it comes to a gang this big, Phelps doesn't have enough . . ." Priest searched for a word, looking upward, rounding a hand to help him find it. "Vision, I suppose you could say. Yes. It takes vision to run an entire operation. Phelps only ran a small part of *Los Pistoleros*, sort of the muscle end of things." He adjusted the wool muffler and smoothed it down his lapels. "Mabrey and I have always been the brains of this organization." He turned to Denver Stanton and spread his hands, posing. "What do you think? Looks good, eh? Fits?"

"Very striking, yes-sir." Denver Stanton cocked his head as he scrutinized him and nodded. "It fits like it was made for you. Now about Phelps. I'm not saying he intended for us to do you any harm—"

Priest cut him off. "I've always been one to say, 'In order to be successful, a man needs to *look* successful.' If you ever go East, you'll find a lot of people there agree with me." Priest opened the black heavy coat enough to highlight the shine of his new pistol in its hand-tooled holster. "Myself, I'm right at home back East." He bent down, lifted a pocket watch from the mayor's vest by its gold fob, and examined it closely. "A pity," he said, then dropped it when he saw blood and a bullet crease along the edge of the watch case. "I enjoy the theater, the countless restaurants, strolls in the park, the women— oh God! the women."

"Cleveland Phelps just said bring you to him. He kind of left it open whether we was rescuing you or just taking you hostage, so to speak." Stanton followed Priest as he adjusted the white straw skimmer hat on his head and stepped out on the boardwalk. It was too late in the year for a straw skimmer, but Priest liked the style of it. "You can't really blame us," he added. "We figured he was the man in charge."

"See? I sensed that right off," Priest said, raising a

finger for emphasis. Looking around at the empty street, he took a deep breath and went on, saying, "I'm just glad I got the chance to straighten you out before something got out of hand. The truth is, after seeing the way you and your boys handled Summit, then this place." He swung a hand, taking in the newly pillaged town. "I'll go so far as to say you might be taking over Phelps's job if he's not careful."

"I'm not out to cause any hard feelings between you two," Stanton said. "But if it's there to begin with, I can't turn down a chance to get ahead."

"I understand." Priest looked across the dirt street to where the two new men, Luther Ison and his son, Bert, stood arguing over a new Winchester repeating rifle, a price tag dangling from its barrel. A few yards from them another new gunman, a black man named Gant, pitched a pair of bulging saddlebags over his horse's rump. "Let me ask you this, Stanton," Priest continued. "For the sake of business, where do you see yourself being, say . . . three to five years from now?" He raised his black cigar to his lips and puffed on it, bringing it back to life.

"Hell, three to five years from now?" Stanton scratched his head up under his hat brim. "I never really gave it any thought. Be alive I reckon. Rob all I can. Drink and whore all I can. Walk as wide as I can get from rattlesnakes and knotted ropes. Why?"

"Stanton, Stanton." J. T. Priest shook his head. "You deserve more than that, *mi amigo*. Any man deserves more than that. Don't you ever think of getting some real power in your hands?" Priest made a thick fist as he spoke. "These are the golden years for our nation, the days of wealth, expansion—of a man stepping forth boldly in this new frontier and squeezing it for all it's worth! Don't you want a big part of all that?" Across the street, Bert Ison had stomped back inside the mercantile store, cursing as he stepped over a body in the doorway.

After a pause for consideration, Denver Stanton said, "No."

Another silence passed as the two of them watched a fire flare up inside the mercantile store. In seconds, tumbling flames spilled out of the doorway and licked upward in a boil of black smoke. "Jesus," Priest murmured, "is he coming out?" In the street, Luther Ison stood staring at the burning store with the new rifle hanging in his hand, the price tag fluttering on the breeze. The other men gathered and watched and stared back and forth at one another, anxious, bewildered. Priest squinted. "Surely to God that fool hasn't set himself afire . . ."

"I don't know," said Stanton in a hushed tone. "They argue and spat all the time, as most fathers and sons are prone to do. But damn . . ."

Luther Ison stepped closer to the raging fire, trying to see through it, leaning forward then drawing back from the heat, his arm raised to shield his face. Even a couple of the frightened townsfolk ventured forward from their hiding places, staring in disbelief.

Suddenly the large showcase window burst forth in a stream of smoke and fire, as Bert Ison launched himself through it and rolled in a spray of shattered glass out into the street. His arms were clasped tight around a bundle of new rifles, and a pistol belt smoked on his shoulder. The black man, Gant, ran forward with a bucket of water from a horse trough and pitched it on him. Steam and smoke billowed from Bert's smoldering back. The townsfolk crept back into hiding, one of them dragging a wounded freight clerk from the street as he went.

Priest let out a breath. "That boy has some serious problems."

"But you can't count ole Bert out," Stanton replied. "I never said they was neither one smart. I just said they're both good gunmen."

"It's none of my business," Priest said, staring out at the steam rising from amid the gunmen gathered around Bert Ison, "but what happened to that boy's front teeth?"

"They say a mule kicked them out—probably was ole Luther did it though. He won't tolerate no sass, and Bert used to be idiot enough to back talk him. What can you expect? Luther kicks like a mule anyway. He's pounded that boy's head his whole life, but it never done any good. If anything, it's made him worse."

"How's Bert going to be at following orders?" Priest asked.

"Bert? Hell, Bert'll kill anything you sic him on. He don't care about the odds either. He'll hone in on the one he's after, and get him . . . worse than a pit dog."

"No kidding?" Priest just stared. The roof of the mercantile caved in, belching fire and smoke upward. Priest shrugged, dismissing it, and turned back to Stanton. "What I was saying is, you need to give some thought to what you want in the future. I know you want to get ahead, you said so yourself."

Stanton scratched his neck, contemplating. "I do want to get ahead as far as I can, money-wise. I'm no fool. I just don't have a head for all that stuff like who owns what in Midwest Investment and so on. That's for you and Phelps to sort out. You want good old-fashioned robbing and killing though, I'm your man." He smiled and righted his Stetson brim.

"That's good enough for me," Priest said. "All this stock ownership, and who owns what, is a bunch of nonsense anyway. I wish I'd never had to fool with it. You take care of what you do best. I'll handle the paperwork."

"See. That's the way I like it." Stanton stepped down onto the street, then turned and looked back at him. "I figure money I didn't steal myself at the end of a gun ain't really mine to begin with."

"I couldn't agree more." Priest grinned, hooking his thumbs in his vest, his cigar curling smoke. "If that idiot hasn't roasted himself, bring him around later. I'd like to get to know him a little better."

"His pa and the black fellow, too?" Stanton asked.

"Naw, just Bert. I sort of feel sorry for the lad. Might take him under my wing, so to speak."

Chapter 7

Back in Summit, Sullivan Hart and Twojack Roth had spent the night and the day before helping the townsfolk get the town back in order. They'd helped board up broken windows until repairmen could get to them, and even loaded burnt debris and swept and raked the large burnt spot from the middle of the street. As they did so, they'd asked questions, gotten descriptions of the pillagers and taken note of how many gunmen had been riding in the gang. There was no doubt that it was J. T. Priest and his men, Martin Tooney riding with them.

Yesterday, the telegraph clerk and three townsmen rode out south of town, traced down the cut lines and repaired them. When the men had returned, Hart sent word back to Fort Smith, letting Judge Parker know they were on the right trail. Now the two deputies looked around at the town, giving it a once over before going their way.

"Ready to ride?" Roth asked Sullivan Hart, gazing up at the graying sky to the north. "We need to get into their tracks before a rain sets in."

"Yep, let's get to it." Hart shoved his rifle down into its saddle boot. It was afternoon, and Hart and Roth had readied their horses at the hitch rail. "We'll probably see more of the same at the next town north of here. It looks like these boys have gone on a spree.'' They swung up on their saddles, turned their horses to the dirt street and rode out past the gathering of townsfolk who walked in somber procession, the wooden casket containing the body of their sheriff raised on the shoulders of six black-dressed pallbearers.

"Kill all them murdering sons of bitches!" cried an old man as the deputies rode by. In the procession were a half dozen young women who ran a brothel on the second floor of O'Rourke's Saloon. They walked along a few feet behind the other citizens, the bruises on some of their faces attesting that they'd done their part in sparing others the same fate. Hart and Roth removed their hats in reverence, but rode on.

They followed the tracks of six horses for the next three hours, Roth having seen the particulars of one horse wearing store-bought shoes with a circled X stamped in its center turn, and another horse in sore need of shoeing. When they came to the place where the tracks led off west toward Luther Ison's place, they followed them for another hour or more until they stopped at the broken fencing two hundred yards from a weathered shack standing in the shadow of a rocky hillside.

On the ground, tracks of the same horses overlapped, coming back out along the trail and cutting north on the side of a broken wire gate. Roth stepped down from his saddle, examined the tracks closely, then looked up at Sullivan Hart. "Looks like they've picked up three more riders."

Hart studied the empty yard in front of the shack, the sagging empty hitch rail, the barren corral, and the small barn with its doors flung open. "Looks abandoned, but we best check it out." A lank brindle hound stood up from the dirt and shook himself, then gazed toward them, uttering a long bawl.

Roth mounted, and as they moved their horses forward at a cautious walk, an older woman dressed in rags stepped out onto the drooping porch and raised a long-barreled shotgun toward them. They stopped their horses. "Whatever you're selling, I ain't buying," she called out to them. Hart and Roth looked at one another and eased their horses forward. "If you think I'm playing," the woman called out, "just keep on coming!" They stopped again fifty yards back.

"Ma'am, we're federal deputies," Hart called out to her above the baying of the brindle hound. As one, he and Twojack Roth opened their riding dusters enough to give her a glimpse of their badges, hoping she could see them from this distance. "We're hunting escaped convicts. Their tracks led us here."

"Then their tracks can just turn you around and lead you out," she said, the shotgun not lowering an inch. "There's nobody here but me and this dog—and either one of us will kill you where you stand!" As if on cue, the brindle hound bounded forward, racing toward them, then skidded to a halt a few yards away, lunging in place, its hackles up, its teeth shining, causing the horses to shy back a bit.

"Whoa," Hart whispered to his horse. His right hand went to his pistol. "Better decide something quick," he said to Roth. "We can't risk him nicking one of these horses' legs."

"Don't shoot yet." Roth turned his big dun and sidled it closer, pressing the dog, making it show its intentions. The dog barked louder, more infuriated. But it gave ground a few feet, then replanted its forepaws and resumed its threats. "He's all bark," Roth said. "Come on, let's get this over with."

"I'm not warning yas again," the woman called out. As they moved their horses closer to the porch, they spread out, putting twenty feet between them by the time they stopped thirty feet away. The woman turned the shotgun barrel from one to the other, unsure of herself. The hound bounded back and forth in the dirt, still barking.

"Ma'am, you have to understand," Roth said, "we mean you no harm. We've got to do our jobs."

"Ha! The law's never meant me anything but harm." Even as she spoke she relented a bit, lowering the shotgun an inch, yet still keeping the stock raised to her shoulder.

"He's right, ma'am," Hart joined in. "We only want to know where these men are headed—and who left here with them."

"Why? So you can kill them, take them in and hang them? I know how you Judge Parker deputies operate." She looked back and forth at them. "My boy ain't done nothing wrong. Neither has my man, for a while anyway. I can't speak for that black devil, Gant."

"If they've done nothing wrong, ma'am, they have nothing to worry about. Maybe we can stop them before they get off on the wrong foot with this gang. We saw what these men did back in Summit. I won't lie to you. If your man and your son ride with them, then there's no doubt they'll come to a bad end. Is that what you want?" The brindle hound circled them, his barking simmering down to a growl.

"It's never mattered what I want." She sighed, lowering the shotgun another inch. "My man is Luther Ison. He's never been any good. If you have to kill him and Gant, I reckon they deserve it. But my boy, Bert, can't help himself. He's never had a lick

of sense. He just does what other folks tells him to
do. Will you not kill him, if you can keep from it?"

"We'll do our best not to, ma'am," Hart said. He
and Roth shot one another a glance. "We know about
J. T. Priest and the prison guard, Tooney. Who are
the others?"

"Denver Stanton," she said. "He's some kind of
third cousin to Luther. The others are Carl White,
and Bobby Crady . . . that's the only ones I know.
They talk like they're headed north to do some dirt.
Luther was fool enough to go along with them. My
boy, Bert, follows him around like a lost dog. I don't
know why though, the way Luther treats him." She
finally lowered the shotgun and held it across her
waist. "There's some coffee left inside. I reckon it
won't hurt if you step down and have some before
you leave."

"Thank you all the same, ma'am," Hart said, "but
we need to keep moving."

"I wish you would," she said, lowering her eyes
to the porch, shaking her head slowly. "I don't expect
I'll ever see Bert again."

Hart and Roth looked at one another. "That coffee
sounds fine to me, ma'am," Roth said. "Can you call
this dog back?"

She stomped her foot. "Get back, Sam!" she
shouted at the brindle hound. The dog slunk back
with a parting growl and slipped underneath the
porch.

They drank coffee seated at a round wooden table
and listened as she told them how all the while the
men had been here, all Priest had talked about was
the money they were going to make riding with him.
"You'd think Luther would know better," she sighed,
brushing a strand of dried dusty hair from her
weathered cheek. "But I reckon he's been here in one

spot too long. He never could sit still long—there's too much meanness in him."

Hart and Roth only listened, nodding as she recounted her life with an outlaw like Luther Ison, and how harsh it had been trying to stay one step ahead of the law while raising a child. At the end of their second cup of coffee, seeing she had gotten a lot out of her system, the deputies stood up, thanked her for the hospitality and Roth asked if there was anything they could do for her.

"Do for me?" She looked stunned that anyone should ask.

"Yes, ma'am," Hart put in. "We could take you to town on our way, see to it you find a place to stay. You'll soon run out of supplies out here. You've got no horse, no way to get around."

"Aw," she fanned the idea away. "Don't worry about me. I'm used to getting left behind. Something will turn up—something always does."

She followed them out onto the porch where she stood watching while they mounted. Roth and Hart tipped their hats to her and rode out along the dusty path leading back to the trail. Before turning onto the trail, they looked back once more and saw her and the brindle dog standing small against the wide hillside behind the shack. "Priest will gather as many men as he can," Roth said, "anybody he can put between himself and the law."

"Yep," Hart replied. "If he's meeting with more *Los Pistoleros* in Cold Ridge, he doesn't want to show up alone. He'll want a lot of men with him to make a strong impression for himself." He gigged his big Morgan forward as he spoke. "We're going to have our hands full with that bunch." He gazed around the endless land, then looked ahead as both horses moved forward at a steady pace.

They followed the tracks of the eight horses for the rest of the day, and spent the night beneath a high-rail trestle where the tracks had gathered together near a burnt spot on the ground—the place where the gang had stopped and made camp on their way north. Empty whiskey bottles lay strewn about. Hart and Roth kicked them aside, gathered dried wood from alongside the dry wash, and settled in around a glowing fire.

By the end of the following day, they'd followed the outlaws' tracks to the town of Benton and stopped at the far end of the main dirt street, not surprised at the sight of a burnt-out hull of a building or at the boarded-up storefronts where the windows had been shattered. "Looks like Priest and his friends haven't wound down yet." Roth let out a breath, seeing three townspeople scurry for cover at the sight of him.

"They won't stop," Hart replied, nudging his black Morgan forward, "not until J. T. Priest figures he's let everybody know he's the cock of the walk."

Before their horses had gone ten yards farther along the street, a rifle shot exploded from around the corner of an alley. The bullet whistled past Hart's head, causing him to duck and rein his horse to one side. "Hold your fire! We're lawmen!" Roth shouted, throwing his duster open as his hand went instinctively to his pistol butt and stopped there.

"Drop your guns," a voice shouted from behind the cover of the burnt tangle of beams and metal sheeting that had been the mercantile store. "We're not taking any chances!"

"Not taking any chances?" Roth looked at Hart. They pulled their horses back a step.

"Listen to me!" Sullivan Hart shouted to the empty street. "We are federal deputies of Judge Parker's court! We're tracking the men who did this to you! We're coming in now. Don't start shooting at us." Atop a roof, Hart and Roth saw the glint of another rifle barrel.

"How do we know you're lawmen!" a woman's voice cried out.

"For crying out loud," Roth said in a low tone, "if they'd acted like this with Priest and his bunch, we wouldn't have to be here."

"They're scared to death," Hart said. He checked his horse back another step then spoke to the woman. "Ma'am, we have badges. We really are lawmen. We've got to come in and find out what's gone on here. Please don't shoot at us!"

They stepped their horses forward slowly, keeping their hands chest high in a show of peace. Out in front of the burnt mercantile store they stopped again and looked at the wary faces as they peered above the debris and from around corners of alleyways and buildings. A big woman carrying a shotgun stepped out from behind a twisted pile of scorched tin roofing. She looked long and hard at the badges on Hart's and Roth's chests. "You can't blame us for being this way. They've just about put us out of business here."

"We understand, ma'am," Roth offered, lowering his hands a little, looking around at the plundered town. "They did the same thing to Summit."

"Then why haven't you done something about them?" As she spoke, the woman glanced at other townsfolk for support. A grumble rose among them.

"We intend to, as soon as we catch up to them," Hart responded, looking at all of their soot-streaked faces. "Can we step down now? We can't spend much time here. There's other towns between here and where they're headed."

"They killed our mayor," an old man said as Hart

and Roth swung down from their saddles and stood among them. "He was the only mayor this town ever had—just took office last week! Now he's dead. One of them even stripped him of his coat."

"They're a bad bunch, sir. That's why we're after them." Hart noted a rifle barrel pointed carelessly at his stomach. He reached out and nudged it to one side as he spoke.

"The worst one of the bunch is that idiot boy with his front teeth missing," the big woman said, propping her shotgun against her side. "He set the fire, then almost burnt himself up. After he came out, another man started pistol whipping him—would've beat him to death if the leader hadn't stopped him."

"The leader is J. T. Priest, ma'am," Roth said. "He's an escaped felon. The boy is Bert Ison—the man beating him was probably his father."

"His father?" She looked stunned. "Lord, no wonder the idiot wouldn't fight back. When they left, the leader had the boy riding next to him."

Sullivan Hart and Twojack Roth looked at one another, offering no further comment. Then Hart turned back to the woman. "We need some supplies. Did they leave much behind?"

"Very danged little," the old man said before the woman could answer. "But you let us know what all you need. We'll get it together some way. But you've got to let us know when it comes time to hang them bastards. I wouldn't miss it if I have to walk all the way to Fort Smith."

Hart gazed out across the northern sky, at the clouds lying low and silver-gray on the far horizon. "The way things are going, I wouldn't count on a hanging if I were you. I don't think they'll ever make it back to court."

Chapter 8

Like the two towns before it, Cedar Bluff was not prepared for what came thundering in on the billowing dust. By the time a few townsmen realized they were under attack, it was too late. J. T. Priest's men had swept down on the small bank, looted it, and began taking what they wanted from the stores along the boardwalk. This time Priest didn't even bother stepping down from his horse. He sat in the middle of the street, young Bert Ison on the horse beside him, and watched the rest of the men plunder the helpless town.

Bert Ison had been riding at Priest's side all day. Now as he started to step down and join in the melee Priest stopped him with a hand on his forearm.

"Take a break, Bert," Priest said, "you've done your part. Let these boys handle it. Some of them look like they need the practice."

Bert Ison just looked at him, his eyes more flat and dull than any Priest had ever seen. Bert looked down at Priest's hand on his forearm. Priest removed his hand and chuckled. "Bert, you don't say much. I like that about you." He nodded at the men in the street, at Bobby Crady kicking a woman out of the way as he forced himself into a bakery shop. "How come I never heard of you before?" He cocked an eye at Bert Ison. "Guess your pa hasn't wanted anybody to know about you. Figures you'd be worth more to an operation like this than he is."

Bert still made no reply. Luther Ison ran up to them carrying two bottles of whiskey in each hand. "Get on down here, boy," he said to Bert in a harsh tone. But before Bert could obey, Priest cut his horse in between the two of them.

"Don't worry about your boy, Luther. He's sitting this one out with me."

Luther squinted up at Priest. "He always does as I tell him, J. T. Don't go butting into family business."

Priest's smile disappeared. "I'll pretend I didn't hear that, Luther. Now get yourself busy. I'm the boss. If I say he stays here with me, that's how it is."

Luther Ison clenched his teeth, his fists balled at his sides. He stood seething at Priest until Gant saw what was going on and ran up and grabbed him by his arm. "Luther! Come on, you've got to see this. Carl White's got an old doctor down on all fours, making him ride him around like a mule! He's even whipping the doc with a riding quirt!"

Luther Ison hesitated for a second, staring up at J. T. Priest. Then, as if something had just clicked in his mind, he turned and grinned at Gant. "What the hell . . . let's go take a look."

"There, Bert, you see," Priest said as Luther and Gant ran off along the dirt street, "as long as I'm the man in charge, you don't have to take orders from nobody else—even your daddy. How's that suit you?"

Bert only stared. J. T. Priest shrugged, a bit uncomfortable at the boy's silence. "Of course, I expect you to do what I tell you. Say . . . what if I were to tell you to take up a pistol, or a knife, and wade in and kill some son of a bitch for me? You'd do that for me, wouldn't you?"

Bert shrugged, a simple unthinking gesture from an empty mind, Priest concluded. He smiled at Bert. "Good boy. Suppose I were to ask you to kill ole Tooney there," Priest nodded to where Tooney stood with a pistol smoking in his hand. "You'd do it for me, wouldn't you?"

Bert started to lunge his horse forward, but Priest caught his arm. "No, not like this. What I'd like is for him to just disappear tonight, no gunshot, no noise of any kind—just *poof!* and he's gone. Will you do that for me, and just keep it between the two of us?" He watched Bert Ison lean forward in his saddle, staring at Tooney, Bert's eyes as flat and empty as slate stone. Then Bert nodded and spread a toothless grin.

"Good boy." Priest patted his forearm. "You get that done for me tonight. I'm counting on you." As Priest turned forward in his saddle, he caught sight of two young men walking toward him straight up the middle of the street, their hands raised. Priest straightened at the sight of them. "Hold up, Bert, what's this coming here?"

"Don't shoot, mister," one of the men said, both of them stopping a few feet away. "We come to join yas, if you'll have us."

On the boardwalk out front of the small bank, Stanton and Tooney turned toward the two men, their pistols cocked and ready. "Easy men, let's hear them out," Priest said, raising a hand toward Stanton. He spread an easy grin at the two young men in the street. "You want to *join* us? Who the hell are you?" Before either of the men could reply, three shots resounded from Earl Mellon's pistol up the street. "Damn it!" Priest shouted, looking all around. "Everybody quiet down! I can't hear myself think!" A second passed as the town street descended into silence. Priest looked back at the two young men. "Now then."

"I'm Tom Bays Junior," said the taller one. He jerked his head toward the young man beside him. "This is my brother . . . everybody calls him Shorty. We want to join up with you, sir."

"Well now, Tom Bays Junior," J. T. Priest said, cutting a glance around at his men as they gathered closer around the two newcomers, "why would you boys want to do a thing like that at a time like this?"

Tom Bays heard low laughter encircle him and his brother. He swallowed to steady his voice. "Well . . . the truth is, me and Shorty have been wanting to ride with a gang for the longest time. Soon as ya'll rode in, I knew we needed to say something."

"So," Priest swept his hand about the dusty street, "you just stroll in here right in the middle of things, as if I had nothing better to do?"

"We apologize for that, sir," Shorty Bays said, taking a half step forward. "But once you're gone, it'd be too late." His hands lowered an inch, but raised back up when he heard a rifle cock behind him. "We figured we'd have to take our chances. Can you use us? If not, I reckon it was just our mistake."

Tom Bays cut in. "What Shorty means is . . . we're both willing to do whatever it takes—"

"Shut up, Tom Bays Junior," Priest said, cutting him off. "I heard your brother loud and clear." Priest chuckled and shook his head. "This beats all I've ever seen. We're right smack in the middle of business, and you just come in and make yourselves at home."

Another ripple of laughter stirred among the gunmen as Priest looked the Bays brothers over. Tom Bays stood bareheaded, carrying an army Colt shoved down in the waist of his tattered wool pants.

The trousers were too big for him and were gathered by a length of rope tied around his stomach. Shorty Bays wore a battered straw planters hat and a tight checkered shirt with the sleeves reaching high up his forearms. Both wore good army boots with the toes scuffed from lack of maintenance.

"You boys are deserters, aren't yas?" Priest said, scrutinizing them closely.

"If we was, we wouldn't admit it, sir," Tom Bays replied. "But we're looking for work, and we don't care what we do."

Priest considered it, then let out a breath. "Ordinarily, we'd kill a couple of wet-nosed bastards, butting in this way, no references, nobody to vouch for yas. But I like men who're bold and not afraid to state their intentions." He looked around at the others, then back to the Bays brothers. "You boys got any horses fit to ride?"

"Yes, sir," Tom grinned, getting hopeful, "if you don't mind that they've got army brands."

"That don't bother me." Priest shrugged it off. "I guess you know you'd have nothing coming from this job?"

"We understand that," Shorty offered. "We ain't expecting something for nothing—next job we'll do our part. We just want a chance to prove ourselves."

Priest nodded. "And that you will. Have either of yas ever heard of a gang called *Los Pistoleros*?"

The brothers looked at one another, then back at Priest. "No, sir," Tom said, "but if that's who you are, we're real proud to be a part of it."

"And well you should be, boys." Priest nodded at Bert Ison beside him. "This is Bert Ison. He'll be seeing to it that you both do your jobs. Bert doesn't say much, so you'll just have to learn what he expects of yas. Cross him, and you're crossing me. Is that clear?"

"Yes, sir." The ragged pair snapped to attention. Laughter rippled once again, low and muffled. "All right then, Shorty and Tom Bays." Priest rose up in his saddle. "Get yourselves over to that mercantile store and get some decent clothes on yas. When we ride out of here, I want you both looking sharper than a Cincinnati clap doctor. Do you understand?"

"Yes, sir," they said as one.

"And I better see some serious-looking rifles hanging in your hands . . . and some shiny pistols in tied-down holsters," Priest added. "Come back here looking like gunmen." He dismissed them with the toss of a hand.

As the two bounded away toward the mercantile store, Stanton stepped off the boardwalk and walked over to Priest, looking up at him. "J. T., are you sure about this? Those boys look like they'd need both hands to find their asses."

"Don't second-guess me, Stanton," Priest said, eyeing him with a crafty smile. "You want to do something? Go help them pick out some warm clothes—don't want them to freeze to death in their saddles. They'd make us all look bad."

"Whatever you say, boss." Stanton looked bewildered, but turned and started off toward the store.

Priest looked at Bert Ison beside him. "There now. Bert, you heard what I told them. Those are your men. You take charge. They give you any problem . . . well, you do what you think is best. Do you understand me?" Bert only stared. Priest added in afterthought, "Only, make sure you don't kill either one of them until after we get to Cold Ridge. Understand?"

Bert only stared. "Shit," Priest said. "Just nod then, Bert, either yes or no. All right? Can you do that?"

But Bert didn't nod. Instead he said, "Me too," in a guttural rasp, a mindless expression on his face. Priest just stared at him for a second, then let out a breath, backed his horse up, and called out to the rest of the men, "All right . . . get back to work! Take plenty of supplies and whiskey. We've got a long ride ahead of us." He cast a long glance northwestward into the low gray horizon. *All right, Mr. Cleveland Phelps, we're on our way. Meet the new* Los Pistoleros.

Snow flurries had moved in by the time the small service engine finished its winding climb toward Cold Ridge. Quick Charlie Sims and Kate McCorkle were the only two passengers. They'd left Harrington's Pullman car sitting on a siding track at Lodgings, a small rail town at the bottom of the mountain. Then they'd boarded a short passenger car at the company depot.

The upward climb had been slow and labored, with streaks of ice shining in the rock ledges and crevices that drifted past the windows in a silver mist. Now snowflakes spun in the chilled air; stepping down from the platform, Kate hiked the fur collar of her winter coat up against her cheeks and looked all around the empty street, taking some comfort in knowing a big Colt .45 lay down deep in her coat pocket.

"I hope you know what you're doing, Charlie," she said to Sims under her steaming breath. Streaks of thin ice clung to shallow puddles of mud. Walk planks ran back and forth from boardwalk to boardwalk. Kate lifted her dress hem enough to keep it off the wet, icy ground.

"It's a little late to be asking that question, Kate," Sims answered with a slight smile, hefting their carpetbag up under his arm. He cupped her elbow, and assisted her toward the wooden building where a faded sign with an even more faded star painted on it hung by rusty chains. "Let's go find this Sheriff Harris Sweet and introduce ourselves to him. What do you say?"

"I say you better watch every step you take. This is Cleveland Phelps's and J. T. Priest's territory. They would kill one another just to get the chance to kill you."

"Now you're getting the picture," Sims spread a devilish grin as they walked on, the planks beneath their feet rising and falling with each step, splattering ice-crusted muddy water on either side of them. Sims glanced at the dirty window in the sheriff's office and saw a figure staring out at them. "Don't look now, Kate, but I think Harris Sweet just saw us coming."

"Oh?" Kate stared straight ahead. "Is that good or bad?"

"Neither," Sims said, stopping at the boardwalk outside the sheriff's office. He paused, looked all around, then said as if suddenly struck by a thought, "You know, Kate, since there doesn't seem to be anyone around, why don't you go to the hotel and get us a suite of rooms?" He nodded down the street toward a ramshackle hotel where a weathered sign hung lopsided.

Kate looked at the rundown building, then back at Sims. "A suite? We'll be lucky if we can settle for a roof we can't see through."

Inside the sheriff's office, Harris Sweet had stood watching as they made their way across the walk planks. He saw the man hand the woman the bulging carpetbag and watched her shake her head and start off toward the Ballantine Hotel. *More damned people* . . . He didn't need this, he thought; and when he saw the man step up and walk over toward his door, Sweet ducked away from the window, went around behind his desk, picked up the one-eyed cat and sat down in his wooden chair.

Sims caught a glimpse of the figure moving away from the window. At first he thought the sheriff had come to open the door for him. After a second when the door didn't open, Sims cocked his head slightly, reached out and started to open the door for himself and go inside. But then he stopped himself, considered it and instead of opening the rough wooden door, he knocked on it and waited. He waited, then knocked again. When it became apparent that no one was going to answer, Sims opened the door enough to stick his head inside. His eyes took in the office, the battered desk, a burnt coffeepot on a woodstove, a polished billiard stick standing against the wall in one corner. *A billiard stick?* Sims made a mental note of it.

"Excuse me? Sheriff?" Sims kept his voice low, courteous, looking across at Harris Sweet sitting idly behind his desk.

Harris Sweet had prepared a gruff reprimand, the same as he'd been giving Phelps and his men for barging in without knocking. But since this man had knocked—twice in fact—Sweet found himself disarmed. "Yeah. What do you want?" Sweet kept his tone as uninviting as possible, staring at Sims's face looking at him through the barely opened door.

"Pardon me, Sheriff." Sims looked taken aback at Sweet's gruffness. "Perhaps I've caught you at a bad time? Sorry. I'll come back later." He began to draw the door slowly shut.

"No. Come on in," Sweet grumbled at the closing door. "Just make it short. I'm busy."

Busy? Sims looked at the big cat cradled on Sweet's forearm, Sweet's hand slowly stroking its back. "Are you sure, Sheriff? I don't want to intrude—"

"Damn it, I said come on in." Sweet rounded a hand, impatiently flagging him inside. "You're going to let all the heat out."

"Certainly, Sheriff." Sims stepped inside and closed the door behind him. He'd already begun sizing Harris Sweet up. Sweet wanted respect, probably hadn't been getting his fair share of it lately. The door was a setup—let a person walk in unannounced, then give them a hard time over it. All right, no problem, Sims thought. He'd played it just right. Now he'd see what else there is to know about Sheriff Harris Sweet. He watched Sweet stand up from the desk and move around in front of him, the big black cat hanging loosely over Sweet's forearm, staring at Sims through its big yellow eye.

Sweet grumbled, "This town's getting busier than New York City." He looked Sims up and down. "Who are you, mister, and what do you want?"

Without answering Sweet, he focused his attention on the big cat. "That's quite a rough-looking feline you've got there, Sheriff!" He eased his fingertips out a few inches from the cat's nose. "Does he bite?" Sims saw the big cat tense up toward his fingers, looking ready to pounce at them.

Sheriff Sweet gave Sims a vapid stare. "He's been known to now and again." He seemed to hold the cat forward, as if offering it a chance at Sims's hand. "Who are you? What's your business here?"

But Sims looked closer at the cat, offering his fingertips once again. This time the big furry animal stretched its neck outward to where Sims's hand stopped. Just as it almost touched its probing nose to his fingers, Sims eased his hand back, making it come to him. The cat gave him a curious look, withdrew, but then leaned forward again. "I'm here looking for Cleveland Phelps and J. T. Priest—although I doubt if Priest has made it up here yet."

"Oh?" Sweet gave the man in front of him a closer look. "I bet you're Quick Charles Sims . . . the one who's caused such a stir for everybody."

"Yep, that's me." Sims smiled, still letting the cat inspect his fingertips. "I've heard of you for a long time, Sheriff Sweet. You've got a tall reputation. To tell the truth, when I heard you were the law here, I almost decided not to come."

"Is that a fact? You'd have been wise not to. There's a lot of men wanting to nail your hide to a board." Harris Sweet's voice was still gruff, but with a more tolerant edge now. Sims knew he'd said the right thing, paying a little uncalled-for respect to this old lawman. His hand established a comfortable distance from the cat's nose and began moving slowly back and forth, the cat's one big yellow eye following it as Sims looked up at Harris Sweet.

"I know, Sheriff. But I figured if you're here, you'll uphold the law—the way you're known to do. Most folks I've talked to about you all say the same thing, that Harris Sweet is a tough lawman, but he always keeps things fair and square."

"That's what they say, huh?" Sweet's chest broadened.

"Oh yes. You haven't been forgotten down there, Sheriff. That's why I thought I better pay you a courtesy call before things start heating up between me and *Los Pistoleros*." On Sweet's forearm, the cat's head

began to sway back and forth gently with the motion
of Sims's hand, as if following the notes to some soft
lullaby. Its eyelids drooped almost shut, its one good
yellow eye looking like a setting sun across a black
horizon.

"*Los Pistoleros?*" Harris Sweet turned cagey now,
not admitting a thing. "What do you know about *Los
Pistoleros*, except that they all want you dead."

"I know a lot about *Los Pistoleros*, Sheriff," Sims
said, now ruffling the cat's head a bit. Sweet glanced
down at the cat, surprised at how the animal had
allowed Quick Charlie Sims to even get so close, let
alone get so familiar. "The fact is, I even own a large
amount of stock in Midwest Investment." Sims
grinned at Sweet. "We both know Midwest is the
real power behind the gang."

Sweet offered no comment, so Sims went on. "I
know Midwest Investment owns this whole mountain, silver mine and all. I know that every month
you get a pay envelope from Midwest. I know it
must stick in your craw a little, stuck up here year
after year, watching all that silver go down the
mountainside, ending up in the hands of people like
Priest and Phelps, and all you get is a monthly wage.
How am I doing so far?"

"You're talking, I'm listening," Sweet said, the cat
purring deeply as Sims's hand stroked its big
scarred head.

"Then I hope you're listening good, Sheriff. Because I've got a notion you've seen your last pay
envelope until Midwest Investment gets some problems ironed out for itself. Since William Mabrey
dropped out of sight, things have really been going
downhill."

"And I suppose you're the man who's going to
straighten all that out?" Sweet stared cold and

steady. "There's a rumor that William Mabrey ain't coming back. Cleveland Phelps even thinks you might have killed Mabrey."

Sims's smile faded, his dark eyes remaining fixed on Sheriff Sweet's. "Who knows how these rumors get started." As Sims spoke, his hand slid beneath the slumbering cat and scooped it up off Sweet's forearm. The cat offered no resistance. Sims nestled the big furry cat against his chest, running a hand along its back. Sweet was stunned. The cat had never let anyone else handle him this way. "But the thing is, Sheriff," Sims went on, "big changes are in the wind. It might be time for you to decide who you want to work for—me, or a couple of wanted outlaws like Phelps and Priest."

Sweet smiled, thin, tight, and knowingly. "You didn't come all the way up here just to see if you and I could strike up an alliance. You'd be a fool to take that kind of chance. What's your real angle in all this, Mr. Quick Charlie Sims?"

Before Sims could give a reply, a knock resounded on the wooden door as it opened. The fireman from the train stepped inside and looked across at Harris Sweet. "Sheriff, we're headed back down. Anything you need the next trip up?"

Sheriff Sweet spoke to the fireman without taking his eyes off Sims. "Yeah, Phelps wants some beef and some more whiskey brought up before the weather sets in."

"It might take a while, Sheriff," the fireman said. "We're pretty backed up down there."

"Then to hell with it," Sweet scoffed. "Phelps will just have to do without." He saw the approval in Sims's eyes. "Did you bring an envelope with my name on it this trip?" he asked the fireman, rubbing

his finger and thumb together in the universal sign
for money.

"No, nothing has come through this month yet,"
the fireman answered shaking his head. "I wish it
would hurry up, though. I need to get paid myself."

"I see. That'll be all, Jake. Just bring it up here to
me as soon as it gets there."

"I'll do that, Sheriff." The fireman nodded and
tipped the brim of his railroad cap. When he'd
backed out of the door and closed it behind himself,
Sweet chuckled under his breath. "Well, Sims, you
called it right about my pay. Maybe you're worth
tagging along with for a while. I've been wondering
how to get these damned outlaws off this mountain
so I can enjoy some peace and quiet."

"I can't promise you peace and quiet right away,
Sheriff Sweet," Sims said, stooping down to set the
big cat on the floor. "But if you'll give me some
playing room with these men, I can promise you
once they leave, they won't be coming back." He
touched the toe of his boot to the cat's rump to get
it started.

"That's bold talk, Sims," Sweet said in a cautious
tone, his eyes watching the cat slink across the plank
floor and slip under the desk. Harris Sweet looked
up from the paw prints across the dusty floor and
shook his head. "What the hell did you do to that
cat? He's never warmed up like that to anybody
before."

"I just treated him the way a tough old cat wants
to be treated, Sheriff." Sims grinned and held out a
hand. "Do we have an understanding?"

"We'll see." Sweet nodded, his expression telling
Sims that it was all he would get for now.

Chapter 9

There was no clerk at the Ballantine Hotel, just a cigar box on the counter with a note saying, "Gone for the winter. Pay on your honor." Sims smiled and dropped ten dollars into the box. In the top corner room of the hotel overlooking the street, Kate McCorkle stood beside the sagging bed, the carpetbag spread open before her. She'd taken out both pieces of the sawed-off shotgun from beneath their personal belongings and fitted the barrel to the rear stock as she spoke to Quick Charlie Sims in a stern voice. "And that's it? You're going to trust this man?" She picked up two ten gauge shells, shoved them into the chambers and snapped the shotgun shut.

"We have to trust someone, Kate," Sims said, picking up a packet of playing cards from the bed, opening it and spreading the deck into a fan. "Harris Sweet is a good man to have on our side. I get the impression that he doesn't care much for Phelps or J. T. Priest. Luckily, we got here while Cleveland Phelps and his men are up at the silver mines." Sims riffled the cards in his hand, double cutting them, then fanning them again. "All I need from Sweet is some breathing room. I need time to talk to Cleveland Phelps without his guns pointed at me. Don't forget, my only interest here is J. T. Priest. As soon as I can cut Priest out of the herd, we'll be out of here. Hart and Roth will take care of the rest of *Los Pistoleros.*"

"If they ever get here," Kate cut in. She gestured a hand toward the window where snowflakes swirled in the wind and melted against the glass. "It's getting worse out there by the hour."

"They'll be here, Kate. That's one thing we can count on." Sims straightened the deck of cards, put it back into the packet and slipped it into his coat pocket. "Meanwhile, I think I'll get back over to Sweet's office." He patted his coat pocket. "See if we can get a little better acquainted. I want us to be best of friends by the time Cleveland Phelps gets here."

"You're going to get him into a card game?" Kate asked in disbelief.

"No. My guess is Sweet's not a poker player. This is just a way of breaking the ice—finding out what his game really is." Sims smiled. "Don't worry, Kate, I've already made friends with his cat."

On the boardwalk out front of his office, Harris Sweet watched the service engine begin its slow descent down the mountainside, gray wood smoke curling upward into the snowy air. He waited with his polished pool cue cradled in his arm, timing it just right until he saw Sims step out through the door of the hotel and start toward him. Then, as if he hadn't seen Sims at all, he hiked up his wool coat collar and walked along the boardwalk toward the saloon, the big cat close at his bootheels. He stopped and turned at the sound of Sims calling out his name.

"I see it didn't take you long to unpack," Harris Sweet said as Sims covered the last few steps along the muddy walk plank and up onto the boardwalk. Sweet adjusted the pool cue under his arm and continued on his way.

"I travel light." Sims caught up to him and nodded at the cue under his arm. "Billiards, huh?"

"Yep." Sweet stared straight ahead as he spoke. "I try to shoot a few games every day . . . if everybody stays away and doesn't pester me. How's your game, Sims?"

"Not good I'm afraid." Sims shrugged, lifting the deck of cards from his pocket. "But I do play a fair hand of poker."

"Not with me you don't," Sweet said. "If we've got anything more to talk about, we'll have to do it over a billiard table."

Sims dropped the deck of cards into his coat pocket and said in a hesitant tone, "Well, I'll do the best I can and try not to embarrass myself."

From the hotel window, Kate McCorkle watched the two of them walk toward the saloon, the big black cat swerving away from Sweet's boot heel and sniffing closer to Quick Charlie Sims. Kate shook her head, then lifted her gaze to the gray sky where the swirl of snow seemed to have grown thicker in the past few minutes. When Sweet and Sims stepped inside the saloon, she looked back and forth along the empty street, sizing the town up, getting a feel for it, familiarizing herself with the muddy sidestreets and alleys.

She looked at the narrow rope footbridge suspended across a rushing creek that ran the length of the town. Across the creek, shacks stood on stilts, their backs against the jagged mountainside. Her eyes followed the narrow trail leading upward until it disappeared into tall slices of ice-streaked rock. This was the trail to watch, she thought. When Cleveland Phelps and his men came down from the silver mines, it would be from that direction. She stared for a moment longer, then turned from the window with a sigh of resignation, picked up the shotgun from the bed and cradled it in her arm as if it were an infant. *Damn it, Charlie! I hope you're not about to get us killed . . .*

Cleveland Phelps stood in the open doorway of the mining shack and looked out at the entrance of the main shaft forty yards away. The entrance had been covered by heavy iron doors and laced with chains, sealed and locked for the winter. In times past, if Cleveland Phelps had wanted into a mine shaft, no amount of chains and locks would have kept him out. But those times were over for him. He held the key to those locks. A large percent of whatever riches lay inside the mountain were now his, legally. Just feeling the key in his gloved hand made him smile to himself.

"So, what do you think, boss?" Benton Rhodes asked, standing close behind him. "Looks like the weather's setting in fast. Think we better get on down to Cold Ridge?"

"Yeah," Cleveland Phelps said over his shoulder, "go round up the boys and bring that old Indian over here. Bring a good strong rope, too."

"We're going to hang him, boss?" Rhodes asked, stepping past Cleveland Phelps and out the door.

"That's right, Rhodes, we're going to hang him and leave him hung till spring—that'll leave a message for anybody else who comes snooping around here."

"Whatever you say, boss." Benton Rhodes tugged his hat brim down against the cold wind and hurried over to the door of the long wooden miner's barracks, where he and the other men had spent the past two nights. Cleveland Phelps watched him step

inside and close the door behind himself. *That's right,
Rhodes, whatever I say . . .*

Phelps looked all around, liking the feeling of
being in charge, of having it all going his way now.
This was his operation now—his gang, his mine, his
mountain. There were other outstanding shares in
Midwest Investment, but that was no problem. He
owned a large portion of the stock and would gain
more control at every turn in the road. He was pretty
sure William Mabrey was dead, and there wasn't a
doubt in his mind that J. T. Priest soon would be.
He'd see to that himself as soon as Stanton and the
others brought Priest to Cold Ridge. Phelps's only
problem was how he would run a big business like
this—but maybe he'd find somebody to do all that.
All he wanted was the income.

He could have let Stanton and his men in on his
plan and had them kill Priest the minute they broke
him out of jail. But he wanted it to be a surprise for
everybody. Besides, killing J. T. Priest was something
Phelps wanted to do personally. He wanted to do it
in front of the whole gang, give them something to
think about, let them know beyond any doubt who
ran *Los Pistoleros* from now on. He could just see the
look on Priest's face as he rode in with Denver Stanton, Bobby Crady, Earl Mellon, and Carl White,
thinking Phelps had sent the four men to break him
out of jail just so that he could turn the gang over
to him. Fat chance, Priest, he thought.

"You stupid son of a bitch," Phelps growled under
his breath, picturing his pistol aimed and cocked at
J. T. Priest's head, the poor bastard seeing too late
what this whole jailbreak had been about. Anybody
dumb enough to get duped by a grifter like Quick
Charlie Sims the way Priest had deserved to go to
jail. Phelps grinned, watching Rhodes and the other

men walk toward him across the mine yard. Rhodes shoved the old Indian along in front of them, the Indian's hands tied behind his back.

"Here he is, boss," Rhodes called out from fifteen feet away, giving the old Indian a final hard shove that sent him tumbling at Phelps's feet like a bundle of rags. Behind Rhodes, a young gunman named Whitten stood with a coiled hemp rope on his shoulder. He took it down and tied a slip knot in one end of it.

Cleveland Phelps kicked the old Indian back with the sharp toe of his boot. "On your feet, old-timer. I don't like looking down when I talk."

One of the men snatched the Indian by his long gray hair and pulled him to his feet. The old Indian looked at Phelps through bruised and puffy eyes. "I am not . . . a thief," the old man rasped in a halting voice. Dried blood covered his chin and his swollen lips. "I am Crow Striker. Every winter . . . I stay in the shack. You can ask Harris Sweet."

"Harris Sweet?" Phelps looked back and forth as if searching for someone. Then he leveled a sharp glare into the Indian's weather-battered face. "Just your luck, I don't see Sweet around here anywhere. I'll be sure and ask him the minute we get back to Cold Ridge, though. If I'm wrong, I certainly apologize to you, in advance." He chuckled, glancing at the rest of the men. "Did any of you boys hear Sweet mention an Indian staying up here in the winter?"

The men shook their heads in unison. "He's lying to us," said Rhodes. "I can tell by the look on his face."

"There, you see?" Phelps said to the old man, leaning in closer to him. "It could take all day to figure out whether or not you're telling the truth—meanwhile, this weather ain't getting no better for us." He spun the old Indian around and shoved him toward Benton Rhodes. "You and Whitten take him over there and hang him from the flagpole. The rest of yas go get your horses and bring mine to me. Let's get on back to town."

The old Indian tried resisting. "No! Wait! You are making a mistake—"

"Come on, old man, you heard him," Rhodes said, cutting him off and shoving him forward. "This just ain't your lucky day." He bullied the old Indian along as Whitten dropped a loop of rope around the man's thin neck.

Phelps stepped back into the door of the shack and watched the men all move away, four of them going for the horses in a barn on the other side of the mine yard, the other two kicking and shoving the old Indian toward the tall flag pole. This was a good bunch of gunmen, he thought, all of them ready to do whatever he told them to do. J. T. Priest or William Mabrey could never have put together this kind of talent in such a short period of time. Phelps had always been the one with a knack for gathering good gunmen. That's why he'd always handled the muscle end of things.

But not for long, he reminded himself. He'd soon be running the whole show—and he'd get somebody else to handle the dirty work. He had a good selection to choose from. Rhodes and Whitten were a couple of Texas outlaws he'd used on a couple of bank jobs in the past year. Both of them were killers with ice in their veins. The other four were just as tough and even more seasoned. There was fat Doc Mason, a paid killer out of California, Lew Spivey, a Kentucky bank robber, kidnapper, and escaped felon, and Matt and Luke Tyrell, two cousins straight out of the Wild Bunch, both wanted for murder in Wyoming. These were the kind of men he could trust—men like himself.

"Rhodes," Cleveland Phelps called out in afterthought, seeing the two men grab the old Indian and stand him back against the flagpole. When Rhodes looked around at him, Phelps called out, "Take his scalp—I want it for a souvenir."

Rhodes looked at Whitten and chuckled. "What the hell does he want this stinking scalp for?"

Whitten shrugged. He reached down to his boot, pulled up a long bowie knife and slapped it onto Rhodes palm. "There, you do it . . . but clean my knife after."

"Hell, I hate doing this," Rhodes grumbled. He turned to the old Indian, saw the horrified look in his eyes and said to him, "Oh, like *you've* never done the same thing before?"

"I have never taken a scalp in my life," the old Indian said, his quiet voice sounding resolved to his gruesome fate.

"Yeah, I bet," Rhodes said. He turned back to Whitten. "I hope he doesn't mean for us to pull this old fart up the pole, hang him, then lower him, scalp him and drag him back up again."

"Beats me," said Whitten. He glanced over toward the shack for some guidance, but saw that Cleveland Phelps had already gone inside and shut the door. He turned back to Rhodes. "It'd be easier if we just shot him first. Don't you think?"

Snow blew in heavier when they left the mining site moments later and began the winding ride down the switchback trail toward Cold Ridge. The Indian's body swayed atop the flag pole in the cold wind, a frosty sheet of clinging snow collecting across his drooping shoulders.

* * *

In the early afternoon, Cleveland Phelps drew his horse up at the head of the riders and motioned toward a deep rock overhang barely visible through the swirling silver mist. He shouted above the roar of wind, "Pull in there! We'll rest the horses and warm up some."

"It's not going to get any better till we get down to town," Rhodes said to Whitten and Doc Mason as they turned their horses, keeping their hat brims ducked down against the blowing snow. Steam billowed from his breath as he spoke.

"He knows we've got to stay ahead of the weather," Doc Mason replied, his thick round face tucked back into his raised coat collar. "But it won't hurt to stop for an hour—get some warm blood circulating."

"I've always been more of a hot weather person," Whitten said, nudging his horse forward. "Give me West Texas any day over this."

At the overhang, Cleveland Phelps stepped down from his horse and flagged the others into the shelter, out of the cutting wind. "One hour," he said, "so don't anybody get too comfortable." He looked around as the five riders filed in past him. They dropped from their saddles, shook themselves off and beat their hat brims against their legs. "Anybody got a bottle?" Phelps asked.

"I knew you'd ask," said Doc Mason, beating the crunchy frost off his saddlebags and lifting its stiff flaps. He took out a half-full bottle of rye, pulled the cork and offered it to Phelps for the first drink. "Guess this is the big blow Harris Sweet has been talking about, eh boss?"

"Yeah . . . the beginning of it anyway," Phelps said, lowering the bottle from his lips and passing it on to Matt Tyrell. "It'll get a lot worse the next few days. Sweet might not know much about anything else, but he should know this weather by now."

The bottle of rye made its rounds, then came back to Doc Mason with only one good swallow left in it. To be courteous, Doc Mason offered it to Phelps before taking a sip. To his surprise, Cleveland Phelps took it, drained it, and pitched it away. "I'll be double-damned," Doc Mason whispered to himself, watching the bottle roll across the floor of the overhang.

Beside him, Whitten saw what had happened and stifled a laugh, nudging Rhodes with his elbow. "Serves him right, brownnosing," he whispered. Doc Mason caught the last part of Whitten's words and shot him a hard glare.

"So, boss," Whitten said, turning away from Doc Mason's gaze, "what's the deal with Sweet anyway? He acts like he doesn't want us around, you especially."

Cleveland Phelps grinned. "I hope you're not one of those sensitive types, who gives a blue-damn what people like Harris Sweet thinks." The men chuckled, huddled against the cold.

"Not me, boss. Just curious." Whitten returned the grin. "Hell, I'm a snake-eating Texan. I'll shut his eyes for you, if you want me to."

"Don't let your El Paso mouth overload your panhandle ass, young man," Doc Mason grumbled, still stinging a bit over his lost drink of rye. "Harris Sweet's eyes ain't all that easy to shut. You better check him out before you try your hand at him."

"Oh, really?" Whitten's grin faded into a sneer, turning to Doc Mason. "You don't know me well enough to talk that way. I expect I can shut most any man's eyes I take a mind to."

"Doc's right, Whitten," Phelps said, seeing where

things were headed between the two and wanting to cut it off. "Harris Sweet is a tough piece of work. But that doesn't mean he can't be killed. A bullet has no respect for reputation, I've always said." He looked back and forth among the men, thought about something for a second then let out a breath. "Boys, while we're here, this is as good a time as any to tell you what's about to happen down in Cold Ridge." The men drew closer, interested. "I told all of you we're waiting for J. T. Priest to show up, and that's the truth. But some things are changing as soon as he gets here."

Cleveland Phelps looked back and forth, letting his words sink in for a second. "Everybody here has rode with *Los Pistoleros* at one time or another. That's all coming to an end. I lost my regular crew of gunman to a couple of Judge Parker's deputies, thanks to J. T. Priest. From now on you boys are riding with me full time, if you've no objections."

"You mean it, boss?" Whitten leaned forward, his voice in awe at the prospect.

"Damn right I mean it. Priest and Mabrey have let this gang fall apart on me. From now on, I'm taking over. I already own a big chunk of stock in Midwest Investment and I plan on owning more. I'm going to make this gang what it once was—the meanest sons of bitches that ever drew iron." His voice rose. "Anybody not with me best clear out before we get back to town. As soon as Priest shows up, we've got some serious killing to do, starting with J. T. himself. If I'm right in my thinking, those two deputies won't be far behind him. They're going down, too." He studied their faces. "Anybody got qualms about killing lawmen?"

"It's right up our alley," Rhodes said with a short laugh. The others nodded in agreement.

"All right then. Boys, there's good times ahead. I want every man here to make his fortune. At some point, I'll be stepping over into running the legitimate part of Midwest Investment. The man who'll take over running this end of things is one of you standing here today." He took his time looking from one to the other in turn. Then he added, "So you better all start showing me what you're worth. Is that clear enough?" Silence set in as each man considered Phelps's words. Outside the shelter of the rock overhang, the wind roared.

Chapter 10

The sound of clacking billiard balls resounded in the otherwise empty saloon. Quick Charlie Sims straightened up from the pool table as the two ball rolled into the corner pocket with a soft sound of ivory on leather. He examined the layout of the balls on the green felt as he sidestepped around the corner of the table. "Three ball in the side," he said, leaning down into position, stroking the cue back and forth through the closed bridge of his hand.

Sheriff Harris Sweet eyed the shot, a bit skeptical. But as Sims straightened up and the three ball rolled over the lip of the pocket and dropped, Sweet murmured, "Good shot," and leaned his own stick against the wall.

"Four ball, two rails in the corner," Sims said. But before he leaned over for the shot, he noticed Sweet had picked up their empty beer mugs and headed over to the bar. "Should I wait, Sheriff?"

"Nope," Sweet said without turning, "I trust you. Anybody who shoots pool like you do has no need to cheat."

Sims smiled to himself. "Thank you, Sheriff." But to be on the safe side, Sims stalled until a bald-headed bartender with a long handlebar mustache had filled both beer mugs. Then as Harris Sweet came walking back with the mugs dripping foam,

Sims took position, stroked the ball with clean, solid, upper-left english and stood back watching the four ball make its run up the table and back down. It struck the end rail and began its smooth angle into the far corner pocket.

"I'll be damned, what a shot," Sweet said. He sat Sims's beer mug on an oaken table against the wall, raised his to his lips and took a long swig. "I thought you said table billiards wasn't your game, Sims?"

"That's what I said, Sheriff." Sims shrugged. "I'm doing everything I can just to keep up. Don't forget, you're seven games ahead." He gestured his cue toward the side pocket. "Five ball in the side," he added. This time, Sims held his aim a fraction to one side of the pocket. This was not the kind of shot a man would miss—it was too easy. The trick was to purposely miss it but not look obvious about it.

Sims let out a breath and slumped when the ball clipped the edge of the pocket rail and rolled away. Sims needed to look surprised at missing the shot, but not so surprised that he gave himself away. Harris Sweet was no newcomer to the game. It was obvious by the look he gave Sims that nothing got past him. "Well, I figured I better miss one, Sheriff, just to keep on your good side." Sims grinned, walked around the table, picked up his beer mug and sipped from it.

"Sure, you did." Harris Sweet spread a stiff smile, dusted his right hand on the cone of talcum powder on the shelf on the wall, then sidestepped around the table, eyeing his shot. "With a little practice, Sims, I could turn you into a hell of a pool player." He leaned down. "Four ball, corner pocket." He shot fast and hard, slamming the ball into the pocket and leaving the white cue ball spinning in place. "But until that happens, I'll enjoy taking your money." As if with a mind of its own, the cue ball broke out of its spin, darted four inches across the felt, clipped the nine ball and sent it into the side pocket. Sweet's stiff smile widened, his eyes gleaming in victory. "Game ball, Sims."

Sims feigned astonishment. "I don't believe it, Sheriff. Nobody can make a shot like that."

"You saw me do the same shot yesterday," Sweet said, rising up from position. "Ten dollars says I can make it again."

Sims leaned his stick against the wall and shook his head. "No thanks, Sheriff. I've had it with you. You're a pool shark. That's two days in a row you've clipped me." Sims slumped down onto a chair at the oaken table.

"Aw, don't get discouraged." Sweet laid his stick on the table and came around to his mug of beer. "You're doing better every game."

The black tomcat slipped from beneath the pool table at the sight of Sims reaching a hand down to him. The big cat leaped up onto Sims lap and rubbed his furry side against Sims's chest. Sims settled him across his knee and stroked his purring back. "Let's see," Sims said, as if working the figures out in his head, "that's seven games today, four games yesterday—eleven games at fifty cents a game. I owe you five and a half dollars, Sheriff. I better settle up with you tonight, in case Phelps and his men show up tomorrow."

Sims made an effort at reaching into his trouser pocket, but Sweet stopped him. "What's your hurry, Sims? Phelps or nobody else is going to tell me what to do."

The old sheriff's eyes took on a serious expression. Sims studied his face for a second. "Have you been thinking things over, Sheriff? Anything we need to talk about?"

"Yeah, I've thought things over." Sweet sat down in a chair across from him, sipping at his beer. "I like your style, Sims. I think you're slicker than socks on a rooster." Sweet jerked his head toward the billiard table. "You haven't fooled me. I believe you could beat the devil out of hell at nine ball if you took a notion and the stakes were high enough." He spread his stiff smile again. "Still, you have a smooth way of doing things, a good way of treating people—I like that. Hell, you've even charmed ole Scratch." He gestured at the purring tomcat on Sims's lap. "And that's not an easy thing to do."

"So, Sheriff . . . you're ready to back me up, keep everybody in line while I take care of my business with Priest?" Sims looked at him, his hand stopping mid-stroke along the cat's back.

"Yeah, I'll keep them off you. How often does an old warhorse like me get a chance to butt heads with a no-good bunch of bastards like Cleveland Phelps and his gunmen. I call it going out in style."

"Whoa, Sheriff." Sims raised a hand toward him. "I want your help. But you sound like a man writing his own epitaph."

"That might be exactly what I'm doing if things get out of hand here." Sweet sipped his beer then set the mug down. "Any man who faces a band of gunmen without giving some thought to dying is a damned fool. So don't go thinking you've won me over with cold beer and a few games of nine ball. I've got bigger things in mind than simply backing your play." Sweet cut a sidelong glance across the saloon toward the bartender, then looked back at Sims.

"Don't worry, Sheriff. Once I get myself in position

with Midwest Investment, you'll be taken care of. Instead of a pay envelope every month, we'll see to it you get a percent of everything coming out of the mine—"

"Aw, hush, Sims." Sweet waved it away. "I said I'll back your play, but it's not for any promises of silver or shares in Midwest Investment, or any of that horse manure. I'll do it just because I'm getting old—because I'm meaner than hell, and still need to prove something before I die."

Sims just stared at him.

"Look around, Sims. This is no real town, and I'm no real sheriff. This is a company town. I'm a paid gun—a guard, you might as well say. All the men I've faced and fought in my life, it wasn't me upholding the real law. It was me protecting the holdings of the rich and powerful. It was never me protecting decent people from the no-good sons of bitches of this world. It was those no-good sons of bitches who always paid my salary. We both know that, Sims."

"Sheriff, I'm not your judge," Sims said, all of this catching him unexpected. "I just came to ask your help."

"And you've got it." Sweet smiled, but it was a tired, ironic smile. "I reckon you just happened to get here about the time I quit fooling myself." He raised the mug, finished it in a long swallow, then stood up and adjusted his holster belt. "Now, if you'll excuse me . . . I've got some guns to clean, and some wanted posters that need to be looked at." He reached down and rubbed the big cat on its head. "You take care of Scratch for me, Sims."

The cat looked up at him with its one good eye, then lowered its head slowly.

* * *

In the hotel room, Sims paced back and forth, the big black tomcat pacing with him, a few inches behind his right bootheel. "I don't understand your problem," Kate McCorkle said. She lay stretched out on the sagging bed with her feet crossed and her hands folded behind her head. The sawed-off shotgun lay beside her. "You wanted his help, you've got it."

"But he's talking crazy, Kate." Sims stopped and raked his fingers back through his disheveled hair. Scratch stopped behind him. "Sure I played up to him, got on his good side. But now he acts like this is going to be his way of going out in a blaze of glory. There's something about this old sheriff I can't figure out, something hiding inside him just beneath the skin. I feel like I've lit the fuse to a powder keg."

"And you don't want to feel guilty afterward, right?" Kate raised up onto one elbow and shook her head. "When you invite somebody into a gunfight, Charlie, you really should consider the possibility that they might get killed."

Sims gave her an exasperated look. "Kate . . . all I want is for him to keep everybody in line long enough for me to talk sense to them. You know my only true interest here is in J. T. Priest."

"Oh? Then owning Midwest Investment doesn't mean anything to you anymore? Because if you really don't want those shares, I'd be happy to—"

"Stop it, Kate. Of course it means something to me, but not as much as getting Priest to show me the cave where my family's wagons are hidden. I can pull this off without Sweet getting himself killed, if he'll let me. When Hart and Roth get here, they can handle Phelps and every gunmen with him."

"So, it doesn't bother you that Hart and Roth could get killed, only Sweet, some old paid killer who ad-

mitted to you that during his entire life, his gun has
gone to the highest bidder?"

"It's Sullivan Hart and Twojack Roth's job to hunt
down outlaws, Kate—and they're good at it. Besides,
I'm not responsible for getting them into this. They've
been after *Los Pistoleros* from the start. Harris Sweet
could have stayed out of Phelps's way, gone on collecting his pay envelope every month, and died of
old age in a feather bed. Now, he's got it in his mind
that this is his way to die!"

"You don't know that, Charlie." Kate swung up
off the bed, snatched up her silk flowered robe and
threw it around herself.

"He gave me his cat! See what I'm saying, Kate?
Sweet is cashing in. I saw it in his eyes. If you'd been
there, you would have seen the same thing."

Kate took a thin cigar from the nightstand and lit
it as she spoke. "I'll tell you what I do see, Charlie."
She blew out a stream of gray smoke. "I see you're
having second thoughts. If it wasn't about Sweet, it
would be about something else. It's dangerous at this
point of the game. You did the same thing back in
Chicago and it got you a bullet in your back. You
get everything going your way, then at the last minute—"

"Don't start on me, Kate." Sims raised a finger for
emphasis. "I got shot in Chicago because at the last
minute I didn't want to risk getting *you* shot. So
there."

She shrugged as she walked over to the window
to look out at the swirling snow. "It's the same thing,
Charlie." The snow had grown heavier throughout
the day and was now starting to stick, forming white
outlines atop tin roofs and around chimney stacks.
Her voice softened, and without facing him, she said,
"I wasn't in Chicago against my will, Charlie."

Sims sighed. "I know that, Kate, but still—"

"I was there because of you," she continued. "I knew the risk, and I took it. If I had died there it wouldn't have been your fault, any more than it will be your fault if Sweet dies here. You have a way of making people want to help you. Sometimes you do it intentionally, sometimes it just happens. Either way, this is no time to question it, or second-guess yourself. The cards are on the table." She turned and faced him, and nodded at the shotgun on the bed. "Hell, Charlie, I'm locked and loaded."

In the sheriff's office, Harris Sweet finished cleaning his Henry rifle, rubbed a cloth along the gleaming barrel, and laid it down on the battered desk. He took his Colt .45 from his holster, unloaded it and took it apart deftly, his fingers feeling along the smooth edges and turns in the steel for any nicks or imperfections, and finding none. He laid each piece of the pistol down on a soft cloth, and as he cleaned, polished and inspected his work, he smiled to himself, thinking about Quick Charlie Sims and Cleveland Phelps, and of the silver gray storm that he knew lay thick and low in a wall of boiling fog on the distant mountain peaks.

When the Colt was cleaned and reassembled, Sweet held it close to his ear, clicking the cylinder gently beneath his thumb, listening to the smooth sound of metal on metal. Satisfied with the sound and the feel of the mechanism, he took a box of cartridges from the top drawer of his desk, loaded the pistol and laid it on the soft cloth. Then he took extra cartridges and filled the empty bullet loops in his holster belt. Some of them had been empty far too long, he thought.

He put his cleaning oil and rag away, closed the

desk drawer with finality, and stood up. He adjusted his pistol belt and holstered the Colt loosely, the clean pistol feeling lighter, more deadly somehow. His awareness of the big Colt's presence low on his hips felt sharper than it had in a long time. Sweet felt younger now, faster, more alert, attuned to everything around him, his senses taking on a new edge, he thought. He liked that. He swung his wool winter coat around himself, cradled the Henry rifle under his left arm, picked up his Stetson and left the office, stepping out into a cold blast of snow-filled wind.

Inside the saloon, the bartender heard the familiar sound of Harris Sweet's boots along the boardwalk and, out of habit, ran a hand back across his bald head, tweaked his handlebar mustache, picked up a shot glass and began wiping it with a bar cloth. The saloon lay empty and dimly lit in the falling evening light. Sweet opened the wooden door just enough to slip inside, then pressed it closed against the resistance of the bitter weather. He swung his Stetson from his head and batted it against his leg as he crossed the floor to the bar. "Evening, Sheriff," the bartender said, his voice crisp, a bit detached. "It's becoming quite a blow out there."

"Cut the sheriff part, Herman, its just us here," Sweet offered, cutting a glance about the empty saloon. "And you know damn well I didn't come to talk about the weather."

"Oh?" Herman Stitz raised his brow. "Well, since you've hardly spoken to me for the past three days, what exactly would you like to talk about, *Sheriff*? Or am I prying again?"

Sweet's face stung red at the bartender's tone of voice, but he let it pass. "You missed the last service train. Why?" Sweet demanded. "Does this mean that even after our little talk, you're still staying up here for the winter?"

Herman shrugged, avoiding Sweet's stare. "I have the mule. I can make it down the mountain anytime." He fidgeted with the bar towel.

"I made it clear to you, Herman, this is one winter I want to be alone." Sweet spread his hands along the bar rail. "If this weather passes and another service run makes it through, I want you on it. Don't make me say this again."

Herman swung the bar towel up over his shoulder and glared at Sweet. "You don't own me, Harris. We've been together our whole life." He cut a glance about the empty saloon out of habit. "But I'm still my own boss. If I decide to stay, you have no say in it." He leaned slightly closer across the bar, his eyes narrowed in defiance. "Do you think I'm blind, Harris? Do you think I haven't seen the way you let that grifter, that two-bit pool hustler waltz in here and dazzle you?"

"Dazzle me?" Sweet's jaw tightened, then relaxed. "Jesus, Herman, I'm so far past being dazzled it ain't funny. You ought to know me better than that, as many towns as we've been through together. I saw through Sims the minute he picked up a cue stick. The way Scratch took up with him? Uh-uh, no way. Five to one odds Sims has a ball of catnip in his pocket. I might be getting old, Herman, but I ain't a damn fool yet."

"Well . . . all right. I've been worried. You can't blame me," Herman relented, his voice and demeanor losing its sharpness. "I know you well enough to see that you've been building up to something ever since Cleveland Phelps and his trash rode in. Maybe this Quick Charlie Sims is your way of bringing things to a head."

"Maybe." Sweet smiled thin and tight, his eyes looking more vacant than Herman Stitz could recall in all the years he'd known him. "But knowing me as well as you do, I'd think you realize when I tell you to clear out, it's time to do it. I don't want you on my mind when the bullets fly."

"Damn you, Harris!" Herman's knuckles turned white, gripping the bar. "What have I ever done to make you talk to me that way? I'm the only person who ever stood up with you—town after town, battle after battle! Who else in God's blue hell ever swabbed your belly wounds, or sewed up your head? Who the hell but me ever covered your back with a shotgun and kept you alive when we both knew we were going to die in some dirt street? For three days you've acted like I'm not even there—now you don't want me on your mind?" His hands trembled.

"Easy, now," Sweet cautioned, seeing Herman's eyes glisten moist in his rage. "I said it wrong, Herman . . . I'm sorry. You know there's nobody I'd trust on my side more than you. But damn it, man, this is my fight, not yours."

"No, Harris!" Herman shook his head. "It's *our* flight. Always was, always will be."

"Not this time, Herman—"

"Yes, this time. Especially this time." Herman slammed a palm down on the bar. "Because this time there's no reason in hell for you getting involved. This time it's pointless and insane, and if it takes me standing up there getting my brains shot out just to show you how crazy this is, then by God I'm going to do it!" he fanned a hand, taking in the whole town. "We have a place here, a home, a way of life. If you're willing to throw all that away just because you're miserable over who you are—"

"Damn it, Herman!" Sweet cut him off. "We've

got nothing here, anymore than we've ever had. An *illusion*! That's what we've got here—me, the badge-toting sheriff, the big gun from the past. You, the bartender friend who just happens to always show up in the same place at the same time." Sweet lowered his head and shook it back and forth slowly. "Lord God, Herman, look at us for what we are."

"So?" Herman Stitz gazed past him, indignant, and tugged down on the edges of his vest and adjusted the black garter on his white shirt sleeve. "Sometimes illusion is all people get, any of us. There's such a thing as accepting what life deals you, you know. So what, your name is not as famous as Wyatt Earp or Bat Masterson? Or that I never got to own myself a fancy gambling hall? Midwest Investment pays me well—both of us, for that matter. We've done all right for ourselves. Better than we might have expected, all things considered."

"Yeah, we're doing all right," Sweet said in a sarcastic tone. "I protect some corporation's silver holdings, and keep a nice quiet town all stocked and ready in case a band of cut-throat outlaws needs to hide out for a while." He raised his eyes to Herman Stitz. "And you keep them drinking, and ignore their insults, and laugh at their profane jokes."

"I'm not complaining, Harris."

"No, you never do. But I'm sick to my guts of it, Herman. There's times like today when I look up into the northern sky, see that winter storm gather its breath, and I wish to God that whole sky would blow through here and cut us all down, every last one of us, right down to the frozen earth." With his head lowered, Sweet sighed and fell silent for a second. When he spoke again, his voice was barely above a whisper. "That's why I'm glad this Quick Charlie Sims showed up when he did. Now I want you out of here, Herman. Don't fight me on this. Get out of here tonight."

Herman whispered in reply, reaching beneath the bar and standing a bottle of rye whiskey up on it beside two clean shot glasses, "Go to hell, Harris." He pulled the cork from the bottle, filled the glasses, and spread his hands along the bar staring at Sweet's lowered head.

Sweet cut his gaze to the glass of whiskey and let out a deep breath. "It's other things too, Herman. I heard all this rigamarole about stocks, investments, who owns the controlling interest, who wants to get their hands on it. I feel like a stranger here all of a sudden. Things have changed so much in this world. I don't belong here anymore."

Herman considered Sweet's words for a second, then said, "Okay. I understand now. You're looking for a place to die, and you don't want me seeing it." He raised his glass of rye whiskey as if in a solitary toast as Sweet's eyes raised up to him. "But guess what, Harris. It's not going to happen that way—I'm staying for better or worse."

Chapter 11

The wind howled low and steady in the night, waking Kate McCorkle from a restless sleep. For a moment she tossed and turned in the darkness until at length she flipped the blanket off her, sat up on the side of the sagging bed and lit a thin cigar she'd stubbed out and left lying in an ashtray on the nightstand. She smoked and thought about what she and Sims had talked about earlier. She looked at his sleeping form in the darkness, breathing peacefully in contrast to the howling wind.

She hadn't admitted it, but it troubled her the way Sims had not been able to read Sheriff Sweet. Quick Charlie never missed a call. What was it about Harris Sweet that had Sims worried? And he really was worried, she could tell. At length she stood up and walked to the window. Through the falling snow she looked down and across the dark street at the single dim lantern glowing through the window of the saloon.

She glanced back at Sims on the bed, then back out the window until finally she came to a decision. Sims wasn't going to like it, but she was going down there. She walked back to the bed and whispered his name quietly. When he didn't stir at the sound of her voice, she stepped back and picked up her clothes from across the back of a wooden chair. She dressed in the darkness, pulled on her lace-up shoes, picked up the Colt pistol from beneath her pillow and walked softly across the creaking pine floor to where her heavy winter coat hung from a rack in the corner.

Inside the empty, dimly lit saloon, Herman Stitz stood behind the bar amid stacks of small packing crates. He'd taken all but a few of the shot glasses and beer mugs from the shelves and placed them down into thatches of packing straw. He'd done the same with most of the bottles of his better-grade whiskey, leaving the bottles of cheap bar rye for the rabble of outlaws who would be holed up there for most of the winter. Inside a small cabinet beneath the bar, he'd placed a few bottles of bourbon for himself and Harris Sweet. Once Stitz had gotten his bar in order, he'd set the single glowing lantern in front of the long mirror behind the bar.

He took the shaving mug with the patty of soap in it, poured a trickle of water in it and began stirring it with a shaving brush, working up a thick lather. He slathered the top of his head, the sides, and down the back of his neck to his collar line. While he waited for the lather to moisten his skin, he took the razor from its leather case on the shelf and stroked it back and forth on a long razor strop, then on the palm of his hand to test its sharpness. The howl of the wind outside muffled the sound of Kate McCorkle's footsteps on the boardwalk, and Stitz did not hear a sound until she opened the door and let it in a roar of cold wind.

"Excuse me . . ." Kate pressed the door closed with her back and stood looking at Herman Stitz from across the empty saloon. Stitz turned, startled, a shaking hand snatching up a towel and hurriedly rubbing it around on his lathered head.

"My goodness!" He ducked his head to one side, embarrassed, as if wanting to hide himself. "Young lady, the bar's closed."

"Yes, I know." Kate offered an apologetic smile, walking to the bar, shaking snow from the front of her coat. "I'm sorry, but I awakened hungry." She stopped at the bar and gestured a hand back toward the door. "The restaurant closed yesterday for the winter. I hoped maybe . . . ?" She let her words trail, looking back and forth at the packing crates along the bar.

Stitz finished vigorously rubbing the towel on his head, then wadded the towel and pitched it beneath the bar. "As you can see, miss, I'm only here putting some things away—getting ready for the off-season, so to speak." He turned, awkwardly fumbling with the wick on the lantern, raising the glow of light as he turned back to her and placed the lantern on the bar top. "We usually don't have anyone around here this time of year, except the sheriff, myself, and—"

"I understand," Kate said, interrupting, "but I'm certain whoever stays here must eat—occasionally. I hoped maybe you'd have something, some cold meats, bread, anything." She smiled, giving him a bit of a pleading expression. As she spoke, Scratch appeared out of nowhere, hopped up on the bar and high-stepped close to her. Kate reached out and ran a hand along his arched back. "Oh, there you are, Scratch. I wondered where you went."

Stitz seemed taken aback for a second, seeing the big tomcat warm up to this attractive young woman, her cheeks pinched rosy with the bite of cold, a sprinkling of snowflakes glistening wet in her dark hair. Then he relaxed, allowed himself a slight smile, saying, "You must be the young lady traveling with Mr. Sims. We haven't met—I'm Herman Stitz." He reached a moist hand across the bar to her. "Where are my manners?" Stitz shook his bald head. "I'm sure we can find something for you." He nodded toward a door at the rear of the saloon, picking up the lantern by its handle. "Come, follow me." As he moved along behind the bar, he added, "Sheriff Sweet and I are a couple of old bachelors. I'm afraid we're unaccustomed to having a young woman around. We often forget ourselves."

"I understand," Kate replied, following him along the front of the bar. In the lantern's glow Kate saw a short streak of shaving soap across the back of Stitz's head, and as they rounded the corner of the bar she felt compelled to reach out and wipe it away. But she didn't. She smiled to herself, noting how Stitz's words included Sheriff Harris Sweet as if the sheriff was with them. *Two old bachelors . . . ?* All right, she thought. Kate McCorkle knew men. She was certain she could find out from Stitz whatever it was about Harris Sweet that had Sims so unsettled. Behind her, Scratch hopped down from the bar top and tagged along.

At the edge of town, two men struggled forward, leading their horses. The horses walked with their heads lowered, their manes whipping sidelong in the blowing sleet. "I'll tell you one thing, Chester." Darby Phelps said, his voice almost a shout beneath the shrieking wind. "If Cleveland has drug me up here for no good reason, he and I are going to have ourselves one very serious discussion, brother or no brother." They trudged across frozen wagon ruts filled with fine powdery snow.

Darby Phelps held his hat pressed down with a gloved hand and continued shouting back at Chester Meins from only a foot away. "But I've got to admit—every time Cleveland has called me in on something, I've come out all the better for it. He must have a big bank somewhere needs robbing."

"Then it better be awfully big," Chester Meins shouted. "I'm near froze to death."

"Nothing a good bottle of rye won't cure, though." Darby Phelps stared ahead through squinted eyes at the dark street before them, the wind holding one side of his Stetson brim flat against his numbed cheek. "If I know Cleveland, he'll have some whores tucked away here somewhere. Or by-God, he better have."

They found the deserted livery barn, stalled their horses, stripped off their wet saddles and tack, and wiped the animals down with a handful of straw. They grained the horses with feed from a bin and stood for a moment in silence with their gloves off, blowing steamy breath into their cupped hands and rubbing their raw hands together. Then, like creatures drawn by sheer instincts, the two men left the barn leaning into the severe weather, and did not stop until they stood on the boardwalk outside the dark saloon.

"It must be closed," Darby Phelps said, his right hand back onto his hat, holding it down as he tried peering through the window.

"Not now it ain't." Chester Meins tried the knob, felt it turn in his hand, then held the knob firmly to keep the wind from blasting the door open as he stepped inside. Darby Phelps followed right behind him. "There you are, see?" Chester pressed the door shut, nodding at the sliver of lantern light seeping beneath the door in the rear corner. "Ole Cleveland even left a light on for us."

Darby Phelps grinned. "I always said, when it

comes to manners, you can't beat my big brother, that obliging son of a bitch."

In his living quarters, Herman Stitz looked up at the sound of the saloon door opening and closing, but then he dismissed it as the sound of the wind and looked back at Kate McCorkle, who sat across the small table from him spooning up a bite of mock apple pie as she continued speaking. "So, anyway, no sooner than the wound in his back healed, we left Chicago and arrived in Fort Smith, about the time J. T. Priest made his jailbreak. Then we came straight here. I tried telling Charlie it was too soon for him to be up and around." She shrugged. "But you know how you men are, once you set out to do something."

"Yes, I know." Herman Stitz broke his gaze away from her, lowered his eyes for a second, then looked back up. "The sheriff is the same way, only . . ." Stitz stopped as if searching for the right words. But instead of finishing, he went on to say, "Look, Miss McCorkle, this is not the sheriff's trouble, nor mine."

"Call me Kate, Herman, I insist," she said.

"Yes, thank you, Kate." Stitz went on. "I'm sure you agree it would be best if the two of you found a way out of here before Cleveland Phelps and his men return. We—that is, *the sheriff* is going through some personal difficulty right now. He doesn't like catering to a band of thugs like Phelps and his men anymore than I do. We know what they are. But you have to understand, this is our livelihood."

"I do understand. All Charlie wanted is for the sheriff to keep these outlaws at bay long enough for him to talk with Phelps. But now Charlie's worried. He thinks instead of the sheriff preventing a gun battle, he might be out to start one! So, you can appreciate my concern. To be honest, that was my real purpose in coming here tonight. I had hoped perhaps the sheriff would be here."

"I don't know why you would think that." Stitz's face reddened a bit. "He doesn't *live* here you know."

"No, of course not." Kate saw Stitz was affronted, although she did not see any impropriety in her words. "I only mean that this being the town saloon and all." She gestured a hand.

"Oh, I see." Stitz looked away again, this time rubbing a hand across his smooth bald head. "Well, ordinarily he would be here until closing time. But with this weather setting in . . ." Stitz also gestured a hand.

"As it turns out, I'm glad it's just the two of us here," Kate said. At her hand sat a steaming cup of coffee. "It's given us a chance to talk. I can see you know Sheriff Sweet pretty well."

"We've become friends," Stitz acknowledged, avoiding her gaze.

A trace of realization began to form in Kate's mind, but it was not quite clear yet. "I want you to know that Charlie isn't out to cause anyone to get hurt, if he can help it." She raised the cup and sipped, taking her time, her eyes catching a glimpse around the small living quarters, noting its cleanliness, with everything in its place, an arrangement of handmade artificial flowers freshly waxed, standing in an ornate vase on a white crocheted doily atop a claw-foot table. On a small divan, Scratch lay licking a paw.

Something clicked for her as she turned her eyes back to Stitz. He must have seen it. He lowered his eyes again, but then seemed to catch himself and leveled them on her. "We both have the same interests here, Kate," he said, his voice soft and sincere. "Our fears are the same, yours and mine. I have

never told this to anyone, but I'm tired of the pretense—''

Stitz's words were cut short as the door to his living quarters flew open and Chester Meins and Darby
Phelps swaggered into the room and slammed the
door behind themselves. ''Well, well, well!'' Chester
Meins looked back and forth between Kate McCorkle
and Herman Stitz, his gaze then locking on Kate,
traveling up and down the length of her supple form.
Startled, she'd risen halfway from her chair, turning
toward him as Chester's expression took on that of
a hungry wolf, ''Talk about hospitality! Ole Cleveland's outdone himself this time. Is this a private
honeymoon, or can anybody join in?'' Chester asked.

Stitz instinctively shot a glance at his double-
barreled shotgun in the back corner of the room.
''Uh-uh now,'' Darby Phelps warned, seeing Stitz
ready to make a leap for the shotgun. Darby Phelps
raised his pistol out of his holster, cocking it on the
upswing, and pointed at Stitz's chest. ''You can't
blame a couple of ole boys if they see something they
like and have to have it. Lord, honey.'' He reached
a hand out, stepping closer to Kate. ''Forget a hot
bath! I'm warmer already.''

Quick Charlie Sims heard the first shot through the
roar of wind and a veil of sleep, but before his mind
could even question what it was, the next three shots
resounded in rapid succession, removing any doubt.
''Kate!'' He sprang from the bed. ''Kate, wake up!''
His eyes went to the place where Kate McCorkle
should have been sleeping. A sliver of cold fear
stabbed him in his chest as another shot exploded in
the night. ''Oh, Jesus! Kate!'' He grabbed his coat
from the rack on his way to the door, not bothering

to grab either his boots or his gun, and slung it around his shoulders on his way down the stairs.

A blast of strong cold wind staggered Sims sideways as he raced barefoot toward the saloon. Through the white swirl he saw the vague image of a man burst from the saloon and run limping toward the livery barn. A pistol shot exploded from the saloon, blue-yellow muzzle fire splitting the night. Sims ducked but kept running, making out Kate McCorkle's figure behind the flash of gunfire.

"Kate, it's me!" he yelled, seeing another shot illuminate the darkness. From the opposite direction another pistol shot barked above the roaring wind as if in reply. Sims dived to the cold ground and scrambled the last few yards to the boardwalk outside the saloon. In the direction of the livery barn, he heard Sheriff Harris Sweet yell, "Stop right there!" But the sound of Sweet's voice only prompted more gunshots. Sims pitched himself up onto the boardwalk and over to the door. Kate stretched her hand down to him, her other hand holding the Colt up, ready, her eyes searching through the blowing snow.

"Kate! Are you all right?" Even as he spoke, Sims shoved her back inside the door of the saloon. He caught a glimpse of her dress, torn down the front, exposing her right breast. Blood trickled from jagged scratch marks running down from her shoulder.

"Yes, I'm fine! Let me go! I'll kill that bastard!" She grappled with Sims, trying to get past him to the door. Another shot rang out from the livery barn.

"Who, Kate? Who did this to you?" Sims held Kate back as she flailed her arms wildly, the pistol barrel nearly clipping Sims's head.

"They killed Herman! The dirty bastards!" she shouted and struggled forward. Sims wrapped both arms around her waist, but just as she broke loose and bolted for the door, Sweet stepped inside, catching her against his chest.

"Where's Herman?" Sweet shoved Kate back into Sims.

"Back there," Kate pointed with her pistol barrel. "They shot him!"

"Oh Lord no!" Harris Sweet ran across the saloon floor toward the open door to Stitz's living quarters. Sims and Kate followed, but stopped at the door as Sweet bent down over Stitz and cried out over his shoulder at them, "Get back, both of you! Give me room! He's alive!"

In the small doorway, Sims looked across the room at the overturned window table, the spilled flower vase, and the body of Chester Meins sprawled face-down in a pool of blood, with three bullet holes in his back. "Jesus, Kate," Sims asked in a rushing breath, "who are they? Phelps's men? Are they here?"

"There's just the two of them," Kate said, shaking her head, her left hand pulling up her torn dress to cover her breast. "I killed that one. The other one got away." She stepped forward. "Sheriff, let us help you."

"Stay back," Sweet barked over his shoulder, tearing the front of Stitz's shirt away. "You want to help—boil some water and get some clean bar towels!" His voice settled as he turned back to Stitz and ran a hand across his brow. "Don't worry, I'm here. You're going to be all right." From the doorway Sims saw Stitz's bloody trembling hand reach up and grasp Sweet's forearm.

"Kate?" Sims whispered, turning a curious expression to her as she backed out of the doorway and headed behind the bar. Sims moved along beside her. "Kate . . . what went on here? Talk to me."

"Not now, Charlie." She frantically searched under the bar, finding a handful of clean towels and stuffing them up under her arm. "I'll tell you about Sweet and Stitz later—not now."

In Stitz's living quarters, Sweet cut a glance over his shoulder, seeing Sims and Kate were gone. "Damn it all, why?" Sweet spoke softly to Stitz, his voice shaky. "You just had to get involved, didn't you?"

"She . . . came to me," Stitz rasped. Blood flowed from the bullet hole in his chest. "She's worried . . . too."

Sweet held him cradled in his arms. "Keep still, don't talk now. Just hang on." He heard Sims and Kate come back from the bar, and he closed Stitz's shirt across his chest, scooped him in his arms and hurried into a small bedroom with him. "Lay the towels there." Sweet nodded at the nightstand beside the single feather bed. "Did you put some water on the stove?"

"Yes, it'll only be a minute." Kate leaned in as Sweet stretched Stitz out on the bed. "How bad is it? What can I do?" But Sweet nudged her back with his forearm.

"Keep back, give him room to breathe," Sweet said.

Sims took Kate by her arm and pulled her away from the bed. He nodded toward the other room. "Come on, Kate, you heard him," Sims said barely above a whisper. In the other room, the two of them stepped around the body of Chester Meins. "What happened, Kate? Tell me everything. What were you even doing here?"

"We—we were just talking, having coffee . . . then they came in." She pointed at Meins's bloody back. "They tried to, you know, take advantage. I shot this one dead, wounded the other one. Herman went for the shotgun. The other one shot him, then ran."

"You said they were part of Phelps's men?"

"Yes." She pushed back a strand of hair. "The other one mentioned Phelps was his brother, I think. It all happened so fast. Luckily, I had a gun."

Sweet called out from the other room. "Did you say Phelps's brother? Darby Phelps?"

Kate stepped back into the doorway, calling across the small bedroom, "Yes, this one called him Darby."

"Good Lord," Sweet said, attending Stitz's wound without facing her, "and I think I only wounded him too. Sims, go see if you can find him. Make sure he's dead. If he gets to his brother, there'll be no question whether or not I'm on your side—we'll have a fight on our hands. We might just as well start blasting the minute Cleveland Phelps rides into range."

"No, Sheriff," Sims said, speaking fast, "Nothing's changed yet. I can still handle Phelps. If his brother's dead, we'll tell him the two of them got drunk and shot each other. I can make that story fly."

"You're out of your mind, Sims," Sweet replied. "He's not going to stand still for some half-baked lie."

Even Kate McCorkle looked a little doubtful.

"I can do it." Sims darted a quick glance back and forth between them. "Give me room to pull it off. People believe what they want to believe. I've got something Phelps wants—I'll make him *want* to believe the lie."

"You've got a high opinion of yourself, Sims," Harris Sweet grumbled, still attending to Herman's wound. "I'm half tempted to see you try it."

"No, Harris . . . we can leave, all of us," Stitz murmured from the bed.

"Leave? Don't talk foolish, Herman," Sweet said,

patting a hand on Stitz's cheek. "You just take it easy. You're lucky to be breathing, let alone trying to leave town." He hesitated for a second, then added, "All those things I said earlier . . . I'm sorry, Herman. You're all that matters to me—all that's ever mattered to me." Sweet glanced around at Sims and Kate as if just remembering they were still there. "All right, Sims, I'll play it your way, but only for a while. The minute I see Phelps ain't buying it, I'm going for a handful of iron. So you better hope you know what you're doing." Quick Charlie Sims stood with a curious look on his face. Sweet's face reddened. "Well, Sims? Are you going or not?"

"Uh . . . yes, Sheriff." Sims turned to Kate McCorkle with a stunned expression. "Come on, Kate," he whispered turning her toward the door, "we need to talk."

Chapter 12

Quick Charlie Sims searched the livery barn barefoot, his feet aching with the cold, Stitz's shotgun in his hands. Kate McCorkle stood right behind him, her six-shooter cocked and ready in one hand, a raised lantern glowing in the other. A blood trail ran into an empty stall where, in his haste, the wounded outlaw had left the stall door open. At the open rear livery door they found another splotch of dark blood in an encroaching drift of snow. "He was alive when he left here," Kate said in a hushed tone.

Sims only looked at her with a flat expression and shook his head.

"You know what I mean," she added, nudging him gruffly. "If he manages to get to his brother we're all in big trouble."

Sims sighed, loosening his grip on the shotgun as he stepped over and forced the barn door closed and latched it. "Well, there's nothing we can do about it now. His tracks will be covered by snow before I can follow them twenty yards. Let's just hope he heads in another direction and they miss one another." Sims walked to the other stall where Chester Meins's horse looked at them with its ears perked, as if listening. "We'll have to stash this other horse somewhere before Phelps arrives. He might recognize it." He nodded back toward the saloon. "Come on, let's tell Sweet."

On their way to the front of the livery barn, Sims asked in a hesitant voice, "Speaking of Sweet . . . have you noticed something strange between him and the bartender?"

Kate McCorkle stopped and looked at him. "Yes. Herman was about to tell me something about him and the sheriff right before the two outlaws barged in on us." She stalled for a second, then said, lowering her voice, "They're a couple, I think." She started to turn back toward the door.

"Whoa, Kate." Sims stepped forward, took her arm and turned her back to him. "A *couple*? You don't just say something like that, then walk away. What do you mean, a couple?"

"What do you think I mean?" Now it was Kate's turn to stare at Sims with a flat expression. "They're . . . you know, a couple," she shrugged, "like you and me, only—"

"No, I don't believe it." Sims cut her off, rubbing his jaw, more astonished that he'd missed seeing it than he was at the fact itself. "I knew there was something. I just couldn't put my finger on it." He digested the information. "Well, if that's the case, it's their business. It has nothing to do with Sweet helping me with Cleveland Phelps, especially now—after what's happened." Sims hesitated, a look of uncertainty on his face. "Does it?"

"I don't know, Charlie. You were so worried, I decided to go to the saloon and see what I could find out. So I did. You tell me if it makes a difference or not. You said Harris Sweet has been a tough gunman all his life. Does this change anything?"

Sims winced, working it over in his mind. "Why should it? Harris Sweet is still what he's always been.

This changes nothing—if it's even true to begin
with." Sims took a deep breath. "You could be
wrong. We could both be wrong." He scratched the
side of his head, his bare feet growing numb beneath
him. "Either way, we keep our mouths shut about
it. There's too much at stake here." He rubbed one
foot atop the other, his legs now stiff, cold and aching. "Come on. I've got to get some boots on before
I get frostbite." They left the livery barn and trudged
through the blustery wind to the hotel, catching a
glimpse of the dim light from the saloon through the
horizontal blast of fine white powder.

In the small bedroom of Stitz's living quarters,
Sheriff Harris Sweet carefully placed a folded towel
on the chest wound and placed Stitz's hand on it.
"Can you hold it there, Herman?" he asked.

"Don't worry . . . I'm not going to break," Stitz
replied in a voice wracked with pain. He rolled sideways, helping Sweet turn him over onto his stomach.
"I was . . . hit worse than this in Brileyville.
Remember?"

"Yes, I remember. Now keep quiet, save your
strength." Sweet touched his fingertips around the
exit wound on Stitz's back, examining it for any lead
fragments beneath the skin. "Thank God, it's gone
through clean." Sweet let out a breath, picked up a
wet towel and swabbed around the wound. He
pressed an edge of the towel to the top of a bottle
of clear alcohol, then warned Stitz, "This is going to
burn like hell."

"Let it burn," Stitz whispered, readying himself for
it. "Do you think . . . they know anything, those
two?"

"No, I don't think so," Sweet said, pressing the
towel to the puffy reddened flesh around the bullet

hole. "If they do, I don't really give a damn anymore. I told you before, I'm sick of the pretense . . . we've nothing to be ashamed of. I've got to the point where I'd rather die being what I am, than go on living being something I'm not. Now help me get you onto your side—get you bandaged and cleaned up before they get back here. I know how picky you are about your appearance." He smiled down at Stitz.

"I'm glad . . . to hear you say that, Harris," Stitz said, slicing his words beneath the burn of the alcohol. "But I don't like what it implies. You've got . . . to clear your head, quit thinking about dying. We've all got to think about staying alive here."

"I know that now, Herman. And I'm sorry for how I've been acting lately." Sweet reached to the roll of heavy gauze lying on the bed, picked it up and unrolled it enough to begin wrapping it around Stitz's chest. "Seeing you laying there with a bullet through you put things in perspective for me." He reached down and worked the end of the gauze beneath Stitz. "Sometimes a person has to come close to losing what's important before they realize—"

"Don't apologize, Harris . . . I'm just glad you came to your senses, even if it took something like this."

Sons of bitches! The dirty, rotten sons of bitches . . . Darby Phelps pressed on through the blinding rush of snow, lost, his left forearm cradling his bleeding stomach, the two bullet holes there pulsing in pain, sapping his strength. Where the hell was his brother, Cleveland? How could his brother have let him ride into something like this? Darby Phelps had only been to Cold Ridge once before, and that was more than a year ago. He had no idea where to head from here, and the front end of a hard blizzard was setting in.

He could see no more than a few yards in front of him. What now? The horse had slowed to a staggering walk beneath him, but he heeled it sharply forward, the horse craning its head sideways to the biting cold.

"Come on, fool! Don't give out on me now . . ." Darby Phelps's voice was low and shallow, his spurs lancing the horse's sides. Was this it for him? Is this the way death came upon a man? he wondered. If it was, then death wasn't fair. It had all happened too fast and there was nothing right about it. There'd been no warning, no standoff in some dirt street where a man might get the chance to look at death in the eye and make some sort of decision about it. He hadn't been expecting this—him and Chester just having a little fun, taking what was there for the taking. It wasn't like they were robbing a bank or anything . . .

To affirm something inside himself, Darby Phelps gathered his failing strength and consciousness into one long shout into the howling wind, *"Cleveeeee-land!!!!"* But his plea brought no consequence, no affirmation of himself; and feeling his circumstance cold, bleak and unyielding around him, he slumped in his saddle, caked with pasty dark blood, and let the horse have its way. "Damn it to hell, Cleveland," he sobbed under his breath, "I never wanted to die . . ."

When morning came, gray and cold, with no sun and only a slight let up in the wind, Cleveland Phelps and his men rose up from the shelter of the deep dry wash where they'd taken refuge the night before. The fire they'd built against the windward side of the wash had gone out before dawn, a slice of wind somehow twisting down into the wash and spinning away in a dust devil of sparks and ashes that they did not bother to attend. Instead, Phelps and his men had huddled close with blankets wrapped around them amid their gathered horses, taking whatever warmth they could from the animals and one another.

"Lord," one of the men said, shaking out his blanket and rolling it up. "We ought to at least gather some brush and boil up some coffee. I'm froze to the bone."

"Forget it, there's no time," Cleveland Phelps said over his shoulder to the others through a wool muffler drawn up around his chin. "As bad as it was, it's not over yet." He swung stiffly up onto his horse's bare back, his cold saddle hanging from one hand. "We'll be lucky if we can make it in today."

Phelps pulled the saddle up behind him, turned it upside down across the horse's rump, and nudged his horse forward, looking around at the land. For all its sleet and snow, the squall had left the ground uncovered, except where the fine white powder had found purchase at the base of trees and brush. There, the snow had stuck and built upon itself, reaching high up the north side of tall pine and spruce as if painting half of their trunks white while leaving the other side untouched. Long stretches of snow stood deep and packed against upthrusts of rock and frozen earth.

They rode on, the men silent and bunched up in their coats with their collars upturned and hat brims lowered, the horses limbering up, their bodies generating heat behind their steaming breath. An hour later, Phelps stopped his horse and stepped down from its back. He turned his saddle and saddle blanket rightside up on the horse, drew the cinch beneath the horse's warm belly, and stood for a moment with his chest pressed against his horse's side, blowing his breath into his cupped hands. Phelps turned his eyes north to a thick wall of fog on the distant mountain peaks, lying lower now than it had only a few minutes ago.

"Boss . . . . ?" Doc Mason stood three riders behind him on the trail, but had gazed forward past the others and along the trail ahead. "What the hell is that out there?" As he asked, he moved forward to Cleveland, leading his horse past the others who now directed their gaze in the same direction.

Cleveland Phelps squinted his eyes along the trail, focusing on the dark lump beside the trail. At a distance of seventy-five yards he saw something fluttering in the wind. *Fur? A downed elk maybe?* "I don't know, Doc. Whatever it is, we've got no time to stop and eat it, if that's what you're thinking."

Muffled laughter rippled across the men. Doc Mason's face reddened. "Hell, I'll go see what it is." He swung up on his horse and gigged it forward. By the time Cleveland Phelps and the others had mounted and pushed forward, Doc Mason was leaning down from his saddle with a hand propped on his thick leg. "It's a horse, boss," he yelled back at the others, "half froze to death!" Doc Mason looked along the trail across a drift of snow, following the horse's tracks back to where they disappeared onto hard bare land.

"Some stray?" Phelps called out as he and the others closed the few yards between them.

"Nope, it's saddled and rigged, boss." Doc fell his horse back a few feet, looking down at the fallen horse, shaking his head as realization set in. Then he said with a level of dread in voice, "Ah, hell, boss! You better get on up here. This don't look good at all."

"What is it, Doc?" Phelps asked, sidling his horse up beside him. The rest of the men circled the dying horse on the ground. But before Doc Mason could say another word, Phelps's eyes widened. "Darby's—" His voice halted abruptly. "Damn it to hell!" He looked all around at the frozen land and yelled to the top of his voice, "Darby? Can you hear me? Fire a shot! We'll find you!"

Rhodes turned to Whitten as Phelps's voice echoed among rock along the trail. "What's the deal? Is that his brother's horse?"

Doc Mason turned to them, hearing Rhode's question. "Don't know the horse," he said. "But that's damn sure his California saddle on it." The men looked down as the dying horse groaned pitifully under its breath and tried to raise its head. Seeing the dark blood frozen on the saddle and along the horse's sides, Whitten and Rhodes gave one another a knowing look.

"Don't just sit there!" Cleveland Phelps bellowed. "Fan out! Look for him, damn it! He's got to be around here somewhere!"

For the next hour the men searched far out along both sides of the narrow trail, the wind building once again in its intensity, whipping fine snow through the frigid air. Rounding a turn in a stand of tall rock back toward the trail, Whitten looked off at the wall of fog that had since dropped farther down, appearing closer now. He turned to Rhodes, who'd been searching with him ahead of the others. "I hate saying it, but from all that blood and last night's freeze . . ." He shook his head and let his downcast expression speak for itself.

"Yeah, I know." Whitten ducked his head a bit and looked back a hundred yards or so farther at Cleveland Phelps, as if making sure Phelps couldn't hear him. "If I thought there was anything good to come out of it, I'd spend the day and half the night looking. But that ain't going to be the case, and we all know it. Best thing for us is to get to Cold Ridge, before somebody finds *our* horses frozen to death out here."

Rhodes sidled closer as they rode on. "Reckon wolves might've got to him?"

"I doubt it." Whitten offered. "No wolf in its right mind would have been out last night."

"That doesn't speak very highly of Darby Phelps then." Rhodes smiled stiffly through chattering teeth, his collar high, his breath billowing in a long swirl on the wind. "Us either, for that matter. How cold you suppose it is in El Paso?"

"What are you talking about? They're dancing naked in the streets about now—or they would be, if I was there." Whitten nudged his horse forward. "And I might just be there soon, if things don't start getting more accommodating up here."

"Me, too, except I've been wanting to ride with *Los Pistoleros* for the longest time." Rhodes took off his gloves as they moved forward and blew breath into his hands.

"So have I. But damn, son. A man who can't pick his weather ain't got no business being an outlaw, I always said—"

"Hold it!" Rhodes raised a gloved hand, cutting him off. "Look up there!" They stopped their horses, but only long enough to get a good view of the body propped back against a length of deadfall pine a few yards ahead of them.

"Lord have mercy." Whitten whistled low at the sight of Darby Phelps. The dead outlaw had snow swept up to his chest, with ice hanging from his nostrils and lips, his face and arms covered with a sheet of frost where the fine powder had melted from his body heat, then formed an icy base. His body had grown cold and his life had faded out like the flame on a spent candle. As they moved closer, Darby Phelps's dead eyes stared at them through a sheen of ice.

"He's deader than hell, ain't he?" Whitten whispered.

"If he ain't, he never will be," Rhodes grunted, pushing his horse to within a few feet of Darby's frozen body, close enough to see the red blood through the drift of snow and thin layer of ice. Rhodes lifted his pistol from his holster and fired two quick rounds in the air, summoning the others. As the shots echoed away, he added, "At least we can get Cleveland up here now, get him to settle down—maybe get on to town before we all freeze to death."

"Yep," Whitten replied and looked down at the frozen body. "Except this man didn't just freeze to death." He nodded at the dark bloodstains on Darby Phelps's corpse. "And I don't reckon Cleveland Phelps is going to settle down much till he gets to the bottom of this."

Chapter 13

In the small rail town of Lodgings at the bottom of the mountain, C. B. Harrington spotted the big Pullman car on the siding track as soon as the train he was riding pulled into the depot. His finger shot up, pointing at the Pullman car drifting past the window. "There it is! Look what he did to my beautiful car!" Harrington shouted, pointing out the streaks of dust, mud and ice on the once bright and shiny private car. "Sims, that low-life snake!"

Across from Harrington, Louisville Ike, Dirk LeMaster, and Steelhead Radner all rose slightly, looking out the window. Recalling how Sims had made him and C. B. Harrington leap from the car into the pitch darkness, Radner gritted his teeth and said, "Don't worry, Mr. Harrington, we'll make him pay." He looked at Louisville Ike and LeMaster as they sat back down. "Hope you boys are ready." He laid a hand on the pistol beneath his suit coat.

"Ready for what, you fool?" Harrington fumed. "Sims isn't in that car—he's not even here! He's gone on up to Cold Ridge. Pay attention, Steelhead."

"Well . . ." Radner's face reddened. He ducked his head a bit, the wind gone from his sails. "I'm just saying it won't be long."

C. B. Harrington said to Radner in a firm tone, "Steelhead, I've got to count on you to take charge of these two." He gestured toward Ike and LeMaster. "So stay on your toes, please!"

"Sorry, Mr. Harrington. It won't happen again," said Radner sheepishly.

"Good." Grumbling under his breath, Harrington stood up as the train slowed to a stop. "Come on, let's make sure he hasn't ruined my private car. I had a case of ten-year-old bourbon in there, not to mention all my personal belongings."

They left the train and walked through a biting wind filled with fine white snow, following a length of rail spur that led off into a long wooden barn, where three men in greasy overalls labored in the open doorway. The three men looked up, then straightened up and watched as C. B. Harrington walked up to them with an air of authority. Radner, Louisville Ike and LeMaster stayed close at his heels. "Who's in charge here?" Harrington demanded.

The three railroad workers looked at one another, almost shrugging. "I've been here the longest," said the taller of the three, sweeping his stained railroad cap from his bushy head. "I'm Jones . . . Merle Jones."

In no mood for introductions, Harrington eyed Jones up and down with an expression of veiled contempt. "Well, Mr. Jones. I'm here to claim that Pullman car." His head jerked toward the car on the siding rail. "And we'll be needing transportation up the mountain in, say, one hour? So whatever preparations you need to make—get to it." Harrington swung around, finished with Jones and now looking out across the yard at his Pullman car, inspecting it for damage.

Jones passed a bemused glance at his two coworkers, then looked at C. B. Harrington's rigid back. "Sorry, mister. But first off, this service engine is up on jacks . . . second off, there's a storm coming down." He stopped long enough to look Harrington's three men over, Steelhead Radner towering above all of them. "Besides, this little work engine wouldn't haul that big Pullman car up this mountain and even if it would, I've got orders not to let anybody use that car. Seems the owner reported it stolen." He shot a guarded grin at the other two railroad men, then back to Harrington. "It could take a long time before the owner gets up here to claim it—"

"I *am* the owner, you imbecile!" Harrington cut him off sharply.

He spun facing him, his face swelling dangerously red. "I'm C. B. Harrington! There, look at that—CBH!" He swung a finger across the wind-swept yard at the initials on the side of the Pullman car. "Does that tell you anything?"

Louisville Ike and LeMaster stepped closer, following Radner and Harrington. The four of them formed a half circle around the railroad man. But Jones didn't budge. He held a long iron wrench in his blackened hand, his fingers tightening around it.

"There's no need to be insulting," Jones said. "I don't care whose car it is, it's not going up this mountain, and neither is this service engine." He pointed the wrench out through the open rear doors at the wall of fog standing deep down the side of the mountain. "There's a blizzard working up there. Now, does that tell *you* anything?"

"All right, I've had it with him," Harrington hissed at Steelhead Radner. "Break his arm—show him I mean business."

Harrington tossed out his order then turned away; but in doing so he found himself looking straight at Sullivan Hart and Twojack, who'd stepped into the open doorway. Twojack's rifle stood poised and

cocked, the butt of it resting on his thigh. He fanned
it back and forth slowly from one of Harrington's
men to the other.

"No broken arms today, gentlemen," Sullivan Hart
said. He and Roth stepped inside the long barn,
closer to C. B. Harrington. Once out of the wind, the
tails of their long riding dusters fell slack and loose,
Hart's badge glinting in the dull morning light. His
gaze hardened on Harrington as if the others were
not there. "Who are you? What are you doing here?"

Harrington was taken aback. "We . . . I mean,
they—" Off guard, he offered a nervous gesture with
his hand. "That is, we're here for my stolen Pullman
car." Having noted the badges, he tried a tight smile,
but couldn't quite pull it off. "That part about the
broken arm was only a figure of speech, I assure
you—"

"It damned better be," Jones cut in, the wrench
still tightly held in his hand, "or I'll open your head
like a cracked gourd. Big-talking son of a—"

"That'll do," Hart said, halting him. He looked
back at Harrington. "Are you the man who ran into
Quick Charlie Sims coming into Fort Smith?"

Harrington hesitated for a second before saying,
"Yes, I'm the one who reported my Pullman car stolen, if that's what you're referring to. I have every
right to be in pursuit of that thieving hustler."

"You'll have to get in a long line if you're out to
settle a score with Quick Charlie Sims," Twojack
Roth said, looking up at Steelhead Radner as if ap-
praising an oak tree. "J. T. Priest and his band of
Los Pistoleros headed up to Cold Ridge day before
yesterday looking for Phelps. We just missed them."

Sullivan Hart watched Harrington's expression
closely as Twojack Roth spoke to him. "But we don't

suppose you know anything about *Los Pistoleros*, do
you?" he asked.

"No, indeed not, sir." Harrington recomposed himself. "I have business with Sims. Nobody else. I'm a
respected gentleman of commerce."

"Whatever business you think you have with Sims
or Priest or anybody else makes no difference to us,
Harrington," said Hart. "But as soon as we catch up
to J. T. Priest, he's going back with us, either sitting
in his saddle or face down across it. Keep that in
mind before you get yourself on the wrong side of
the law."

Behind C. B. Harrington, LeMaster looked at Louisville Ike and said in a hushed tone, but still loud
enough for Radner and Harrington to hear, "*Los Pistoleros?* Nobody said we'd be getting involved with
that bunch."

C. B. Harrington glared back over his shoulder at
LeMaster, then looked back at Hart and Roth. "I have
no intention of getting involved with Priest, sir. I
know he's a wanted felon. Sims is my only interest
here."

"Then you better be awfully careful traipsing up
that mountain. We figure Priest and his men got
pinned down by the weather about halfway up the
mountain. If you're crazy enough to head up there
in a coming blizzard, you better at least make sure
you don't run headlong into them."

"Thank you for your advice, I'm sure." Harrington
took on a haughty tone now that he saw he had
nothing to answer to. "We're quite capable of handling any situation. Meanwhile, since you're both
lawmen, be kind enough to inform this railroader
that I own that Pullman car, and shall do as I damn
well please with it." C. B. Harrington turned a cold
stare at Jones.

"It's his," Roth said to Jones and the other two. "We heard about it being stolen before we left Fort Smith."

"And I also have my ownership receipt, sir," Harrington said, reaching into his coat pocket and taking out a folded document and waving it around for everyone to see.

Jones glanced at the paper and raised his brow in a show of unconcern. "It's your name on it all right. But I don't care if you own every Pullman car from here to China. It's not going up that mountain until the blizzard's spent itself out—and that's that."

"Oh, really?" Harrington reached inside the coat and took out his wallet. "Step over here with me, Mr. Jones. Let's talk this over in private."

Hart and Roth stepped back, looking Radner, LeMaster and Louisville Ike over one more time. "If you boys are smart, you'll remember what we said here. Anybody hooks up with *Los Pistoleros* is automatically on our list."

Steelhead Radner only sneered.

"Don't worry, Deputy," LeMaster said, "I want no part of that gang. Neither does Ike here." Louisville Ike shook his head vigorously.

When Hart and Roth had stepped back out of the doorway and turned toward the depot, Radner turned toward LeMaster and said in a mimicking tone, " 'Don't worry, Deputy, I want no part of that gang.' You sniveling chicken-shit!"

"Hey, Steelhead!" LeMaster raised a hand toward Radner's broad chest as if to stay him in place, at the same time taking a cautious step backward. "*Los Pistoleros* was not a part of the deal. If you think me and Ike is going to tangle with them murderers, you're worse than just wrong . . . you're out of your mind. How do we know you're able to ride in there without them killing all of us? We don't know that you used to ride with them, now, do we?"

Radner sneered. "Then you just sit back and watch."

He walked over a few yards to where Harrington stood huddled with Jones. Harrington looked over at LeMaster and Louisville Ike, and said to Steelhead Radner, "If either one of those idiots tries to duck out on us, you have my permission to break them in half."

"Whatever you say, boss." Radner grinned, popping his big knuckles. LeMaster and Louisville Ike, seeing the gesture, looked at one another with sickly expressions.

Outside the building, Hart and Roth walked to the depot with their duster tails whipping in the cold wind, their Stetson brims standing up flat on one side, their collars pressed against their cheeks. "For a minute there I thought we'd cornered some of Priest's rats," Roth said above the slight roar.

"We couldn't have been that lucky," Hart replied. "We'll have to face them on the heels of this blizzard, I expect." He looked off to the north into the thick wall of haze on the side of the mountain. "I wonder how Sims and Kate McCorkle are making out with Cleveland Phelps and his bunch about now."

"Knowing Sims," Roth smiled, the wind licking at his long black braided hair, "he could be through with them and gone by now."

"He could, but I doubt it," Hart said as they stepped up onto the wooden platform at the depot, out of the pressing cold. "We're going to have to move up closer, in case Priest turns his men back from the weather." He gazed once again toward the wall of fog. "He might expect us to be here waiting for him . . . but he won't think about us already being up on the trail." Hart spread a stiff ironic smile, his breath running out in steam. "He'll figure us to have better sense."

Roth bunched up inside his duster and the wool coat beneath it, his rifle cradled in his arms. "Yeah . . ." He let out a long frosty breath. "And this is one time I wished Priest was right."

When Bobby Crady came back inside the small cave, he sat down across the fire from J. T. Priest and batted his cold gloved hands together before holding them close to the flames. "It's colder than a welldigger's ass out there, boys," he said. Gathered around the fire, the others looked at him and nodded. "Anybody ever figure what happened to Tooney?" he asked, looking around the area.

"Boss said he thinks Tooney had a change of heart and lit out on us in the night, right boss?" Mellon eyed Priest from across the fire.

Priest only shrugged, dismissing it. "So, Bobby, how are the horses doing?" Priest sat with a blanket across his shoulders, a black cigar between his teeth. There was something cagey in Priest's tone and expression. Bobby had seen it all day, ever since he'd started asking questions about Tooney, and harping on Priest to pull back down the mountain until the weather spent itself. He knew Priest hadn't liked hearing him say it, especially when he'd seen Bobby talking to some of the other men about turning back.

"The horses are fine, boss—a hell of a lot better shape than we are," Bobby Crady replied, avoiding Priest's stare. "I've got a feeling this is going to get a whole lot worse before it gets any better."

The men all sat huddled in quiet reflection, giving Bobby Crady a gnawing feeling that they'd been talk-

ing about him in his absence. Outside the small cave
the wind wailed like some large beast, mournful and
lost. "So, Bobby," J. T. Priest cut into the lull, "I don't
suppose you happened to leave your horse saddled?
Maybe left it a little apart from the others, did you?"
He smiled flat and mirthless across . the fire at
Bobby Crady.

"What's that supposed to mean, boss?" Crady cut
a glance around at the others, then settled his eyes
on Priest. To one side of the fire, Bert Ison snickered
under his breath and lowered his hat brim over his
dull eyes.

"Oh . . ." Priest dragged his words out. "Just heard
how unhappy you've been the past couple of days.
Heard how you told ole Stanton and Mellon here
how you'd like to cut out, get on back down the
mountainside. I thought maybe you'd decided to
leave in the night without saying good-bye."

Bobby Crady had seen this sort of thing happen
before, somebody being singled out, used as an example to let the rest of the men know how things
stood. "Now, damn it, boss, I mighta bellyached a
little, but that's just me." He shook his head,
avoiding Priest's eyes, turning his gaze to Earl Mellon and Denver Stanton and adding, "You both know
how I am. I wouldn't have said anything if I thought
you'd take it the wrong way."

"Or if you thought they might let it get back to
me, eh, Bobby?" Priest interjected.

"That ain't what I meant, boss. Anybody's ever
rode with me will tell you the same thing." He
thumped himself on the chest. "I stick to the last of
it—sure I might piss and moan about it. So what?
You see me still here, don't you?"

"Indeed, I do." Priest nodded slowly, keeping his
deep stare on Bobby Crady. "But in keeping with the

true democratic spirit of things, I want to let you
know . . . if you don't like the looks of things, you're
freed to ride out right here and now. Nobody will
stop you."

"Hell," Bobby chuckled, his voice sounding shallow and weak, "a man would have to be a damned
fool to strike out in this weather, this time of night—
not that I would anyway." He shrugged, as if dismissing the subject, and reached out for a tin cup
near the fire. With the cup in hand, he tested the
coffeepot handle, then started to pick it up off a bed
of glowing embers.

"Leave it be, Bobby," Priest said in a lowered
voice.

"What? Boss, are you serious?" Bobby tried a
shaky smile, his gloved fingers wrapped around the
pot handle. "There's plenty here. I'm cold to the
bone." He started to lift the coffeepot anyway.

Priest's pistol cocked, coming up from beneath the
blanket wrapped around him. "Do I look serious?"

"Jesus, boss!" Bobby Crady took his hand back
from the coffeepot, spreading both arms toward
Priest in a cautious show of peace. "All right. I
thought you were only joshing me, you know? It's
all yours."

"It ain't about the coffee, Bobby. I don't want you
here with us. You're bad for morale," Priest said, low
and even. "Now get up from this fire and get the
hell out of here."

"But, boss, I—I'll die out there," Bobby Crady
pleaded, his eyes looking to the others around the
fire, then back to Priest.

"You're prospects here ain't one damn bit better.
Now get going," Priest hissed. "And don't even
think about taking your horse. We might just have
to eat him if we're stuck here long enough. Walk

yourself down the mountain, Bobby-boy. Maybe it'll give you some time to think."

"Boys? Is any of you going to do something here?" Crady implored. But even as he spoke, he wasted no time scooting back from the fire and rising to his feet, Priest keeping the cocked pistol aimed at his chest. "I meant no harm, complaining like I did. Stanton, Carl? Somebody, damn it! Say something for me!"

"You heard the man, you sniveling idiot," Luther Ison said to Crady. "All you've done is sore-mouth and bellyache all day. He's giving ya better than I would if it was up to me running things."

Bobby Crady gave Priest one more pleading look, but saw no change in Priest's hard expression. "All right then, I'm gone. I never thought I'd be treated this way. Things have gone a long ways from what they should be around here . . . I'll say that." He inched toward the entrance of the cave, then disappeared out into the wind.

A silence loomed. J. T. Priest uncocked his pistol but left it hanging in his hand. He looked around at the others in turn—at Stanton, Mellon and White. They sat gazing into the flames, their blankets drawn around them, their hat brims streaked where ice had melted in the fire's heat. He looked at Luther Ison and his idiot son, Bert, then at Gant, then at Tom Bays and his brother, Shorty.

"You see, boys, there's a time to complain and a time not to," Priest said. "I knew Bobby Crady well . . . like a brother, you might say. Rode with him for quite a while." Priest raised a finger for emphasis. "But I can't tolerate having a man second-guessing me behind my back. Can you blame me?" He stared as eyes lifted to him, then turned away. "See . . . everybody here is a part of my team. Now where would this team be if I allowed one man to go against me that way?" He shook his head and started to continue, but at that second Bobby Crady busted back into the cave, interrupting him.

"Damn it, boss!" Crady shouted. "I can't go out into this freeze! I won't last ten minutes before I—" His voice was cut short beneath three rapid blasts from J. T. Priest's pistol. One shot went all the way through Crady's chest, slamming him against the stone wall of the cave and ricocheting with a thin whine. The men ducked their heads, then turned toward Crady's body lying limp on the cave floor. Crady's boot toes quivered for a second before falling slack to one side.

"Well, shit," Stanton grumbled, breaking the ringing silence as he stood up, dusted the seat of his trousers and walked over to Crady's body. "Now I've got to drag his dead sorry ass out of here—" He stopped abruptly, shooting Priest a quick grin. "Not that I'm complaining though." The men chuckled at his words, but turned their eyes back to the fire. J. T. Priest sat stone still, smoke coiling upward from his slumped pistol barrel.

As burnt powder smoke filled the cave and intertwined with the wisps of smoke from the fire, Stanton bent down and took Bobby Crady by his shoulders. "Come on, Bobby-boy," he said and dragged him outside. When he returned, he dusted his hands together, sat down by the fire and drew his blanket across his chest.

"You might have been right on the mark about having to eat his horse, boss," Stanton said, his hands and lips shivering from his brief trip into the cold. "It's getting worse out there by the minute."

Chapter 14

"Let him sleep, Charlie," Kate McCorkle whispered, looking down at Harris Sweet's haggard face in the dim glow of the lantern in her hand. "I'll check on Herman." Sweet sat slumped back in a chair just outside the door to Herman Stitz's small bedroom. A rifle lay across Sweet's lap.

As Kate stepped away, carrying the lantern into Herman's bedroom, Sims stepped over to the table and turned up the wick on another lantern. With the light spread in a widened circle, Sims stepped back over to Sweet, reached down and tugged lightly at the rifle barrel to see just how sound asleep the sheriff might be. Sweet caught the movement right away and snapped his eyes open, his hand clasping instinctively around the rifle stock.

"Take it easy, Sheriff, it's only me." Against the windowpanes and on the tin roof, the sound of ice pelted like buckshot in the wind. Sweet stretched his eyes open wide to clear them. He looked all around the small room. The window table had been turned upright, the vase now back on top of it. Chester Meins's body was gone and the blood had been cleaned from the floor.

"How—? How long have I been asleep?" Sweet rubbed his bleary eyes with his knuckles. He appeared astonished that it was night again, that the chilled windy afternoon had somehow slipped past him.

"Not long. Don't worry, everything's all right . . . for the time being anyway." Sims pulled a wooden chair from the table, turned it to face Harris Sweet and sat down, leaning comfortably forward, his elbows on his knees. "You were up all night and all day. We figured we'd leave you alone for a while."

"How's Herman?" Sweet almost stood up, glancing at the door to the bedroom. But Sims stopped him by not giving him the room he needed.

"Herman's fine. We've kept an eye on him. Just sit still for a while. We need to talk."

"Talk?" Harris Sweet cut another glance toward Herman's bedroom door. "There's not much left to talk about, Sims. We're here, and we couldn't leave if we wanted to. Cleveland Phelps is coming. If you hid that outlaw's body good enough, and Phelps doesn't run into his brother on the trail, you'll get your chance to talk to him. That's all you wanted to pull off, wasn't it? For me to cover your back? You wanted to find a way to stick here long enough to get J. T. Priest, then get out?"

"Yes. That was all I wanted." Sims studied Sweet's eyes as he spoke. "That's still all I want. But I won't put you and your friend at risk. I won't pull out of here and leave you to face Cleveland Phelps alone."

"Don't concern yourself with me and Herman, Sims. We've been in worse spots. If it wasn't for the weather, I'd have already sent you and Kate packing. My thinking was bad for a while there . . . but I'm over it." He jiggled the rifle on his lap. "We'll play this out however it's dealt." He cut another glance at Herman's bedroom door. A nervous glance, Sims thought. "If that's all you needed to talk about, we're through talking."

"No, there's something else." Sims fell silent for a second. Throughout the day he'd given thought to Harris Sweet and Herman Stitz's relationship. He had no problem with it. Yet, he felt he had to say something. There was an uneasiness in his knowing it and not mentioning it. He wasn't sure why. "Sheriff . . ." Sims's voice grew low, personal. "Don't ask me why, but I've got to tell you this. Kate and I know about you and Herman." Sims stopped and watched his eyes, not discounting his hands on the rifle in his lap.

"What about me and Herman?" Harris Sweet's eyes flared with a sharpness. He stiffened a bit in his chair. "Where's Kate? Is she in there? What kind of snooping around have you two been—" He almost rose from his chair. But once again Sims settled him, cutting him off, raising both hands toward him.

"Easy, Sheriff. Listen to me, please." Sims spoke fast but calmly. "Yes, Kate's in there. But we haven't been butting into your business. Herman told her earlier, before the shooting. If he hadn't wanted to tell someone, he wouldn't have. I'm only mentioning it to let you know it makes me no difference."

Sweet settled, staring at Sims, his jaw tight, his eyes searching Sims's for something. "All right, Sims . . . so now you know." Harris Sweet let out a heavy breath. A crushing weight seemed to have just been thrown off his shoulders. He sank into the chair. "All right, the cat's out of the bag. Now what, you'll be spreading it around, I suppose? Going to let the world know that ole Harris Street is really—"

"Cut it out, Sheriff," Sims snapped, already seeing that his rifle wasn't going to be coming into play. "It's your secret, yours and Herman's. It'll remain that way. I don't know why I even needed to bring it up—but I had to."

"Well . . . to tell you the truth, I've been sick of hiding it lately—you wouldn't believe how sick." His eyes lowered. "Now that somebody knows it, so what? We've never been ashamed of it. But we've always had to hide it. That's been the hard part, keeping something a secret just because the world has its own set of rules—rules that don't fit you." He offered a stiff, tired smile. "The world has its way with all of us, eh, Sims?"

"I suppose so, Sheriff." Sims spoke quietly, letting Harris Sweet take the lead, letting him get it out of his system.

"But you needn't worry," Harris Sweet said. "What I am won't affect my aim, when the time comes. That's one thing I've proven over the years."

"I never doubted it, Sheriff," Sims offered quietly. "I knew your reputation long before I got here. Nothing I've learned here has changed my opinion."

"Thanks," Harris Sweet nodded. "I have to admit, I always envied people like you and Kate . . . real people, with nothing to hide of themselves."

"We're all real people, Sheriff. I've come to know that much," Sims said. "No matter what else we might be, or what else we might consider ourselves."

"Yes, I suppose . . ." Sweet reflected in a short silence, then said, "You know, you two coming here upset me at first. Made me feel sorry for myself—reminded me too much of what I am instead of who I am. You'd think, as hard as I've lived in this man's world of ours, that I would have gotten over that sort of thing years ago. But I hadn't. It took seeing Herman shot apart on the floor to put things in perspective for me."

Sims nodded, listening, knowing it had been a lifetime since Harris Sweet had spoken to an outsider this way. "It must have been a hard trail to ride, all these years," he offered.

"Oh yes, for Herman and me both. We started out as quite the prim and proper little ladies, you might say. Our mother always saw to that. Herman was only seven, and I was nine when we lost mother and father. We saw right away how life was going to be without them . . ."

Harris Sweet continued speaking, even as the door to Herman's room opened and Kate McCorkle stood in the doorway with the bloody bandage in her hand, a stunned look on her face. "Charlie . . . ?" She whispered, breathless, her voice too hushed to disturb Harris Sweet as he spoke.

"Kate? What is it?" Sims rose halfway from his chair, still bewildered at the turn Sweet's conversation had just taken, even more bewildered now by the look on Kate's face.

Kate said, "Herman is a—" Her eyes went to Harris Sweet, as if shocked at something the sheriff had done. "He's a woman!"

Sweet's eyes darted back and forth between Kate and Sims. "But, you said you knew—that you both knew. You said Herman told Kate!"

Stunned, Sims's mind went blank for just a split second. But he saw the look on Sweet's face, and worked hastily, trying to sort through it, desperately trying to make sense of it all. "Uh . . . yes. We knew! Didn't we, Kate?" Sims responded, nodding for emphasis. "About Herman being a woman. Sure, we knew that."

Kate stood staring, bemused, giving no response. Harris Sweet took on an expression of clarity, his gaze narrowing on Quick Charlie Sims. "Tell me, Sims, what exactly did you think we were, Herman and I?"

"I thought—" Sims spread his hands in abandon, then shook his head, still bewildered by the whole situation.

"We're women, Sims," Sheriff Harris Sweet said with finality, leaning close to Sims as if that would help it sink in. "We're sisters, to be exact!"

"It's true, Charlie," Kate said, blinking her eyes, seeming to snap out of a trance. "I should know. I just changed the bandages." She stepped over to Sims and held out Herman Stitz's fake handlebar mustache on the tips of her fingers.

Harris Sweet stood up with the rifle in hand and looked down at Sims. "Now what did you say earlier, about how your opinion hadn't changed?"

In the hotel room, Quick Charlie Sims paced back and forth again, Scratch close at his heels. Kate McCorkle poured them both a drink and handed his glass to him. "Here, Charlie." She stopped him midstep. "You look like you need a drink."

"Thanks." Sims stopped and tossed back half of the whiskey in one gulp. He let out a quiet hiss. "But the day I need a drink is the day I'll quit drinking." He swirled the whiskey in his glass and paced some more. Kate stood back and smiled. The cat swung away from Sims and stood beside her.

"You should have seen your face, Charlie, when Sweet told you he and Herman were both—"

"Stop it, Kate." Sims came to a halt and turned to face her. "That was humiliating. I've never been caught so completely off guard in my life." He pointed his whiskey glass at her. "It was *you* who said they were a couple, you know. You're the one who planted the thought in my mind."

"They are a couple—a couple of sisters," Kate beamed.

"This is serious, Kate. We're stuck here, with no way out. My plan on talking a deal with Cleveland Phelps is shot to hell if he finds out we killed his brother. Now I find out the sheriff is a woman." He sipped his drink and ran his fingers back through his hair.

"Jesus, Charlie, listen to yourself. Harris Sweet is the same person he's been all his life! So what if he's a woman?"

"I know, Kate. I keep telling myself that over and over, but it doesn't stick for some reason. I feel wrong now thinking I've got him—or I should say, *her*—involved in all this. I can't ask a woman to face this bunch of killers."

"Charlie, Charlie," Kate shook her head. "Sweet has spent his whole life involved with these kind of killers. Notice I have no problem saying *his*? That's the life he built, the image *he* wanted in front of the world. Don't deny him that—not at this late stage of the game."

"Don't you think I realize that, Kate? This isn't a problem about Sweet, who he is, or what he is. This is all my problem, all in my head." He swiped his forehead and sipped his whiskey. "Now that he's a woman I feel different, *responsible*, whether I want to or not! I can't help it."

"You've never minded me standing beside you in a tight spot, Charlie."

"That's because I don't think of you as a woman, Kate."

"Gee, thanks, Charlie."

"You know what I mean. You're always up to whatever comes at you. You're cool, calm and tough."

"But nothing like Harris Sweet has been his whole life," Kate cut in.

"I've learned to trust you from experience, Kate. I know Sweet is capable, though—you don't have to keep reminding me. But it's different now. I can't even explain how. It's just how men are brought up I suppose. It's how we look at things. We can't help it." He finished the drink and put the glass down on the nightstand. After a few moments' pause, he turned to his heavy coat lying across a chair, picked it up and put it on. "I'm going to look this town over, check out those empty shacks across the foot-bridge—clear my mind a little." He picked up Herman Stitz's shotgun leaning against the chair, checked it, then swung it up under his arm.

"I'll meet you back at the saloon," Kate said. She watched him stop at the door and turn to face her, his hand on the doorknob.

"Do you notice something different out there, Kate?" Sims cut a glance to the window.

"No." Her eyes followed his to the window. She stood still for a second, listening with him. "Nothing at all. It's quiet out there."

"Yeah, that's what I mean," Sims said. "It's too quiet. What happened to the wind?" He gave her a curious look.

"Be careful, Charlie." She watched him leave, and when Scratch stood at the door, looking up expectantly, she stepped over, picked the big cat up and cradled it against her bosom. She walked to the window stroking its furry back and looked down in time to see Sims crossing the walk planks toward the foot-bridge. "I know what it is that's bugging you, Charlie . . ." she murmured to herself.

Though neither one of them had mentioned it, and though she knew Quick Charlie Sims did trust her, they both knew what had happened in Chicago the day Sims took a bullet in his back. Sims had managed to keep a dangerous situation under control until Kate had shown up. But with her there, for all his cool calculation and calm resolve, at the last moment when the bullets started to fly, Sims had thrown himself to the gunman to protect her. Heroic? Yes, she thought, but foolish.

Kate knew what was going on in Sims's mind. She knew his weaknesses as well as his strengths. Sims had laid out his plans on his way here. For all she knew Sims had started putting this together the day on the train when Steelhead Radner told him about Harris Sweet being the sheriff here. Sims had elected Harris Sweet to hold off the wolves while he dealt with Cleveland Phelps. But now that idea was out the window, and Sims knew it. He wouldn't admit it to her of course—or to anyone else—but with the death of Darby Phelps, Sims was left without a plan. He was now falling for his old weakness, his need to protect what he considered the weaker sex.

Kate shook her head slowly, stroking Scratch's back. "Men," she whispered, looking down at the cat for a second, then back out the window. "You're all alike . . ."

She watched Sims cross the footbridge, noting the stillness, the deathlike calm that had set in—no snow, no wind, not even a stir of cold breeze. To the north, she saw where the plumes of fog had dropped low and thick, completely hiding the taller peaks of the mountain range. Was that it? Had the storm played itself out? She didn't think so. Somehow she felt that the passing wind and snow had only been a preview of bigger things to come. This was the lull, the calm before the *real* storm.

Well, there was nothing she could do about the weather, she told herself. Kate bent down, dropped Scratch to the floor and walked over to the shotgun and pistol lying on the bed. She didn't know if Sims's plan had counted on the two lawmen, Hart and Roth, getting here at the right time or not. Sims was good at timing things just right, counting on every player in his game to make their move when he expected them to. If he thought he had planned it correctly this time, he was sure in for a disappointment, she thought. Kate picked up the guns from the bed and walked to the coatrack, Scratch tagging along a few inches from her heel.

Down on the street, Sims steadied himself with one hand on the rope handrail and crossed the foot-bridge, the rope-entwined walk planks swaying beneath his boots with each step. On his way, he looked down at the raging icy water, its rush strong after gorging itself steadily for three days and nights on snow and ice. Sims stopped for a moment, after crossing the bridge and looked back on it. He took a hold of one of the two thick hemp ropes supporting the footbridge and shook it, as if testing it.

As he stood inspecting the thick support ropes, Sims caught a glimpse of Kate crossing the street to the saloon. At the sight of her, he reminded himself of what a fix he'd gotten them into here. He'd had things worked out in his mind, and it should have gone smoothly. Risky yes, but simple and straightforward. He had something Cleveland Phelps wanted and Phelps knew it.

Sims could have reasoned with Cleveland Phelps, traded him the shares of Midwest Investment in exchange for J. T. Priest when Priest got here. Phelps would have jumped at the deal. Then Sims would have taken Priest with him and made him show him the cave where the old wagons of his family were hidden. But so much for that plan now, Sims thought. He looked warily northward at the low distant fog; and he let out a sigh and turned and walked upward along a narrow path to the line of stilted mine shacks against the slope of the mountain. Once Phelps knew about his brother, this town would turn into a bloodbath. There was no way to stop it.

Inside the saloon, Kate walked back to the door of the living quarters and knocked softly. When she heard Harris Sweet tell her to come in, she stepped inside, took off her coat and draped it over a wooden chair. "How's Herman?" she asked, seeing Sweet close the bedroom door behind him.

"Sleeping," Sweet said in a lowered tone. "He's doing as well as can be expected." Sweet offered a tired smile. "How's Sims?"

"He'll be all right," Kate said. "That was a lot for him to take in all at once."

"I thought he already knew, or I wouldn't have told him," said Sweet. "Herman and I have never told a soul before. But it was getting to be too much for me—for both of us. Herman has always done better with it than I have."

"Is—is Herman his, I mean, your sister's real name?"

"It was Harmony," Sweet said, his mind seeming to reflect back to a long time ago. "My real name is Harriet . . . Harmony and Harriet, the Sweet sisters." Harris Sweet smiled wearily. "Herman took the name Stitz from our mother's side of the family."

"I see." Kate listened.

"I know this must seem strange, us doing what we did. But after our parents' and our older brother's death, we were alone, out in the Missouri Breaks. We knew what was in store for us if we went back to civilization. We didn't want it. It would've been bad enough being orphans as boys, let alone as a couple of young girls. We weren't about to be shipped back to some orphanage, and made to live indoors. We'd been born and raised out there on the frontier. So we managed to bury our ma and pa and our older brother, Harris. Then we cropped our hair, took Harris's clothes, and lit out. Even at our young ages, we found work here and there for room and board—imagine how that would have been for two girls on their own. It was better for us, being boys in a man's world. That goes without saying. Somehow we kept our secret all this time."

"That's quite a story," Kate said quietly.

"The more we came to see of men in a man's world, the less use either of us ever had for them--not that we're any different from you. We just happened to become what we pretended to be."

"Maybe we all do that in some way," Kate smiled in acceptance.

"Maybe we do." Sweet studied her eyes. Kate saw a difference now, something she would never have noticed or believed had she not learned otherwise. "Perhaps the difficulty was that Herman and I always knew the illusion we lived—some folks live their whole lives never knowing theirs. I think that's better for them, don't you?"

"I don't know." Kate shrugged a shoulder, her smile loose and guileless. "I stay too busy being what I am to stop and wonder what's real or illusion about me. Call me simple, but that's too far over my head."

Sweet still studied her eyes. "No, Kate, I wouldn't call that being simple. There's nothing simple about you. If I might be so bold as to say it, you strike me as living the very kind of life my sister and I avoided, yet you seem to have done it on your own terms."

"We all do what we must," Kate replied in a soft voice, "to be what we need to be."

Sweet nodded, then leveled a firm gaze back at her. "You're afraid Sims is going to die here, aren't you?"

"I'm afraid we all will," Kate said, aware of the weight of the pistol in her dress pocket.

"Yes . . . but mostly, you're afraid for him, this man Sims that you're so in love with. You're more afraid for him than you are for yourself."

"I don't stop to think about it, but yes, I suppose that's true. Is that so bad?"

"No, Kate, that's not so bad. Not bad all. That's something I envy. Of course I feel that way toward my sister—she's family. But to feel that way toward someone else, someone who is a part of my life only because I let them in? I've never felt that—and I miss it."

A silence passed, and in it Kate felt an awkwardness, hearing a woman's feelings speak to her from inside this shell of a hardened old gunman. She looked away from Harris Sweet's eyes, not knowing what to say, not liking how uncomfortable she'd become. To change the subject, Kate gestured a nod to the window. "The wind has stopped. Did you notice how calm it's gotten?"

"Oh yes, I noticed. It's grown far too calm." Harris Sweet looked toward the window with her, the streaks of thin ice on the windowpanes obscuring their view. "I'm glad we talked now, while we still had the chance . . ."

Chapter 15

Sullivan Hart and Twojack Roth stood readying their horses at the hitch rail out front of the depot at Lodgings when the sound of the small service engine gave out a short blast on its steam whistle and came clacking along the rails a few yards from them. The two deputies caught a glimpse of C. B. Harrington's stern expression through the window of the only car behind the engine—a small passenger car. Twojack Roth shook his head. "Thought Jones said it would take all day to get that engine serviced and railed?"

"Nothing like a handful of money to get the wheels rolling, I suppose," said Hart. "We warned them. That's all we can do. If they're stupid enough to go, I'd rather have them in front of us than behind. Harrington must think that if he runs into Priest, he can just swing around him."

Twojack Roth turned back to his horse, strapping his saddlebags down, gazing off at the low rolling fog creeping farther down the distant mountains. "Notice how the wind's flattened?"

"Yep," said Hart, "I noticed."

"That's a bad sign. This storm hasn't finished with us yet. Not by a long shot." Roth finished preparing his horse without another word.

* * *

In the small railcar, C. B. Harrington stood up from his seat and walked forward to the engine. As soon as the door closed behind him, Louisville Ike and LeMaster turned to Steelhead Radner sitting in the seat across the aisle from them. "So, Radner," LeMaster said, trying to keep the tone friendly, "assuming you really did used to ride with some of these *Los Pistoleros* . . . just how bad are they? What kind of men are we getting ready to run into?"

Radner cut him an icy stare and growled under his breath, "Oh I rode with them all right . . . long enough to know they'll rip your heart out, you green sack of horseshit."

"Well then," LeMaster nodded. "There we are." He looked at Louisville Ike. The two sat staring straight ahead. In the rear of the car, four horses stood in the aisle with their reins hitched to the handrail.

In the service engine, Harrington spoke to Merle Jones above the clank and roar of the engine. "Now that you've agreed to take us halfway up, how much more money will it take to get us all the way to Cold Ridge?"

"There ain't no amount of money going to get this engine to Cold Ridge, Harrington. I already told you. We'll be lucky to get you halfway up and get ourselves back down before this storm rips through."

"Goodness, man! Look out there!" Harrington gestured with a gloved hand toward the looming grayness outside the window. "The storm has spent itself. It's calm out there!"

Jones cut a glance and a guarded smile to the fireman standing beside him and said to Harrington in a voice ripe with veiled contempt, "Whatever you say, Mr. Harrington . . . whatever you say." The small engine pushed on, Jones directing his attention toward the rails ahead, ignoring Harrington until after a few minutes of silence, Harrington turned and huffed out of the small compartment, slamming the metal door behind him.

"He's one hardheaded peckerwood," said the fireman. "I'll give him that."

"I don't care how hardheaded he is," Merle Jones said over his shoulder. "I'm not getting up there and getting stuck. He ain't seen nothing till he sees what that fog is going to drop on these mountains."

"Don't I know it," the fireman said, leaning on his short shovel handle above a small pile of coal. "Only reason I came was to keep you from coming alone."

Jones stared ahead. "Stoke her up some more, Vance, she's dropping on us."

The fireman opened the iron door, threw in a shovelful of coal as the flames licked out at him like snakes tongues. For the next two hours the engine hissed and puffed and climbed upward. In the small railcar, C. B. Harrington and Steelhead had moved to the front seat, to where the small potbellied stove in the corner glowed red at its base. Louisville Ike and LeMaster had moved forward with them, but remained a seat farther back, Harrington and Radner getting the most benefit from the heat of the stove.

"I don't suppose it'd do any good to tell you I'm not much of a shot, would it?" LeMaster asked C. B. Harrington in a cowering voice, huddling inside his coat, his nose red and puffy from the cold.

"No," Harrington replied without turning to him. "Not at all. You agreed to do a job, and by thunder, you'll do it."

LeMaster started to say something more, but Louisville Ike gigged him in his ribs and whispered in a hiss, "Let it go, LeMaster. We're in . . . we might as well make the best of it."

"I hate a coward and a liar worse than anything," Harrington said to Radner as LeMaster and Louisville Ike slunk back. "It's good to know that you're neither, Steelhead." He paused for a moment, then added, "You are certain you can get me introduced to these gunman without any problem?"

"You can count on it, Mr. Harrington. With me with you, you're safe."

Harrington settled. "I can't help but think it was providence that brought us together, Steelhead. You're going to come out of this a rich man, sir." Harrington raised a finger for emphasis. "Mark my words, we're all going to come out of this with a big smile on our faces." He reached a hand over and patted Radner's thick shoulders while the train pressed on through the wind and the fine spitting snow.

In the gray stillness high up the mountainside, J. T. Priest and his men stopped their horses on the icy trail. "What's that sound?" Priest raised a hand toward the men to quiet them. They listened closely until the sound of the distant engine became more clear. "It's the damn service engine," Priest said bemused, a trace of a grin coming to his cold red face. "They never come up the mountain in this kind of weather."

"Think maybe it's the law?" asked Denver Stanton.

"The law?" Priest looked at him. "To hell with the law. Whoever it is, they've come at the right time. I'm sick of this cold. What about you boys?"

The men nodded, grumbling under their steaming breaths.

Priest looked around, judging their position, then listened again to the distant sound. "It's still a good hour or more down the mountain. There's a stretch

up ahead where we can take it. Let's get up there
and get ready." He slapped his reins to his horse
and kicked it forward.

At the top of a steep turn in the trail a hundred
feet above the rails, Priest slid his horse to a halt and
swung down from his saddle. He took the field lens
from his saddlebags, pulled it open, squatted down
and steadied his elbow against a rock, then scanned
down the mountainside through an encroaching drift
of fog.

He spotted the engine laboring upward, pulling
the small passenger car behind it. But before lowering the lens from his eye, he swept it farther down
the mountain and caught sight of the two deputies
moving through a stretch of cedar on horseback.

"Aw, hell!" Priest followed them with the lens
until they moved out of sight behind a jagged jut
of rock.

"What is it, boss?" Denver Stanton asked, having
dropped from his saddle to join Priest. The rest of
the men had gathered back a few yards waiting to
hear what Priest had in mind.

"Nothing," Priest said to Stanton in a clipped tone.
He clapped the lens shut behind his palms. "Go send
the idiot up here with me. The rest of you drop back
down the trail. Get down as close to the tracks as
you can. Don't let that engine come to a complete
stop, or it'll take all day to get it going again up this
grade. Just slow it down. Get in there and take over
the engine."

"Then what?" Stanton stared at him.

"Then the idiot and I will get on as you come by
here. Hurry up, Stanton. Get the men in position."

Stanton moved toward his horse, stepped up into
his saddle and swung back to face the men. He didn't
like the way Priest was acting all of a sudden, not

wanting to join them when they took the train. What was it down there that spooked him? Whatever it was, Stanton wasn't about to get left behind here. He reined his horse around sideways to the gathered men. "All right, boys, we're going to take a train ride." He pointed at Bert Ison. "Bert, you get over there with Priest. The rest of yas, follow me."

"Hold it, Stanton." Luther Ison looked suspicious as Bert nudged his horse away from the others and over toward J. T. Priest. "Why's Priest and my boy staying up here? Why ain't they riding down with us?"

Stanton thought quickly. "Because if we can't slow that train down enough to get on, they will. Now, does that suit you, Luther? Let's go!" He swung his horse away, the men falling in behind him. Luther Ison lagged back for a second, staring after his son, Bert. "I don't like one damn thing about this," Luther murmured to himself. But then he turned his horse and gigged it along with the others.

Winding down a narrow elk path to the rails, Denver Stanton held his horse to one side, letting the other men pass him. "All of you get down along that turn and spread out. As soon as the train comes into sight go to work on it—grab on and hold on as soon as it slows. The first man who gets to the engine, make that engineer slow down some—but don't let him stop."

"What about you, Stanton?" Luther Ison asked, giving him a distrusting look.

"What about me, Luther, damn it!" Stanton's hand went to his pistol butt and rested there. "Do I look like I want you holding my hand on this? Slow the damned train and get on it! Don't back talk me!"

Luther Ison spat, giving Stanton a harsh lingering

gaze. Turning to the Bays brothers, Luther said, "Come on you two, stick with me."

Tom Bays Junior looked confused and started to say something, but Luther Ison snapped, "Keep your mouth shut, boy, and come on. This whole bunch is gone to hell if you ask me."

Merle Jones stood beside his iron seat in the engine room, the fireman busy throwing in another shovelful of coal as the engine puffed upward around the turn. When Jones first spotted the two horsemen on the tracks a hundred yards ahead, his first instincts were to reach out a hand to the throttle and shut it down. "What the—?" But he caught himself just as the fireman looked out the windshield with him. "Hang on, Vance, these boys ain't making a social call!"

"Uh-oh," the fireman said, seeing two more horsemen come into view. "I best pour the coal to her!"

"Do it then, damn it!" Jones opened the throttle the rest of the way, the train already giving the steep grade everything its boiler had. "Steam's the only thing that'll get us through! They ain't blocked the tracks—they must want the engine!"

Riding behind the Bays brothers and Luther Ison, Earl Mellon saw the three of them stop in the middle of the tracks. Mellon shouted, "What the hell are you doing?" just as Tom Bays Junior raised the pistol and fired at the engine.

"Those stupid bastards!" Carl White shouted, gigging his horse out of the cover of rock and stopping it beside Mellon. "The train might've slowed if they'd acted like they had some sense! Where's Stanton?" He looked back along the tracks, the sound of the shrill train whistle partly drowning out his words.

"He's back there!" Mellon shouted, kicking his horse forward. "He should have stayed with Luther and these boys. They don't know what the hell they're doing!"

The train seemed to speed up, boring toward them. Mellon and White saw Luther and the Bays brothers jerk their horses out of the middle of the tracks. "What do we do now?" White yelled, pulling his pistol form his holster. From out of the rocks came Gant, spurring his horse up beside Carl White.

"Grab something as it comes by and hang on!" Mellon heeled his horse off to one side, not even drawing his pistol.

Back in the small car, C. B. Harrington stiffened at the sound of the shrill whistle. "Come on, Radner! Something's wrong!" He bolted from his seat, Steelhead right behind him, LeMaster and Louisville Ike trailing. Moving through the cold air from the car to the engine, Harrington caught a glimpse of one of the horsemen. A pistol shot exploded, the bullet thumping with a loud ring against the iron frame-work of the passenger car.

"They're shooting at us!" Harrington ducked, lunging forward and throwing open the door to the service engine, then scurrying across a mound of coal. Behind him, Radner, LeMaster and Ike huddled inside the closed door. Radner rubbed his coat sleeve on the soot-coated glass and looked out in time to see Carl White and Gant drift past, their pistols leveling toward him.

"Hell, that's Carl!" Radner shouted. "I know him!"

"Then do something!" Harrington demanded. "Let him know it's you!"

Louisville Ike and LeMaster stared at each other, stunned. The engine roared hard and steady, shuddering a bit beneath their feet as it struggled upward.

"What are you doing up here?" Jones screamed, seeing Harrington hurrying into the engine compartment. Beside Jones, the fireman shoveled fast, two scoops, three, four, then slammed the iron boiler door shut, threw down his shovel and snatched up the rifle from its place in the corner.

"They're after the engine," C. B. Harrington shouted.

"Hell, I know it!" Jones jerked his head back toward the passenger car. "Get back there and keep them off us, you damned fools!"

Radner bristled and took a step toward Jones, but Harrington grabbed his arm. "Come on, you heard him! Let's show these ruffians we're game for a fight." With Radner's help, Harrington forced Louisville Ike and LeMaster through the door and back to the passenger car. But before Harrington could get himself across the few exposed feet between doors, a bullet whistled past his head, and he ducked back into the engine. Harrington gasped. This wasn't working out the way he wanted it.

From the door of the passenger car, Steelhead Radner called out to him, "Mr. Harrington! Are you all right?" Another pistol shot exploded alongside the train.

"Yes," Harrington shouted. "Keep them off this train. I'll stay here!" He slammed the door to the engine and turned to the fireman. "What can I do to help?"

"For starters, you could shoot at somebody!" The fireman bellowed, shooting his rifle out toward the horsemen.

Behind the train, Mellon and White raced along the side of the tracks, their horses struggling with the loose rock. "Come on, White," Mellon yelled, stretching out of his saddle toward a metal handrail.

"If they reach that flat spot ahead, we'll never catch up!" But even as he shouted, the train leveled onto a stretch of flatter ground and began building speed.

"Damn it!" Carl White could see the train pulling away from him, and he let up on his horse. In a second, Mellon did the same, letting his horse drop back until he and White sat side-by-side. "We better hope Stanton or Priest does better than we did." White looked around at Luther Ison and the Bays brothers as they came riding up beside them.

"Don't blame me," Luther Ison growled before White or Mellon could speak a word. "I figured these two knew better than to start shooting."

The Bays brothers looked ashamed.

"I ain't blaming nobody," said Mellon. "Priest or Stanton should have taken charge here." The men spurred their horse forward alongside the rails.

As soon as the train started across the stretch of level ground, Denver Stanton sailed out from ten feet above on a rock ledge, and landed with a loud thump atop the passenger car. He flattened for a moment, then raised into a crouch and ran along the top of the car, bullets from Radner's pistol kicking up splinters of wood from inside the car.

At the rear of the car's roof where a brakeman's platform offered more protection from the bullets below, Denver Stanton kneeled down with one hand on the brake wheel. He looked forward and saw J. T. Priest and Bert Ison hurl themselves out of a shelf of rock and scrub juniper and land atop the service engine.

"All right!" Stanton shouted, feeling better, knowing that Priest couldn't abandon him, even if he did leave everybody else behind. "You didn't outfox me, you son of a bitch!" he raved, knowing his voice would be lost beneath the roar of the engine and the clack of the rails.

Hearing the sound of boots atop his engine, Jones looked up, then yelled at the fireman, "Vance, they're coming in! Shoot 'em!" C. B. Harrington lay in a corner, cringing against a mound of coal.

Bert Ison and J. T. Priest tumbled down between the engine and the railcar. As the fireman raised his rifle and fired up through the engine's metal roof, Priest kicked open the back door and Bert Ison fired two shots into the man. "Okay, lad, hurry now," Priest commanded Bert. "Grab that coupling pin and cut the car loose." He kept his cocked pistol aimed at Jones and Harrington. "I've got these two covered."

Jones looked at the fireman lying wounded on the floor, the rifle only inches from his hand. "Don't even think about it," Priest hissed at Jones, "I'd hate to have to kill you and drive this thing myself." He stepped over, picked up the rifle, and stepped back to the open door. From atop the railcar behind them, Priest and Bert heard the sound of pistol fire—Stanton firing down through the roof of the car, Radner inside the car beneath a thick seat firing back at him, splinters flying. Louisville Ike and LeMaster scurried along the aisle on their bellies beneath the frightened horses' hooves.

"Pay them no attention, lad," Priest said to Bert. "Pull that pin! Stanton and the others can take care of themselves! You're with me now, my second in command!" Priest roared with dark laughter.

"Lord, God! He's cut me loose . . ." Stanton spoke aloud to himself, seeing the growing separation between the engine and the car. He jumped up and raced forward along the roof of the car, the gap growing wider and wider. At the edge of the railcar, he flung himself out with a loud yell and managed to catch the metal roof of the engine by his fingertips. On the small platform below Stanton, Priest looked up and saw him flailing his legs wildly, trying to hang on.

"Damn it!" Priest cursed under his breath. But then he reached up and caught Stanton around his legs and helped him down. "Get down here, Denver. I was afraid we'd lost you."

"I bet you were." Stanton glared at him, his breath heaving in his chest. He looked back and saw the gap between the engine and the passenger car widen, the passenger car slowed down against the upward grade.

"What's that supposed to mean?" Priest stood nose to nose with him, his pistol cocked.

"Nothing." Stanton managed to swallow down his anger. "What do we do about the others?" He nodded toward the slowing passenger car as the engine pulled farther away from it.

"They'll have to look out for themselves," said Priest. "Bert and me saw our chance and took it, right, Bert?" Priest looked at the blank face of Bert Ison as the young man stood up, swaying to the rhythm of the engine. Bert made no response. Priest continued to Stanton, "Just be glad I managed to bring you along."

Bring him along? Stanton stared at him for a moment, fighting the urge to draw his pistol and put a bullet through Priest's smug face.

"I better make sure this engineer doesn't try something stupid." Stanton turned and threw open the door to the engine.

Chapter 16

"Now then, gentlemen, on to Cold Ridge." J. T. Priest spread a crooked smile and looked around at the faces of the others inside the small engine compartment. Jones only cast a glance back over his shoulder, then turned his attention to the rails ahead. The fireman lay groaning on the floor, his hands clasped to his bleeding chest. C. B. Harrington stood crouched in the corner, his soft hands raised chest high, a streak of coal dust across one cheek. Stanton and Bert Ison stood with their pistols cocked. Priest lowered his pistol and shoved it down in his holster.

"There's a blizzard dropping down on us, in case you don't know it," Jones called out above the fast throb of the engine.

"That's your concern," Priest shrugged. "It just means you better squeeze this bucket of bolts for all the speed it's worth." He looked at Harrington. "Now what have we here?" He cocked his head in reflection. "I've seen you before, haven't I?"

Harrington straightened up cautiously. "I—I'm C. B. Harrington. Yes, we may have met at a stock convention or somewhere over the years." Harrington settled himself and tapped a finger to his temple. "Come to think of it, I believe we met at just such a convention in Chicago."

"Do tell." Priest studied him for a second.

"Yes." Harrington ventured his hands down to his vest, tugging it into place. "We listened to the vice president discuss national growth and expansion in precious metals."

"I'll have to take your word for it," said Priest. "Good to see you again though. Stanton, shoot him!"

Denver Stanton stepped forward and raised his pistol toward Harrington's chest. "No! Please! Hear me out, sir!" Harrington spoke fast. "I came to help you, Priest. I have major holdings in Midwest Investments! I can restructure—!"

"Hold it, Stanton." Priest raised a hand just in time. Denver Stanton pulled the trigger, but caught the hammer with his thumb as it dropped. Harrington's face turned ashen white. "Let's hear what dear Mr. Harrington has to say," Priest grinned.

"I don't mean to interrupt," Jones said over his shoulder, "but somebody's going to have to stoke that boiler if we're going anywhere."

Priest reached out with his boot toe and nudged the wounded fireman. "You there, ready to get back to work?"

"He can't do nothing! Look at him," Jones shouted without turning to Priest. "He's shot all to hell."

"Oh, I understand," Priest said. "Bert, shoot him!"

Bert Ison aimed his pistol down without hesitancy and shot the wounded fireman dead. Jones stiffened, but kept his attention on the rails ahead. "Now then," Priest continued, looking back at C. B. Harrington, "I trust you can shovel as you talk, sir?"

Harrington hurried, picking up the shovel and opening the door to the firebox. He threw in a shovelful of coal and scooped up another as he spoke. "I heard what happened in Chicago a while back, how you were arrested—how Mr. William Mabrey disappeared. I began buying up outstanding shares of Midwest Investment in a bid for a take-over." He tossed the coal into the firebox, scooped up another shovelful and held it. "I have a list of stockholders in my coat pocket, and proof of my purchases. I came here to force—that is persuade—Quick Charlie Sims to sell me the shares he took from you. With those shares—"

"Sims?" Priest cut him off. "Quick Charlie Sims is around here?" He shot a glance outside the soot-blackened window as if Sims might be out there watching.

"He's in Cold Ridge, I'm pretty sure," said Harrington. "He stole my Pullman car and left it back there at the depot. He's after the same thing I am: control of the corporation. If he gets it, all of you lose. Sims will cut out *Los Pistoleros* and run the business straight." He cut a glance at Denver Stanton and Bert Ison long enough to see they had no idea what any of this meant. Then he looked back at J. T. Priest. "But if I make my move, there's room for you in it, Priest. I'll restructure, issue additional stock, restore your shares through a proxy—at discount, of course—and you're back in the game. I'll even put it all in writing!"

"At discount . . . ?" Priest thought about it for a second rubbing his chin, pretending to know what Harrington was talking about. "Let's see this stock-holders list, and that proof of purchase certificate." Priest looked at the shovel in Harrington's hands, then added, "Stanton, stoke that fire. Give me and Mr. Harrington a chance to get acquainted."

Back at the abandoned passenger car, Steelhead Radner, Louisville Ike, and LeMaster stepped out onto the rear deck with their hands raised. Gant searched each of them for weapons, and in turn shoved them down off the deck platform to the ground. Radner stumbled on the edge of a cross tie, then stood up and faced Carl White and the others. "Howdy, Carl . . . remember me?"

"I'll be damned," said Carl White with a bemused smile, dropping his pistol hammer to half cock and letting the barrel tip upward away from Radner's chest. "What are you doing up here, Steelhead, you overgrown son of a bitch? I heard they strung you up for murder back in Houston." Earl Mellon and the others grabbed Louisville Ike and LeMaster as Gant shoved them to the ground.

"Houston was a big misunderstanding," Radner said, lowering his hands. "I got hooked up with this Harrington fellow a couple weeks back—he's on that engine right now. I told him I used to ride with some of you boys." He grinned. "Told him I had no qualms against killing any of you if I had to. They always like hearing that kind of talk, you know."

"Don't they though," Carl White chuckled, nudging his pistol barrel toward Earl Mellon. "You remember Earl Mellon I reckon? He's the one you was just shooting at."

"Earl the Pearl. Sure I do. How's it going, Earl?" Radner asked, touching his bowler brim. "Sorry for shooting at you."

"Think nothing of it, Steelhead," Mellon replied, "I was shooting back."

White nodded toward LeMaster and Louisville Ike. "What about these two scared-to-death-looking fools? Are they with you?"

"Shit." Radner turned with him, looking LeMaster and Ike up and down as if for the first time. "These boys couldn't find their dicks in a rainstorm. Shoot 'em if you feel like it."

LeMaster and Louisville Ike turned sickly green.

"Naw," said White, "we need our ammunition in case we catch up to Priest. I can't believe that bastard did us that way. He told us we was the new *Los Pistoleros,* then lit out like dogs was on his tail."

"He knows what's on his tail all right," said Radner. "There's two of Judge Parker's deputies headed up here right now."

"Well, hell, that's what Priest must've spotted through his field lens." White looked back at Radner. "J. T. had it all made up to ride into Cold Ridge with a show of force. Reckon he saw the lawmen and had a sudden change of plans."

"If he gets my boy hurt, I'll kill him flat-out," Luther Ison growled. He snatched his horse by its reins and led it away from the others.

"Who's that?" Radner asked.

"Just one more sore loser," Mellon said, stepping in, handing Radner a twist of tobacco. "His son's a complete idiot. There's no telling what Priest has in mind for him." Mellon shook his head. "I can remember when this used to be a fine gang to ride with. Nowadays, it's just one more lick-and-a-promise operation. They promise you everything, then the first thing you know you're standing in the cold with an empty railcar, and the law climbing down your shirt."

"Don't start getting misty on us, Earl," said Gant, stepping in and looking Radner up and down. "We've got a big blow moving this way. Are we going on up, or holding out here till it passes over?"

"This is Gant," Mellon said to Radner. "A good gunman, but a little distracted by the weather as you might have noticed."

Radner eyed the black gunman. "It makes no sense fighting a storm when there's a hot stove inside that railcar."

"A hot stove? Hell . . . what are we doing out here?" White jerked his head toward the railcar. "Come on."

"What about us?" Louisville Ike asked in a weak tone of voice.

"What about you? You can gather some wood for the stove, can't yas?" White grinned. "That'll keep you on our good side—for awhile, anyway."

"What about the two deputies coming?" Radner moved beside White and Mellon on their way to the railcar, the Bays brothers venturing forward now at the prospect of a warm stove, Gant shoving Ike and LeMaster ahead of him.

"To hell with them," said White. "If they come snooping, we'll take care of them. I've been wanting to shoot somebody all morning." A few yards from the tracks, Luther Ison sat staring upward in the direction of Cold Ridge, with his reins hanging in his hands. His lips moved as he cursed to himself. "Luther, come on," Earl Mellon called to him. "Ain't no point in grumbling about it. Get in here and warm up."

"I'm all right out here," Luther said in a sore tone, without facing him.

"Suit yourself then," said White. "You're on lookout for those lawmen."

As the others filed up on the platform and into the car, Radner looked back at Luther and said to White, "Is he an idiot, too?"

"Starting to look like it, ain't it?" White replied. "Did your man Harrington bring any whiskey with him."

Radner gave him a look. "Think I'd be here otherwise?"

Sullivan Hart and Twojack Roth had heard the gunfire from farther down the mountainside. For over two hours they'd pushed their horses as hard as they dared, leading the switchback trail, cutting the time short, getting above the winding rails by taking elk paths the last few miles. When at last they spotted the abandoned passenger car, smoke now coiling up from the stack of its small woodstove, they edged closer, keeping in the cover of rock.

"What do you think?" Hart asked Roth in a whisper, seeing Luther Ison sitting huddled at his horse's hooves with a ragged blanket wrapped around his shoulders.

Roth looked northward toward the wall of fog that seemed ever closer. "I think whatever we're going to do, we need to get busy doing it. I've never seen a blizzard take this long to hit, but when it does it'll be one for the books." He looked to their left at a long crevice in the tall upthrust of rock. "Looks like we could get these horses in there if we had to."

Hart nodded at the car. "I'd like to know how many are in there before we get started." Alongside the car stood the gunman's horses and the four horses C. B. Harrington and his men had brought with them.

"That's easy enough to find out. Here, hold my reins. Cover me." Roth handed him the horse's reins, then eased around the cover of rock and dropped out of sight into a stretch of scrub cedar whose roots clung like claws to the steep slope. Hart didn't hear so much as a brush of trousers or the turn of twig. In a moment, Roth appeared as if out of nowhere, moving forward in a crouch to within a few feet behind Luther Ison, who sat with his chin slumped on his chest.

Hart watched with his hand around his rifle stock, his finger across the trigger. Roth crawled the last few feet, keeping out of sight should anyone from the railcar come out unexpectedly. Three feet from Luther Ison's back, Roth heard him snoring. As quiet as a spirit, Roth slipped up against his back, threw his thick arm around Luther's face and lifted him like a sack of flour. At first Luther Ison kicked and clawed and tried to yell. But when Twojack Roth tightened his arm around Luther's face and said in a harsh whisper, "Keep still or I'll crush your little pea head!" the old outlaw relented and raised his hands in a show of surrender.

Roth lifted Luther's pistol from his holster as he dragged him into the cover of the cedars. Sullivan Hart watched the two men disappear as he kept an eye on the rear door of the passenger car. Once Roth had made it to Hart's position, and had pitched Luther Ison to the ground at Hart's feet, the outlaw went into a spiel. "Deputies, I'm not with those men. Me and my boy came upon them last evening, looking for a place out of the cold—"

The sound of Hart's pistol cocking cut his words short; the sight of the big pistol barrel poised an inch from his nose caused him to swallow a dry knot in his throat.

"There's a blizzard coming down on us, and we don't have much time," Hart said. "Be real careful about lying. We're not in a mood for it."

Roth bent down almost nose to nose with Luther. "You mentioned your boy? You're Luther Ison, aren't you?"

When Luther hesitated, Hart added, "You heard him, Luther, don't lie to us. I'm having a hard enough time keeping this man from setting that car on fire and shooting every one of your buddies as they run out. He's real upset at what happened in those towns back there."

Luther looked back and forth at the deputies, his

eyes like that of a trapped raccoon. "This was all my boy's idea—him and that Negro Gant that was living with us. I just came along to try and stop them!"

"We talked to your wife, Luther," Roth said in a flat tone as he cuffed Luther's hands behind his back.

"Oh . . ." Luther regrouped his thoughts, then said with a look of dejection, "I never could get her to go along with anything."

"How many are in there, Luther? Start talking." Sullivan Hart leaned down beside Roth. Together they stared into Luther's eyes.

In the passenger car, Radner passed a bottle to Earl Mellon as the lot of them gathered in a close circle around the glowing woodstove. "All that fancy talk about Midwest Investment, and controlling stock never meant a thing to me. I'm like you boys—just a working outlaw trying to stay ahead." He sighed a whiskey-laden breath. "It's not getting easier these days."

"Ain't that the truth," White agreed, holding out a hand for the bottle as it made its rounds. "Phelps sent us to bring in J. T. Priest, then Priest led us to believe he'd take us on full time with *Los Pistoleros.* Now he's run out on us. No wonder people don't trust each other anymore—you can't afford to!"

"Well, boys," said Mellon, a trace of a drunken slur to his voice, "it's a simple fact, you have to go where's the money's at." The men all looked at him, unsure of just what he meant. Having difficulty with it himself, he shrugged and looked away from the circle of faces and cut a gaze to Louisville Ike and Dirk LeMaster sitting behind the circle of men. "One of yas get out there and bring in some more wood. This time bring enough to last a while."

When both Louisville Ike and LeMaster appeared

reluctant, Steelhead Radner looked back at them over his broad shoulder. "You heard my friend. Go get some wood!"

"Come on, Ike." LeMaster nudged him. "We'll both go." They stood up and slinked away, out the back of the car.

"Check on Luther while you're at it," Steelhead Radner called out to them. "Tell him to get in here and warm up . . . the dumb son of a bitch."

"Is that a good idea, letting both them yardbirds out of our sight?" Mellon asked as the door closed behind the two men.

"Hell, they can't run off," Radner chuckled. "Where they gonna go?"

Just as Louisville Ike and LeMaster moved into the cedars gathering scraps of wood, LeMaster felt the big Cherokee deputy's gloved hand clamp around his neck from behind. Before he could make a move, he was on his tiptoes, his feet scuffling along in a hurry trying to keep up as Roth pulled him over to where Louisville Ike was stooping down to pick up a chunk of pine deadfall. With a big hand around each of their necks, Roth dragged them back to the crevice where Hart stood waiting with his rifle covering the passenger car.

"If it keeps on like this, we'll soon have them all," Hart said, grabbing LeMaster and throwing him over against Luther Ison. Luther sat with his hands cuffed behind his back, his teeth chattering from the cold.

"Listen," Louisville Ike pleaded with the deputies, "you know we're not with these men. This whole thing went wrong on us! Harrington is gone—got caught on the engine when it got uncoupled. We're not outlaws, you both know that! We didn't put up a fight. We're glad you got here!"

"Sit down and shut up," Roth snapped at him. "We tried warning you fools about coming up here."

"It wasn't us who wanted to come! It was Harrington and Steelhead Radner," LeMaster cut in. "Radner knows these men—he used to ride with them!"

Roth reached over and thumped LeMaster on the head. "Sit there and keep your mouth shut." He turned back to Sullivan Hart and cast a glance toward the stark looming grayness in the distance. "We better start making our move if we're going to. I don't like the looks of that sky."

The glow of the woodstove had dimmed as the bottle of whiskey was slowly emptied by thirsty mouths. The circle of men had inched closer to the stove instinctively, until Radner and White looked at one another, both coming to a realization at the same time. "What the hell's taking them so long?" White asked. "I could have chopped a cord of firewood by now." He looked at Gant and jerked his head toward the rear door. "Gant, check them out. Tell Luther to get in here, too."

The black gunman stood up stiffly, drew his blanket tighter across his shoulders. "I'll go this time," Gant growled in protest, shooting the Bays brothers a cold glance, "but don't get my name stuck in your mouths every time there's fetching to be done." He stepped over to the back door and opened it, with his right hand resting on his pistol butt.

Mellon, Radner and White gave one another a smug grin. "He just don't know, does he?" White gave them a secretive wink.

"Then he better learn," Radner said.

Gant stood on the rear platform and looked all around, seeing no sign of LeMaster, Louisville Ike, or Luther Ison. He did see Luther's horse milling close to the stretch of scrub cedars, and it gave him pause. He eyed the cedars with caution, then called out, his right hand deftly raising the pistol from his holster, "Luther? You there?" He waited for a silent second. "Luther? You hear me?" His cagy eyes scanned the rocky terrain, sensing something amiss, his feet already stepping back slowly toward the half-open door.

"Don't let them get that door closed," Roth whispered, standing a few feet from Hart with his rifle propped over the edge of a rock.

"I won't," said Hart, already taking aim, the knuckle of his trigger finger growing whiter.

"Damn it all, Gant," Luther Ison whispered, wincing, lowering his head at the sound of Sullivan Hart's rifle shot.

Inside the car, Radner had risen halfway to his feet, ready to chastise Gant for having left the door open. But all of a sudden, a hard blast of cold wind jarred against the side of the car as if trying to lift it off the rails. "Damn, boys, it's getting—" His words stopped at the sound of Hart's rifle shot. The bullet picked Gant up and hurled him backward through the door, a wake of blood streaming the air.

Chapter 17

Shorty Bays was the next to die. A bullet from Two-jack Roth's rifle caught him in the side as the young outlaw tried crashing through a side window of the car toward the horses. His brother Tom Bays Junior would have followed him had it not been for a hard blast of wind rocking the car far over onto one side. Tom Bays fell backward and rolled into the wood-stove, knocking it over. The stove pulled loose from its tin pipe and spilled its bellyful of fiery coals onto the wooden floor. Tom Bays batted out the streak of fire on his coat sleeve and yelled at the others for help.

"Jesus!" yelled Mellon, looking back for a second at the fire already licking up the door at the other end of the car. "We're on fire!" Mellon and Steelhead Radner crouched inside the rear door, exchanging fire with the deputies. Hart and Roth kept a steady, deliberate volley of rifle fire pouring through the open door, keeping the men pinned down inside. Splinters of wood spun in the air. Chunks of white stuffing spewed upward from holes in the leather seats. "We've got to get to the horses!"

A loud long roar of wind blasted along the mountainside, bending scrub cedars over onto their sides. The wall of fog had finally released its stormy fury. Behind his cover of rock, Hart felt the impact of the

wind-driven sleet try to lift him from the ground.
But he ceased firing long enough to duck down out
of the cold blast and fling himself over against the
prisoners. Deeper inside the rock crevice, Roth and
Hart's horses nickered wildly. Part of a scrub cedar
bough lashed the edge of the rock above Hart's head,
then tumbled away.

"Twojack! Are you all right?" Hart held a hand on
his head, keeping his hat from spinning away. He
yelled out again to the big deputy. Twojack Roth had
dropped flat to the ground behind his rock cover. He
only raised his head enough to nod in reply.

The sound of the outlaws' guns fell silent in the
screaming wind. Hart crawled on his belly to the
edge of his cover and managed to peep around it
long enough to catch a glimpse of the railcar shaking
and quivering in the gale, the wind now strong
enough to lift the car up onto two wheels for a second before crashing back down onto the rails.
Steelhead Radner came spinning out of the door with
a long yell in the grip of some relentless icy wind
devil, flames from the spreading fire belching out of
the broken windows.

"Oh, my God!" Hart murmured, seeing the outlaw
come tumbling down off the platform of the car, the
blizzard wind pummeling him. Steelhead scrambled,
flailing his arms, trying in frantic desperation to grab
something to keep himself from being blown away.
"Help me!" Radner screamed. But the roar of the icy
blast swallowed his words. As he sailed backward
and across the fattened cedars, he caught onto the
tangle of branches and wrapped his long arms
around them, his feet fluttering up and down, suspended in air.

"Stay down, Twojack," Hart shouted, diving back
into the crevice amid the prisoners and the terrified

horses. But his shouting was pointless. The icy roar
engulfed all other sound. But Twojack had already
taken deeper cover beneath a low overhang of rock.
The scream of one of the outlaws' horses reached
them as the animal sailed by overhead. Twojack Roth
caught a glimpse of the poor beast thrashing in the
air, its scream lingering as it spun out of sight. Roth
gritted his teeth and hugged the ground, feeling the
suction of the wind draw the back of his coat upward. His Stetson was ripped from his head. His long
black braid lashed wildly like a whip.

"We're all gonna die! We're all gonna die!" Luther
Ison crawled deeper into the crevice, his hands cuffed
behind his back, his boots digging fiercely into the
ground. A loud crash resounded in the wind. Broken
pieces of the passenger car swept above the edge of
the rock cover. LeMaster and Louisville Ike followed
Luther Ison, scrambling for deeper shelter. Sullivan
Hart held his position, clutching a spur of rock with
both hands, his hat gone and his duster tails lapping
out like the wagging tongue of some rabid cur.

Earl Mellon and Carl White had dived out of the
railcar just before the ice-filled wind lifted it completely off the tracks and dashed it against the tall
slope of rock, the fire inside streaking away as the
car burst apart. "Lord God!" Carl White shouted,
rolling on the ground unable to stop himself. Somehow in the stir of things, he managed to roll to his
feet, but the wind kept him moving as he backped-
aled, screaming, seeing the edge of a steep ravine
drawing closer.

White was powerless. Beneath him the ground disappeared. He looked down as he tumbled through
the air, the tops of tall pine and spruce whipping
in a valley two hundred feet below. "I'm dead!" he

shouted, his voice fading behind him as he sailed forward through the air like a large wingless bird.

In the shelter of the crevice, Sullivan Hart saw Tom Bays Junior bounce down out of the passing streak of ice and shattered wood and debris, like something spit from the angry mouth of hell. Before that same angry mouth could suck him up again, Hart dove forward, threw his arms around Bays's chest and hurled the two of them back into the deep crevice. In an instant, Twojack Roth came diving in atop them, ice clinging to his hair and his chest. "It's the hardest blow I've ever seen!" Roth shouted.

Ice grew thicker in the wind, capping the rocks and filling the front of the crevice waist high in a matter of seconds. In the close quarters, the four outlaws and the two deputies lay piled like corpses in a common grave, each man listening to the screeching sound of ice-filled wind slicing across rock and through open crevices. For a full half hour they lay there, the lawmen and the lawless, united in their state of siege.

When the wind lessened, the cold frightened faces looked at one another. The remaining horses milled nervously, but settled. "Is it stopping?" Tom Bays Junior whispered, as if to keep the weather from hearing him.

"It's trying to," Roth said. They lay there for a few moments longer until the roar turned into a low mournful whir. Roth stood up first from the tangle of limbs, then reached a hand down to Hart and pulled him up. Hart looked at the men on the ground. Louisville Ike and LeMaster were both trembled out of control, Luther Ison still had his hands cuffed behind his back. Hart reached down, pulled Tom Bays's pistol from its holster and shoved it down into his belt.

"Help them up," Hart said to Bays.

"I—I think my arm's broke," Bays replied.

Hart helped him to his feet and leaned him back against the rock wall. He looked at the sliver of white bone poking out through the skin in Bays's forearm. "Yep, it's broke. Stay here and don't move it. We'll set it first chance we get. Can I trust you not to run?"

"Run where?" Bays asked. His arm hung limp against his side.

"It wouldn't be the first stupid thing I've seen out of a prisoner," said Hart. He raised Louisville Ike and LeMaster to their feet. "Come on, you two, stick close to me. We don't know who's still alive out there."

Upon leaving the shelter of the rock crevice and looking around at the area, it became apparent that there was no one left alive. Except for the scattered remains of the railcar and a hat pinned high up in the branches of a swaying spruce, there was nothing to indicate that man had even been present less than an hour ago. The crushing force of the blizzard had passed, yet the wind was still raw and hard and filled with driving sleet.

Louisville Ike and LeMaster pressed their shoulders forward against the weather, each of them holding their coat collars tightly closed at their throats. "Lord, Deputy, what was that? I've never seen anything like it!" Louisville Ike asked, squinting, taking in the land with his eyes half closed.

"I have," said Roth. "But nothing that hard. Usually a blizzard has spent itself by the time it comes through the mountains." He looked back and out across the sky. "This one will do some killing down on the flatland." Taking the lead, Roth guided the others to where a tall flat rock provided a wind break.

In the shelter of the rock, two horses stood with bits of cedar and gravel tangled in their manes and tails. One horse's saddle was drooped down under its belly, a broken piece of rail dangling from its reins. The other horse's reins were missing, a trickle of frozen blood showed on its lip.

Sullivan Hart stepped in next to Roth. Hart settled the horses and inspected them for injuries. The horses were shaken but sound, a few cuts showing on their flanks and legs. The dried blood on the one horse's lips revealed a cut where, in the trashing of the storm, the reins had pulled hard on the horse's mouth before breaking loose. "They've been tossed around pretty bad," said Hart, "but they'll do."

"We're not going to try traveling in this, are we?" LeMaster asked with an expression of disbelief. "It's still rough out here."

"Yep, we're pushing on," Hart said. "You haven't seen rough yet. If there's a head of snow behind this thing, we could get trapped here for the next month."

"You mean there's more?" Louisville Ike sounded on the verge of sobbing.

"More than likely, yes, there's more weather coming," said Hart, taking the rope from the reinless horse's saddle horn and fashioning it into a harness. "What do you think a blizzard is? Some heavy snow, a drop in temperature? A blizzard is more like a Kansas twister—only with ice in it and a heap of snow right behind it."

"Jesus," LeMaster whispered, hunkering once more against the icy wind, as he and Ike followed the deputies as they led the horses back toward the rock crevice. "Do you suppose C. B. Harrington made it through on the engine?"

"If not, I expect we'll find out along the trail," Roth

answered, cutting a glance along the bare rocky earth where earlier the stretch of scrub cedar had stood. Now only a sheet of ice remained, and above it a swirl of fine snow.

In a winding narrow canyon where towering walls of rock rose up on either side of the tracks, Jones helped Denver Stanton and Bert Ison clear a fallen aspen from the rails. He stretched his back, followed Stanton and Bert to a spill of rocks, and began pitching them to one side. "I shoulda had my damned head examined, coming up here, for any amount of money," he grumbled. Snow swirled along the canyon, the wind not nearly as hard in this deep corridor, and the storm itself not nearly as bad as it had been farther down this side of the mountain.

"Me too," Stanton replied. "You think I like this any better than you do? I know what was about to happen to me if I hadn't hopped a ride on that engine."

Jones just stared at him.

"That's right," Stanton added, "he was leaving me and the others hanging down there. You think it's all whiskey and good times riding with a bunch of outlaws?"

"Never gave it much thought," Jones said, picking up a big chunk of rock and tossing it away. Bert Ison snickered and turned in circles, studying the rocks at their feet. "If it's any harder than railroading though, I feel sorry for yas."

"How much longer before we get to Cold Ridge?" Stanton asked as he tugged a wool muffler up around his cheeks.

"Ordinarily, just a couple more hours," Jones said, "but if there's a lot of spill on the tracks it could take us a whole other day—that's not counting any heavy snow we have to deal with."

Denver Stanton cursed under his breath. "Think those two give a damn?" He gestured toward the engine sitting a hundred feet away, smoke rising in slow steady puffs from its stack. "They couldn't care less if the sun never shines, what with them and their business deal."

In the warm compartment of the service engine, C. B. Harrington sat close to the firebox, with the glove off of his right hand and a pencil and notepad resting on his knee. J. T. Priest sat with his pistol across his lap, watching engrossed as Harrington worked with a scribbled column of figures. "You see," Harrington said as he worked, "this is why I can't understand Midwest Investment even having anything to do with *Los Pistoleros.* It's simply bad business."

"Now that I'm a wanted man," Priest said, "I tend to agree. But old habits die hard, sir. There was a time when it was just me, William Mabrey and a handful of others. We robbed enough banks and pay-rolls to foot the bill for everything else. I always said when something works you stick with it."

"Too bad then," Harrington said, "because if I re-structure this corporation, it will be with the under-standing that *Los Pistoleros* has nothing more to do with it, including owning any of the outstanding stock, which I'm assured Cleveland Phelps does." Harrington held up the notepad, pointing the tip of the pencil to a long, impressive figure. "On the other hand, this is what I'm prepared to pay you as a si-lent partner."

J. T. Priest's eyes gleamed, but he shrugged, trying not to look too impressed. "That's fair perhaps, but don't forget, I'll be on the run for the rest of my life.

That costs money." He nodded at the figure on the pad. "Once this figure runs out, then what?"

Harrington shook his head as if to clear it. "Mr. Priest, I'm afraid you don't understand." He tapped the pencil to the notepad. "This is the amount you'll receive *per year*, deposited in an account at the bank of your choice, anywhere in the world."

Priest just stared, knowing that this was the answer to his problems. "How do I know you'll make that deposit every year?"

Harrington gave an indignant lift of his fleshy chin. "You'll have my word as a gentleman, sir."

"Horse shit. No gentleman ever started from scratch the way you say you did and come out rich with a word that's worth any more than the air that formed it." Priest jiggled the pistol in his hand. "Don't insult my intelligence. Things might have gone wrong for me lately, but I'm no fool. I've still got enough sense to pull a trigger."

"All right, sir." Harrington lifted a clean soft hand, as if closing the subject. "We'll put it in writing. As soon as all the other shares are in my name, you'll receive your first year's payment. Do we have a deal, sir?"

J. T. Priest scratched his jaw. "You realize that Sims will have to die?"

C. B. Harrington smiled. "I wouldn't have it any other way, sir."

"It seems like a mighty generous offer," Priest said.

"And well it is, sir." Harrington leaned closer to him. "But you realize of course this is all providing that you can deliver the shares Quick Charlie Sims owns, and the shares that presently belong to Cleveland Phelps."

Priest looked around as if making certain Denver

Stanton was out of hearing range. "There's a lot of *Los Pistoleros* scattered all over this country. They won't stand for being cut out this way."

"Let me worry about that, J. T.," Harrington said, hooking his thumb in his vest. "Once your name is off the stockholders' list and the corporation is mine, I'll simply claim ignorance, tell the authorities my new company is riddled with outlaws and sit back and let the law do its job."

Priest chuckled. "It could take an army to handle a gang this size."

"Than an army it shall be." Harrington smiled in satisfaction, now hooking both thumbs in his vest. "Make no mistake, Mr. Priest, I will lead this corporation to heights you and William Mabrey could only have imagined."

"Yeah?" Priest returned Harrington's smile, holstered his pistol and rubbed his hands together. "Then what say we take a look at that figure one more time . . . just for the hell of it."

Chapter 18

Before the blizzard wind had even made its way down through the mountain passes, it had struck Cold Ridge hard. The cold squall moved in so fast it would have caught everyone unexpectedly had it not been for Quick Charlie Sims. He'd crossed the footbridge, and was headed for the saloon when the first slicing blast swooped down the street, nearly lifting him off his feet. Luckily he managed to struggle to a hitch rail and get a grip on it for a second. He caught a glimpse of what was to come in the billowing swirl of gray fog. Before the main thrust of the storm hit, he was able to crawl up across the boardwalk and inside the saloon door.

"What was that?" Kate McCorkle shouted. She and Harris Sweet had run out of the back room at the sound of the doors swinging open and batting back and forth in place. Before Sims could even answer, Sweet saw what it was and grabbed Kate by her arm.

"Get back there with Herman! I've got Sims!" Sweet shoved her hard.

Sims struggled forward, the wind sucking him backward toward the wide open door. With one hand thrown around a thick support timber, Sweet grabbed Sims by his coat and helped him press forward. Then Sweet swung his weight around the support timber for leverage and threw Sims toward the rear of the saloon. Sims caught a grip on the bar with one hand then pulled Sweet to him. They clung to the bar for a second. Sims's breath pounded in his chest.

"Ready?" Sweet shouted above the roar as chairs tumbled across the floor and sailed out, some of them missing the front door and crashing through the large windows. Before Sims could even nod, Sweet hurled him to the back door. As if on cue, Kate pressed the door open enough for Sims and Sweet to squeeze through in turn, then the three of them shouldered the door closed and Sweet propped a chair back beneath the knob.

That had taken place nearly an hour ago, and for the first few minutes they'd hurried as fast as they could, tossing and shoving heavier furniture against the door, dragging Herman from his bed so that the four of them could lift a trapdoor to the small cellar beneath the floor. Sims had pulled the trapdoor shut and thrown the timber latch. Through the worst of the blasting wind, they'd watched the trapdoor rattle in place, Sims pulling with all his weight on the wide latch. Now that the wind had abated, Harris Sweet let out a breath, sitting on the earthen floor and cradling Herman in a protective embrace. "It's gone, Sims. You can let go."

Sims had to force himself to turn loose of the timber latch. When he did, he let out a gasp of relief and looked at Kate in the dim glow of the lantern she'd found and lit for them. "Are you all right, Kate?"

Kate only nodded. But Sweet spoke for her, trying to hurry things along, "Yes, she's fine. Let's get out of here and see what we need to do. Once this kind of wind has passed, you can expect tons of snow."

"Do you often have this sort of thing up here?"

Sims asked as he slipped the timber latch out of its brace.

"Yep, but nothing this bad," said Sweet, scooping Herman up off the floor. "This one will be talked about in the low country for a long time."

"I believe you're right, Sheriff." Sims threw open the trapdoor and felt cold wind and ice on his face. "God almighty," he whispered to himself. The greater part of the saloon had been ripped away. What remained was the floor, the west wall, and part of a sagging roof held up on the two remaining support timbers.

"It's—it's gone!" Kate McCorkle gasped, stepping behind Sims, drawing her coat collar closed against the pelting ice.

Sweet stepped up also, carrying Herman, seeming to give no regard to the missing saloon or the disheveled town around them. "Come on," Sweet nodded toward the hotel, seeing it damaged but still standing, "Let's get Herman out of this weather."

They made their way across ripped siding boards, broken furniture and debris to the boardwalk of the hotel. The wind was still cold and strong, but nothing like the brutal force of what had just passed through. As the others filed inside the hotel, Sims stood for a second longer looking up and down the razed streets of the town.

The footbridge was still in place although it had tossed wildly, becoming entangled in some spots. The sheriff's office was missing a wall, its sagging tin roof forming a slope to the ground where crystalline ice had already begun forming. The livery barn lay flattened to the ground. Two horses had miraculously escaped and they stood fifty yards away, badly shaken. Sims took one more look back and forth and shook his head. Large snowflakes were

starting to infiltrate the fine darts of ice. "Damn it,"
Sims cursed, "this is all we need."

Once inside the hotel door, Sims took off his hat
and batted it against his leg. "Well, at least Phelps
and his boys can't sneak up on us. The bridge will
take some straightening out before anybody can
cross it."

Sweet had climbed the stairs with Herman. Kate
McCorkle stood leaning against the hotel desk, her
hair hanging wet and tangled. She only looked at
Sims for a moment without answering, her breath
settling. "Maybe we've lucked out . . . maybe the
wind got them."

"I wouldn't count on it, Kate," Sims said.

She shook her head, "Neither would I," and raked
her fingers back through her hair.

Four miles up the trail beneath a tangle of broken
ash and cedar, Cleveland Phelps rose up to his knees
and crawled to the low rock overhang where most
of the men and horses had taken cover. The horses
were down on their sides, the men lying atop them,
covered with a layer of snow and ice. "Who's left?"
he asked, brushing bits of cedar from his coat sleeve.

Doc Mason stood, shaking himself off, his horse
scrambling up beside him and doing the same. "Lew
Spivey's gone, boss. So's your brother's body. I
watched them get blown away." Along the rock
overhang, Matt and Luke Tyrell rose up, followed by
Rhodes and Whitten.

"You didn't even try to help them, did you?"
Whitten asked in a demanding tone.

"Try hell, I was barely hanging on myself."

"I bet," Whitten spat.

Fat Doc Mason flared instantly. Even in the cold
wind he spun, facing Whitten and Rhodes with his

thick hand wrapping around his pistol butt. "Listen, you little bag of Texas pigshit. If you've got something to say, you get it said plainly. Nobody's gonna dog me unless they've got the guts to—"

"Hold it, damn it!" Cleveland Phelps yelled, steam bellowing in his breath. His pistol came up cocked, waving back and forth between the men. "We've got enough to worry about getting to Cold Ridge before we get stuck by more snow! You men settle down right now, or there'll be more killing than you bargained for."

Matt and Luke Tyrell moved back a few cautious steps, pulling their horses with them. "We're not taking sides, boss, but we both saw them blow away," said Matt. "There was nothing that could be done about it." He gave Whitten and Rhodes a flat stare.

Doc Mason stood firm with his hand on his pistol until Whitten relented and tugged his ice-encrusted hat down onto his brow. Then Doc turned to Cleveland Phelps. "Want me to scout around? Look for your brother's body?"

Cleveland scanned the wind-ravaged land surrounding them, taking note of the larger snow flakes moving in. "Naw . . . he's dead anyway. I reckon so's Lew Spivey." He looked around again, this time for a horse, yet seeing none. "One of yas is going to have to double up till we get to town."

Luke Tyrell had stepped up onto his horse before the others. He nudged it forward and reached a gloved hand down to Cleveland Phelps. "Here you go, boss, hop up here."

Cleveland Phelps just stared at him. "Did I say double up with me?" His gaze narrowed until Luke Tyrell lowered his eyes and stepped down from his saddle. Phelps snatched the reins from his hand

when Luke held them out to him. "That's more like
it," Phelps growled.

When Phelps had stepped up into the saddle and
nudged Tyrell's horse toward the narrow trail, Rhodes
and Whitten chuckled looking down at Luke Tyrell
as they filed past him. "Way to go, Luke," Rhodes
said down to him in a guarded voice, "you stupid
son of a bitch."

Luke bristled, but before he could respond, Matt
Tyrell sidled his horse up to him. "Come on, cousin.
Get on up here." He reached a hand down to Luke.
"You can keep my back warm for me."

Herman looked up from the bed at Harris Sweet,
Sims and Kate McCorkle. "We could all stay in the
cellar until they've come and gone. If they think
there's nobody here, maybe they'll ride on."

"Uh-uh, not a way in the world," said Harris
Sweet. "They can't go no farther than here, the way
that snow's coming down. If we got snowed in,
down in that cellar, we'd all die." Sweet raised a
spoonful of hot beef broth to Herman's lips. "You
just worry about getting well. We'll handle the rest
of it." Scratch stood on the foot of the bed staring at
Herman and sniffing the hot broth as its aroma
wafted on the air.

Sims stepped away from the bed over to the window, where he looked out at the heavy falling snow
and let out a sigh. He looked over at the collapsed
rail depot, seeing it and the railroad tracks only
vaguely within the white swirl. "We're lucky to have
food and coal here. We might bargain with Phelps
for some of it, if all else fails."

From the bedside, Sweet looked over at him. "Forget bargaining, Sims. What little we've got downstairs, we'll have to ration as it is. It could be a long

while before anybody brings the service engine up here. They might have been blown away down there for all we know." Sweet raised another spoonful of broth to Herman's lips, then said to Sims, "There's no point in figuring on anything now but a shoot-out."

"I'm afraid you're right, Sheriff." Sims let out a breath of resignation, stepped over to the shotgun leaning against the wall, picked it up and walked to the door. "I'll be downstairs, keeping an eye out for them. If I hear them trying to straighten out the bridge, I'll let you know." He stepped out the door and closed it behind himself.

"Poor Charlie," Kate said when he'd left the room.

"Poor Charlie?" Sweet gave her a bemused look. "Didn't you tell me how unpredictable he is to deal with? How he never lets anybody know what he's up to till he's good and ready?"

"Well, yes, sometimes," said Kate.

Sweet spread a tired smile. "Then it looks like the weather's just treating him the way he's used to treating others."

"Oh, don't worry, Charlie's going to be all right," Kate said in Sims's defense. "He gets this way when he's got everything all planned out. He'll settle down once his plan starts falling into place."

"His plan?" said Sweet. He and Herman looked at one another questioningly.

"Oh yes, Charlie has a plan," Kate said, nodding. "You'll see. He'll come up with something. I've never seen him without a couple of aces in the hole."

On the cold street, Sims looked all around at the ruined town and shook his head. Now what? he asked himself. What on earth had he been thinking coming up here, hoping he could pull off something like this. He looked forlornly through the thickening falling snow toward the empty rails trailing out of sight down the side of the mountain. Where were Hart and Roth? Where was J. T. Priest? Where were C. B. Harrington and the others? Timing was everything. Didn't they all know that? He walked to the rails and let his gaze follow them until they grew obscure in the white swirl. At his heels he felt something brush against him, startling him for a second.

"Come on, Scratch," he said, letting out a steaming breath. He bent down, picked the big cat up and held him against his chest and brushed snow from its back. "If you're smart, you'll find yourself a deep hole and crawl into it for a few days," he whispered to the big furry black ball, feeling the cat purr against him. "I don't think they're coming . . . that's right, you heard me. I'm afraid this weather's bigger than anything I came up with." He gazed once more along the rails, feeling the cold bite of the wind clutching him deep in his bones.

Chapter 19

It was evening in Cold Ridge when Quick Charlie Sims heard the soft plodding sounds of horses moving through the snow on the other side of the twisted footbridge. The snowfall had slackened, a thick blanket of white scalloping the damaged walls of buildings and lying nearly a foot deep on the ground. Sims had just stepped out from the door of the hotel with a cup of steaming coffee in his hand. At the sound of the horses, he tensed, then pitched the coffee out into the street, stepped inside the hotel door and placed the cup down on a vase table.

"They're here," Sims said, picking up the shotgun leaning inside the door. Kate swung her coat across her shoulders and hurried over to him as he checked the shotgun and handed it to her. "Nope. You stay here. I don't want Cleveland Phelps seeing anybody's face but mine until I've had a chance to talk with him."

Kate took the shotgun. "You can't go out there alone, Charlie. You're not even armed."

"I'm armed, Kate. Go tell Sweet they're here. The two of you wait until you hear something from me."

"You mean wait until we hear gunfire, don't you?"

"That's right." Sims stared at her. "Kate, help me out here. Don't fly off and try something without me knowing it."

"But by the time we hear gunfire, you could be dead, Charlie."

Sims spread a weak smile as he reached for the door. "Then let's hope you don't hear any. Now go get Sweet." He nudged Scratch back with his boot toe, opened the door and stepped out into the cold.

"Look at this damn mess, boss," said Rhodes, sidling his horse up to the footbridge, looking at the way it lay twisted over itself. Beneath the bridge the water ran fast and was clogged with long skiffs of ice. Thick snow mantled the meandering banks. "We'll be all night getting this straightened out."

Cleveland Phelps moved his horse up closer, looked the twisted bridge over, then stepped down from his saddle and waded over to it through the deep snow. "How the devil do you straighten out a bridge that's been tossed around like this?" he asked no one in particular, one hand on the thick suspension rope as if checking its strength.

"I've seen 'em do it back in Texas," said Whitten, "only not in this kind of weather. We'll have to have some long rope."

"Anything you do in Texas requires long rope, I expect," Doc Mason grumbled.

Whitten and Rhodes just stared at him until Cleveland Phelps turned to all of three of them. "Cut it out, Doc. All right, everybody give Whitten some rope. Whitten, let's see you do your stuff."

A coiled-up rope sailed from Doc Mason's hand. Whitten caught it just in time to keep it from smacking him in his face. Another rope slapped against his chest, this one coming from Matt Tyrell. Then Whitten ducked as the rope Luke Tyrell flung at him sailed past his head. "Hey, damn it! This ain't funny," Whitten cursed.

He stepped down from his horse, waded a few feet over to the rope lying half buried in the snow, picked it up and walked over beside Phelps.

"Now what?" Phelps asked.

"I got to climb out there some way, hook this rope up and climb back. Then we take a couple of these horses and twist that sucker straight."

"Then get to it," said Phelps, "before the snow starts up again." He turned to the others. "You heard him. Rhodes, you and Doc get your horses ready."

Across the creek, Sims stayed back out of sight, listening and watching Whitten tie the ends of two rope coils together, then doing the same with the other two. "Here I go," Whitten said, taking off his hat and tossing it up for Rhodes to hold for him. He turned and reached out with a boot, testing the bridge. "Hope this baby ain't damaged. That water looks awfully cold."

"Get to it!" Phelps demanded.

Sims smiled to himself and waited.

Whitten crawled out on trembling knees with the ends of the two long ropes in his hand. On the snowy bank, Rhodes stood next to Cleveland Phelps, feeding the ropes out. "I'll tie the first one here," Whitten called back to them.

"Shut up and do it!" Phelps barked.

Whitten tied one of the ropes in place, then cautiously crawled a few feet farther and tied the other one around the swaying length of upturned walk planks. Twenty feet beneath him, the freezing water churned thick with mushy ice. Whitten looked down, then sliced his breath short as the whole tangled, twisted contraption swayed and shuddered in place. "Aw-Jesus, boss! I can't make it back. This sucker's shifting back and forth too bad."

"Get back here, Whitten, or we'll starting pulling it over with you on it!" Phelps raged.

"Please, boss, damn it, this thing's making me dizzy!" Whitten looked terrified, the upturned bridge wobbling beneath his knees, his teeth chattering.

Now's the time, Sims thought. He stepped out into the open with his hat brim lowered, hiding his face. "It's closer coming this way," he called out.

On the other side, Phelps and the others stared at Sims in the gray evening light. "Who are you?" Phelps yelled, his hand reaching for the pistol on his hip.

Sims kept his face partly hidden and raised a hand in a show of peace. "I'm the man who's going to keep this fool from drowning himself, that's who." He waved Whitten toward him, stepping over to the suspension rope, holding it in one hand while he reached his other hand out toward Whitten. "Come on . . . it's steadier on this side."

Even with his teeth chattering and his whole body trembling, whether from the cold or in his fear, Whitten managed to snarl at Sims, "Who you calling a fool? Damn you!"

"No offense," Sims said, leaning out toward him as Whitten crawled one tortured inch at a time along the shifting swaying rope and boards. "Come on, keep moving, give me your hand."

From around the corner of a ragged wall left standing on one end of a small mercantile store, Sweet and Kate watched Sims help the man down from the upended footbridge. "What's he doing helping him down?" Sweet whispered.

"From the looks of it, I'd say Charlie is unloading his pistol," Kate whispered in reply. "Charlie's good at that sort of thing."

"Easy does it," Sims said to Whitten, his hand deftly lifting the pistol from Whitten's holster, letting the bullets fall into the snow, then slipping it back into the holster all in one smooth, seamless move. "There you go," Sims added, steadying Whitten until the trembling man righted himself and leaned with a hand on the thick suspension rope.

On the other side of the bridge, Cleveland Phelps stood staring across at them while Rhodes and Doc Mason tied the ropes to the horses. "Okay, Phelps," Sims called out, lifting his face, letting Phelps get a good look at him. "Get that bridge straightened out. I've been waiting here to talk to you."

"Son of a bitch!" Cleveland Phelps's face twisted into a mask of boiling hatred as his hand snapped the pistol up from his hip. "It's Sims!" As he raised his pistol, Phelps saw how long his odds were of hitting Sims from that far away. He shook the pistol back and forth in a tight fist. "Hold him there, Whitten! Don't let that snake get away!"

"Don't move!" Whitten's pistol streaked up, cocked, and pointed at Sims's head, two inches from his temple.

Sims shrugged. "Settle down, Phelps. I'm not going anywhere. We need to do some talking," he called out across the creek, seeing Phelps pace back and forth, enraged but powerless.

"You're damn right you're not going anywhere," Whitten growled.

Behind Phelps and the Tyrell cousins, Doc Mason and Rhodes hurried, coaxing the horses forward, the animals leaning into the heavy swaying weight as the upturned bridge groaned and creaked on its way back over. Loose snow fell down in clumps from the bridge into the icy water.

"Sims, when I get over there you're dead, you slippery dog! What happened to my brother? We found his body! Don't lie! You killed him, didn't you?"

"Stop acting like an idiot, Phelps." Sims smiled to himself, watching Phelps stomp in place, steam swirling in two jets from his nostrils like an angry bull. "Think I'd be stupid enough to be here if I killed your brother? Him and his friend got drunk, got in an argument and shot one another—that's the plain truth of it. The bartender tried stopping them, but he got a bullet in his chest for his efforts. I saw the whole thing. Take my word for it."

"Your word? *Ayiieee!*" Phelps let out a strange raging shriek, stomping in place. "God! I've got to kill him!" His fingers flexed like talons. He bellowed at Doc Mason and Rhodes, "Hurry up, damn it to hell! I've got to rip his heart out." He turned back facing Sims, pointing at him across the rushing water. "Don't move an inch! Do you hear me?" He shouted back over the thick shoulder of his coat, "Get that damned bridge turned over right now!"

"I hear you, Phelps," Sims replied calmly. "I told you I'm here to talk business. I didn't kill your brother . . . and I'm not worried about this fool shooting me. I figure if he shoots me, he'll soon be dead too, once you realize how much money he caused you to lose." Sims cut Whitten a sharp glance, seeing his finger tighten on the trigger. "Don't try it . . . you'll be sorry."

"There ain't no *trying* to it," Whitten snapped. "I drop this hammer and you're dead!"

"But you won't, so shut up," Sims said. Then he turned back to Phelps across the water. Whitten stood stunned by his brashness. "Listen to me, Phelps," Sims called out, "I know J. T. Priest is on his way here. But he doesn't have what you want . . . I do."

"You've got nothing I want, Sims! Whitten, if he opens his mouth again, shoot him!" Phelps spun in place. "Get that damn-blasted bridge turned over, or I'll shoot you both!"

"I have Priest's share in Midwest Investment, Phelps. You sure you don't want to talk about it?"

"You heard what he said, Sims," Whitten growled. Sims turned facing him in time to see the hammer snap down on the empty chamber. At the sound of the impotent click, Whitten gave his pistol a stunned, puzzled look.

"Now you've done it," Sims said. He stepped in fast, grabbed Whitten's wrist, turned his back against Whitten's chest and flipped him high and headlong into the icy water licking the bank near their feet. Whitten let out a scream and thrashed in the mushy ice, the frigid water up to his chest, trying to pull him down stream as he struggled to right himself.

"He's getting away!" Phelps shouted. Two shots pierced the water toward Sims, falling short by five yards.

"Hold your fire," Sims yelled, "I'm trying to keep this man from drowning." He stepped down through the snow to the water's edge, reaching a hand out and snatching Whitten by his coat. "I'm getting tired of saving you, young man," Sims said in a chastising tone. He dragged Whitten up into the snow on the bank. "Now lay there and keep quiet. Next time I'll hurt you really bad."

"What on earth is Sims doing?" Sweet whispered to Kate.

Kate stood staring for a second, a confounded look on her face, a wisp of steam rising from her warm breath. "Maybe he's softening them up?"

"I hope to God he's got something better than this in mind," Sweet murmured. "I better get across the street. If he gets them gathered on this side, let's be ready for anything."

Cleveland Phelps had been watching, running Sims's words through his mind as the horses pulled with all their strength to set the bridge straight. "Sims," he shouted, his pistol still smoking in his hand, "what have you got in writing?"

"I've got the whole transaction between me and Priest. It's even filed and on record in Fort Smith. I own every share J. T. Priest had to his name."

"Why'd he do that?" Phelps was getting interested now that the prospect of money was coming into play.

"Because he was stupid, Phelps. And if you harm me before you listen to what I can do for you, then you're as stupid as he is."

Luke Tyrell stepped in beside Cleveland Phelps with a rifle in his hands. He kicked a clearing in the snow at his feet and took position, levering a round into the rifle chamber. "I've got him for you."

"Wait, hold on, Luke," said Phelps, still keeping his eyes on Sims across the rushing creek. "Sims, what about my brother?"

"I told you, Phelps. He should have told you the same thing."

"He was already dead when we found him. What happened, Sims?"

Good . . . Sims took a breath of relief. "They shot one another. He killed the other man. We begged him to stay so that he could get his wound taken care of." Sims shook his head, making the story up as he went. "He was too hardheaded to listen. Has he always been that way?"

Phelps ran it through his mind. "Yeah, he was." The bridge gave way to the pull of the horses and with a mighty yank, flopped over into place. A few walk planks broke loose and fell into the creek, showering snow. "You stay put, Sims," Phelps added, his tone of voice less enraged, "we'll be right there."

All right . . . Sims took another deep breath, turning a bit to one side and catching a glimpse of Harris Sweet taking position on the opposite side of the street from where Kate stood peeping around the corner of a wrecked frame wall. He winked in Sweet's direction, then looked back across the water as two of the men started stepping slowly out onto the righted bridge.

"Hurry up, damn it!" Phelps demanded. "It's not getting any warmer here." He turned and snatched his horse's reins up from the snow-covered ground. He spun the reins around a short stubby hitch post beside the bridge, cursing under his breath. "What the hell kind of town cuts itself off this way?"

As Sims watched the men move closer, he reached down, took Whitten by his wet, stiffening coat shoulder and pulled him to his feet. "Here you go. Let's get you brushed off." As he spoke and dusted a hand on Whitten's back, his free hand lifted Whitten's pistol from his holster. "I bet you're about frozen, aren't you?"

"I—I—I've never been so cold in my life," Whitten offered in a strained voice through chattering teeth.

"We'll have to get you indoors, get some hot coffee in your belly." Sims reached inside his coat pocket, took out three cartridges, quickly loaded them into the pistol and lowered the pistol back into the stiff, ice-encrusted holster, all in a sleek, singular motion.

"Some whiskey would be even better," Whitten chattered.

Behind Luke and Matt Tyrell, Phelps walked along on unsteady legs, stepping over the gaps left by the missing planks. "Don't be talking to this snake, Whitten," Phelps said, stepping off of the bridge into the deep snow. "Why didn't you shoot him like I told you to?"

The Tyrell cousins had their guns pointed at Sims's belly, Luke with his rifle, Matt with his cocked .45 Colt.

"My pistol wouldn't fire, boss," Whitten said, astonished. "I don't know what happened!"

"Let me see it." As Phelps put out a hand for the pistol he kept his eyes on Sims.

"Sure, check it out, boss." Whitten took a step back.

Phelps pointed the wet icy pistol straight down, cocked the hammer and pulled the trigger. Fire blasted from the barrel; snow kicked up from the ground. The sound of the shot resounded across the snow. "Um-hmm," Phelps said, skeptically, "seems to be working fine now."

"Boss, I swear to God!" Whitten's eyes widened. "I cocked it and pulled the trigger right up close to his head! It didn't do a thing!"

"I'm not surprised," Phelps said. "They say things go a little haywire anytime this grifter's around."

"I'm sorry, boss," Whitten chattered.

"No matter," Phelps replied. "I'm glad you didn't shoot him anyway." He stepped closer to Sims, stopping inches from his face. "I bet you're just smug enough to think you're coming out of this alive some way, ain't you, Quick Charlie?"

"I'm calling it even money right now." Sims gave him a flat stare, not backing down an inch. "But we'll see how it goes." Sims listened to the distance, needing to hear something coming up the mountainside—train, horses anything. He had Phelps settled now, but that was just part of the plan. Timing's everything, he reminded himself.

"You arrogant son of a bitch!" Phelps drew his pistol back for a good swipe at Sims's forehead.

"Hold it, Phelps!" Kate's voice seemed to come from every direction out of the surrounding snow. "Charlie's not alone here."

A shotgun blast exploded upward and Phelps and his men all flinched at the sound. "I'm here, so's the sheriff. Like he said, we're here on business. But you know how I can get if I lose my temper."

"That crazy bitch," Phelps hissed. But he settled himself down, ran a hand across his damp lips and said to Sims, "You even took Priest's woman, you sneaking—"

"She was with me long before she was with him." Sims cut him off. "Are we going to talk business or what?"

Cleveland Phelps stared at him for a silent moment, then called out over his shoulder into the falling snow, "Is that right, Sweet? You're backing this swindler's play? Against all of us? That don't sound like you."

"It's me all right," Sweet's voice rang out. "Bring harm to him or the woman, I'll cut you in half for cat food." The sound of a shotgun clicking shut caused Phelps's expression to sharpen.

"So, you think you've got a deal that's in my best interest, Sims?" Phelps pitched Whitten's pistol back to him. "Then let's hear it." Whitten caught the pistol and looked at it as if in awe.

"I knew you'd listen to reason," Sims grinned. "Let's go to the hotel."

Chapter 20

The small engine struggled the last mile up toward Cold Ridge, the short cattle-catcher blade barely handling the foot of snow on the tracks. At times the train had to force itself slowly through deeper drifts. "It'll be easier coming down," Jones said, staring ahead, "provided we don't stay long and this snow gets no worse."

Stanton looked at Bert Ison, then at Priest and Harrington. He cursed under his breath and looked down at his wet boots. Three times in the past hour he'd had to climb out and heft downed trees from the tracks. J. T. Priest took note of Stanton's sour mood and said to him above the roar of the engine, "Look at it this way, Stanton—once we get Phelps to go along with C. B. here, we'll be chasing naked women along a breach somewhere, probably have some island chieftain begging us to father him some grandkids."

"Shit," Stanton hissed. Bert Ison sat chuckling under his breath like a lunatic, the gap showing wide and wet where his front teeth were missing.

Less than a thousand yards down the mountainside, Sullivan Hart looked up through his binoculars, catching only a vague outline of the engine through the falling snow. He lowered the binoculars and rubbed his eyes. "They're not doing much better than us," he said to Twojack Roth behind him. The two horses ahead of them carried Luther Ison, Tom Bays Junior, LeMaster and Louisville Ike.

"At least they're shoveling us a path," Roth replied, nudging his horse on along the center of the rails, the horse stepping with care, feeling its way among the icy cross ties beneath its hooves.

In the lobby of the dimly lit hotel, Sims pulled out a wooden chair and gestured a hand toward the chair on the other side of the table. Phelps looked at the chair, but didn't sit down. Instead, with his pistol still in hand, he looked around the lobby at Kate McCorkle and Sheriff Harris Sweet. Sweet stood on the fourth step of the staircase, commanding the room. Kate McCorkle stood in the opposite corner of the room, a large oak buffet ready to offer her cover if she needed it.

Cleveland Phelps's men were standing in an open spot a few feet from the wooden table with the two shotguns covering them. Phelps took note of their position and pulled the chair out from the table but still did not sit down right away.

"You've bought yourself nothing more than a few minutes, Sims. I've wanted to kill you ever since Chicago. So make this fast."

"A few minutes is all I need, Phelps." Again Sims gestured toward the chair. Again Phelps ignored the invitation.

"I haven't forgot about my brother, Darby." Phelps cut his gaze to Harris Sweet. "Tell me *your* version of what happened to him, Sweet." As Phelps spoke, Scratch slipped across the floor and purred at Sims's feet. Sims nudged him away with the side of his boot.

"Whatever Sims told you is how it went," Sweet said with firm resolve.

"Oh? So you've let this swindler get into your ear? Forgotten who your friends are, Sweet?"

Sims watched them both closely, noting that Phelps seemed to have settled down some. That was good— let things cool for a couple of seconds, he thought. But then he heard Sweet's reply.

"It's *Sheriff* Sweet to you, Phelps. We've never been friends and we ain't likely to start this evening. You want my version? Your brother's dead because he was nothing but the hole at the end of a skunk's belly—it must run in the family."

The hole at the end of a skunk's—? No! Not now, Sweet . . . Sims felt this spine stiffen. "Hey, everybody . . . let's keep our heads here." He cut Sweet a sharp warning gaze, then looked back at Cleveland Phelps. "We're all a little tense. What say we crack open a bottle of bourbon and get down to business."

Phelps stood seething, his eyes fixed on Sweet, his hand tightening on his pistol. "When I've heard this snake's deal, whatever comes of this, I might kill you anyway, Sweet." He glanced around at his men. "You boys watch my back. I happen to know how this *sheriff* got his reputation."

Now Sweet stiffened, taking one step down the stairs. Sims made a quick move to one side blocking them from one another's sight—a dangerous thing to do, but he had to give them a reason to unlock their horns. "Your brother was coming here to help you do something for both of your benefit, right, Phelps?" Before Phelps could answer, Sims went on, "I know he'd wish the best for you, wouldn't he?"

"Hell," Phelps sneered, "he never did. But he was still my brother."

"Well." Sims had to blink to clear his line of thought. "All right then. Let's sit down like gent— that is, *businessmen*—and let me tell you my offer."

"Start talking," said Phelps, jerking the chair the rest of the way out with his boot and sitting down slowly, laying his pistol down atop the table and keeping a hand on it.

Sims sat down, stared across the table at him and loosened his shirt collar. As he did so he listened beyond the door for any sound of horses, hoping the deputies might show, or J. T. Priest. "Like I told you, Phelps, I have the shares of stock J. T. Priest owned in Midwest Investment. He's on the run, coming here. Before he gets here, I'm offering you the stock, every last share of it."

"Yeah?" Phelps tilted his head a bit to one side, skeptical and cautious.

Sims hesitated for a second, then said in a lowered voice, "For free, Phelps. But you've got to give me Priest. He's got to go with me."

"But then I wouldn't get to kill you, would I, Sims?" Phelps leaned back in his chair.

"You're not killing him anyway," Kate cut in from her spot in the corner, the shotgun in her hands turning toward Phelps. "So take him seriously, you son of a bitch."

Phelps showed her a thin cruel smile, his fingers tapping silently on the pistol. Phelps wasn't about to mention that his intention was to kill Priest anyway once he got the shares of stock. All Sims was doing was making things easier for him.

"Easy, Kate," Sims cautioned.

"Why do you want, Priest?" Phelps asked. He couldn't believe how this was all going his way without him having to lift a finger.

"It's a personal matter," Sims replied. As he spoke,

he reached inside his coat—Phelps's eyes closely following his hand—and pulled out a folded document. He unfolded it, laid it on the table, and slid it over to Phelps. "There's the ownership transfer form. All it needs is my signature of release then it's all yours, or whoever you want to assign the shares to."

"Now ain't that nice," Phelps grinned, his hand still on the pistol. "What's to keep me from making you sign it anyway? Or what if I just took it and signed it myself. All I have to do then is—"

"Forget it, Phelps," Sims cut him off. "You're smarter than that. You know I'd die before I'd be forced to sign anything. Besides, you've never seen my signature. If this signature doesn't match the one on record in Fort Smith, you can't take ownership."

Phelps rubbed his cheek, making it look like he had to think about something. "I don't know, Sims. Priest means a lot to me . . . not to mention how bad I want to kill you." Evidently Sims wasn't as slick as Phelps had always heard he was. Phelps was starting to enjoy this, watching Sims bargain for something Phelps had no interest in at all. "Besides, if those lawmen are on Priest's heels, I can't guarantee they won't snatch him away from you."

"That will be up to me to deal with, Phelps. All I want is for everybody to stay back and let me settle up with Priest."

"And for that I get the shares in Midwest Investment, signed, sealed and delivered?" Phelps turned his eyes from one of his men to the other in turn, his expression alone telling them he was about to outfox the one and only Quick Charlie Sims.

"That's the whole of it, Phelps. I sign the papers over. You don't even have to sign them right now. You can leave your part blank for the time being, put the shares in your name or anybody's you want later on." Sims reached his hand across the table to him. "Deal?"

Phelps spread a smug, superior grin. "Get your hand down, Sims, we ain't in church." He nodded down at the paper in front of him.

"But, sure, go ahead and sign. I'll stay out of the way between you and Priest."

Sims took out a nibbled pen and a small traveler's bottle of ink. He stalled, taking his time opening the bottle, cleaning the tip of the pen. This wasn't quite what he'd wanted or what he'd planned, but with everything getting knocked off balance, and with him out of time, he'd take this setup just to keep his hand in the game. Once Priest and the others got here, he'd make whatever changes he needed to put his plan back in order. But what plan? his inner voice asked him. He ignored it, dipping the pen into the ink, then reaching out and pulling the ownership papers back over in front of him. He positioned his wrist to sign.

Outside, the blast of the service engine's whistle screamed in the snowy evening air. Sims halted and looked up toward the sound.

"What the hell's that, the supply train?" Whitten asked, standing shivering wet near the glowing woodstove in the center of the lobby. All heads turned in the direction of the toppled depot, the sound of the pulsing engine clearer now as it came to a halt and idled with a long blast of steam.

Phelps spread a cagey grin and snapped his eyes back to Sims, his hand still on his pistol grip. He saw the look on Sims's face, telling him Sims wanted to change his mind now for some reason. "Get it signed, Sims," he demanded.

Sims swallowed hard, his expression unsure now. "Sure thing, Phelps," he said, with a lack of convic-

tion in his voice. His hand poised over the paper, he
then slowly formed his signature across the line.

"There now." Phelps snatched the paper, folded it,
and stuffed it inside his coat. "I gave my word I'd
stay out from between the two of yas. So if that's
J. T. Priest at the depot, he's all yours. You better
have the guts to kill him, and kill him quick. I hope
you have better sense than to think he won't try to
blow your head off the second he lays eyes on you."

Sims just stared.

Cleveland Phelps turned to Whitten. "Get over
there and see if that's Priest. If it is, bring him right
over."

Shuddering, Whitten stepped away from the hot
stove, knowing better than to protest. "What if it's
not Priest, boss?"

"Who the hell else would it be?" Phelps stared
at him.

"The deputies maybe?" Whitten kept a submis-
sive tone.

"If it is, then you start shooting, Whitten." Phelps
grinned. "We'll keep an ear out for you."

The men chuckled. Whitten flashed them a harsh
gaze, walked over to the door and stepped outside.
"Luke, Matt," Phelps said to the Tyrell cousins, "get
an eye out the windows, see who comes back with
him. Doc—you and Rhodes make sure dear Miss
Kate and this old gunman don't decide to make a
play on us."

He cut a sharp glance at Kate and Harris Sweet,
then looked back at Sims. "I always heard you're a
hell of a gamesman, Sims. I have to say I'm a little
disappointed in you.

Sims raised his eyes to Phelps. "Oh? How do
you mean?"

Phelps chuckled. "You'll see."

"You're not going to double-cross me are you, Phelps? You gave me your word—"

Phelps guffawed, cutting him off. "Naw, he's all yours, Mr. Quick Charlie Sims." His eyes slid across Sweet on the stairs and Kate in the corner. "I'm just anxious to see if you can handle him."

A swirl of snow proceeded the men through the open door. Denver Stanton stepped in first and moved to one side, looking all around, his right hand poised near his pistol butt. Next came Jones, looking scared stiff and shivering from the cold. Behind him came J. T. Priest and Bert Ison as one, Priest's hand on Bert's shoulder, guiding him. Priest stopped and looked around without saying a word until his eyes fixed on Sims. "Evening, boys." He didn't appear at all surprised to see Sims there.

"It's about time you got here, J. T.," said Cleveland Phelps. His eyes cut to the hulking figure of C. B. Harrington as he shoved Whitten inside the door ahead of him, then stood rigid and stately, looking around the lobby at the dimly lit faces. "Who the hell is this?" Phelps added, rising halfway from his chair toward Harrington.

"Easy, Cleveland," Priest cautioned him, already taking charge of things. "This is C. B. Harrington. He's with me." Priest stopped it right there, then took his time looking from one face to the next as he plucked each finger of his glove then took it off. "Well, well, well," he whispered, his eyes lingering for a second on Kate McCorkle. Kate returned his stare in silence.

Denver Stanton took a step forward from his spot against the front wall. "Well, boss, here he is," he said to Cleveland Phelps. "I delivered him to you just like I promised—"

"Shut up, Stanton," Phelps snapped, quickly rethinking now that J. T. Priest was standing before him. He didn't have to kill Priest after all—so much the better, he thought. "And don't call me boss. Now that J. T.'s back where he belongs, he's the leader." Phelps managed to throw Stanton a look that told him to keep everything to himself for now. Priest caught the look exchanged between them, but didn't let on.

"Cleveland is right, boys," Priest said, offering Phelps a flat smile. "There can only be one boss of *Los Pistoleros*." He hesitated a second for effect, then said, "And from now on it's going to be *Cleveland Phelps*."

A murmured stirred amidst the gunmen. Cleveland Phelps cocked his head to one side as if in question. "That's right," Priest continued, gazing straight into Phelps's eyes. "You had me broke out of Parker's jail, sending Stanton and the boys to escort me here. It doesn't matter what your motives were, I'm here in gratitude." He pushed his hand out to Cleveland Phelps. Phelps shook, but with an air of caution.

"That's all well and good, J. T.," Phelps said, lowering his hand back onto his tabled pistol. He jerked his head toward Harrington. "But what's this man got to do with anything?"

"I'm glad you asked." Priest turned and brought Harrington forward to the table. "Mr. Harrington here is the man who's going to keep you and me rich for the next hundred or so years. Right, C. B.?"

But Harrington stood rigid with his eyes glaring down at Quick Charlie Sims, his gloved fists drawn tight at his sides. "What's this son of a bitch doing here?" Before anyone could answer, Harrington lost control and let out a scream, hurling himself over the table at Sims. *"I'll kill you!"*

"Jesus!" Priest grabbed Harrington around his

shoulders and pulled him back. Stanton jumped in, helping him. Harrington bellowed in rage, his fists pounding on Sims before Sims could duck back out of range. "Take it easy!" Priest demanded of the entire room, hearing the click of the shotguns coming from Kate in her corner and Harris Sweet on the stairs.

Sims spilled backward onto the floor, then scrambled back to the table as Priest and Stanton jerked Harrington back and settled him. Sims slinked back into his place, picking up his chair and righting it beneath him. Kate McCorkle noted the crestfallen look on Sims's face. "I'm here, Harrington," Sims managed to say, trying to hold his ground, "so you might as well accept it. Phelps and I have a deal— don't we, Phelps?"

"What kind of deal?" Priest cut in before Cleveland Phelps could respond. His eyes flashed to Phelps, his hard gaze pinning Phelps in place. "What's been going on here, Cleveland? You know what this swindler has done to me. What's he talking about?"

Phelps considered it, then smiled and relaxed, leaning back in his chair and propping his boot up on the table. "You'll get a kick out of this, J. T." Priest was relieved to notice Cleveland Phelps had left his pistol on the table. Phelps went on, nodding toward Sims, "Quick Charlie here told me how he bamboozled you out of your shares of stock, back before you got arrested—"

"Hold on, Cleveland, there was more to it than that." Priest's face reddened in embarrassment. But Phelps raised a consoling hand toward him.

"That's water under the bridge—anybody might have done the same thing." Phelps smiled and patted his coat pocket. "The thing is, I have those shares back now, signed by his own hand."

Priest's jaw dropped. C. B. Harrington stepped into the conversation abruptly. "Signed, did you say, Phelps? I hope *you* haven't signed anything! If you did, you take it back from him right now! Nobody will ever know!"

"Well now, Harrington," Phelps chuckled, "ain't you the sterling example of American commerce at work?" A ripple of muffled laughter stirred among the gunmen. Phelps shrugged. "Naw, I didn't sign nothing—didn't have to. Once they're signed out of his name, the shares can be signed into anybody's name I want. But I did give him my word on something."

"Jesus," Sims whispered. He slumped his shoulders, lowered his eyes and shook his head slowly. Seeing him from the corner, Kate McCorkle wasn't sure what would happen next. She shot a bewildered glance at Harris Sweet for some direction. Sweet only gave her a look that said stand still and watch.

"Oh?" Priest looked curiously at Phelps. "You gave him your word on what, exactly?"

Phelps leveled a flat stare deep into Priest's eyes. "I promised him when you got here, I'd step back and let you two thrash things out between yas. I could be wrong, but I have a hunch he wants to kill you, J. T." Phelps added that part just to fuel whatever fire might start. Then he fell silent, his face slack, shifting his eyes between Sims and Priest.

"You . . . did what?" Priest's mind seemed to be struggling to put it together. "You meant it?" As he and Phelps stared at one another, C. B. Harrington took a slow step back. Jones managed to slip behind the woodstove for cover.

A silence passed as Priest searched Phelps's eyes.

Then Phelps said in a lowered tone, "Look at me, J. T. Do I look like a man who'd break his word?"

A pin-dropping silence descended, which seemed to clutch everyone by their throats, keeping them from breathing.

"You sneaky son of a bitch," Priest said in a low purr, eying Phelps. Only the quiet crackling of the woodstove could be heard. Then Priest's belly shook slightly, a small breath of laughter moving upward from his chest.

Phelps's chest made the same muffled sound. He looked at Quick Charlie Sims with a smug grin, then back at Priest, now unable to keep his laughter from spilling out. "What an idiot!" Phelps slapped his hand down hard on the table, both him and Priest now laughing aloud. The men all looked relieved as nervous laughter made its way across them now that the tension had dissipated. Sims slumped further into his chair and avoided the eyes on him.

Harrington relaxed, fanned a hand in front of his face and patted a hand on his heart as if to restart it. "Whew! Gentlemen! You certainly have a way of thickening the air!"

"Sorry, C. B.," Priest said, gesturing him back to the edge of the table. "Cleveland and I haven't seen one another for a while. We needed to clear the air, eh, Cleveland?"

Phelps only nodded and smiled. "Yeah, we never meant to soil your britches."

Harrington recovered quickly, his hand disappearing inside his coat pocket and coming out with the folded paperwork. "Think nothing of it, gentlemen . . . sometime these mergers and acquisitions can get quite spirited."

"Mergers?" Phelps cut his gaze back to Priest.

"What's this peckerwood talking about, J. T.? How do we know he's even on the up and up?"

C. B. Harrington took exception and cut in before Priest could even answer. "*Peckerwood*, you say? How dare you, sir!"

Priest chuckled, raising a hand to settle Harrington. "No offense, C. B., I assure you. Mr. Phelps here is more used to dealing with the less delicate end of the business."

"Yeah," Phelps cut in. "I'm the one in charge of raising thick dust and quick money. Right, boys?" He swung a nod toward the gunmen for support, their answer coming as one in a low murmur. Priest saw that Cleveland Phelps wanted him to know that the men were all behind him. *All right, you son of a bitch*, Priest thought, smiling at Phelps. He saw what would have been waiting for him here in Cold Ridge. For a second he wished things would have worked out differently—him coming to town atop a horse, his new gang members surrounding him. But this was fine. He'd get this thing done with Harrington, and that was all that mattered—that and putting a bullet through Sims's head.

"I vouch for C. B.," Priest said. "So would Steelhead Radner if he was here. Radner was bringing him to us. Seems Harrington was out to take the shares from Sims here, but Sims and his girlfriend pulled one of their stunts and threw them off Harrington's Pullman car, then stole the car and rode it all the way to the lower depot."

C. B. Harrington cut a sharp glance at Sims. "That's right, Sims, you smug bastard! Don't think you're not going to pay dearly for what you did! It could have killed Radner and me both, jumping from a moving train! I've never seen a person like you,

Quick Charlie Sims! I could wring your neck like a chicken's and think no more of it!"

Priest shrugged at Sims. "See? You should have killed him and Radner when you had the chance. Leaving an enemy alive always comes back to haunt you." He tossed the subject aside and added to Harrington, "C. B., calm down . . . go on and explain this whole deal to Cleveland. He's going to love it."

"Well, then," Harrington settled himself once more, giving Sims one more threatening glance. He drew an empty chair from beneath the table and seated himself. "You must pardon me, gentlemen. I'm not accustomed to a snake like Sims." He smoothed out the paperwork with his thick palm, cleared his throat and looked at Cleveland Phelps. "Now, sir, to the business at hand."

Chapter 21

As dark set in, Sullivan Hart sat kneeled behind an overturned rain barrel half covered by snow. A few feet to his left, behind the partial wall of the flattened mercantile store, Tom Bays Junior and Luther sat in the snow, Luther with his hands still cuffed behind him, Bays with his broken arm in a bandanna sling. Next to them, LeMaster and Louisville Ike stood holding the horses. Hart gazed forward through the falling snow and the encroaching darkness at the dim light glowing from the windows of the hotel. He glanced over at the idling engine on the tracks, then back at the hotel, trying to get a picture of what was going on in there.

"Careful, Twojack," Hart whispered to himself, watching the Cherokee's dark figure slip away from the front hotel windows. Roth moved smoothly in a crouch, down off the low porch of the hotel, around the side of the building, and slowly up the outside stairs toward the landing at the second-floor window. He tried to keep the sound of crunching snow beneath his feet as quiet as possible, moving with his pistol drawn.

Hart watched his partner stop at the landing, the wind blowing loose snow from the stairs in a silver-white stream. He tightened his grip on his rifle stock, seeing Roth brush snow from the window ledge and lift the window open. "Don't do it," Hart whispered. But Roth slipped inside the window and lowered it behind himself. Hart waited. "Get out of there . . ." Then as if hearing his partner's plea, Roth stepped out through the window, closed it and began working his way down the stairs.

"What was that all about?" Sullivan Hart asked when Twojack Roth finally made his way across the deep snow-covered street and dropped down beside him.

"I couldn't see through the upstairs window— figured we needed to know who's up there." He took a deep breath, let down the hammer on his pistol and put it into his holster. "There's a woman up there with a bad chest wound. She's unconscious."

Sullivan Hart winced at the thought of more hostages to worry about. "Is it Kate McCorkle?"

"No, it's not Kate. This is an older woman." Roth's expression turned bemused. "She's bald."

"She's what?"

"Bald." Roth shook his head slightly. "I mean completely bald."

"How could you tell it's a woman then?" Hart gave him a puzzled look.

"The covers were down a little. She's wounded right here." Roth cupped a hand to the center of his broad chest. "I—I couldn't help but see . . . it's a woman. A short, stocky—" He hesitated, then added "—bald-headed woman." His voice had a certain amount of disbelief in it.

Hart looked at him, but wasn't going to question his judgment, however uncertain he sounded. "They'll bargain with her. They'll bargain with Sims, with Kate . . . with whoever they can."

Roth nodded at the idling engine car, smoke puffing slowly from its stack. "They left it running for a reason. Maybe somebody's going to be coming out soon. We can wait and hit them then—might make it safer for everybody."

"Meanwhile, it's getting awfully cold out here," Hart said, biting his lips and considering their best move. "What's it look like in there? Does Sims seem to have anything going his way?"

"If he does, he's hiding it. He looks whipped to me." Roth tugged his collar tight against the blustering wind and snow.

"How many guns are we talking about?" Hart studied the dim glow of light as he spoke.

"I counted seven gunmen, plus J. T. Priest and Cleveland Phelps. There's an old sheriff in there—I figure it's Harris Sweet. He must be on Sims's side."

"What makes you think so," Hart asked.

"Because I could have sworn he saw me through the window. But he didn't let on about it. It looks like him and Kate McCorkle are at a standoff with the rest of them. C. B. Harrington and Merle Jones are in there, too. Jones looks pretty worried. Harrington looks right at home."

"It'd be good to know the sheriff's on our side," Hart said, "if we have to rush the place and start shooting."

From a few feet away, Luther Ison heard their discussion and whispered, "My boy's in there! My only begotten son! Don't go charging in there and kill him! You've got no call to—"

"Shut up, Luther!" Hart hissed at him. "Your boy's in there because you put him there."

"No. I didn't. J. T. Priest just snapped him up and took him along. I never meant for Bert to die! I've been a good daddy to him. He's always been hard to handle."

"Your wife told us what a good father you've

been, Luther. She told us the boy is slow because you've smacked him around his whole life . . . said now you use it to make him do whatever you want him to. So don't try to sell us on what a kind and decent man you've been. You raised him to be an idiot and a gunman. He's just following orders."

"Hey, hey," Roth nudged Hart to direct his attention back to the hotel. "Somebody just walked past the window. It looked like J. T. Priest." They both stared at the hotel windows, Hart's finger inside the trigger guard of his rifle, his thumb taut across the hammer ready to cock it.

"Maybe that's a good sign," Hart said calmly. "If they start moving around it could mean they're ready to come out."

"Let's hope so," said Roth, settling down beside him and picking up his rifle, which he'd left leaning against the rain barrel.

Inside the hotel lobby, Priest took the bottle of bourbon he'd removed from behind the counter and stood it on the table. He looked at Kate McCorkle, then at Harris Sweet. Then he said to Cleveland Phelps, "Well, Cleveland, you heard his deal. Do we drink to it?"

But Phelps held out for a second, even looking at Sims, as if to see what Sims's expression might reveal. Sims saw his chance and cut right in. "Listen to me, Phelps . . . you think I'm a swindler? You haven't seen anything as shifty as this man in your life. C. B. Harrington will skin you!" He shot a glance at Priest. "He'll skin you both! I didn't come here to kill you, Priest—not that I would mind doing it—but I came here to make a deal, to offer my shares—"

A powerful backhanded slap shot across the table from C. B. Harrington. Sims's head swung as if on a hinge. Blood flew from his lips. But before he even righted himself in the chair, Sims cried out over his shoulder, already knowing what Kate's reaction would be. "No! Kate! Don't do it!" Without seeing her, Sims could feel her raising her shotgun, one split second away from dropping both hammers. "Sweet!" Sims cried out, "Keep her under control! Tell her not to shoot! We'll all die here!"

Sweet, with a shotgun leveled toward the gunmen, saw them ready to throw down on Kate McCorkle. "You heard him, Kate. Hold fast there." Kate saw something more than just a warning in Sweet's eyes. The old sheriff saw something at work in the way Sims let these men take the upper hand on him so easily. Kate McCorkle took a deep breath, stilling herself.

She'd have to play it the way that Sweet saw it for now. She watched closely as Sims straightened in his chair and ran a hand across his bloody mouth.

"Listen to me, Phelps—you too, Priest," Sims said in a rush, sounding a bit desperate to Kate McCorkle's ears. "How do you know Steelhead Radner was backing Harrington's plan? Steelhead's not here. He can't tell you one way or the other what—"

"That's enough, Sims." Harrington cut him off, then turned to Merle Jones, who cowered on the other side of the stove. "Jones, tell him who was with me down there, claiming my Pullman car after this man stole it."

Jones looked terrified. "I don't want to make nobody mad at me, but there was three men with Harrington—one of them a big mean-looking fellow. They called him Steelhead, that's true." Jones nodded and cowered back behind the stove.

"Can't you see what this man is going to do to you, Phelps?" Sims exclaimed, but not sounding too convincing, Kate thought. "If you go along with him, he'll waltz out of here with both of your shares in Midwest Investment! You'll never see a penny!"

"That's all for you, Sims." C. B. Harrington stretched toward him, his arm swinging back for another smack in the mouth. But this time Phelps jumped forward and caught his wrist.

"Not so fast, Harrington. Let this swindler say what he's got to say, if you've got nothing to hide."

Way to go, Charlie. . . ! Kate McCorkle almost let out a breath of relief. He'd take it over now, she thought, put some of the ole Quick Charlie spin on things, get them all confused, maybe fighting among themselves . . .

"Go on, Sims, get it said." Cleveland Phelps stared at him. "But you better say something worth hearing this time."

Sims looked worried, too worried, too unsure of himself. Kate had never seen him this way. *Come on, Charlie, damn it, snap out of it!*

Sims stammered, "I—that is, how do you know he'll pay you the amounts he said? He takes those shares with him . . . who says you'll ever see him again?"

Kate looked stunned. *Was that it? Was that all Charlie had?*

Harrington jumped on Sims's question. "Gentlemen, I hate to agree with this snake, but he's absolutely right." As he spoke he took out both ownership documents, the one Phelps had received from Sims earlier, and another one for the shares Phelps himself owed in Midwest Investment. "If there's any doubt in your mind, we'll postpone the actual transaction until spring." He dropped the documents on the table. "Of course that will shorten your first year's income considerably, you must realize."

"Like hell," Priest said. He picked up the documents and forced them back into Harrington's hand. "Cleveland can do what he wants. You and me has already signed an agreement." He shot his gaze to Cleveland Phelps. "Are you going to listen to a rat like Sims, or to a man who's known all over the world of commerce?"

"We had a deal, Phelps. You better listen to me," Sims said in one last weak effort.

"Shut up, Quick Charlie Sims," Phelps grinned, "or I'll backhand you myself. You ain't showed me much since I got here. I'm still wondering about my brother, Darby."

"What about Darby?" Priest asked.

"He's dead, that's what. Sims claimed Darby and ole Chester killed one another, but I've still got some doubts."

"There's only one way to be sure," said Priest. "Kill him."

"Whoa, gentlemen." Harrington cut in, casting a glance at Kate and her poised shotgun. "Only one problem there." He hurriedly stuffed the paperwork back inside his coat and looked at Sims with satisfaction. "I'm taking Sims with me when I leave here. We're going to the first attorney we come to. Only then will I sign them into my name. He's going to sign this over to me in front of a legal witness. I'm not taking any chances on him. Any objections?"

"Here's one!" Kate sidestepped closer to the stairway below Sweet. She leveled the shotgun at them from five feet away.

"Kate, this is not the time or place to argue," Sims said without turning toward her.

"No way, Charlie. You're not going along with this man just because you think I might get hurt. Only way you leave here with him is over my—"

Her words were cut short when Sweet's hand

swung in, snatching the shotgun and wrenching it from her grasp. She spun toward Sweet, swiping a hand at the shotgun, but Sims moved fast. He darted around the table, grabbed her around the waist and wrestled her to a standstill. "Easy, Kate, easy." Sims settled her, turning with one hand raised toward the gunmen in a show of peace. "She's okay, boys, see? I've got her under control. Everybody stay calm." Sims flashed a glance at Harris Sweet. "Thanks, Sheriff."

Sweet nodded, then with both shotguns covering the edgy gunmen, the sheriff backed up three steps. "Everybody be good now. If Sims wants to go with you, it's up to him. If he don't, a bunch of us can die right here." Sweet's jaw tightened. "Sims, you call it."

Sims looked around as if weighing their odds—his, Sweet's and Kate McCorkle's. He swallowed a knot in his throat. At his feet, Scratch moved in and rubbed against his leg. Sims brushed the cat back with the side of his boot. "It's all right, Sweet. I'm going with them. I played the game, and I lost. There's no point in all of us dying." He kept an arm around Kate's waist.

J. T. Priest chuckled under his breath, turning to Harrington. "How do you plan on making him sign? He's slick, C. B., I've got to warn you."

"Oh, I can promise you, he'll sign." Harrington hooked his thumbs in his vest. "She's going along, too." He nodded at Kate McCorkle. "If he refuses to sign before an attorney, he'll simply find this young lady splattered all over the wall of my Pullman car."

Cleveland Phelps rose halfway from his chair. "I only just met you, Harrington, but I already like the way you do business."

"Maybe I better tag along with you C. B.," Priest said, "just to keep this snake in line."

C. B. Harrington stiffened. "Don't you trust me, sir? You have my address in New York. All you have to do is let me know where to send your money."

"Naw, that's not it. I trust you, C. B. . . ." Priest stalled for a moment. "The truth is, I'd kinda like to spend some time alone with Mr. Quick Charlie Sims—the woman, too, once you're through with them."

Kate started to struggle once again against Sims's arm, but Sims pulled her to the side, whispering close to her ear, "Settle down, Kate, this is the only way."

She fought with him for a second longer to make it look good, then collapsed against him, her expression saying that she hoped he knew what he was doing. "You don't need us both with you, Harrington. Take me . . . leave Kate out of this. I'm asking you as a gentleman."

"You're in no position to ask us for anything, Sims." Harrington stepped closer, Priest right beside him, Priest's pistol raised, cocked and pointed at Sims's head.

From the stairs came Harris Sweet's voice. "Sims, are you sure about this? If you're not, just say the word."

"No, Sheriff, it's all right," Sims said. "You didn't ask for any of this. You take care of Herman—he needs you." His eyes turned to Harrington and fixed on him. "If C. B. Harrington is half the businessman he thinks he is, I've got information for him that'll keep Kate and me alive."

"Oh really?" Harrington cocked his head. "Then I can't wait to hear it. Perhaps you'll tell me as we're dragging you by a rope behind the engine."

At Harrington's threat, Kate McCorkle struggled to free herself from Sims's grip. Sims notice that she didn't struggle nearly as hard this time. It was only for show—Kate's way of telling him she would play the game his way. Sims hadn't shown her much yet, but she wasn't about to count him out. "Easy, Kate," he whispered.

Outside in the snow, Sullivan Hart and Twojack Roth had grown colder and more restless. Against the partial frame wall, snow was starting to cover the men sitting on the ground and the horses standing next to him. "We've got to make our move before long," said Hart, "before we all freeze to death out here."

He studied the glow of light from the hotel window, once again seeing a figure pass by.

"I'm with you on that," Roth said, batting his gloved hands together for circulation. "You can start the ball rolling any time you're ready, far as I'm concerned." He looked at Hart and saw him run a hand along his rifle barrel, getting ready. "Want me to get around behind the building, in case they make a break through the back door?"

"Nope," said Hart. "No matter which door they come out of, they still have to come to us." Beyond the hotel there was nothing but cold and darkness, and the swirl of falling snow.

Chapter 22

"Don't think just because they're leaving, that you and I are through with each other, Sweet," Cleveland Phelps sneered. "Me and the boys are going to be here for a quite a while. You might want to think about clearing out of here yourself—you and your bartender friend. I won't forget how you turned on us."

"I'm ready for anything you've got, any time you feel like bringing it to me, Phelps." Harris Sweet stood, boots spread shoulder width on the stairs, both shotguns cocked and poised toward the gunmen. "Maybe there ain't much left here, but it's still my town. Me and my bartender friend will be here till we're damn good and ready to leave."

"Listen to me, Sheriff," Sims called out, seeing the look in Sweet's eyes. "Get up there with Herman. We're through here. Let this thing go, will you? Please?" Denver Stanton finished wrapping a length of rawhide around Sims's wrists and stepped away.

Beside Sims, Rhodes finished doing the same to Kate McCorkle and then stood by Stanton, both of them keeping a cautious eye on Sweet and the cocked shotguns.

"I hate a shotgun cocked at me worse than anything," Rhodes said to Stanton in a near whisper as they both moved slowly across the room. "I had an ole uncle cut in half by one down in Tex—!"

The shot from Sullivan Hart's rifle shattered through the window glass and through Rhodes's head, lifting him off the floor in a spray of blood. "Lord God!" Denver Stanton shouted, warm blood splattering across his face. The next shot came through the same broken window, grazing Stanton's shoulder as he dove to the floor. The other gunmen were stunned, but they recovered quickly, seeing Rhodes's body slam down lifelessly across the hotel counter.

"Move it!" Priest screamed, shoving Harrington, Sims and Kate toward the door at the back of the lobby. He spun around toward the woodstove long enough to shout at Bert Ison and Merle Jones. "Bert, Jones, come with me, boys! Hurry up!"

Cleveland Phelps scrambled to his feet. He flipped the heavy oak table up on its side and crouched behind it, already firing out the broken window. "Back here, Phelps, hurry!" Priest yelled, directing Bert Ison past him into the other room.

On the stairs, Sweet moved quickly but kept calm, backing up the stairs one at a time, still keeping the shotguns ready. At the top of the stairs, the sheriff ducked sideways into the hall and ran to the room where Herman lay on the floor in a nightshirt, trying to draw a pistol from a worn leather holster. As Sweet burst through the door, Herman called out in a weak voice, "Harris! Harris! Are you all right?"

Sweet hurriedly locked the door, the sound of gunfire blazing beneath them. "I'm all right, Herman." Sweet pitched one of the shotguns across the foot of the bed and bent down to Herman. "Here, let me have that." Herman resisted letting go of the pistol, but Sweet managed to loosen it from his grasp. "Sims

sent me away, Herman. He's got something up his
sleeve and didn't want me involved. So we're out
of it."

"Are—are you sure?"

"I'm sure. Here, let's get you back into bed. We'll
hold out here if we have to."

"I can handle a gun, Harris . . . I always want to
do my part."

"This time your part is to take it easy." On the
bed, Sweet propped a pillow beneath Herman's head.
"I'll get you dressed in case it gets too risky here.
Meanwhile, we'll let the law handle those killers."

"I'm glad to hear you say that, Harris." Herman
sank back on the bed, the sound of guns pounding
away downstairs.

In the room just off the lobby, Phelps leaned
against the closed door with his pistol raised, his
breath heaving. "I know damn well that's Sullivan
Hart and his Injun partner out there, Priest! Didn't
you have any notion they were right on your tail?"

"They've been dogging me ever since Fort Smith,"
Priest said, brushing broken glass from his forearm.
"I had no idea they were *this* close."

"Gentlemen," C. B. Harrington cut in, flinching at
the exploding gunfire. "Perhaps we should table all
of this for the time being. We can get together some
other time—"

"No, C. B.," Priest spat. "We're going right on with
this deal. We'll slip out the back and around to the
train."

"I say they've got the back covered," Cleveland
Phelps interjected.

"We'll see." Priest turned to Bert Ison. "Boy, get
out there and see what's what. Hurry now, then get
right back here."

Cleveland Phelps and the others stared in disbelief

as Bert Ison ran along a hallway, threw open the back
door, jumped out into clear view and looked back
and forth with his pistol raised. J. T. Priest grinned
and called out to him, "All right, Bert, if they were
there, we'd know it by now."

Bert Ison slammed the back door and came running up to Priest like a trained dog. "Makes you
wonder how they live this long, doesn't it, Cleveland," Priest chuckled. He reached out and patted a
hand atop Bert's battered Stetson.

"Jesus, where'd you find him, J. T.?" Phelps looked
Bert up and down, astonished.

"He's one in a million." Priest took Bert by the
shoulder and pulled him up closer. "Bert, I want you
to remember what I told you earlier on our way
here—how I wanted you to stay and take care of Mr.
Cleveland Phelps after I leave. Remember me telling
you that?"

Bert nodded, lifting a toothless leer at Phelps. In
the other room gunshots tore chunks of wood from
the oak counter; splinters pelted the door. "Got to
go now, Cleveland," Priest said. "But I'm leaving
Bert with you—call him my going away present. He's
like a bulldog. Anything you sic him on, he'll kill it
for you."

Cleveland Phelps eyed Bert, then turned to Priest.
"Well, much obliged, J. T. I won't forget you for
this." He turned from Priest to C. B. Harrington.
"Make sure you get us all taken care of, Harrington."

"Consider it done, sir." A bullet sliced through the
closed door leaving a gaping rugged hole. Harrington ducked away, grabbed Sims and Kate by their
shoulders and shoved them ahead of him. "My goodness!" Harrington cried out. "Come, Mr. Priest,
quickly now! This isn't exactly my cup of tea!"

In the lobby, Doc Mason, Whitten and Denver

Stanton pumped shots through the large broken window on the left while the Tyrell cousins did the same through the window on the right.

"I only saw flashes from two rifles out there," Matt Tyrell said, leaning down against the wall beside the window, reloading his pistol. "They've spread out some—got us in a cross fire." He glanced around the bullet-riddled lobby, clicking his reloaded pistol shut with the jerk of his wrist. "Where's Phelps?"

"Don't worry about Phelps," said Luke, "he's around." No sooner than he'd said it, Cleveland Phelps came back through the rear door with Bert Ison right at his heels. The two slid down behind the overturned table just as a rifle shot thumped into it.

"What's the play, boss?" Doc Mason called over to Phelps as the rifle fire slackened for a moment while one of the deputies outside reloaded his rifle. "Are we going to stick here or what?"

"Yep, for the time being," Cleveland Phelps replied. "Where else can we go?"

Doc Mason's eyes turned to the back door.

"Don't even think about it, Doc," Phelps said, seeing his suggestion. "We've nothing out there but the cold, same as the deputies. They'll have to rush us soon or pull back before they freeze to death. This is as good as we can do." He ducked down when the second rifle came back into play, a shot taking a chunk of wood off the table edge.

Twojack Roth fired from across a snowcapped water trough fifteen yards to Sullivan Hart's right. From his position he could cover the upper window atop the outside stairs. He saw movement up there, the lantern inside the window glowing brighter now. He leveled a new round into his rifle chamber and swung his arm toward the upper window. A hand raised the window enough to hold the lantern out and swing it back and forth slowly. Okay, Roth thought. He got the signal. Whoever was up there was not with the gunmen. He found his aim back down to the pistol fire coming from the front of the hotel.

Over by the partial wall where Louisville Ike and Dirk LeMaster stood holding the horses, a stray bullet struck something solid in the snow and ricocheted past them. The frightened horses lunged, but the two men managed to hold them in place. On the ground, Tom Bays Junior cowered beside Luther Ison, his broken arm pressed to his chest. "Lord, we can't stay here!" His words were almost a sob. "If they don't kill us, we'll freeze to death!" Snow mantled his shivering shoulders.

"He's right," Louisville Ike whispered to LeMaster. "Think it's time we make a move?"

LeMaster looked over in the direction of the smoke puffing upward from the idling engine. Without a word, LeMaster nodded, stepped the horse back a few inches and tied the reins to a stub of broken frame sticking out of the wall. "Hey," Luther Ison hissed up at them from his seat in the snow, "you can't leave me here. Take me with you!"

"Keep your mouth shut," LeMaster snapped at him. "We're not prisoners like you two. We've got a right to leave if we want to."

"Then you won't mind me hollering at them, will you?" Luther Ison threatened.

"I'm warning you," LeMaster growled.

"I will . . . I swear I will," said Luther.

"Yeah?" LeMaster drew back a boot and kicked him hard across his jaw. Luther Ison rolled across Tom Bay's lap and lay there half conscious. Tom Bays struggled to get Luther's head off of him.

"Are you going to give us a problem, too?" Louisville Ike whispered down to Bays. Ten yards away, fire exploded steadily from Sullivan Hart's rifle.

"No, sir," Tom Bays said, hugging his broken arm to his chest to protect it. "I don't want no more trouble."

Behind a pile of rubble and broken timbers, J. T. Priest ventured a peek out along the snowy street toward the flash of the deputy's rifles thirty yards away. The falling snow had thickened, the night looking ghostly and surreal. Rifle fire streaked like crisscrossing lightning in some dark netherworld. "One at a time," Priest whispered. "You first, C. B. Then you, Jones." He looked at each of them in turn. "Sims, Kate, don't forget, you're both going with my gun in your backs. Either one of you makes a sound, it'll be your last."

Sullivan Hart had moved closer toward the front of the hotel and had dropped down behind a pile of storm rubble. As he fired at the broken windows, he caught a glimpse of the figures moving across the street in the direction of the tracks. But when he turned and leveled his rifle, he saw the high collar of a woman's coat and kept himself from firing. "Roth, behind you!" he called out. "They're headed to the engine."

"I've got them," Twojack Roth responded. Yet as he tried to turn and move away toward the tracks, a hail of fire from the hotel pinned him to the ground.

Hart returned fire and kept the gunman at bay. "Are you all right, Roth?" he shouted.

"Yes . . . I'm going for the engine." He tried to rise up into a crouch, but the thick lead buzzing in the air wouldn't allow it. Even with Hart's rifle pounding at them, they managed to hold Roth in place, their bullets kicking snow high around him. A blast of steam from the engine resounded along the street. "They're getting away! Cover me!" Roth yelled through the relentless barrage of gunfire, then rolled flat across the snow, firing back at the hotel as he went.

Behind the partial frame wall, Tom Bays Junior ducked down against the ground as the gunfire followed Roth. When Roth rolled into cover, he looked around quickly and shouted at Bays, "Where's the other two?" With their reins hitched firmly, the horses nickered and stepped back and forth nervously.

"They lit out," Bays shouted. "Said you had no reason to hold them anyway!" Beside him, Luther Ison had regained consciousness and sat shaking his head, trying to clear it.

"Stay put," Roth shouted at Tom Bays, "I'll draw their fire away from you." He sprang to his feet and ran from behind the wall, firing, giving the gunmen his muzzle flash to follow. As the shots from the hotel windows drew closer to him, he leaped behind a cord of firewood near the flattened rail depot. Twenty yards ahead of him he saw the vague outline of the engine pulling away in the falling snow. He struggled toward the rear of the engine, the deep snow clinging around his boots, hampering his efforts.

Sullivan Hart emptied his rifle, then drew his pistol and kept firing, knowing what Twojack Roth was up to and trying to cover him as best he could. Once in between the rails, Roth found better footing and raced forward along the cross ties. But the engine was headed backward over the edge of a short flat stretch of ground, gaining more speed gradually as it moved downhill. Roth forced himself on for another fifty yards, his gloved hands snatching out at a handrail on the front of the engine, only missing it by an inch, then two inches, then four inches as the engine built up speed.

Roth came to a halt, gasping for breath, seeing the engine farther away, the face of Merle Jones in the narrow smudged window looking shadowed and grim in the dim light of the firebox.

"Don't shoot him," C. B. Harrington said to Priest. "He's no problem now."

J. T. Priest drew himself back inside the engine and uncocked his pistol. "Any chance I get to kill one of those two, I take it." He looked around at the faces inside the crowded engine compartment. "If that was your rescue party, Sims, you can kiss them good-bye." Quick Charlie Sims and Kate McCorkle stood against the wall of the engine, Sims staring down at the floor, helpless with his hands tightly bound.

"What can I say, Priest," Sims murmured in a resigned voice. "I was counting on them getting here a little sooner. Looks like I overplayed my hand."

"Yeah," Priest gloated, "so much for all of that Quick Charlie luck and timing. Now it's all going my way, Sims." He reached over with his pistol barrel and bounced it on the tip of Sims lowered nose. "I can take all the time I need and kill you real slow now."

"Don't get carried away, Mr. Priest," C. B. Harrington cautioned him. "Nobody dies until I get this deal finalized and in the bag. Then you do what you want with these two." His eyes moved slowly up and down Kate McCorkle in the dim light, a cruel thin smile spreading on his lips. "I dare say . . . I may even join you."

"Put a hand on either one of us, you son of a bitch," Kate McCorkle hissed, "and I'll rip your throat out with my teeth." She strained against the rawhide binding her wrists.

J. T. Priest and C. B. Harrington both chuckled. "My, but she is a spirited little cat," Harrington said, his voice turning husky and suggestive. "I have to admit . . . I like that."

"There's nothing there you'd want, C. B.," said Priest. "Believe me, I know." He cut a disgusted glance at Kate, then looked back at Harrington. "She was with me for a while, back when her boyfriend here was running from the law. I did everything for this strumpet. Got her out of jail, set her up like a real lady—now look at her. Right back in the dregs, where she belongs."

"You bastard," Kate spat. "You got me out of jail after framing Charlie for robbing a bank—after causing me to be there in the first place. You want Harrington to hear what you are? I'll tell him!"

"Easy, Kate," Sims whispered beside her.

But Kate shunned his warning. "J. T. Priest, you're nothing but a small, stupid pig—when I say small, I think everybody here knows what I mean—"

Priest drew back the pistol barrel. Sims saw his intention and lunged in between Priest and Kate. C. B. Harrington caught Priest's wrist, snatched the pistol from his hand and stepped back, laughing. "My goodness! She certainly knows how to get your goat."

"Give me the pistol, C. B." Priest's eyes took on a killing darkness. "Nobody jerks a gun out of my hand."

"Now, now." Harrington pressed back against the wall of the engine, hiding the pistol behind his back as Priest reached out a hand for it. "Not until you cool off. We've got some traveling to do. You must promise to settle down and control yourself."

Priest stared at him for a tense second in the ghostly flicker of firebox light. All right, C. B. Harrington wasn't used to this kind of life, or these kind of people, Priest thought, struggling to gain control of his rage. Harrington had no idea what it meant to take a man's gun away from him, shaming him that way. Priest took a deep breath, feeling foolish and childlike, and said, "Okay, C. B. Look, I'm all settled down now." He snapped his fingers toward Harrington's large belly. "Now give me my pistol."

Harrington hesitated. "Are you sure?"

J. T. Priest gritted his teeth, keeping himself from flying off the handle and blowing this deal. "Yes . . . I'm sure."

"All right then." Harrington handed him the pistol barrel first, which just proved even more to J. T. Priest how out of place this man was. "But I mean it, J. T." Harrington raised a thick finger for emphasis. "We've got to keep our heads and get everything taken care of."

"I understand," Priest said grudgingly, too embarrassed to even look at Sims and Kate. He shoved his pistol down into his holster and cast a glance at Merle Jones, seeing Jones's eyes on him. "What are you looking at, you railroad bum. Keep your mind on your business."

"You got it, mister," Jones said. He propped an elbow on the ledge of a small open window, leaned his head out into the cold and stared along the side of the engine. After a moment he said, "Uh-oh," and looked over at Harrington. "Hate to tell you, but we've two men hanging onto us out there!"

"What?" Priest snatched up his pistol, forced Jones back from the open window and looked back along the engine.

"Don't shoot!" cried Louisville Ike as Priest's first

pistol shot whistled past his head. "It's us, Ike and LeMaster! Don't shoot us Mr. Harrington!"

"Who's that?" Priest asked, pulling his head back inside, looking at C. B. Harrington.

"Sounds like the two peckerwoods I brought up with me and Steelhead Radner. Let them in . . . we might find use for them if the tracks are covered between here and the flatland."

"Damn," said Priest, "we're awfully crowded in here as it is."

"Nevertheless," Harrington snapped, "do you want to shovel these tracks? I certainly don't."

"Okay." Priest walked to the small door and opened it in a swirl of snow. "Get in here." He stepped back as Louisville Ike and LeMaster spilled through the open door shivering, snow clinging to their faces and hair.

"Lord have mercy, Mr. Harrington," Louisville Ike exclaimed through chattering teeth. "We was afraid we'd never get out of there."

"Find a spot and keep quiet," Harrington growled at them.

"Yes sir," LeMaster said in a meek voice, casting a glance at Sims and Kate with their wrists bound. "All we want is to get home in one piece."

"Somebody get ready to stoke up the fire," Merle Jones cut in. "We've got a short uphill climb coming half a mile ahead." He turned back to the open window, one arm stretched out to keep a hand on the throttle while the engine churned down the side of the snow-covered mountain.

Chapter 23

The lull in the firing brought Cleveland Phelps closer to one of the broken hotel windows, where Stanton and Doc Mason hunkered down beneath the splintered window ledge reloading their pistols. Phelps ventured a look out into darkness and the gusting snow. "See? They can't hold out much longer. They either have to rush us or leave us be. Either way, we're holding all the cards here."

As he spoke, he felt Bert Ison looming too close to his back. He turned to the leering face. "Bert, boy, get back a little! Give me room to breathe." But Bert only pulled back an inch and sat with the same blank empty expression.

"What about him, up there?" Doc Mason jerked his head toward the staircase. At the top of the stairs, Scratch sat looking down at the gunman through his one shiny yellow eye. When Phelps and Doc Mason looked up in his direction the big cat hunched down, turned and slipped away.

"Who? Our fine Sheriff Sweet?" Phelps grinned, shoving bullets into his pistol. "To hell with Sweet. I never thought he was much. He should have died years ago when his reputation played out on him. Far as I'm concerned, that's all he ever had."

"Think if we put a gun or two up there, it would help us any?" Doc Mason asked.

"We'll see how it goes," Phelps shrugged. "So far we ain't doing bad right here." He felt Bert Ison breathing too close to his neck. "Damn it, boy!" He spun toward him. "Don't make me keep telling you—stay the hell back a little! You're starting to get on my nerves."

In Herman's room, Sheriff Sweet called out in a hushed voice through the narrowly opened door, "Scratch, come here, boy." But the cat only sauntered a few feet toward Sweet's outstretched hand, then stopped in the hallway, sat down and licked his big forepaw, seeming not to notice all the commotion one floor below. "He's just being stubborn," Sweet said, turning back to Herman, who lay back on the bed. "I can't afford to worry about him right now." Sweet had helped Herman pull on a pair of trousers and a pair of socks.

Herman's high-topped shoes stood on the floor at the foot of the bed.

"We can't . . . leave Scratch out there," Herman said in a strained voice.

"I'll get to him. First let's take care of you." Sweet stepped in close, helping Herman sit up. "Here, let's get some shoes on." Sweet hurried, slipping one shoe onto Herman's foot, then the other, fussing over Herman like a mother hen.

"Harris . . . settle down. This isn't the first time I've been shot." Herman picked up a shirt from the foot of the bed with a weak hand and struggled to get an arm in the sleeve.

"I know that." Sweet took Herman's arm and pulled the sleeve over it. "I just want to make sure it's the last."

When the shirt was on both arms, Herman looked down and sighed. "I can't go anywhere looking this way . . . I've got no binding on." Herman's fingertips went to his lip. "No mustache either."

"This is one time you'll have to forget about appearance, Herman. I'll get a heavy coat on you—nobody will notice."

"But . . . they might, Harris." Herman's voice grew weaker with each word. "I don't . . . want to be . . . seen like this."

"Herman? Herman?" Sweet saw Herman's head and shoulders slump forward. "Answer me, Herman!" Sweet shook him gently. "Oh no, Herman! Don't die! Do you hear me? Don't die, Herman!"

Herman's words were faint, as if from a great distance. "I fear I must, Harris . . ."

From beneath the ledge on the broken hotel window, Cleveland Phelps and the others stopped reloading and turned quickly, looking up the staircase. "What the hell was that?" Stanton asked.

"It sounded like a woman screaming," Doc Mason said, pulling more bullets from his holster belt and shoving them into his pistol.

Outside, Hart and Roth had finished reloading and began firing. Bullets sliced through the air, one of them so close to Matt Tyrell's head that he dropped to the floor and placed a hand to the side of his head.

"Are you hit?" Luke Tyrell called out from the broken window and had started toward his cousin.

"No, Luke! Get back!" Matt yelled to stop him, but a rifle shot caught Luke in the shoulder from behind and sent him sprawling on the floor amidst strewn glass and wood splinters. The other gunmen began returning the deputies' fire, Phelps still cutting quick glances at the top of the stairs.

"There's supposed to be nobody up there but Sweet and that damn wounded bartender."

"Well, that was a woman's voice all right," Doc Mason called out beneath the roar of gunfire.

"Damn right it was," Phelps said. Then, trying to dismiss it, he turned and fired three shots out toward the flash of Sullivan Hart's rifle. But his curiosity wouldn't leave him alone. "Hell!" Phelps turned, looked up the staircase again, then looked at Bert Ison sitting a few inches from him. "Boy, get up there, see what's going on." A shot thumped into the window ledge. "Hurry back now."

"What's that weird-acting peckerwood doing here anyway!" Doc Mason said, firing out the broken window as he spoke.

"J. T. Priest left him here for me," Phelps said through a hail of rifle fire. "Called that boy my going-away present."

"Going-away present, huh?" Doc fired the last round from his pistol and dropped down beside Phelps to reload. "Anything J. T. Priest gives away might not be worth having."

"You tend to what you're doing," Phelps said with a snap. "I'll worry about that boy." From the other window, Whitten let out a short yelp, like the sound made by a kicked dog. He stood up with blood streaming down his face and staggered in place.

"Get down, Whitten!" Denver Stanton's warning came too late. Another rifle shot knocked Whitten two steps backward. Before he could right himself, another shot put him in a complete circle, then a third shot dropped him backward and limp on the bottom of the staircase.

"Damn it all!" Matt Tyrell shouted, helping Luke rip his shirt open and stuff a wadded-up bandanna against his gaping shoulder wound. "We've got to get out there and kill them bastards before they cut us to pieces!"

Phelps cut his gaze from Whitten's body at the foot of the stairs to Matt and Luke Tyrell. "Use you head, boys! You go jumping out there into their rifle sights, they won't have to pick you to pieces! You'll be dead before you get five yards. Now stick in here and hold them off!"

The rifles began pounding harder. Cleveland Phelps ducked down beneath the broken window ledge. Hearing Bert Ison's boots hurrying down the stairs, he raised up long enough to get off two rounds beside Doc Mason, then dropped down as Bert Ison dove across the floor and rolled up against him. "All right, boy, what's the deal up there? Was that a woman's voice we heard?"

Bert Ison looked at him with a flat expression and only nodded.

"I thought so," said Phelps. "Sweet must have been hiding himself a little honey here for the winter—no wonder he wanted everybody to leave."

Doc Mason dropped back down to reload. "We could use a hostage or two here. Want me to go up and get her?"

Phelps looked around, seeing the dead and wounded beneath a thick cloud of burnt gun powder. "Naw, you stick right here. I'll go up there."

Phelps waited for a moment until the rifle fire tapered off. "Keep 'em busy, boys," he shouted, springing up into a low crouch and running to the staircase. Halfway up the splinted, bullet-riddled stairs, he stopped short at the sound of Bert Ison right behind him. "No, boy! Stay down there! We need some firepower."

Bert Ison only leered at him. As the rifles started again, Phelps cursed under his breath. "All right then, damn it, come on. Cover my back."

In the bedroom, Sheriff Harris Sweet had stripped to the waist, taking off the winter coat, a vest, and shirt and laying them across the foot of the bed. Sweet had taken off the binding he wore, wrapped it tight around Herman, and pinned it in place. Sweet then put a shirt on Herman's corpse and buttoned it all the way to the collar. Sweet had even taken Herman's mustache from his pocket and pressed it into place above Herman's lip. "There now, Herman," Sweet whispered close to the corpse's deaf ear, "it meant so much to you, nobody will have to know. You look as much a man as any of us."

The sound of boots running along the hall didn't distract Harris Sweet. The old sheriff stood before a full length dressing mirror, studying the half-naked figure staring back through the wavering glass. The flicker of dim lantern light cast a pale unwholesome glow on the hard flat stomach and the aged protruding ribs. Sweet raised a flattered withered breast, then let it down and ran a calloused hand across the indentation left there by years of hiding beneath lengths of tight cloth.

"Lord, Lord . . . Look at you, Harriet," Sweet whispered, still paying no attention to the sound of boots pounding closer to the partly opened door. The wispy thin mustache smiled back wearily, and Sweet reached a hand out to the mirror and touched the cheek in the flat glass as if touching the cold face of a stranger. In the mirror, Sweet saw Herman's drawn still face on the bed behind him.

In the hallway, Cleveland Phelps pressed his back flat against the wall outside the door. Bert Ison stood next to him, his pistol still in his holster until Phelps nodded and whispered, "Get that gun out, boy. Do like Priest told you! Take care of me."

Bert Ison cocked his head with a strange toothless

grin, raised his pistol, and pointed it an inch from Phelps's stomach. Phelps shoved the barrel away. "Watch what you're doing with that, you damn fool!"

At Cleveland Phelps's feet, Scratch appeared out of nowhere, looking up at him with a low hiss. "Git, you hairy son of a bitch!" Phelps kicked the cat ten feet down the hallway. Scratch let out a squall, rolling and finally coming to halt as he slammed against a closed door.

Harris Sweet turned from the mirror at the sound of the cat. "Scratch?" the sheriff said as if snapping out of a trance.

"Sweet, it's me, Phelps! Who's in there with you?"

Harris Sweet looked around the dimly lit room, then at Herman's pale body lying with his hands folded neatly on his chest. Sweet said in a lowered tone, "Nobody here but us womenfolk. Come on in, Phelps."

But Phelps caught the strangeness in Sweet's voice. "No way, Sweet, you come out here. Keep your hands high! Whoever the woman is in there, bring her with you. I might have to use her for a way out of here." Phelps turned to Bert Ison, whispering, "What did you see when you peeped in there a while ago? You said you saw a woman?" But Bert only shrugged and spread the vacant grin of an imbecile.

"Damn it!" Phelps hissed, turning away from Bert. "Next time J. T. Priest gives me a present, I'll think twice before taking it." He leaned his cheek close to the slash of dim light through the partially opened door. "I've got no time to waste on you, Sweet. If I come in there, you ain't going to like what I'll do to you."

"Come on in, Cleveland Phelps," said Harris Sweet, taking a step forward. "My gun's in my holster."

Sweet spoke in a resolved voice, reaching down to loosen the pistol in its holster, keeping a hand poised near it, feet spread shoulder-width apart in a fighting stance. The sheriff's shadow spilled slantwise through the door.

"All right then, you contrary son of a bitch!" Phelps swung the door wide open and sprang into the room, his pistol up and cocked, his thumb across the hammer ready to let it drop. But he was stunned motionless at the sight of Harris Sweet standing there bare to the waist, the wispy gray mustache looking profane somehow in the dim glow of the lamp. "Lord God . . . !" Phelps looked at the sagging withered breasts facing him. "You—! You're—! You're a—"

"A woman, Phelps," Sweet said, finishing his words for him. "The one who's going to nail your hide on the gates of hell."

Phelps's pistol drooped in his hand. He stared, numb and speechless. "What happened to you? You're some kind of . . . deformed freak," he finally whispered in awe.

Sweet chuckled low in irony. "Nothing like being blunt about it, is there, Phelps?" Sweet's poised hand drew nearer to the holstered pistol. "Let's get this done."

"Wait now! Damn it! Hold everything!" Phelps raised his free hand toward Sweet as if to stop things. Bert Ison slipped inside the room and stood at Phelps's shoulder. Phelps shook his head slowly, trying to recover. He hissed over his shoulder at Bert, "Get the hell back, boy! I can't stand being crowded this way!"

"I'll count to three," said Harris Sweet. "One."

Phelps swallowed hard, settling his mind to what stood before him. What he'd wanted was a hostage—

not this, he thought, whatever *this* was. Downstairs, the firing continued relentlessly.

Phelps felt that he needed to say something, ask something, but there was no time for it. No time for anything now, except to raise his pistol and fire.

"Two," said Sweet, the sheriff's stance growing more poised, more deliberate.

Beads of sweat glistened on Cleveland Phelps's brow. "To hell with you then!" His hand snapped up, level to Sweet's chest, his thumb already releasing the hammer. As his shot went off, Sweet's pistol came up in a glint of iron, the blast of it sounding as one with Phelps's shot—two gunfighters in a fatal waltz, whatever trails past having led them both to this spot in time, to this finality of circumstance.

"Jesus," Cleveland Phelps grunted, feeling his back slam into the wall with no clear idea of how he got there. He slumped down halfway to the floor, his gun nearly slipping from his hand. The warmth spilling from his chest spread down his belly. He sensed that the middle of his back was missing and that, had it not been for the flowered wallpaper clinging wet against him, his spine would spill like broken chalk onto the wooden floor.

"Get it up," Harriet Sweet rasped, nodding at Cleveland Phelps's pistol, her left hand clasping the gout of blood between her withered breasts. She staggered forward as if to give Phelps a better target. "Go on, raise it . . . we're not finished yet." Sweet leveled her pistol out and down, only inches from Phelps's forehead.

Phelps shook his head. "No, that's enough," he said in a strained whisper. His eyes went to Bert Ison, signaling for help. Sweet caught the gesture and swung his pistol at the boy, standing unsteady, her deep chest wound taking its toll on her strength.

But with Sweet's pistol on him, Bert cocked his head slightly, raised his own gun slowly and lowered it into his holster. He squatted down beside Cleveland Phelps and drew a long knife from his bootwell. "What's . . that for?" Phelps asked, his eyes leaving Sweet and fixing on the gleaming blade in Bert Ison's hand. "You're . . . supposed to take care of me."

Downstairs the gunfire slackened. Along the broken windowledge, the gunmen looked up the stairs. "Was that a gun up there?" Doc Mason asked. But with no response, the others turned back toward the flashes of rifle fire coming from the swirling snow.

In the smoke-filled bedroom, Sweet rocked unsteadily on her feet, her hand still pressing the oozing chest wound. She looked down at Bert Ison for a moment. Seeing nothing to fear in the boy, Sweet turned, stumbled to the bed, picked up a heavy coat and wrestled herself into it. She picked up one of the shotguns at the foot of the bed, then struggled with Herman's corpse until she managed to get a dead arm looped across the barkeep's shoulder.

"Boy, what's wrong with you?" Phelps said to Bert Ison, unmindful of Harris Sweet staggering past them and out into the hall, with Herman's corpse drooping across one shoulder, a shotgun hanging in her free hand. "You can't . . . do me no good with that knife. The bullet . . . went plumb through me." He looked at Bert Ison and tried to shy back from him as the boy came closer, taking the pistol from Phelps's weak hand and pitching it across the wooden floor. "Damn it, boy . . . what are you fixing to do? Answer me . . . you damn lunatic."

Chapter 24

Sullivan Hart left his position and slid beside Two-jack Roth. "How are you on ammunition?" he asked panting, steam billowing around his ice-streaked face. At the broken hotel windows, Doc Mason reloaded as Stanton and Matt Tyrell fired.

Twojack Roth rose slightly and tipped his hat brim up. "I'm down to about thirty rounds. How about you?"

"Fourteen," said Hart. He took off his left glove and blew breath on his stiff hand. "We're going to have to rush them. That's all there is to it."

Twojack looked over at Luther Ison and Tom Bays Junior, the two of them huddled against the wall, almost hidden by a mantle of snow across their shoulders. The horses stood near them with their heads lowered, snow covering their saddles. "You're right," Roth replied, "but we're going to get shot all to pieces doing it."

"I make it to be only three left in there. They could be running low of bullets themselves." Hart squinted through the snow, barely seeing anything save for the occasional flash of pistol fire. "I don't think we've got much choice. We won't last another hour out here."

Roth nodded toward the two prisoners. "What

about them? I haven't seen them move around for a while. Haven't heard a peep out of them."

"I'll check on them." Hart slipped his glove back on his hand and rubbed his hands together. "Get ready."

Twojack Roth loaded his rifle as Sullivan Hart hurried in a crouch over to Tom Bays and Luther Ison. "Bays? Luther? You boys all right?"

"I am," Luther Ison said, his voice shaking uncontrollably in the cold. "This poor bastard's froze to death—has been for the past few minutes."

Hart winced. "Why didn't you say something?"

"Say what? He'd of been no less dead if I'd hollered to high heaven."

Hart forced Tom Bays's face up from his chest. Bays's eyes were partly open and glazed with ice, one corner of his coat collar stuck tight to his stiff blue lips. "Shouldn't you have done something?"

"Done what?" Luther said, shivering badly. "He went to sleep. I couldn't stop him . . . he ain't my charge anyway. You going to get me somewhere warm, or do you plan on freezing me, too?"

"We're making a move right now. Just sit tight." Hart started to turn and leave.

"Wait, damn it! What about me? You can't leave me here handcuffed! What if you don't come back?"

Hart thought it over for a second. "Come on, get up. Let's go. We're taking you with us."

"Like hell!" Luther struggled against him as Hart raised him to his feet. "I ain't going in there! You've got no right making me." He stepped up and down in place. "Besides, I can't feel nothing in my toes." He turned his back to Hart and wiggled his hands. "Are my fingers moving?"

"Yes, they're moving," said Hart. "Any feeling in them?"

"Very damn little, if any." Luther turned back facing him. "At least take these cuffs off me."

Hart hesitated a second, then reached into his coat pocket for the key. "I'm going to take the cuffs off, but you better not try something stupid, Luther."

"I understand. I'll lose all my fingers, my hand too, if I don't get to circulating them some. I won't try anything, you've got my word on it."

"If you do, we'll kill you," Hart said. "You've got *our* word on that."

The firing ceased momentarily as Hart and Luther Ison moved through the snow and dropped down beside Twojack Roth.

"What's he doing loose?" Roth turned his rifle barrel toward Luther Ison. The old outlaw shied back from him.

"I had to uncuff him," Hart replied. "He's about frozen. Tom Bays is already dead."

Roth looked Luther up and down, then turned back to Hart. "I'm ready when you are."

Hart checked his rifle and looked up toward the silent hotel through the white snowy shroud. "Let's get it done while they've stopped firing."

Roth rose up stiffly from the cold ground and started forward, Hart three feet to his side, moving as quiet as possible. But before they'd gone five yards, Luther Ison came boring past them in a wake of snow, shouting toward the broken windows, "Bert! They're coming, boy! Kill these lawdog sons of bitches!"

Before either deputy could put a bullet in Luther Ison, three shots rang out from the hotel, two of them lifting Luther off of his feet and pounding him backward. Sullivan Hart and Twojack Roth dove to either side beneath more pistol shots. "We can't stop now!" Hart called out, rolling in the snow, coming back up to his feet and firing, his rifle and hands coated with thick white snow. Together they charged forward, bullets whining past them.

Inside the hotel lobby, Luke Tyrell lay wounded on the floor, his back propped against the splintered counter. He looked up the staircase just in time to see Sweet standing there, her coat open down the front, blood still spewing down her chest. "What the hell is this?" Luke Tyrell tried to raise his pistol toward the top of the stairs, but one barrel of Sweet's shotgun exploded down into his face.

The three gunmen turned from the windows at the sound of the blast. The second barrel of Sweet's shotgun flashed in a streak of fire, the spreading buckshot hitting Stanton full in the chest and slapping into Matt Tyrell's face like a handful of fiery hornets. Stanton's gun bucked twice in his hand as the shotgun blast drove him back through the broken window. The first shot hit Harris Sweet low in the stomach, causing her to lose hold of Herman's corpse. The second bullet grazed Sweet's head as Herman tumbled forward down the stairs.

Twojack Roth had just scampered up onto the boardwalk, his rifle firing. But he ducked to one side as Stanton crashed through the window and fell face first at his feet. Blinded by the buckshot, Matt Tyrell turned screaming, firing wildly until a shot from Sullivan Hart's rifle silenced him, jackknifing him forward, face down on the floor.

The deputies stood in the ringing silence on the boardwalk, drifts of burnt gunpowder wafting around them. Twojack Roth looked himself up and down in disbelief—no sign of a wound on him. Hart did the same. Both of them stood a moment longer, hearing only a low groan from Stanton. Hart aimed his rifle down at Stanton, but instead of firing, he waited, watching the outlaw's hand stretch toward the pistol butt only an inch from his fingertips. When Stanton's hand closed around the pistol, a quick shot rang out from just inside the broken windowframe and nailed Stanton's head down against the boardwalk.

In reflex, Hart and Roth swung their rifles at the pale bleeding figure leaning almost lifeless out the window toward them. Sweet's eyes were trying hard to focus, but not doing a good job of it. Her bloody head swung from one deputy to the other, a string of blood stretching long from her chin. "Come in . . . fellows . . . we been . . . expecting yas."

Hart lowered his rifle, reaching out quickly to catch her slumping body.

"I'm a . . . lawman myself . . . you know?" She collapsed into Sullivan Hart's arms. Hart and Roth only stared at one another, then Roth cut a glance inside the broken window. "Take care of her. I'll see what's left in there." He raised a boot and stepped cautiously over the bullet-riddled windowledge. Hart waited until Roth had looked all around the lobby and shuffled through shards of broken glass to the stairwell. As Roth ascended the stairs with his rifle poised and cocked, Hart lifted Sweet over the ledge, carrying him to the glowing belly of the woodstove and laid her down on the floor in front of it.

"You hang on," Hart said, stripping off his cold gloves and rubbing his hands together in the stove's heat. Sweet had regained a drifting consciousness, and when Hart turned back, the old sheriff had reached a trembling hand to the front of her coat, trying to draw it closed across the wounds in her chest and lower belly. "Here, let's take a look." Hart moved Sweet's hand away and opened the coat wide. He froze dumbstruck at the sight, looking back and forth between her blood-caked breasts and the tin star glinting on her coat. "Are you . . . Sheriff Sweet?"

A weak rasping laugh came from Sweet's throat. "It's me all right . . . no hiding now." Sweet's hand moved in a show of modesty, trying to cover herself up.

Sullivan Hart batted his eyes in order to get himself moving again. He reached up and untied the bandanna from around his neck, pulled it loose and shook it out. "I understand, Sheriff. It's not important right now. Let's get the bleeding stopped." He ripped the bandanna in half, gently laid Sweet's hand aside and pressed part of the bandanna against her gaping wounds.

As he pressed the bandanna, the big cat appeared at his forearm and reached its probing nose into Sweet's face. Hart started to shove the cat back out of the way, but Scratch would have none of it. Its back arched high as the cat swiped a paw full of claws past the palm of Hart's hand. "Leave him be . . . deputy," Sweet said in a strained voice. "He's . . . been mine and Herman's for . . . a long time now. Nobody else . . . would have put up with him."

"Lie quiet, Sheriff Sweet," said Sullivan Hart, "I believe we can pull you through this."

"Don't . . . kid me, Deputy. I know a killing wound when I see one." Scratch licked Sweet's pale face and stood watching curiously with his one good eye.

Hart heard footsteps coming slowly down the stairs and looked at Twojack Roth's blank distant expression. "What's the matter, Roth?" he asked, keeping one hand against half of the torn bandanna on Harris Sweet's chest wound and the other half pressed to her stomach.

"Nothing," Roth said flatly. "They're all dead. You

don't want to go up there." He nodded back toward the top of the stairway.

"Why? What do you mean?" Hart studied his dark eyes. "What's up there?"

"Just take my word, you don't want to go up there." Roth stepped down beside Hart as Harris Sweet drifted out of consciousness. He looked down at Sweet's bare chest and appeared startled. "What in the world?" he whispered.

"I know," said Hart in a whisper, "It struck me the same way at first."

Roth looked around at the blood and bodies lying stretched out on the floor, at the top of Herman's bald head, Herman's dead eyes staring up at the ceiling. He whispered close to Sullivan Hart's ear, "That's the woman I saw in the bed upstairs. What sort of place is this?"

Sweet heard Roth and turned his drowsy eyes to him. "That's my sister, Deputy . . . it's a long story."

"I bet it is, Sheriff," Roth said. He reached out a gloved hand and patted Harris Sweet's slumped shoulder. "Take it easy. Thanks to you, we're both alive to hear it, soon as you're able to tell us."

Hart spoke as they lifted Sheriff Sweet and carried her to an overturned sofa. "Any sign of J. T. Priest anywhere up there?"

"No," said Roth. He reached out with one hand, righted the sofa and brushed splinters and glass from the seat. "J. T. Priest was on the engine when it took off. So were Sims and Kate McCorkle."

Hart glanced up the stairs. "Then who's up there?"

"Just Cleveland Phelps, as best I can tell—or I should say what's left of him."

"What do you mean?" Hart stared at him as they laid Sweet down on the sofa.

"I mean . . he looks like something a mountain lion got a hold of."

They both turned and looked at Scratch, the big cat sitting a few feet away licking its paws. "You don't mean . . . ?"

Twojack actually considered it for a second, then shook his head. "Naw, no way. This was a larger animal—had to be. Whatever it was, it must've liked what it was doing. Cleveland Phelps looked pretty bad."

"And there's nobody else up there?" Hart caught himself looking upward along the top of the stairs.

"Not that I saw," Roth replied. He looked down at Harris Sweet on the sofa. "I'll go find a pot to boil some water in, and some cloth clean enough for bandages." He moved away, casting a sidelong glance up the empty stairwell. "Watch yourself here," he added over his shoulder in a lowered voice.

It was gray daylight before Harris Sweet's bleeding was staunched. The snow had fallen throughout the night, growing thicker as the wind lessened until by morning, the bodies of Luther Ison in the street and Tom Bays Junior leaning against the frame wall were only smooth rises on the rolling white terrain. While Sullivan Hart kept a fire glowing in the woodstove and tended to the wounded sheriff, Twojack Roth had scraped through the snow at the site of the flattened mercantile store and brought back heavy canvas tarpaulins large enough to cover the broken windows and help keep the cold out.

"I must still be alive," Sweet said in a weak voice, stirring at the sound of Hart closing the iron door on the woodstove.

"Yep, and you're going to stay that way, Sheriff." Sullivan Hart lifted the coffeepot from the stove, poured a steaming cup and set the pot down. From the rear of the hotel a horse nickered, causing Sweet to turn her head toward the sound. Hart smiled, stepping over to her with the cup of coffee. "My partner brought the horses inside . . . there's not much left standing here in the way of shelter." He bent down beside the sofa and held the coffee out to Sweet's lips. "Here, see if this will warm you up some."

Sweet sipped the coffee, then settled back onto the sofa. "If I make it, I'll be down all winter."

"We'll stay as long as we can, Sheriff. There's a lot that needs to be done here." Hart held the cup out for him again, but Sweet turned it down. She glanced at the row of bodies lying at the foot of the staircase where Hart and Roth had dragged them and covered them with sheets from the linen closet.

"Is—is Herman over there with them?" Sweet asked.

"No, Sheriff. We took Herman into the other room. Figured you'd want it that way."

"Thanks . . ." Harris Sweet fell silent for a moment with her eyes closed. At length, she opened her eyes again and said in a weak voice, "You men need to get on. You don't have time to fool with me all winter."

"We've just about put *Los Pistoleros* out of business," Hart replied. "We'll get J. T. Priest and the rest once the weather breaks."

"But Priest . . . is the head of the snake," Sweet said, her strength flagging. "As long as he's running loose, the chase is still on. I know . . . how that goes."

"He killed my father, so I've got a personal stake in bringing him down." Hart sipped the steaming coffee. "But we've got time to get you back on your feet. You probably saved our lives, doing what you did at the same time as we rushed these men."

"I had . . . no idea what you two were doing right then. That was just lucky timing."

"Well," Hart smiled, "as Quick Charlie Sims would say, timing is everything."

"Sims, that rascal . . ." Harriet Sweet closed her eyes, seeming to reflect on something. "I hope he makes it . . . him and that young woman."

"If I know Sims and Kate, they will find some way to do just that." Hart sipped the coffee and studied Sweet's pale face. "Get some rest, Sheriff. That's enough talking for now."

"I'll get plenty of rest," Harris Sweet said without looking at Hart. "You boys have to get on . . . I know you want to stay on their trail."

A silence passed as Sullivan Hart sipped the coffee and studied Sweet's drawn face. When he spoke to Sweet again his voice was barely above a whisper. "You'll have to decide, Sheriff. We won't force it on you."

"Thanks, Deputy . . ." Sweet let out a labored breath. "Healing's long and painful . . . sometimes it's not worth the end result."

Chapter 25

At midmorning the snow had stopped. A ray of sunlight had broken through the looming gray sky and streaked through the kitchen window at the back of the hotel. Here the horses stood near an open cupboard full of airtight bags of dry-food supplies. They tested the edges of counters and cabinets with their wet muzzles, finding scents of things long past and foreign to them.

"Easy, boys." Twojack Roth pushed the horses aside with his palm as he prepared broth made from jerked elk on the kitchen stove. The horses milled in place and studied their strange surroundings like visitors from another world, here not by their own choosing but rather by unquestioned circumstance. Snow lay scalloped high up the windowpanes.

Roth poured the broth into a large bowl and stepped up from the stone kitchen floor into the wooden hallway toward the front lobby. Sullivan Hart met him halfway and stopped him. "Sweet's dead, Twojack," Hart said quietly. Without a word, Roth turned and walked back to the kitchen and set the broth down on a long counter.

"I figured he was going to make it, the way he was feeling this morning." As Roth spoke, he took down another bowl from a cupboard in which he poured half of the broth from the other bowl. He then slid one of the bowls over to Hart.

"Yeah, me too. But Sheriff Sweet didn't want to be here any longer. He—or *she*—as much as said so." Hart cupped his hands around the bowl and lifted it to his lips and sipped. "Must've been a strange life for those two," he added, looking around at the kitchen, the horses and back at the streak of dried blood along the hallway. "I think this one part we'll leave out of our report to Judge Parker, if it's all the same to you."

Roth shrugged and sipped his elk broth. "They lived as men and died as men—what more needs to be said."

"There's some who would say it's not right what they did, not natural to the order of things." Hart set the bowl down and rubbed a finger across his lips. "But I'm no good at judging."

"Me neither." Roth thought about it as he picked up a piece of jerked elk from a plate on the counter, tore off a bite and chewed passively. "I figure the world makes us all what we are, some way. How we take it and go with it is all that matters. Sweet was a hell of lawman at one time, or so I always heard. Think Sims knew about all this?"

"I don't know," said Hart. "I'll never mention it to him. If he brings it up though . . ." He let his words trail.

"Yeah, that's right enough." Roth swallowed his elk jerky and looked out through the window. "It's let up as much as it going to for a while. If we're going to make it down this mountain at all, we best head out pretty soon."

Sullivan Hart gazed out along the hallway toward the bodies beneath the blood-soaked sheets. "Grounds too hard for burying. What do you think?"

"You already know what I think," said Roth. "This town's about gone anyway."

"Yeah, that's what I was thinking, too." Hart sighed. "That blasted Sims . . . how come he's never around for the hard part of this work?"

"What part's ever easy?" Roth asked.

Hart shook his head. "Do you realize we're working with a man we haven't laid eyes on since back in Chicago?"

Roth chuckled. "Ever stop to think maybe he's smarter than we are?"

'Oh yes, more than once." Hart smiled. "But I'd give a hundred dollars to just one time see him get his hands dirty."

"Save your money," said Roth.

"Well," Hart let out another sigh, "I'll go get what kerosene's on hand. Might as well get started."

Roth stepped in close and said near Hart's ear, "Think Luther Ison's boy is still in here somewhere?"

"If he is," Hart whispered in return, "we'll soon find out."

By noon they'd taken on staples for their journey and gathered their horses from the kitchen then left the Ballantine Hotel. Now they stood gazing back at the building from near the flattened depot that was only one more gentle rise of pure white snow in a town of many such rises. They watched flames lick high and fast from the windows and door of the hotel. When the fire had eaten through the timbers supporting the roof and the top of the building sagged down in bellowing flames and black smoke, Twojack Roth turned and stepped up into his saddle. "If Luther's boy was in there, he's turned to charcoal by now."

"Yep." Hart stepped up into his saddle with Scratch nestled in his arm and turned for one last look. "He must've slipped out some way during the shooting. If he did, somebody will find him frozen to the ground come spring." He looked down at the big cat as they turned their horses in the deep snow. "What are we going to do with this thing?"

"Give him to Judge Parker," Twojack Roth said, spurring his horse forward to a more shallow dip along the trail. "His wife loves animals."

"But this thing is wilder than a buck. I'm surprised he's letting me hold him."

"He knows what's going on," Roth said, his horse lunging through the snow. "He'll settle into what comes to him, like everything does."

"Are you getting philosophical on me?" Hart asked, pushing his horse forward, following his partner's tracks.

"Nope, just tired . . . wanting to get out of this cold."

"Ain't we both," Hart said almost to himself. In the crook of his arm, the big cat looked back at the licking flames, reflections of fire dancing in his bright yellow eye. "Our part of this job is done. Let's go home."

The crash of the falling roof had not startled Bert Ison. He sat on the sofa on the dead outstretched legs of Sheriff Harris Sweet and stared blankly up and around at the fiery mass surrounding him. He held his breath, the same way he'd learned to hold his breath all of his life when things roared or crashed or grew too hot around him. He was not hiding from the deputies. In fact, he'd had no idea they might be waiting out there to see if he would flee from the burning building. He liked sitting inside a fire and watching it bluster and rage. He hadn't given a thought to the deputies or to anything else since finishing his gruesome task on Cleveland Phelps. He'd kept the knife in his blood-soaked hand and simply rolled under the bed and lain there, staring at the bottom of the feather mattress and feeling the skin on his wrist and hand draw tight as Phelps's blood dried there.

With the knife still in his hand, he felt the heat and smoke cause his eyes to water, tears drying down his scorching cheeks. He knew it was almost time to go—almost, but not quite, he thought. He timed it in his mind, feeling the heat and forcing himself to stand it. The hair atop his head singed down to his skull. He raised his free hand and patted out the spark from a stray ember. Short pieces of timber fell around him and he ducked slightly to one side. His lungs throbbed in his chest until he knew he was losing consciousness.

As Bert grew weaker, he dropped to the floor, to where he knew he could always find a thin layer of air; and with his lips perched almost against the hot wood, he expelled his breath, drew in a hot lungful of air, then crawled fast like a tortured snake, coming to his feet through a wall of flames and throwing himself through the thickest part of it, letting out a terrible scream.

"Did you hear that?" Roth asked, turning partly around in his saddle, already down around the mountainside and out of sight of the burning hotel.

"I heard something . . . I don't know what," Hart said, stopping his horse and looking around as well. He studied the rising black smoke above the jagged wall of rock. "Maybe we better go back."

"It's up to you," said Roth, "but there's no one alive back there, if that's what you're thinking." He gazed up into the rising smoke a hundred yards behind them, listening for the sound to come again.

After a moment when no sound came except that of the whole building crashing down, Roth added, "If there was anything to it, we'd have heard more by now."

"You're right." Hart turned forward in his saddle, as did Roth and together they heeled their horses along the deep winding trail. "I'm anxious to get back to Fort Smith. Sims said he'd take J. T. Priest into custody. Let's hope he does. With any luck Sims will have Priest hog-tied before they're halfway across the flatlands. If he doesn't, we'll be right back on the trail."

"Wouldn't surprise me if Sims had him in custody already," Roth said, adjusting his coat collar against the cold. "Sims doesn't know it, but he's turning into quite a lawman." He nudged his horse forward. "He's a devil to work with, but you've got to give that devil his due."

In the snow out front of the collapsed hotel, Bert Ison rolled back and forth, sobbing under his breath in pain as he let the cold soothe his burning skin. Steam rose from him as he rolled farther away from the searing heat. At length he lay flat in the snow, and his quiet sobbing turned to silent laughter in his chest. The bloody knife was still in his hand. He pitched himself up onto his knees, rubbed snow on his face, then stood up and started walking, his shirt nearly turned to ashes, the holes burned in his trousers exposing split and blackened skin underneath.

He walked across the deep snow-filled footbridge, feeling the iced contraption sag and groan under his feet. On the other side of the bridge he walked on, cold and shivering, through a make-believe world where all signs of man had been covered beneath the thick white blanket of snow.

When Bert rounded a sharp turn in the trail that led upward toward the mining yards, three old Indians on horseback drew up quickly at the sight of him. Ison would have walked right through these vaporous apparitions had it not been for one of them sidling his horse against him and deliberately knocking him off his feet.

The two other horses drew close around him, the riders looking down bewildered, then looking at one another with curious detachment as Bert's feet still tried to walk although he lay on his side in the clinging snow. "You, Burnt-man," said the tallest of the three, wearing a battered silk top hat of a fashion long outdated. "What are you doing up here?"

When Bert only rose to his knees with the bloody knife in his hand and stared up at them, one of the others jumped his horse a step closer and aimed an old flintlock rifle down at his face.

"What do we care what he's doing up here?" he said to the other two, impatiently. "You see the knife, the blood."

The Indian in the battered silk top hat raised a hand to stop him from pulling the flintlock's trigger. "That doesn't mean he killed Crow Striker. Don't be foolish. Would he be carrying the knife around this long? Would he be out in the cold?"

"No, but this is a sign, Henri Kettle," said the other Indian.

"It's not a sign," replied Kettle, adjusting his top hat. All three of them looked off at the dark boiling rise of smoke. "This poor child did not kill Crow Striker. Can't you see it in his eyes? He could kill no one. We come to take vengeance for Crow Striker. It does him no honor if we kill the wrong man." Henri Kettle nudged his horse down the snow-covered trail and added over his shoulder, "Bring him. He will tell us something."

A second passed as Henri rode slowly forward. When he heard no horses behind him, he stopped and looked back. "Well . . . ?"

The other two were where he'd left them, and seeing Henri Kettle look back, the one with the old flintlock called out, "He does not come. I have poked him and poked him. Still he sits here! I think he has no mind, this one."

Henri Kettle turned his horse with a deep grunt of disgust and heeled it back through the snow. "I think the one with no mind is the one who does the poking," he grumbled to himself. The three had spent the night before in a small cave, their old bones aching from the cold. They had been cross and testy with one another all day. Henri Kettle stopped at the other Indian's side and cursed in French. Then he swung his tired body down off of the blanket and pelt covered saddle and stood looking at Bert Ison, taking little heed of the knife in Bert's hand.

"You are burned from head to toe," Henri said, as if the boy may not have known it. "Were you with the men who hung Crow Striker, up there?" He gestured toward the rising trail up into the mountain.

Bert Ison only leered at him and mimicked his gesture toward the mountain trail.

Henri Kettle turned stiffly to the two Indians still on their horses. "See, I told you, Red Horse. He did not do it."

Red Horse shook his flintlock in protest. "He did not answer you at all! How can you say he did not do it?"

"Because some things I can tell. This boy is no killer. If you had grown wiser over the years as all *good* men do . . . you would see it, too."

"What is that supposed to mean?" Red Horse asked in a huff.

The third Indian watched his aged friends bicker back and forth for a moment. Finally he cut in, saying, "It is too cold to sit here and argue. Ask him to come with us, Henri Kettle. Perhaps he feels better when he is not being poked with a rifle." He shot Red Horse a look of disdain.

"Come with us, Burnt-man," Henri Kettle said. He reached an aged hand out to Bert Ison as if to help him stand. But Bert came to his feet with a low guttural growl, a string of saliva swinging from his blistered lips. He slashed the knife at Henri Kettle's hand, barely missing it. Henri Kettle jerked his hand back and examined it.

"Let me shoot him, Henri Kettle," Red Horse implored of his ancient friend.

"Silence, Red Horse." Henri Kettle reached his hand out again toward Bert Ison, this time slower. "Come with us. You are cold and in much pain. We will find some clothes and a coat for you. We will make a salve for your burns."

Bert Ison still snarled at him, the knife poised for another swipe. But when Henri Kettle neither backed away nor tried moving closer, Bert settled, the growl in his chest soon winding down like the tail end of a passing storm. "See? I won't hurt you, neither will he." He nodded at Red Horse. "He just wants to talk bold to you, to make you think he is not afraid." He turned a stern look to Red Horse. "Isn't that right, Red Horse?"

A brief silence passed, then Red Horse, relenting a bit, said to Bert Ison, "Yes, this is true. Come along with us. I will not hurt you, Burnt-man."

Chapter 26

It had been slow going down the mountain in the service engine for the first few miles as it chugged backward against the heavy snow. But once Merle Jones reached an old siding rail leading back to an abandoned mine, he backed the engine onto it, turned it around and came out forward onto the tracks, the cattle-snatcher serving as a snow blade. The rest of the trip had taken all night through the falling snow, Louisville Ike and Dirk LeMaster having to get out twice in the bitter cold to clear high drifts out of their way. By the time Jones rolled the engine into the depot, his eyes were red-rimmed, his hand shaky and tired on the throttle.

"Well, it's been a rough one, gentlemen," Jones said, rubbing his eyes and stretching his arms out with a yawn.

"There's an extra three hundred dollars in it for you," C. B. Harrington said in a quiet tone, "if you take us on across the flatland."

"You've got to be kidding me!" Jones exclaimed, rubbing his closed eyes. "I wouldn't go another mile for all the money in the—"

His words cut short when he felt the barrel of J. T. Priest's pistol jam into his belly. He looked down at the cocked pistol, then back up into Priest's eyes. "It's illegal, forcing me against my will this way."

"Haven't you been paying attention, railroad man?" Priest spread a dark smile. "I'm on the run from the law now for murder and jailbreak. You think putting a bullet through you is going to make me any difference one way or the other?" Behind Priest, Harrington, Sims, and Kate looked on with flat tired expressions.

Jones swallowed a dry knot in his throat. "Three hundred you said?"

"Make it five," Priest replied. He jiggled the pistol toward the throttle. "Now back this sucker into Harrington's Pullman car, and let's get moving."

Within minutes, Louisville Ike and LeMaster had loaded coal, and Jones had taken on water from the tank inside the service shed. The storm wind had left the depot and service shed ravaged. The railroad workers had all gone three miles north, up the flatland rails to clear a heavy rock slide. An elderly station attendant came forward toward the tracks as Jones backed the engine in and coupled it to the Pullman car. The snow on the flatland was only a few inches deep, but the old attendant wanted no part of it. He stood back behind a three foot pile of snow the workers had cleared from along the depot tracks.

"You can't take that engine out of here, Jones!" the attendant shouted from fifty feet away. "You've been gone too long as it is!"

"Just watch us!" Priest yelled. A shot from J. T. Priest's pistol resounded along the flatland.

Still the attendant persisted, ducking his head and jumping back a step. "You leave that Pullman car where it sits! It was stolen from C. B. Harrington! He's coming for it!"

"I *am* C. B. Harrington, you meddling old fool!" Harrington shouted at him. A second shot cracked from Priest's pistol. This time, not wanting to push

his luck, the attendant scurried away, slipping sideways back to the shelter of a storm-torn work shack.
He peeped through a soot-covered window and
watched until the Pullman car rolled out of sight.
"Can't shoot worth a damn though, can you?" He
shook a balled fist at the line of smoke in the
distance.

The single-car train rolled on for the next two
hours, gray morning breaking in streaks of sunlight,
revealing the aftermath of the high wind that had
roared down from the mountain passes with deadly
force. In some places the wind had swept the land
clean; in other places the snow lay in drifts six feet
high along cut banks and rock cliffs. Dead cattle lay
iced and glistening in sunlight, some of them
wrapped in tangles of barbed wire where they'd tumbled and rolled across barren fields.

Quick Charlie Sims turned his face from the destruction outside the Pullman car window and
looked straight into C. B. Harrington's malevolent
eyes. "Never thought we'd make it down the mountain, did you, Sims?" Harrington swirled bourbon in
a glass and spread an insidious grin. "Whatever plan
you had involved the two deputies catching up to
us, eh?"

As Harrington spoke, Priest grinned, raised his pistol from his holster, took two bullets from his belt
and replaced the two he'd spent shooting at the railyard attendant. He snapped the pistol closed and
shoved it loosely back into his holster.

Sims took note of the bullets going into the gun.
He slumped on the wooden bench, Kate McCorkle
beside him, the two of them facing J. T. Priest and
C. B. Harrington sitting on a plush sofa. LeMaster
stood at the bar on the other side of a card table—
the same table where Sims had made a fool of him

and exposed him and Louisville Ike as card cheats. Ike was in the engine, keeping an eye on Jones.

"If that was my plan, you've got it screwed up tight, Harrington."

Sims let out a whipped sigh, looked down at his bound wrists and tapped the tips of his fingers together. "Suppose there'd be no harm now in cutting us loose, letting us finish this trip in comfort."

"Not a chance in hell, Sims. I'm watching every move you make, every flicker of an eyelid." Priest cut in before Harrington could speak. "I know you too well. First I'll let your hands loose, then you ask for something more . . . pretty soon we're having to deal with you all over again."

"Careful you don't watch me so close that you forget to keep an eye on ole C. B. here," said Sims. "He's the one about to clean your clock. Isn't that right, C. B.?" Sims grinned.

But Harrington ignored Sims. "Come now, J. T.," Harrington chuckled, "I think you give this man too much credit. So far he hasn't showed me much. He got the drop on Radner and me . . . but thinking back on it, I believe that was merely a stroke of luck."

Sims perked up. "Oh, really? Then why not be a sport? Cut us loose. I promise I won't try anything, and neither will she, right, Kate?" He cut Kate a glance.

Kate nodded slowly, her eyes fixed coldly on J. T. Priest. "That's right," she said in a low growl. "Cut us loose, you low dirty son of a bitch . . . see if I don't rip your lousy eyes out of— "

"Kate!" Sims cut her off, nudging her with his elbow.

"My." Harrington tossed back a drink of his bourbon and shook his head. "I was seriously considering it." He bored his gaze at Kate McCorkle. "But that would have been a bad idea." He settled back into the sofa, crossed one knee over the other, and studied Sims and Kate with curiosity as the Pullman car rolled along. Then he looked at J. T. Priest and propped an arm up along the back of the sofa. "J. T., I look at the three of you and can't help but wonder what twist of circumstance ever brought you together."

"Humph," Kate McCorkle grunted in disgust, still staring at Priest. "This worm framed Charlie for bank robbery, then while Charlie was in jail for it—"

"Take it easy, Kate," Sims interrupted. "That's all water under the bridge. Don't give him the satisfaction. It's the only good scheme he ever pulled off in his life."

"Ha!" Priest leaned slightly forward. "Good scheme? Let me tell you both something. I set you both up like tin ducks in a shooting galley." He offered C. B. Harrington a self-satisfied smile, making sure Harrington was listening. "Yeah, I put this fool on the run for a bank me and my boys robbed." Priest thumbed himself on the chest. "And her? When the law held her for questioning about his whereabouts, I stepped in, bailed her out and cleared her name. She followed me around like a lap dog until he skipped jail and showed up again."

Kate sprang forward, but Sims caught her arm with his bound hands and pulled her back. "Kate! For crying out loud!"

"Fascinating," Harrington commented. He paused, then asked Priest, "This life you lived as the gang leader of *Los Pistoleros*. It must have been extremely interesting."

"Oh yes." Priest looked smug, tugging his vest down with a superior air. "I have to admit, nobody ran an operation the way I ran mine."

"He's lying," Sims cut in. "He was never more

than the second-in-command—he was more like a bagman for William Mabrey. He started out pushing stolen cattle for Mabrey. Then he became a hired gun, and did some killing for him. Later, Mabrey kept him on, probably to keep him from starving to death. Mabrey fed him the scraps . . . and kept the big money for himself.''

"Why, you bastard!" Priest's pistol streaked from his holster, cocked and ready to fire. C. B. Harrington jumped up from the sofa, wild-eyed, stunned speechless. He waved a thick hand at LeMaster, hurrying him over. LeMaster bounded around the card table, looking scared, his pistol wavering in his shaky hand.

Sims slid a cool glance around at everyone, then said in a calm voice, "I bet you won't shoot me, Priest. I bet Harrington won't let you . . . will you, Harrington?"

"Everybody calm down," C. B. Harrington said, raising his hands in a cautious show of peace. "J. T., please lower that pistol. We have too much at stake here. Don't let Sims rattle you now. Use your head, man! You're almost home on this deal."

Priest thought about it and took a deep breath, seeing the gun in LeMaster's hand. "All right." He lowered the pistol, uncocked it and slipped it back into his holster.

Harrington settled back onto the sofa. "My goodness. Perhaps we shouldn't engage in any more conversation."

Kate McCorkle had caught a glimpse of the calmness in Sims's eyes when he looked down the barrel of Priest's pistol. He'd been too calm. What was going on here? What was Charlie's angle? she wondered, settling herself down and folding her bound hands on her lap.

"You're right, Harrington," Sims agreed. "Maybe

we better not talk any more. I might slip and tell you something about Mabrey and Priest that would change the whole flavor of this deal you've cooked up."

"Don't even start, Sims, " Priest hissed. "Neither C. B. nor I are buying your bill of goods."

"Oh, I wouldn't be selling this bill of goods," Sims said, lowering his tone. "This is one I'd be giving away." He pointed a finger at Priest and winked.

C. B. Harrington cocked a curious brow. "What's he talking about, J. T.?"

"Who knows? He'll say anything he can think of right about now. He knows I'm going to kill him once this is over . . . her too." He gestured his chin toward Kate McCorkle. She sneered at him. "You see, C. B., Sims tried to imply a moment ago that you're the one I need to watch. Now he's wanting to tell you that I'm up to something." Priest grinned with satisfaction. "He knows he's played out his hand—now he's desperate."

"Yes, of course," Harrington said, settling back again. He raised his whiskey glass toward LeMaster and summoned him back from the bar with the bottle of bourbon. As LeMaster filled Harrington's and Priest's glasses, Harrington smiled and added, "We'll just let him rant if he needs to—it's entertaining, to say the least.

They rode in silence for the next fifteen or twenty minutes. But finally Harrington's curiosity got the better of him. "Let me ask you one more thing, Sims. You had what you wanted . . . you got yourself cleared of the robbery, you got your woman back, and a nice chunk of stock in Midwest Investment. Why didn't you leave well enough alone? Why the vengeance?"

Quick Charlie Sims leaned toward C. B. Harrington, saying, "For the gold, of course . . . the same thing you're really after." Sims then leaned back, letting the words fall where they may, seeing what affect his words would have on them.

"Gold?" Harrington asked.

"'What gold?" Priest murmured.

"Don't play dumb, Harrington," Sims said, ignoring Priest. "The gold, you told me about before I threw you and Radner off the train. The gold Priest hid in the caves over in the badlands years ago."

C. B. Harrington only stared, as if Sims had just spoken in a foreign language. "You're out of your mind! We never talked about any gold. He's lying, J. T.!"

Now Sims turned his gaze to Priest, ignoring Harrington. Kate McCorkle paid close attention but kept her mouth shut, knowing that Charlie was working an angle. "He knows about the gold, Priest, the gold you hid for Mabrey?" Sims poised it as a question to jar Priest's memory. "'The gold in the false bottom of those wagons you stashed after killing the gypsies? Come on, J. T.! Harrington knows about it, you know about it . . . and I know about it! Why else would I be chasing your worthless hide all over the country?"

J. T. Priest turned a puzzled look at Harrington. But Harrington only shrugged saying, "Believe me, I have no idea in the world what he's talking about."

J.T. Priest then turned his lost gaze to Sims, his mouth slightly agape. He studied Sims's eyes.

"The gold, Priest!" Sims slashed at him. "It was Confederate gold being shipped out of the country! The gypsies were only a ruse! They were working for the Confederate States of America! Don't act like you don't know about it!"

Priest only stared, dumbstruck. After a pause, after

Sims studied Priest's blank eyes, Sims said almost in a whisper of astonishment, "My goodness . . . you really *don't* know about it, do you?"

J. T. Priest shook his head slowly, his eyes locked on Sims.

"What gold?" Harrington asked, trying to cut in, Sims and Priest not allowing it. Kate McCorkle breathed a guarded sigh of relief, not knowing quite what Charlie was up to, but liking the way he'd drawn everybody's attention.

Sims spoke low and directly to Priest, knowing Priest had to remember going up into the badlands after Mabrey and some others had done the killing. "The gypsies? You remember the gypsies?" It had been Priest's first big favor for William Mabrey, making sure the weapons were never found. As Sims talked about it now, he felt as is he were unearthing old graves.

Priest only nodded, confounded by this sudden revelation of something so long ago. "What gold?" Harrington demanded again, rising halfway from the crate he was sitting on.

"There were false beds in their wagons, Priest," Sims said directly to J. T. Priest, barely above a whisper. "They had a lot of gold in those wagons. You mean to tell me you had no idea? That you never even searched the wagons?"

J. T. Priest gave no response, still totally stunned at the prospect of having had riches at his fingertips and never knowing it.

"*What gold?*" Harrington's question had turned into a shouting rant. He flailed his big arms in the air, standing now, his pistol butt dangerously close to Kate McCorkle's bound hands.

She could snatch it, she knew she could. But should she risk it? No, it was better to wait and see what Charlie had going here. She bit her lip, holding herself back.

"Jesus," whispered Sims, as astonished now as Priest, it seemed. "I know Mabrey didn't know about it—but I thought for sure you did." Priest just stared as Sims went on. "There was close to four million dollars in gold on those wagons. All the money the Confederate army had. Most of those gypsies were actually Confederate soldiers, guarding the shipment."

"Hold it!" Harrington demanded. "You say gold? Confederate gold? Four million dollars?" He tossed his head back. "Ha! There was never that much gold in the whole—"

"Then why are you after it, Harrington," Sims lashed out at him, cutting him off.

"Don't listen to this man, J. T.," Harrington barked. "You just said yourself he'd try anything, didn't you?"

"Yes, I know . . ." Priest sounded like a man speaking in a trance, his mind working, remembering how heavy those wagons were to move.

Harrington pointed a thick finger at Sims. "Listen to me, Sims. It's obvious what you're doing! I won't have it. Open your mouth again, I'll have LeMaster put a bullet in it. You're not going to ruin what I've got going here . . . For J. T. and myself." He reached a comforting hand down and squeezed Priest's shoulder.

Sims leaned back and let out a breath. "All right, forget it, Priest. He's right . . . it was only a scheme I came up with at the last minute." He turned to Harrington. "I've got to use the jake. Can LeMaster take me?"

"Me too," Kate McCorkle chimed in, "really bad."

"Damn it." Harrington calmed himself, breathing deep through his wide nose. "LeMaster, take them both." He gestured a hand toward a small door near the back of the car. "Take her there . . . walk him out back on the platform. Watch him close." He turned to Kate McCorkle. "Young lady, if you stick your head out that door before LeMaster comes back for you, I'll have J. T. Priest shoot you. Are we clear on this?"

Kate only nodded, she and Sims rising at the same time, LeMaster keeping a safe step back from them with his hand on his pistol butt. Harrington stood watching them until Kate McCorkle stepped inside the small door, and LeMaster shoved Sims forward, and out onto the rear platform. "Now then." Harrington smoothed down his vest and looked down at Priest. "What is all this about gold, sir—and need I remind you we're about to become partners in a tremendous business undertaking?"

"I—I don't know," Priest shrugged. "There was a time, up on the badlands—some gypsies Mabrey and his boys killed. That much is true. I went back later on and took their bodies, wagons and all, into a cave. But this other thing about Confederate gold? I have no idea what he's talking about." He shook his head in confusion.

"If it's about a missing shipment of gold from Atlanta, I know a lot about it," said C. B. Harrington. "I had investments in the South. I lost a ton of money in that blasted war! There was talk about a large shipment of gold being smuggled out of the country for safekeeping. It was never heard of again. Some say it may have cost the South the war. If you know anything about it, I suggest you tell me, sir—no, I *demand* you tell me, if you expect us to go through with our deal as planned."

J. T. Priest looked at him, bewildered. "He said you were after the gold all along. Is that true?"

"No," said Harrington, "he's lying through his

teeth. But apparently there's some truth to what he's talking about. Why else would he be chasing you all over the land? Like I said earlier, he's already got what he set after—he's free, and you're running from the law. If you know where there's four million dollars in gold hidden out there, we need to go see about it, don't you think . . . *partner*?"

J. T. Priest studied Harrington's eyes, still a bit confused, needing time to work this new development out in his mind. "This could all be a trick of some sort. I don't trust anything Quick Charlie says."

"What possible trick could there be to this? He knows he's a dead man once we settle this deal."

"I don't know . . . but I don't trust it, not as long as Sims is alive. There's no way I'd head out for the badlands with him around."

On the rear deck, Sims straightened his trousers and turned to LeMaster in the cold wind. "How've you been, Dirk?" Sims grinned.

"I've been better," LeMaster said. "Think I'm catching a head cold, this damned weather."

"It's been a rough one, that's for sure," said Sims, stepping ahead of him to the rear door. "Think we'll ever have another card game like that one on the train, you, Ike and me?" Sims tossed his words back over his shoulder, stepping through the door.

"I hope not. I hate being looked at that way by everybody."

"Well," Sims chuckled, moving forward, "maybe next time we'll—" His words stopped short at the sight of C. B. Harrington reaching down and snatching Priest's pistol from his holster. "Oh no!" Sims said, stopping in his tracks.

"What the—?" J. T. Priest saw his pistol streak up in Harrington's hand.

"You're so worried about this swindler, I'll settle

your mind, Priest!" Harrington cocked the pistol and aimed it. Priest only stared in surprise.

"No, wait!" Sims yelled, but it was too late. The first shot went wide of him by two feet, Sims and LeMaster both ducking to one side. The second shot went wide as well, slicing across the small door just as Kate McCorkle started to step out. The force of the shot threw the door closed, launching Kate backwards and to the floor. If there was ever a time for her to draw the derringer from under her skirt, it was now. She hurried, her bound hands fumbling upward for the small pistol.

Outside the small door, Sims and LeMaster were still scrambling away from the second shot when Sims saw Kate McCorkle swing the door open and jump forward with the derringer in her hand. "No, Kate, get back!" Sims yelled, moving toward her, his chest exposed toward the third shot as it exploded from the pistol in C. B. Harrington's thick hand.

Kate was behind Sims now. He'd jumped in front of her, perhaps to shield her, she thought fleetingly. And as the third shot exploded loudly in the closed engine, she saw Sims falter backward a step. Then the fourth shot exploded, and he bucked backward again. "God, noooo!" Kate screamed, but her voice was eclipsed by the fifth shot as Sims spun around with the impact of it, facing her on his way to the floor where he fell flat and limp at her feet. Kate's scream was torn from deep in her bosom. Yet even as she flung herself to Sims as if to cover him, the derringer came up cocked and aimed and the small bullet stung C. B. Harrington's face like a mad hornet before LeMaster could jump forward and wrench the gun from her hand.

Chapter 27

Within seconds, Louisville Ike ran in from the engine, a pistol in his hand. "God almighty," he whispered, looking down at Sims on the floor. He stooped down, ran a hand beneath Sim's chest and held it there for a second, ignoring Kate McCorkle's screams. When he stood up, he raised his bloody hand and looked at it. *"Charlie Sims is dead . . ."*

"Don't just stand there, help me!" LeMaster shouted, trying to hold Kate around the waist. She screamed and clawed at him with her bound hands. Louisville Ike jumped forward and helped hold her back.

"Damn it, C. B.," J. T. Priest chuckled, staring at the bloody scene before them, "I didn't think you had it in you."

Beside Priest the pistol cocked again in Harrington's thick hand. He turned his eyes to it, hesitantly. "You have no idea what lengths I'll go to at the sniff of gold, sir," Harrington rasped. "You wanted him dead? There he is. I have one shot left here. Are we going to talk about that gold or not?" Harrington stood with a white handkerchief pressed to his grazed cheek, dark blood already soaking through it.

"Easy, C. B., Jesus!" Priest looked concerned by the sudden crazed look in Harrington's eyes. "Sure, we can go get the gold. We can go right now! But how will we settle our deal with Sims dead?"

"That's something we'll take care of when the time comes. If there's gold, I want it. You better want it, too!"

"No problem at all," said Priest, cutting a glance at Kate McCorkle struggling with Louisville Ike and LeMaster. He saw her settle down a little as Louisville Ike pressed his face against her cheek.

"Tell her she's dead, too, if she keeps fighting us," LeMaster said to Ike, cutting a glance at Priest and Harrington. "Ain't that right, C. B.?"

"Tell her what you want. I don't care what you do to that foul-tempered wench." Harrington pressed the handkerchief tighter to his wound. He turned back to Priest. "Where is it?"

It took Priest a second to respond. "Huh?"

"The gold damn it! Where's the cave? Don't fool with me, Priest! I just killed a man because you said you didn't trust having him along." He shoved Priest down onto the sofa with the pistol barrel. "Now start talking!" He held the pistol close to Priest's forehead.

"Okay, okay! It's not easy to explain." Priest seemed to be stalling. Harrington pitched the bloody handkerchief down onto the sofa, took a pencil and writing pad from inside his coat and dropped them in Priest's lap. "There, draw it out! Surely you can do that, can't you?"

Priest took the pencil and pad and started drawing a map. Then he stopped and looked up at Harrington. "Where did you say you ran into Steelhead Radner?"

"I didn't say. What of it?"

"Nothing." Priest started drawing again. "You took a big chance, hoping he'd bring you to us—and an even bigger chance coming on your own after losing him on the way." Priest chuckled under his breath, drawing as he spoke. "I'm starting to think you're not C. B. Harrington the businessman at all."

"Are you, now?" Harrington studied the crude map as Priest drew.

"That's right," said Priest without looking up from his map work. "I'm thinking you're C. B. Harrington, a cutthroat outlaw, no different than me, Cleveland Phelps or the others."

C. B. Harrington let out a short breath, keeping the pistol leveled on Priest as he finished the drawing and held the pad up for him to see. "Too bad we're doing away with the criminal part of this business. You and I could do well for ourselves."

"I don't think so," said Harrington, snatching the pad from Priest's hand and studying it. "So this is where we're going, eh? This is where the wagons are hidden?"

"That's the place." Priest leaned back into the sofa. "We can be there in a day."

"You're certain this is the spot?" Harrington asked.

"I know it like the back of my hand. If there's gold in those wagons, we'll be running our fingers through it this time tomorrow."

"LeMaster, come here," Harrington said, motioning him over from where he stood holding Kate McCorkle. LeMaster passed Kate to Louisville Ike, Kate looking much calmer now. "You're familiar with that country. Think this is the right place?" He held the map out for LeMaster to scrutinize.

"Hell yes, it's the right place," Priest interjected. "Why would I lie about it now—we're on our way there, ain't we?"

"Yep, I just want to make sure," said Harrington.

LeMaster looked up from the pad. "I'm familiar with those buttes there," he said, pointing a finger.

"This map looks real enough. I can't say beyond that."

"Of course it's real!" Priest started to rise. Harrington shoved him back down with the pistol barrel.

"What do you think, Ike?" Harrington called out over to Louisville Ike.

"I have no idea," Ike shrugged. "But I can't see why he'd lie about it now." Ike turned Kate McCorkle loose, reached out with his boot and nudged the body of Quick Charlie Sims. "Why don't we ask ole Charlie here? What do you think, Quick Charlie . . . this is your show, after all."

Priest chuckled at Louisville Ike's little joke. But then his expression changed. "Oh no," he murmured breathlessly. His jaw went slack, his mouth hung open. He watched Sims's body come back to life as Sims rose stiffly from the floor, the rawhide binding dangling from his freed wrists. J. T. Priest shook his head slowly as the realization sank in. "Damn you, Sims," he whispered to himself.

Sims dusted his hands together. "That's it, fellows. He's telling the truth." Sims grinned, reached a hand out and braced himself as Kate McCorkle flung herself into his arms. "J. T. never could hold out in the long game, once things start happening fast," Sims added, his dark eyes flashing, looking past Kate McCorkle's shoulder at J. T. Priest.

"*Aiiii!*" J. T. Priest's face swelled purple-red until he shot forward screaming, his trembling hands outstretched toward Sims's throat. "I'll kill you, Sims!" he shrieked like a lunatic. But Sims sidestepped and allowed Priest to dart past him, straight into the waiting arms of Louisville Ike and LeMaster. They dragged Priest away as he screamed, sobbed, and babbled mindlessly.

"Gets quite emotional too, doesn't he?" Sims grinned.

In the small village where the drifts of snow rose high up the sides of the tepees and ragged old army tents, and where across the frozen land the only sound to break the crystalline silence was the barking of a dog at play, old Henri Kettle stood up from the warmth of the glowing fire and stepped over to the fly of the tent. He raised the fly far enough to look out and see Bert Ison shaking a stick above his head. Then Bert tossed the stick a few yards across the snowy ground. A big yellow cur had jumped up and down for the stick as Bert waved it. Now the dog loped, bouncing high in snow to its belly to fetch the stick and start the game all over again.

"I think Burnt-man will talk someday," Henri Kettle said, dropping the flap of the fly and walking back to his pile of rabbit pelts and elk skins near the fire. "We may never know what has passed before his eyes and caused his tongue to go silent." He sat down, shrugged, gathered the blanket across his bony shoulders, and added, "Is it important that we should know?"

The two other old Indians looked at one another, then Red Horse turned to Henri Kettle. "No . . . if you take him in, he is your son. I will ask no more about him. It is enough to know that he did not kill our brother, Crow Striker." Red Horse nodded, staring into the low flames. They were back now in a high rock valley above the mines. Their bellies were full, their old bones were warm and, their voices were less testy with one another. What more was there? Henri Kettle thought. He looked at his two friends and almost smiled.

Red Horse said without raising his eyes from the

fire, "I marvel at how Burnt-man shows no pain. Already he is out in the cold, as if nothing happened to him."

"He shows pain," said Henri Kettle. "We do not see it because we not yet know where to look." He raised a bent ancient finger for emphasis. "All men show pain . . . yet the greater the pain, the less men show it."

Red Horse closed his eyes, saying, "So, we know a man is in great pain only when we see no sign of it at all?"

Henri Kettle thought about it. "Yes . . . I think that is so. I think Burnt-man has been in such pain that he has forgotten to feel it . . . he does not know what it is."

"You don't know this," said Red Horse, opening his eyes, lifting them to Henri Kettle.

"Oh yes, I know this."

"No, you cannot know this. You have not known Burnt-man long enough to—"

"I do know this." Henri Kettle cut him short.

"No, you don't."

"Yes, I do."

On the other side of Red Horse, the other old Indian sighed and whispered under his breath, "Here we go . . ."

Outside, Bert Ison bent down in the snow and slipped the knife from his belt. He held the knife behind him, hiding it from the yellow cur as it ran up to him and dropped the stick in the snow at his feet. *Good boy . . . good boy.* He could hear his words in his head, but could not form them aloud. *Nice dog . . .* Bert Ison reached his free arm out and looped it around the dog and pulled it against his chest, feeling the outer cold of the animal's fur, and yet feeling a warmth beneath that reminded him of

something from a long time ago. His free hand encir-
cled the dog's neck and felt the beating pulse there,
the fast blood racing beneath his fingertips.

Behind his back, Bert's hand tightened around the
handle of the knife, and his eyes went flat and empty
for a moment. The dog panted and rubbed against
him, its breath swirling away in long cottony steam;
and as if seeing something in Bert's hollow eyes, the
yellow cur threw open its wet muzzle to the tender
flesh on Bert's jaw where the raging fire had left its
mark, gently licking him there as if knowing of
Bert's pain.

Bert's hand loosened on the knife handle and let
it drop to the ground. With both arms around the
yellow cur, the dog warm against him, its tongue
soothing, Bert Ison struggled deep inside his chest
and his mind until at length he turned his face from
the animal and managed to say with more effort than
most men ever would think it worth, "Goood booooy."
Then he turned his tired eyes out across the quiet
frozen land and told himself that he had no idea how
he'd gotten here . . . or where he'd been those long
times before.

As the train rolled on across the blizzard-swept
plains toward the badlands, Kate McCorkle looked
around at the smiling faces of Dirk LeMaster, Louisville Ike Woodson, and the man she had known as
C. B. Harrington. "You mean—this has all been one
big stage show?"

"I'm afraid so, Kate. I told you J. T. Priest would
never tell me the location of those wagons. This was
the only way I knew to get it out of him—the only
way to clean up Midwest Investment and put an end
to *Los Pistoleros.*" Quick Charlie Sims walked over
and sat down in a chair, Kate standing beside him,

still a bit shaken by everything that had happened. "Kate," Sims said, "it gives me great pleasure to introduce you to Uncle Stanley Czech." Sims gestured a hand toward the man who had been impersonating C. B. Harrington.

Kate blinked a few times, already seeing a difference in the gruff strong-handed manner of the man she'd known as C. B. Harrington. Now that this man Charlie introduced her to was out of character, there was a friendly, almost jovial aura about him. Uncle Stanley rose halfway from his seat with the handkerchief pressed to his bleeding cheek. "A pleasure indeed, young lady." He touched a polite kiss to the back of her extended hand, then sat down. "Please don't take anything I said personally—I really get caught up in any role I play."

"Oh, my no!" said Kate. "Here let me take a look at that wound, you poor dear. I feel just awful, doing that to you!"

Quick Charlie Sims relaxed and shook his tired head, watching Kate busy herself with Uncle Stanley's face wound.

The train rolled on.

Kate McCorkle could not apologize enough for having shot Uncle Stanley in the face. She attended the deep graze along his cheek and bandaged it for him, Uncle Stanley explaining to her all the while that he realized how these things could happen in a game this intense. "Charlie told me you had a temper and could be hard to handle sometimes," Uncle Stanley told her, still sipping bourbon from the same glass he'd used earlier, his gestures and manners the same as when he was C. B. Harrington. "Perhaps we should have let you in on things," Uncle Stanley added, "but Charlie insisted we play things out as naturally as possible. I'm glad you're not angry."

Kate turned to Quick Charlie Sims with a hand on her hip. "Well, I should be, you scaring me like that—I really thought you were dead when Ike raised his bloody hand from under your chest."

"Theatrical makeup," Louisville Ike said. "Dirk and I always carry some in our pocket, especially when we work with these two," he gestured toward Sims and Uncle Stanley. He smiled. "You never know when you're going to need to 'die' real quick."

From his spot on the floor at the bar with his hands cuffed around a foot rail, J. T. Priest lay grumbling under his breath. Kate looked at each of the three men in turn, Louisville Ike, Dirk LeMaster, then Uncle Stanley. Each of them cordially returned her smile. "But how could you have possibly had everything planned to go the way it did?"

"We didn't," said Sims. "You can never run something this widespread by the numbers and expect everything to fall into place. But everybody knew their role and played things accordingly—sort of like starting out in a chess game." As Sims spoke, a coin appeared in his hand as if out of nowhere. He rolled it back and forth across his knuckles. "You don't know what to expect entirely, but as long as you know how all the pieces should move, you anticipate, and play the game out."

Uncle Stanley chuckled. "So *that's* what we were doing? I was starting to wonder. We played a lot by ear on this one, because of the weather. But we got lucky, I suppose."

"Lucky? Don't get modest on us, Uncle Stanley." Sims laid a hand on Uncle Stanley's shoulder. "There are few people who can work this way . . . these three gentlemen just happen to be the best at it in the world, for my money. Uncle Stanley set things up, got Steelhead Radner to go along with him just to make sure *Los Pistoleros* would hear him out. Ike and Dirk here played the go-betweens—their jobs were to create a diversion, first by the card game incident, then by keeping Radner busy goading them on. Nobody ever stopped to think that this could all be a scheme. Phelps and Priest just turned their stock over to the all powerful C. B. Harrington without question." Sims grinned, tipping a salute to Ike and LeMaster. "They did well, these two. They would've also been safety men, working as backup in case something went wrong."

"Yes," said LeMaster, "and a lot of things did! Like the old man back at the station saying C. B. Harrington was on his way to claim his stolen Pullman car. That was quick thinking, Stanley, you telling him *'I am C. B. Harrington, you fool!'*"

"It got a little too close for comfort a couple of times, I have to admit," said Stanley Czech. "I'm just glad I never had to sign anything into C. B. Harrington's name. That would have been more problems to deal with. This way it's all clean and simple."

"Yep, you sure pulled it off," Sims pointed out. "We set out to bust up *Los Pistoleros'* financial holding, and we did it. I wanted to know where my family's wagons were hidden, and now I know. At long last my family can rest in peace."

"What about those two federal deputies," Louisville Ike asked. "Are they going to understand what was going on? I don't want them down on me for any reason."

"Hart and Roth? They're the best in the business," Sims said. "By the time they reach Fort Smith, I'll have Judge Parker filled in on everything. We work together well, me and those two—they just don't always realize it." He grinned. "But by now they're starting to know it." He stopped rolling the coin across his knuckles, flipped it, caught it, and out of force of habit made it disappear.

Kate beamed, looking around at them. "But wasn't it awfully risky? Uncle Stanley shooting at you that way?"

"That had me worried," Sims said. "Uncle Stanley switched blanks into Priest's pistol when he held it behind his back last night. When I saw Priest replace those two blanks he'd fire at the rail yard attendant with real bullets, I got a little tense. But I always get tense when there's guns involved . . . that's why I avoid them. Look what could have happened had your shot been just a couple of inches to the right."

"I know . . ." Kate looked worried just thinking about it. "But I had to do something. I thought he had killed you."

"I know, Kate. There's times when nothing comes in as handy as a loaded pistol. The problem is knowing when that time is at hand. Most times a pistol is simply the quick cure. I like to think there's always a better way if a person has time to look for it."

"Well," Kate sighed, "I just thank God you're okay—all of us for that matter," she added, passing a glance at the others. "You got what you wanted, the deputies will get what they wanted once Priest is back in his cell . . ." She paused, then said to Uncle Stanley, "What about you? What do you get out of this?"

Uncle Stanley shrugged his big shoulders. "They were my people too, the ones who were murdered and left in the caves." He raised a finger for emphasis. "All Roma Gypsies are of the same family." He lowered his eyes coyly, then said, "Of course, owning the largest part of Midwest Investment Corporation is not a bad reward either." He patted his coat pocket where the stock ownership papers lay signed and ready for recorded transfer into his name.

Sims and the others laughed. "We'll have to ditch this big Pullman car pretty soon," said Louisville Ike. "Evidently C. B. Harrington is looking all over the country for it."

Uncle Stanley sighed. "Yes, I know. Too bad though. I could really get used to traveling this way."

"Well, with the money the family will be making from the investment stock," Sims threw in, "you can soon afford one of your own."

"Ah, but it won't be the same," Uncle Stanley said, raising a thick finger. "There's something appealing about traveling freely on a Pullman car that doesn't belong to me." He ran a hand along the back of the plush sofa, looking all around. "But to be honest, this will never replace the Roma wagons."

"No, never," Dirk LeMaster said, him and Louisville Ike raising their whiskey glasses in confirmation.

Sims smiled and turned to Kate McCorkle. "See? I told you I might have a gang of my own."

"If you gentlemen will excuse us," Kate McCorkle said, pulling Sims forward by his lapel, "I have some things I want to discuss with Charlie in private."

"We understand," said Uncle Stanley, as Louisville Ike and Dirk LeMaster stepped aside to let Kate lead Quick Charlie Sims toward the bedroom door.

When the two had closed the door behind them, Uncle Stanley looked up at Ike and LeMaster. "Ah, that Charlie." He swept a hand toward the bedroom door. "If this and this alone is all a man is due in life . . . what a lucky man he is, eh?"

"Yeah," Louisville Ike breathed. "You should have seen her face when I leaned in and told her Sims was alive—that this was all being staged so Priest would tell us where the wagons are."

"Yes," said Uncle Stanley, "it makes us realize there are far more precious things than wealth, doesn't it?"

Ike and LeMaster smiled and nodded. "Yes, that's true. There's far more than wealth—" LeMaster stopped short, staring at Uncle Stanley. "Hey, hold on. Shouldn't we sit down and decide how we're going to divide the shares in Midwest Investment?"

"Of course," Uncle Stanley shrugged. "We can do that now."

"Okay," LeMaster said with a shrewd tight smile, "don't start trying to soften us up with all this flowery, 'more important than wealth' malarkey."

"That's not what I was doing," Uncle Stanley smiled. "You know we always share and share alike." He reached out, picked up the bottle of bourbon and refilled each of their glasses in turn. "Now then, let's divide things up . . . maybe have time to play some poker on our way to the badlands, eh?"

"Don't even think about it, Stanley," said Louisville Ike, pulling up a chair, sitting down and fingering the deck of cards on the table. "I'm not about to gamble my shares away. Are you, Dirk?"

"No, but—" Dirk stared at the deck of cards. "I suppose we could play a few hands though, just to pass the time?"

"Sure, why not!" Uncle Stanley laughed, then looked off toward the platform door and shook his head slowly. He picked up the deck, riffled the cards, fanned them, spread them out across the felt, then brought them back into a neat stack, all in one dazzling sweep of his hand. "That Quick Charlie, I swear . . ." Uncle Stanley stopped for a second as if reflecting back on everything that had happened. Then he shook his head, still chuckling. "I don't know where he gets it from."